P9-DCH-916

Dinosaur Thunder

Also by James F. David

Footprints of Thunder
Fragments
Ship of the Damned
Before the Cradle Falls
Judgment Day
The Book of Summer
Thunder of Time

Dinosaur Thunder

James F. David

A Tom Doherty Associates Book  New York

This is a work of fiction. All of the characters, organizations, and events portrayed in this novel are either products of the author's imagination or are used fictitiously.

DINOSAUR THUNDER

A Forge Book
Published by Tom Doherty Associates, LLC
175 Fifth Avenue
New York, NY 10010

www.tor-forge.com

Forge® is a registered trademark of Tom Doherty Associates, LLC.

Library of Congress Cataloging-in-Publication Data

David, James F.
Dinosaur thunder / James F. David.— 1st ed.

p. cm.

"A Tom Doherty Associates book."

ISBN 978-0-7653-2378-1 (hardcover)
ISBN 978-1-4299-4872-2 (e-book)

1. Time travel—Fiction. 2. Dinosaurs—Fiction. I. Title.

PS3554.A9155D56 2012
813'.54—dc23

2012024907

First Edition: December 2012

Printed in the United States of America

0 9 8 7 6 5 4 3 2 1

Looking back through the dedications in my other books, it is easy to see the biggest change that has taken place in my life—my family keeps growing. Gale continues to be my primary reader, although I know I can always call on Abby, who reads at warp speed, or Drew, who devours books just as fast. Now that Katie is back from Arizona, it will be easier to impose on her, and soon Bethany and Mark will have time to read Dad's stuff. Until my granddaughter, Adelaide, learns to read, or James, my grandson, I'll have to settle for reading to them.

This book is dedicated to my constantly growing and changing family, which provides all the characters, relationships, conflicts, dialogue, happiness, frustration, and hope that a writer needs.

Personae Dramatis

Florida

Dr. Norman "Norm" Gah—Paleobiologist, Ocala Dinosaur Preserve
Jeanette Johns—Office manager, Dinosaur Wrangler
Fanny Mills—Married to Marty Mills
Marty Mills—Married to Fanny Mills, owner of a weekend hobby farm
Emmett Puglisi—Special Consultant to the Office of Strategic Science
Carson Wills—Owner, Dinosaur Wrangler
Les Wilson—Deputy sheriff
Carmen Wynooski—Senior dinosaur ranger, Ocala Dinosaur Preserve

Florida Dinosaur Wranglers

Lymon Norris
Robby Bryson
Nate Simpson
Doris Melton

Marines

Melvin Kelton—Private, personal security detail for Nick Paulson
Michael Kwan—Sergeant, personal security detail for Nick Paulson
Nash Sampson—Private, security detail, Mills Ranch
Lance Snead—Private, personal security detail for Nick Paulson
Afa Tafua—Private, personal security detail for Nick Paulson

Toby Washburne—Private, personal security detail for Nick Paulson
Sam Weller—Lieutenant, personal security detail for Nick Paulson

NASA/Astronauts

Sarasa Chandra—Mission specialist
Rick Maven—Mission specialist
Rosa Perez-Roberts—Aurora pilot, married to John Roberts
Mike Watson—Mission commander
Connie West—Deputy flight director

Neverland

Betty Brown—Member of Reverend's Community, wife of Lincoln Brown
Lincoln Brown—Member of Reverend's Community, husband of Betty Brown
Crazy Michael Kramer—Member of Reverend's Community
Jacob Lewinski—Member of Reverend's Community, husband of Leah Lewinski
Leah Lewinski—Member of Reverend's Community, wife of Jacob Lewinski, mother of Beatrice (six years old) and Bonnie (three years old)
Grandma Reilly—Sewing master for Reverend's Community
Reverend—Leader of the "Community"
Jack Williams—Youngest son of Willy Williams
Mel Williams—Butcher for Reverend's Community, oldest son of Willy Williams
Willy Williams—Master hunter for Reverend's Community

Orlando

Kris Conyers—Officer, Orlando Mounted Patrol
Morgan Nara—Officer, Orlando Mounted Patrol

Washington, D.C.

Wilamina Brown—President of the United States

Elizabeth Hawthorne—Former White House Chief of Staff, defense lobbyist for Weinert and Goldfarb, wife of Nick Paulson

Kaylee Kemper—Nick Paulson's administrative assistant, Office of Strategic Science

Nick Paulson—Director, Office of Strategic Science, husband of Elizabeth Hawthorne

John Roberts—Director of Field Operations, Office of Strategic Science, married to Rosa Perez-Roberts

Mike Stott—Deputy Director of Field Operations, Office of Strategic Science

Dinosaur Thunder

Prologue

It has been eighteen years since the planet was swept by time waves, intermixing the Cretaceous and modern periods. In that disaster, whole cities disappeared, never to be seen again. Millions of people were displaced in time, their homes and businesses gone with them and replaced with dinosaur-infested forests. Some called it God's punishment, but the investigation of the disaster eventually linked the catastrophe to the testing of nuclear fusion weapons in the fifties and sixties.

To detonate a fusion bomb, the heat and pressure of a fission explosion is used to fuse hydrogen atoms, to produce helium atoms, resulting in the release of massive amounts of energy. The resulting thermonuclear explosion sends out several destructive waves, including electromagnetic, blast, and thermal. Unknown at the time of fusion testing was the existence of a fourth wave: a ripple in time and space. While a single time wave was insufficient to cause more than localized time effects, the convergence of several time waves accounted for the worldwide disruption of the space–time continuum.

As civilizations have done for centuries following catastrophe, people adapted to the losses, rebuilding their homes, their highways, and the railroads. Power grids were restored, and holes in the data networks filled. Cities sprouted in and around the chunks of Cretaceous wilderness. Economies boomed as unemployment dropped to record lows and resources poured into urban renewal. As civilization recovered, the most difficult problem was what to do with the dinosaurs.

Some countries exterminated their dinosaurs. Other dinosaurs died naturally, unable to adapt to the climate they found themselves in. Still other countries, like the United States, rounded up dinosaurs, confining them to preserves. Special rangers were recruited and trained, and given responsibility for dinosaur management. Quickly, the people of the world adjusted to cohabiting with the prehistoric animals, and then became fascinated with them. Dinosaur preserves became popular tourist attractions.

Then, ten years after the Time Quilt, as the popular press dubbed the disaster, a group of ecoterrorists infiltrated a secret government project hidden in Alaska. Scientists at the Fox Valley site had created a special pyramid to gather orgonic energy, the same energy used by the Egyptians to help preserve their pharaohs. These researchers had discovered that the pyramid form focused orgonic energy, and by lining a pyramid with a high-tech material, the Fox Valley scientists created a highly efficient capacitor capable of storing orgonic energy. Not widely known at the time was that orgonic energy also influenced the time ripples and could be used to manipulate them.

Taking control of the Fox Valley site, ecoterrorists simultaneously detonated three nuclear weapons, sending the facility back in time ten years, and to the moon. Those three symmetrical and simultaneous explosions also created connections through time and space between the Fox Valley pyramid, the Fox Valley pyramid transported to the moon, and a newly discovered pyramid in the Yucatán. By using the orgonic energy stored in the Fox Valley pyramid, the ecoterrorists were able to manipulate the time waves still rippling across the planet, planning to create a massive new Time Quilt that would shred space–time, jumbling past and present and destroying modern civilization. If successful, the planet would return to a primitive state, where animals would once again thrive. Fortunately, Nick Paulson and his team thwarted their plan, and all three pyramid sites were destroyed.

The public was told the nuclear explosions were terrorist attacks, the attack on the time line classified. Next to the Time Quilt, the terrorist attack paled in comparison, and gradually the public settled once again into complacency, unaware of the damage done to space–time.

1

Moon

You look at that photo on my website, and then you tell me there wasn't an explosion on the moon. You've got to start listening to me, America! Wake up! The government blew up a secret alien base on the moon, and it's time we-the-people know why.

—Cat Bellow, host of *Radio Rebel*

Present time
Flamsteed crater
The moon

"We are approaching the debris field now," Mike Watson said, his message relayed from his PLSS suit to the lunar lander to the orbiting lunar shuttle and then on to Earth.

As mission commander, Watson led the way, the rest of his crew fanned out behind him. Mission Specialist Sarasa Chandra trailed on his left, Mission Specialist Rick Maven on his right. They used the gentle hopping motion perfected by Apollo crews. In one-sixth gravity, walking quickly became bounding, so planned bounding was more efficient.

Watson checked the radiation reading in his heads-up display. He ignored the UV radiation; his suit could handle routine lunar exposure. What concerned Watson was the particle radiation. The team's specially insulated PLSS suits would protect them for a time, but Watson kept an eye on the rems. He and his wife wanted more children, and wanted them to have all the usual body parts.

They passed random bits of man-made debris—strips of metal, chunks of rubber, pieces of concrete, the brass knob of a door handle. They came to a larger object—a refrigerator. Dented and half buried, it stuck up out of the regolith like modern art. The door was partially ajar. Watson did not bother to look inside. According to the intelligence briefing, the last residents of the structure ahead had eaten everything. Watson snapped a picture and moved on.

"Over here, sir," Chandra said.

Watson stopped, turning his shoulders to turn his helmet toward Chandra. She was holding up a long bone.

"It's a human leg bone," Chandra said. "It's been picked clean."

"Photograph it and leave it," Watson said.

They kept moving toward the deep shadow of the crater wall, where the structure hid.

"Sir, this might be what we came for," Maven said.

Again, Watson stopped, turning his shoulders and head. Maven was holding a jagged piece of black material. Watson walked to Maven, Chandra following. They formed a small circle so they could make eye contact. Maven held what looked like a thin piece of black plastic with a dull surface. About a foot long, and eight inches at the widest point, it resembled a piece of ice broken from the surface of a pond. Maven tapped it, knocking off a bit of dust. Taking the material, Watson turned it on its side, seeing that it was made up of a dozen thin layers.

"It's light," Watson said, passing it to Chandra.

Chandra held the material close to her faceplate, studying the layers through two sunscreens.

"This is it," Chandra announced. "This is what they spent a billion dollars to get."

"Well, that was easy," Maven said. "And we have rems to spare." Maven tapped his faceplate where the radiation readings would show on his side.

"That's half the mission," Watson said. "Collect more samples as we go."

Maven put the sample in a bag, labeled it, and then followed the others. They spread out again with Watson in the lead. The regolith was soft, Watson sinking an inch with each bounce, sending up a small puff of dust. When they came to an edge of the rim shadow, Maven stopped them again.

"This just gets weirder and weirder," Maven said.

Maven had angled away and was now twenty yards to the right. He was standing by a large object, his lunar boot resting on top. With a shove, he tipped the object over.

"It's a snowmobile," Maven said. "I don't remember this in the mission briefing."

"They told us to expect the unexpected," Chandra said.

"They tell you that kind of stuff, but you never really believe them," Maven said. "Until now. A snowmobile on the moon?" Maven mumbled as he resumed hopping.

Watson checked his display. The rems were increasing, but well within the safe zone.

Entering the shadow, they took a dozen bounds before one of the sun shields lifted, allowing them to see farther into the shadow. Now Watson could see the objective. What had once been the most famous building on the moon—and the only building—was now nothing more than two vertical walls marking one corner. They moved forward, Watson's eyes on the radiation meter. Then he found a body.

"Chandra! Maven!" Watson called, coming to a stop.

His crew hopped over, closing ranks around the body. Any clothing and hair had been burned away. The genitalia was male, the body mummified through the combination of vacuum and UV radiation. Chandra photographed the body. Maven took samples of the regolith around the corpse, storing them in plastic bags. When they were finished, they continued toward the ruins.

"We should bury him," Maven said.

"And the leg bone we found?" Chandra asked.

"If there's time," Watson said, understanding the feeling. Even on the moon, the cultural need to return humans to the soil was strong.

Now well into the rim shadow, another sun shield retracted and they could see even more detail. What had once been a large rectangular structure had exploded, leaving two intersecting walls standing, the tops crumbled, bent rebar protruding from broken edges. What surprised Watson was that anything still stood. According to the mission briefing, a twenty-megaton warhead had destroyed the site.

The rems continued to creep up but nowhere near the level Watson had feared.

"Sir, there are bones here," Chandra said.

"Photograph them," Watson said, not bothering to turn and look this time. "We'll bury them if we have time."

"They're not human," Chandra said.

Now Watson stopped, turning. Chandra held a long thin bone.

"Dinosaur," Chandra said.

"Snowmobiles and dinosaurs on the moon," Maven said. "They said expect the unexpected, not expect the weird."

Moving on, the texture of the regolith changed. Kneeling in PLSS suits was impossible, so Watson used a long-handled scoop to sample a piece of the surface. The material looked like gray straw. It crumpled when touched.

"I think it's organic," Chandra said. "It may be grass."

"Take a look at this," Maven said.

Hopping over, they found Maven looking at another chunk of the black material they had collected earlier.

"I'm having trouble focusing on this piece," Maven said.

An eight-inch chunk of the black material lay on the surface, coming in and out of focus.

"Its refractive properties keep changing," Chandra said.

"Mike, this is Mission Control," a voice cut in. "Do not touch that material. Use tongs and store the material in a lined bag."

"Tongs?" Maven said. "Now they tell us."

The team carried special sample bags, now understanding what they were for. Using long-handled tongs, Maven picked up the chunk and dropped it in a bag held open by Chandra. Chandra sealed the bag. She put the sample in a pouch on the side of her suit, and they moved on, now picking their way through chunks of concrete, careful to skirt exposed rebar and other jagged material. The debris here was larger, heavier, the smaller pieces having been blown well across the moon's surface. Finally, they reached the foundation for the original building. Up close, Watson could see that more of the building stood than appeared from a distance. Concrete several feet high still formed a perimeter. There was a gap near the astronauts, and they carefully worked through concrete chunks toward the opening.

"Sir, look at that," Chandra said, pointing over the jagged wall.

They stopped to see where Chandra pointed but saw nothing. Then over the broken wall they saw puffs of dust.

"Something's kicking up dust," Maven said.

Few things kicked up dust on the moon, Watson knew. Seismic activity could, but they felt none. Meteor impacts also, but the dust they were seeing came regularly, inconsistent with a random micrometeor strike. Rapid heating of the frozen regolith could cause surface fracturing, but the rim shadow prevented rapid solar heating.

The dust continued to puff.

"Let's take bets on what's causing it," Maven said. "I'll take a Russian women's hockey team."

"Residual volcanic activity," Chandra said. "Left over from the nuclear detonation."

"Not weird enough," Maven said. "Take my word for it, whatever is causing that dust cloud is going to be closer to a Russian women's hockey team than volcanic activity."

Watson stayed out of the betting, but leaned toward Maven's point of view. The path through to the opening was narrow, so they walked single file now with Watson in the lead. Coming to the opening, Watson stopped, the others coming to stand shoulder to shoulder. What they saw left them speechless.

"Impossible," Chandra said.

"Yeah," Maven said.

One end of what had been a building was rubble, but in one corner of the remaining wall was a dinosaur, standing on a flat black surface. Not a dead, mummified dinosaur, but a living, thrashing animal, trying to break free from some invisible restraint.

"That's a tyrannosaur," Chandra said.

"No, too small," Watson said. "That's *Deinonychus*."

"Those are the ones they call 'dine on us,'" Maven said.

"The jaws are too big and the arms too short for *Deinonychus*. It must be a juvenile tyrannosaur," Chandra insisted, "or something in the tyrannosaur family."

"It has to be an illusion," Maven said. "A projection."

"Looks real to me," Watson said.

"What's holding it?" Chandra asked. "It's like its feet are glued down."

Like an animal trapped in quicksand, the tyrannosaur struggled, its tail swinging wide, sending up the occasional cloud of dust.

"Mission Control, are you seeing this?" Watson said.

"Affirmative, Mike," came the reply. "Do not approach until we advise."

"No problem," Watson said.

"How can it breathe?" Chandra asked. "It can't," she said, answering her own question. "It shouldn't even be alive. Nothing can live in a vacuum."

"It's alive, all right," Maven said. "Let's just hope it doesn't get loose, or we'll wish there were a Russian women's hockey team here to protect us."

"Look at how hard it's struggling," Chandra said. "It should be exhausted."

"Commander Watson?" a new voice cut it. "This is Nick Paulson. I am director of the Office of Security Science."

"I know who you are," Watson said. "What can we do for you?"

Watson knew Paulson through reputation and rumor. By reputation, Paulson was world-renowned for his work on the time quilting that had swept the planet, bringing dinosaurs to the modern world, and was a confidant of presidents. By rumor, Paulson was said to be one of the few people on the planet who knew what was really behind the time distortions.

"Can you probe the surface of the interior without stepping on it?"

"Stand by," Watson said.

Watson unsnapped the long-handled scoop, extending it full length. Carefully stepping around concrete rubble, he worked his way to the edge of the perimeter. Inside, Watson could see chunks of what once had been a concrete floor. Most of the floor was gravel-size rubble arranged in elongated piles, looking like ocean waves. Watson touched the surface with the scoop.

"It feels solid," Watson said.

After the long pause for relay to Earth, Paulson came back. "Advance slowly, probing every six inches," Paulson said.

Watson paused long enough to rotate his shoulders and to exchange looks with Chandra and Maven. Maven shrugged his shoulders while Chandra rotated her shoulders back and forth, indicating *Hell no.* Watson could switch off the Earth link and talk to his team, but decided against it. Having Paulson suddenly commandeer the mission was unorthodox and even weird, but Watson was as curious about the conditions in the interior of the structure as Paulson was. Even without the order, Watson was going in.

Inching toward the still-struggling dinosaur, Watson felt like a soldier probing a minefield. Six inches at a time, he worked toward the dinosaur, always one eye on the tyrannosaur. Suddenly, the carnivore stopped struggling. Cocking its head, it stared at Watson with one eye.

"I think it spotted me," Watson said.

"Get out, sir," Chandra said.

"I'm coming in," Maven said.

"Everyone stay where you are," Paulson said, stopping Maven as he started into the perimeter. "Keep your cameras on the dinosaur."

They stood, locked in a staring contest with the tyrannosaur. Then abruptly, it turned its head, using its other eye. Suddenly, it lunged, but the invisible restraints held, and it barely moved. Twisting and turning, it repeatedly lunged, jaws snapping silently in the vacuum.

"Try moving sideways," Paulson said.

"Moving? I thought prey were harder to see if they didn't move."

"Please move sideways," Paulson said after a long pause. "It's safe."

In a PLSS suit, sidesteps were impossible, so Watson turned, hopping to his left. The tyrannosaur struggled another second, and then stopped, cocking its head from side to side as if searching for Watson. Finally, it gave up, ignoring Watson, resuming its frenetic struggles.

"Commander, I won't ask you to go any further," Paulson said.

"That thing is cemented in place," Watson said. "It's safe enough to get closer."

"If you are comfortable," Paulson said.

"Do you have a goal in mind?" Watson asked as he resumed inching forward.

"Yes," Paulson said. "I would like a sample of the material the dinosaur is standing on."

Watson studied the predator, estimating the sweep of its tail and the length of its neck. Watson did not think it could reach him.

"You don't want to get that close," Maven said.

"I'll be careful," Watson said.

Inching slowly, Watson worked his way over waves of rubble, the tyrannosaur ignoring him, still wrenching back and forth violently. Reaching the edge of the black mass the trapped animal stood on, Watson used the long-handled scoop, touching the black material. It was solid. Watson tapped the material and then turned the scoop over, using the serrated edge to scratch the surface. No marks.

"It's hard like rock," Watson reported.

There was a long moon-to-Earth pause.

"Try probing it with the orgonic material you collected."

"Orgonic?" Watson said.

"The pieces of black material," Paulson said.

"Why?" Watson asked.

A long silence followed. Watson imagined an intense argument taking place on the other end of the Earth link.

"Try the collected samples because they may be made of a related material."

That explained nothing, but Watson knew he would not get anything more. Maven came forward, detaching his sample bag, offering the first piece of the material they found. Watson snapped the scoop head off his long handle and attached the tongs. Then he used a multitool folded into pliers to extract the material from the sample bag and transfer it to the tongs. Now using the long-handled tongs, Watson touched the material to the surface.

"Same result," Watson said. "What were you expecting?"

After a long pause, "We're just experimenting. Try the sample Dr. Chandra is carrying," Paulson said.

Watson returned the sample to Maven's bag, and then Maven backed away as Chandra came forward. Using the same procedure, Watson extracted the sample from Chandra's bag. As before, the surface of the piece was hard to focus on. The tongs gripped it, however, and Watson lowered it to the surface. When the material touched, it slowly sank.

"It's melding with the surface," Watson said.

"Extract it," Paulson radioed after a pause.

"This just gets better and better," Maven said.

"Major Watson," Paulson said. "Please collect as much of the black material as you can. From now on, that is the only mission priority."

"Yes, sir," Watson said.

"What about the dinosaur?" Chandra asked.

"I say we leave it," Maven said. "The Russian women's hockey team will be along soon, and they can deal with it."

2

Pest Control

I did find a statistically significant increase in the number of unlicensed dinosaurs appearing outside of ranges and licensed habitats (see attached). I have not been able to identify the source of these dinosaurs, or a pattern, but I will work on it again next summer if I receive another internship.

—Chad Barrett, university intern, memo,
Department of Dinosaur Control

Present time
Hillsdale, Florida

Carson Wills turned his van down the access road, driving through an open security gate onto fresh blacktop. A sign over the entrance read MILLS RANCH. "Ranch" was a grandiose term for a weekend farm owned by yuppies. Ahead, a large two-story "farmhouse" sat on the highest point on the property, where the masters could look out on their estate. A large deck on the second story overlooked the pool below and the shallow valley beyond. Carson pictured young executives, girlfriends and trophy wives standing on the deck, drinks in hand, admiring the view of what had once been a productive farm—tomatoes and lettuce, Carson guessed by the look of the fields.

From the deck, visitors would see land that generations of farmers had fought nature for, taming the lush subtropical forest piece by piece, making a living for their families and feeding the state and the nation with year-round crops. The crops, livestock, and sense of purpose were gone, replaced by pastures for horses, llamas, or the newest fad, domesticated dinosaurs. Apatosaurs were the most popular, but only for the very rich. These massive animals with their long necks and tails took more acreage than the Mills Ranch could offer. Smaller sauropods were common on ranches like the Mills Ranch, and even armored dinosaurs like *Monoclonius,* triceratops, or smaller ankylosaurs. Managing beasts like triceratops was difficult, however, and took a professional staff. Carson guessed these paddocks would hold small sauropods or maybe a hadrosaur, probably a duck-billed hadrosaur.

Carson pulled into the circular drive, parking his cream-colored GMC van next to a red Audi. The decal on the side of his van showed a cowboy lassoing a *T. rex*. Above the image was painted DINOSAUR WRANGLER, the name of Carson's company. The same cowboy logo was embroidered on the chest of his yellow cotton shirt. For a five-hundred-dollar minimum, plus expenses, Carson or one of his employees would come on call and deal with dinosaurs that had escaped from preserves or broken through fences. Despite the decal, Carson had never encountered a tyrannosaur and never would, since carnivores were strictly regulated. There were only a few in Florida, all federally owned and managed. Private ownership of carnivores was a felony, and there were only two ranges in the United States where they roamed free. The only carnivores roaming free in Florida preserves were small scavengers like the seven-pound *Bambiraptor.*

Ignoring the brass knockers, Carson rapped on the front door with a knuckle. Marty Mills opened the door, wearing Levi's and a long-sleeved denim shirt. He was clean-shaven, with dark hair trimmed neat, blue eyes, and a genuine smile that showed off his bright-white teeth.

"Hey, Fanny, the dinosaur guy's here," Marty called over his shoulder. "Thanks for coming."

Marty Mills took Carson's hand, shaking it and pulling him in at the same time. The entry was walnut hardwood. A staircase led to the second floor, a spacious living room opened to the right, and on the other side, a set of French doors led to a library.

"I'm so glad you're here," Fanny Mills said as she came down the stairs. "We called the preserve, but they don't have any rangers available. They put us on a list."

Fanny Mills wore cargo shorts with a navy blue polo shirt. She was pretty—very pretty—with short black hair, large expressive brown eyes, and another smile full of bright-white teeth. Her face, arms, and legs were genuinely tan, not the spray-on fake tan that gave you the color without the cancer risk. Coming directly to Carson, Fanny took his hand, shook it, and then held it while she spoke to him sincerely.

"You're not alone, are you? It's too dangerous to do it alone. We won't let you, will we, Marty?"

"No, of course not," Marty said.

It took Carson a few seconds to realize the Millses were genuinely concerned about his safety. "Mr. and Mrs. Mills," Carson began.

"Marty and Fanny," Fanny said, finally releasing Carson's hand after a final squeeze.

The squeeze gave Carson a warm rush.

"Look, I have been doing this for a long time. Let me take a look at what you've got, and if I need help I'll call in one of my crew."

"It's a velociraptor," Marty said.

"Probably more than one," Fanny said, taking him by the arm. "They run in packs. Of course you would know that."

"Velociraptors are illegal," Carson assured them. "If it's a carnivore, it's more'n likely an oviraptor. They keep them in the ranges as scavengers to keep the range free of carcasses. The problem is that they keep escaping because the barriers are built for the big animals. If it is an oviraptor, there's not much to worry about. Might eat your cat if you have one, but that's about it."

"I heard an oviraptor killed a baby in California," Marty said.

"Urban myth," Carson said. "Do you have a baby?"

"No, but we're trying," Fanny said, taking Carson's arm, and leading him down the hall.

Fanny and Marty were uncomfortably open, Carson thought, but Carson liked them. The Millses took Carson down the hall to the biggest kitchen he had ever seen, with a breakfast bar and kitchen table. The back wall was glass, with more French doors that opened out to the pool deck. The tile floor in the kitchen was the same as the tile around the pool, so with the French doors open, the pool area and the kitchen would seem to be one large room. There was another set of stairs along one wall of the kitchen, and the Millses took Carson to the second floor and another large open space sprinkled with arcade games and a foosball table. A large wet bar sat against one wall, and another glass wall led out to the deck. Two pairs of binoculars sat on the bar. Marty picked them up, and Fanny led Carson onto the deck.

Fanny was unusually physical for a married woman, holding Carson's arm, leaning against him, guiding him with a hand on his back. Carson enjoyed the contact, feeling it was somehow illicit. Carson also knew that if the plumber showed up later that day, Fanny would be just as attentive.

"Here you go," Marty said, handing Carson one of the binoculars. "We saw the velociraptor down the valley by the old barn."

Marty took the binoculars, following Marty's point. The binoculars had image-stabilization technology, and the view through the lenses was as stable as looking out a window. Carson found the old barn. It was a half-collapsed structure that looked like a pile of weathered scrap wood.

"We saw it run from the tree line on the south into the barn," Fanny said.

Carson studied the barn but saw nothing.

"We've seen it twice now," Marty said. "Fanny saw it yesterday early in the morning, and I saw it last night."

"Have you been to the barn?" Carson asked.

"No!" Fanny said emphatically. "Marty wanted to go, but I said, 'Don't even think about it.' I told him, I said, 'Marty, we need a professional,' and so we called you."

"Did you find me in the yellow pages, online, word of mouth?" Carson asked.

"Online."

Carson made a mental note to drop his yellow pages advertising. Only one call in fifty was coming from print advertising.

They watched the barn for another couple of minutes.

"I'll go take a look," Carson said.

"Not alone?" Fanny said, touching his arm.

"No worries," Carson said, feeling her genuine concern. "I'm a professional."

The Millses followed him to his van. Carson loaded his tranquilizer rifle with a dosage for an animal the size of an ostrich, still expecting an *Oviraptor.* Putting on his camouflaged hunting vest, he put a pouch of darts in his shirt pocket, preloaded with a range of dosages.

"Those tranquilizer darts are a lot bigger than I thought," Fanny said.

"They're nothing like they show on TV," Carson said. "Each dart is really a full-size syringe with an explosive charge on the end," Carson explained as he put on his gear. "The rifle is CO_2 powered. I can adjust the power setting so I can shoot an animal from as close as two feet or as far as thirty yards without hurting it."

Carson opened the rifle, extracting the dart.

"When the dart hits, this blue end compresses and this brass rod strikes the firing pin, setting off a charge. The explosion drives the plunger and injects the drug."

"Cool," Marty said.

"How long before the animal is sedated?" Fanny asked.

"Depends on the size of the animal. Too small an animal, and I could kill it with this dosage. Too big, and it won't go down at all. If the dosage is right, it takes five to ten minutes for the animal to get manageable."

"Five minutes with an angry velociraptor," Marty said, whistling.

"It's not a velociraptor," Carson said.

"We're going with you," Fanny said.

"It can't be a velociraptor or any of his bigger cousins," Carson said. "Dinosaur rangers tag any predator, and besides, there aren't any large predators in the Ocala preserve. If any of the scavengers they do keep start probing the fence line, they put them down. Predators just can't get loose, let alone this far from a preserve."

Carson snapped the bag with his throw net to the loop on his left side, checked the load in his pistol, and put it in his holster. Then he took the leash pole—an extendable aluminum pole with a wire loop on the end. With the loop over the head of the dinosaur, Carson could tighten the wire and keep the animal at bay with the pole.

"Aren't you taking a rifle?" Fanny asked, pointing to the guns hanging on the wall of the van.

"I've never had to use one of those," Carson said, closing the van door. "I'll take a look in the barn and check the area for animal signs. Depending on what I find, I'll either handle it or call in for help." Carson pulled a phone from his vest pocket and showed it to them. "If I need help, it will cost more than the five-hundred-dollar minimum."

"I would hope so," Marty said.

The Millses walked with him to the edge of their carefully watered and trimmed lawn and then stood on the edge as he walked down the hill into the valley leading to the old barn.

Most of the former lettuce and tomato fields spread across the valley to the north. The pastures were to the south. Carson skirted two pastures green enough for Kentucky Thoroughbreds and then through the scrub growth beyond. Ahead to the south, Carson saw the original farmhouse, its windows and doors boarded. The barn sat a hundred yards behind the house. The barn was in bad shape, the end nearest Carson partially collapsed. The rest of the structure still stood but listed to the south, looking ready to fall at the slightest breeze. Given the regularity of hurricane winds in Florida, it was a miracle the structure still stood.

Carson slowed his pace, now choosing his footing to avoid sticks and dried leaves. Approaching the barn, Carson paused often, listening. With virtually no breeze, there was no downwind approach. Assuming the barn was as boarded up as the old house, Carson crept to the collapsed end. Part of the wall was gone, leaving a hole he would have to duck through. That was good, since only a medium-sized animal could get through the opening. He did not want to come face-to-face with triceratops with only a dart gun and a leash pole.

Waiting and listening, Carson heard nothing and saw nothing. Then he duck-walked through the opening, the tranquilizer rifle in one hand, and the leash pole in the other. Inside, he stood and moved right until he could stand with his back against a portion of the wall. Waiting for his eyes to fully adjust, soon Carson could make out details. The floor was dirt, giving the interior an earthy smell mixed with the stink of manure. Light leaked through cracks and joints, illuminating slivers of the interior but creating deep shadows too. Looking around, Carson found the interior disequilibrating, the slanted barn boards giving the illusion that the floor of the barn was tilted. There was little left in the barn except for a pile of blue plastic crates, a stack of hay bales, some circular saw blades hanging on the wall over a workbench, and a pair of snowshoes hanging from a ceiling beam. A set of dilapidated stairs led to a loft. Under the stairs was a pile of hay that looked out of place.

Alert for any movement, Carson walked to the hay pile. The mound was roughly circular and filled with a mix of straw, dried leaves, and dirt. Carson leaned the leash pole against the stairs, then squatted, digging into the mound. It was warm. Upon feeling an object, he pulled it out of the pile. It was a brown oblong egg. An egg like he had never seen before.

"Shit!" Carson said, shoving the egg back into the mound and standing, grip tight on the gun.

Sweeping the room with his tranquilizer rifle, he calmed down. The barn was empty, and even if the animal nesting in the barn was an *Oviraptor,* Carson could shoot it and fend it off long enough with the leash pole for the tranquilizer to take effect. He felt like an old woman for being so nervous. All the talk about a velociraptor by Fanny and Marty had put him on edge. Turning back to the nest, Carson studied it, trying to remember if he had ever seen an oviraptor nest before. Then he heard movement behind him.

Turning, Carson saw a velociraptor trot out of a dark corner of the barn. Spotting Carson by the nest, its head went low and its tail straight out. Hissing, it cocked its head back and forth, sizing up its target.

Velociraptors were small predators, this adult about the size of a German shepherd, but equipped with curved claws used to slash prey to ribbons. Carson was six feet tall and 190 pounds, just big enough to give the velociraptor pause, but not for long. Velociraptors could bring down prey several times its own size. Slowly raising his tranquilizer rifle, Carson backed up, making sure when he moved, he moved away from the nest. The velociraptor continued to hiss, watching Carson's movements, sizing him up, plotting an attack. Fanny had been right when she said velociraptors hunted in packs. It also nested in pairs. Carson had to get out of there before the mate showed up.

In his peripheral vision, Carson saw the stairs. Guessing the barn doors were nailed shut, Carson backed up faster, never taking his eyes off the hissing velociraptor. Before he got to the bottom of the stairs, another velociraptor trotted out of the shadows of the collapsed wall. This velociraptor was larger, the size of a Rottweiler, and just as fearless. Assuming the attack posture, it was more impulsive than its partner. It charged.

Carson shot it in the chest. The rifle was set for a fifteen-yard shot, and at this range the hit and explosion of the dart surprised the velociraptor, knocking it out of its charge. Spinning, the velociraptor reached for the dart with its jaws and then clawed with a foot. Carson turned, took two steps, and climbed onto the stairs. The smaller velociraptor jumped onto the stairs just behind Carson. Carson threw his rifle. The velociraptor caught the rifle in its jaws and twisted its head, the rifle coming free, clattering down the stairs. Carson pulled his pistol and shot the velociraptor three times at near point-blank range. Squealing, it snapped at Carson and then twisted, clawing at its chest, falling off the stairs.

Taking the stairs two at a time, Carson reached the top. The clicking of claws alerted him, and he turned just in time to see the larger velociraptor jump into the loft, a hypodermic dart hanging from its chest. Carson fired twice but missed the moving target. Surprised by the crack of the gunshots, the velociraptor retreated toward a dark corner. Carson fired again, the shot splitting a barn board, releasing a sliver of sunlight. Carson looked around. The loft held ancient hay bales but nothing else. There were double doors. Carson ran to the doors, finding a bar holding them closed. After lifting it out of the brackets, Carson shoved, the doors swinging open on rusty hinges. The blast of sunlight blinded him. Blinking, he turned, seeing the velociraptor crouched in a corner. Blinking furiously, Carson fired again, then sat with his feet dangling, holstered his pistol, and then grasped the edge of the opening, lowered himself, hung for a second, and then dropped.

An ankle crumpled when he hit—sprained but not broken. Lying on his back, Carson saw the velociraptor leaning out the opening, estimating the drop. Then it turned, disappearing inside. Carson got to his feet, limping back the way he'd come. Pulling his pistol, he aimed it at the opening in the collapsed end of the barn. He was just past the opening when the velociraptor shot out of it. Carson turned to fire, but hitting a target as fast as a velociraptor with a pistol was almost impossible. Carson stumbled, turning, falling to his back, bringing the pistol up. The velociraptor jumped feetfirst, raking claws extended. Carson fired and at the same time Carson heard two almost simultaneous gunshots. The velociraptor was shredded midair, landing next to Carson, dead.

Carson got to his feet. The Millses were behind him, each carrying a smoking shotgun.

"I told you it was a velociraptor," Marty said.

"And I told you we wouldn't let you go alone," Fanny said.

"I had it under control," Carson said, limping toward them. "I'm a professional."

"Any more in there?" Marty asked.

"One other. It's dead."

The Millses came to look at their kill. Carson looked the velociraptor over, searching for a tag—he could not see one.

"Where is the tag?" Fanny asked, squatting by the velociraptor.

"It's subcutaneous," Carson said, telling a half truth. "The carcass has to be returned to the Park Service or you would have yourself a nice trophy."

"I thought you said there weren't any velociraptors at the Ocala Preserve," Marty said.

"Must've brought a couple in. They'll get rid of them for sure now. I'll go get my van and clean up the site," Carson said, not mentioning the eggs.

"Lunch first," Fanny said. "I've got steaks in the fridge."

"And beer," Marty said.

"Sounds good," Carson said, distracted by the thought of the eggs.

The Millses were paying five hundred dollars for the job, but each egg was worth ten times that much on the black market—maybe more. The beer was cold, the steaks were thick, and by midafternoon, the velociraptor carcasses and the eggs were safely stowed in the Dinosaur Wrangler van and on the way home.

3

To Live and Die in Neverland

That's right, Senator, by passing through the passages inside the pyramids, we were able to travel forward and back in time and to quite remote locations. While we traveled only a few thousand years back in time, the fact that dinosaurs traveled to our present is proof that much more distant travel is theoretically possible.

—Dr. Nick Paulson, testimony to the Senate Committee for Security Affairs

Unknown time
Unknown place

Jacob Lewinski was a Realtor by trade, back when "Realtor" meant something. Jacob doubted any of the children born since coming to Neverland had ever heard of a Realtor. Now, instead of his chosen profession, Jacob was a rifleman in a hunting party. A rifleman hoping he would not have to use any of his precious ammunition, since it was almost as rare as batteries. If Jacob had been a carpenter or a farmer or even a butcher, he would have skills too precious to risk in a hunt, but Jacob was a Realtor, and Realtors were useless in Neverland.

The bulk of the hunting party was spreading out before him, creeping through the low vegetation at the edge of the meadow, moving as slow as the minute hand on a clock. A mixed herd of ankylosaurs, *Protoceratops*, and other armored dinosaurs grazed well away from the tree line, a few always on watch, heads up, eyes and nostrils busy. Looking at all the armor plate in the clearing, Jacob shook his head. Something was wrong in Neverland. Only the armored dinosaurs remained, the sauropods gone, driven away by the strange high concentration of predators. Sauropods were big quadrupeds like the *Apatosaurus,* with long necks and tails and no armor. Too big to be hunted even by tyrannosaurs, adult sauropods were relatively safe, but their young were vulnerable. There were also the old, and the sick, and they could be taken. Unfortunately, the sauropods were gone, leaving behind dinosaurs built like a Sherman tank.

The hunting party was downwind so if they moved slowly and carefully, they could get close enough for a chance at a kill, and they were desperate for a kill. Spreading out, a small group worked around to the far side of the herd. No specific animal had been picked out yet, the master of the hunt still studying the herd. If fate was kind, one of the young might get reckless, wandering too far from its mother, or if the herd stampeded, one of the old or crippled might fall behind. If not, the humans might still get lucky and pick off a healthy adult.

Ankylosaurs were easier to kill but did not provide as much meat as *Protoceratops. Protoceratops* were a hard, dangerous kill. Thick hides, layers of fat and muscle, and a bone shield protecting the neck were hard to penetrate even with a rifle bullet, and the hunters were using arrows and spears. The precious bullets in Jacob's gun were for emergencies, not hunting.

The low-riding quadrupeds carried a long thick tail, a parrot beak for snipping off vegetation, and that armor plate covering the vulnerable neck. The beefy *Protoceratops* could outsprint a man but quickly tired, and with a little luck, a well-placed hunter could make a crippling or even killing strike. Armed with spear throwers, compound bows, and crossbows, the hunters spread along the most likely escape route. Most of the arrows and spears had steel shafts, and the hunters were well practiced and well motivated. An adult *Protoceratops* could be butchered into five hundred pounds of meat. Two kills would mean they would not have to leave their fortress for weeks.

They were far from the Home Depot they called home, ranging

farther than they normally dared. Hungry families depended on the meat and increasingly on the skins, as usable fabrics went the way of batteries and ammunition. Since a pod of tyrannosaurs had moved into the valley, most of the herds had migrated to safer pastures. Unfortunately, the humans could not risk following. Ranging even this far from the Home Depot was a risk they seldom took.

The ankylosaurs and *Protoceratops* that stayed behind when the tyrannosaurs moved in were a wary bunch and easy to stampede, and that made them difficult to hunt. Undetectable to the humans, the scent of the tyrannosaurs was in the air, keeping the herd on edge. The pod of tyrannosaurs hunting the valley was small as *Tyrannosaurus rex* went, but with dinosaurs, "small" was a relative term. Jacob's head would barely reach the shoulder of even the smallest of these tyrannosaurs, and like all tyrannosaurs, they had a huge head with five dozen teeth they put to good use, snapping the neck of prey, or biting smaller animals in half. And while the biggest *T. rex* hunted individually, smaller tyrannosaurs like these often hunted in packs. The pod working the valley included six or seven adults, usually breaking up to hunt in threes and fours.

This far from their fortifications, there was another danger for the humans. Hunting grounds were disputed even when game was plentiful. In times of scarcity, like now, hunters jealously defended their territory. The humans were hunting outside their normal range. If the Inhumans caught them, the fragile peace could be shattered.

Now spread along the length of the meadow, weapons ready, the hunters held perfectly still, peeking through leaves, watching, waiting. The master of the hunt signaled their quarry, a fat sow with a calf orbiting its mother, eating, rooting, and throwing dirt. It was an ambitious choice, but both sow and calf had drifted to the back of the herd and near the hunters who would give chase. The master of the hunt gave the sign, and from the far side of the meadow, six hunters charged, shouting and waving weapons. As if one, the herd lurched and then stumbled into a confused mass as panic gripped it. In the few seconds of confusion, the hunters charged in a cone shape, cutting the sow and calf off from the rest of the herd, driving them toward the far edge of the meadow. The rest of the herd stampeded, tearing up turf, sending up sprays of moist earth as animal hooves dug for traction.

Lying flat, weapons at hand, hidden hunters waited, watching. Sensing the trap, the sow turned to follow the stampeding herd. As she turned, the hidden hunters sprang to their feet, rushing into the meadow. The sow completed her turn, running parallel to the hunters, the calf right behind, bleating. Arrows flew, glancing off the neck armor, sounding like fingernails on a blackboard. One arrow buried deep behind the shoulder of the calf. It stumbled, digging its parrot snout into the earth, bleating. Hearing the distress, the sow looked back and then started a turn, an enraged mother giving in to her instincts. A spear pierced the calf's belly, eliciting a loud, long, sharp squeal. As the mother finished her turn, two arrows struck simultaneously, the shaft from the crossbow disappearing into her shoulder. Still she came, driven by maternal instinct. A spear took her down, striking just behind the right leg, severing a key tendon. Crippled, the sow collapsed, three legs still working, but she was unable to lift herself to her feet. Hunters ran forward, plunging spears in mother and calf, slicing through the neck behind the shield, sawing deep, probing for a major artery. Blood spurted, then flowed, both animals continuing the struggle but growing weaker by the second. Quick deep breaths slowed to occasional gasps, and then, like a clock winding down, the breaths became shallower and slower, and then irregular. Finally, it came, the long slow exhale that marked the end of life.

Jacob hated hunting. He hated the blood, the death, the gutting, the butchery, and the danger. He had always been that way, ever since his father dragged him out to get his first pheasant. Jacob hated hunting, but he liked shooting, getting good enough to become a junior skeet champion. And it was Jacob's skill with a rifle that turned the Realtor into a hunter. So he hunted.

The hunters were celebrating now, cheering and slapping each other on the back, a couple dancing a victory dance. Most of the hunters were bearded, Jacob one of the few who took the trouble to shave. Jacob did it for Leah, who liked him clean-shaven. Shaking hands, Jacob joined the revelry, and then he helped settle a dispute over whose arrow struck the sow first. Jacob declared it a tie. The sow and the calf continued to bleed out, blood pooling below the wounds. An animal the size of an elephant held gallons of blood. Crazy Kramer, one of the spearmen, put his finger in the sow's pool of blood and then sucked his finger.

"Finger-lickin' good," Crazy said.

No one laughed. Crazy was a good hunter because he was big, powerful, and too stupid to know what was dangerous, but no one wanted him around when the hunt was over. Overbearing, crude, and dumb made for poor company, but he was human, and that meant Crazy was one of their own. With each passing year, there were fewer left in the Community, and that made even a life like Crazy Kramer's precious.

Then the ground trembled, then shook, and then settled back to a dying tremble. Suddenly wary, the hunters searched for signs of attack. Tremors were the early indicators of predators. Seven tons of animal were not good at sneaking through the forest, although every one of the hunters had been surprised by one at some time or another.

"Just an earthquake," Willy Williams said.

Just an earthquake, Jacob mocked silently, amazed at how quickly something so dangerous could be dismissed. And it was not just another earthquake. Small earthquakes had been occurring regularly in recent months, and getting more frequent.

Willy Williams was the master of the hunt and now took charge of field dressing the kills. Ironically, before the rest of the world disappeared, Williams worked at the Portland Zoo, preserving animals. Now he led the hunts. Removing the entrails was a messy job, so during the gutting, Jacob was happy to be a rifleman. The blood from the kills would attract scavengers, so experts did the butchering and did it quickly. These men unsheathed their knives and rolled up their sleeves, ready to begin the cutting. Willy Williams led one team of butchers, and his oldest son, Mel, the other. Once the meat was butchered, each man would pack home one hundred pounds of it.

Willy Williams and his men worked on the sow while his son's team dressed the calf. The sow rolled to her side as she died, but the calf died on its belly. Six men rolled the calf up onto its side so Mel Williams could cut through to remove the intestines. The baby was male. Mel cut off the penis and testicles, passing them to his younger brother, Jack, who held the foot-long penis in his crotch and waggled it at the others. Ribald jokes and laughter followed. The penis and testicles were good eating, however, so they were packed to go home. Willy Williams was further along, pulling out intestines, digging for the liver and heart—more good eating.

Small pterosaurs flushed from the forest were the only warning. Jacob spotted them, a dozen in flight, screeching, whiplike tails swishing the air as their featherless wings beat the air for elevation. The crack of breaking limbs came next, and then the vibrating ground as hundreds of tons of carnivores broke from the trees, charging across the meadow.

"Run!" Jacob yelled.

He could have saved his breath. The others were moving as he spoke. Unslinging his rifle, Jacob hung back, even knowing it would take a bazooka to stop a charging tyrannosaur, not a .30-06. Two other men carried rifles, and like Jacob let the others flee first, backing away from the kill, rifles ready.

The tyrannosaurs came on, the alpha male in the lead. Careful not to stumble, Jacob and the others continued to back away from the kills, picking up speed but not turning their backs on the attacking carnivores. Approaching the sow, the alpha male deviated, charging around the carcass. Jacob and the others continued to back away, rifles ready, knowing they were more effective as noisemakers than as weapons. Just when Jacob thought he was dead, the alpha male skidded to a stop, opened his jaws wide, and screamed at the humans. So close was the carnivore that Jacob felt the warmth of the tyrannosaur's breath and smelled the rot of its breakfast.

"Keep walking," Jacob said to steady the others. "Just keep walking."

The alpha male took another step, repeating the screeching. Behind it, the other tyrannosaurs reached the sow and calf, digging in. Snapping jaws and butting heads, the bigger tyrannosaurs took prime positions, snapping up the entrails from the meadow, ripping out chunks of flesh. Hearing the feast behind him, the alpha male snorted at the retreating humans and then turned back, forcing his way between two smaller tyrannosaurs, tearing off one of the sow's legs.

"Now we can run," Jacob said, giving the others a head start and then following.

"Damn, I hate hunting," Jacob muttered as he ran.

Back in the trees, the hunters gathered, nothing to show for the hunt but two balls and a penis.

"Man, that was intense," Crazy Kramer said, visibly excited. "Let's do it again!"

Ignoring Crazy, the others watched their meat disappearing down massive gullets.

"Better move on before they come looking for dessert," Willy Williams said.

Following Williams, the dejected hunters walked in the general direction of the Home Depot.

"We can't go back with nothing," Mel Williams said, walking next to his father. "Everyone's counting on us."

"There was going to be a feast," Jack Williams said, ending with a whine.

"Yeah," Willy Williams said. "I know."

"You know where we need to go," Mel Williams said.

Jacob knew what Mel was suggesting, and he watched for Willy's reaction.

"Yeah," Willy Williams said after a long pause.

"We can't go there," Jacob said, pulling on Willy's arm, looking the man in the eye.

Willy and Mel stopped, the other hunters surrounding them, listening to the argument.

"It's too dangerous," Jacob argued. "Even if we got away with the meat, they would come after us. It would trigger a war."

"It's better than starving to death," Mel argued.

"The tyrannosaurs will move on soon," Jacob argued. "They'll follow the herds any day now. We can wait them out."

"Something's keeping the tyrannosaurs here," Willy said. "They should have moved on weeks ago. Unless you want to hunt a tyrannosaur, I don't see that we have any choice."

"Fishing," Jacob argued.

"Fishing!" Mel said, rolling his eyes and tilting his head back. "Even if you can dig one of those sonsofbitches out of the ground, it's like eating a bag of glass."

Lungfish were the only fish of any size near their village, and this time of year, the fish burrowed, surviving the dry season by hibernating. This long into hibernation, the fish were essentially bones held together by tough skin.

"Yeah, but they don't kill you," Jacob said.

"One bit my little girl's finger off!" one of the hunters grumbled.

The lungfish were aggressive predators, with jaws and teeth capable of crushing shells.

"We can go to the big river," Jacob said.

Nervous mumbling spread through the clump of men. There were edible fish in the big river to the south, but the Inhumans lived between them and the river. If they skirted their territory, it would take days to reach the river, and that meant days of living in the forest, vulnerable to predators.

"We'd have to dry the fish on the bank," Willie said. "Otherwise, it would rot by the time we packed it all the way back to home."

"Yeah, and we would stink like fish on the way back," Mel Williams added. "You want to walk through the forest smelling like bait? For three days?"

The argument continued, some hunters taking the side of the Williams brothers, a few Jacob's, the rest sitting it out. Jacob's best hope of persuading the hunters came when Crazy Kramer joined those who wanted to raid the Inhumans. Crazy's support worried the others, but not enough to win the debate. With Willy in the lead again, the hunters changed direction, following a dried-up stream to the valley of the Inhumans.

"This is a mistake," Jacob muttered over and over as the hunters walked past. When the last of them was by, Jacob took up the rear, still muttering, "This is a mistake."

4

Visitors

The states with the fewest earthquakes are Florida and North Dakota. The last recorded earthquake in Florida was three years ago.

—USGS: Earthquake Hazards Program

Present Time
Near Hillsdale, Florida

Carson Wills pulled off the highway onto the dirt road leading to the old wood-frame house and steel building that served as his home and business. The road connected three farms: one abandoned; one housing the Dinosaur Wrangler; and one functioning as a flophouse for thieves, drug dealers, and transients. Carson had seen so many vehicles, late-night visitors, and young men smoking on the porch of the drug house that he had no idea who actually paid the rent. Today, three men occupied the porch, two sitting on folding lawn chairs with ragged yellow webbing, another leaning against the wall. One was shirtless, one in a muscle tee, and the one leaning against the wall was in a denim shirt with the sleeves cut off. All held beer cans; a small pyramid of empties sat between the chairs. Carson nodded as he passed. The leaner one gave Carson the finger.

At Carson's, Jeanette's chickens pecked their way through the overgrown grass in front of the small porch. Jeanette was into organic eating, and in addition to the chickens had a garden in the back with carrots, lettuce, squash, tomatoes, and snap peas. Carson liked organic food—liked all food—but warned Jeanette regularly that if she went vegetarian, he would kick her vegan ass out the door. "We'll see who kicks whose ass," Jeanette always replied.

The front door of Carson's office/house was open. Through the screen door Carson could see into the living room that served as his office. Carson hoped the air conditioner was turned off. Jeanette hated air-conditioning, blaming it for global warming, pollution, erectile dysfunction, and the decline in honeybee populations. She tolerated refrigerated air when Carson was home, but opened the doors and windows as soon as he left. "Move to Seattle," Carson suggested once. "The sun doesn't shine there." "You can stick it somewhere the sun doesn't shine," Jeanette shot back. Jeanette had attitude, and Carson liked that in a woman—at least he liked it in Jeanette.

Carson's golden retriever came from the shady side of the house, tail wagging, tongue lolling, scattering the chickens. Too old to give chase, Sally ignored the chickens, finding them annoying, not tempting. Jeanette pushed the screen door open, wearing boxer shorts and a pink T-shirt with the dinosaur wrangler character on the back, and the words DINOSAUR WRANGLER over her left breast—and what a nice breast it was, Carson thought, waving at Jeanette as he passed. The screen door screeched on opening and slammed when she released it, reminding Carson that he hadn't gotten around to fixing the closer.

Carson pulled up next to the steel building that was once a barn, got out, scratched Sally's head, and then kissed Jeanette, patting her bottom.

"You came back horny," Jeanette said. "Hornier," she corrected.

"What did you do to the neighbors?" Carson asked.

"Called the county and reported them for code violations. They've got four junk cars in the front yard, and none of them have current tags. An inspector showed up a little while ago and wrote them a citation. They have ten days to get rid of those cars. When he left, it got kind of ugly. They were dropping F-bombs on him like B-1s over Afghanistan. The inspector stopped by here when he got done and checked us out too. I think he was pretending to be fair. He hit on me."

"Yeah?"

A lot of men hit on Jeanette. She had the kind of body men noticed, but what made them hit on her was the persistent naughty look on her face. Short brown hair framed a freckled face, a wide mouth, almond eyes, a small gap in her front teeth, and a suggestive smile made Jeanette look just a little trampy. She wasn't easy, though; Carson dated her for six months before she took him to her bed.

"I came back a little richer," Carson said, opening the back of the van.

"Raptor carcasses?" Jeanette said, surprised.

"They're Visitors," Carson said.

"What? You're kidding."

"They're not tagged," Carson said.

Jeanette wore her pants tight and her tops loose, but no matter how loose the top, her figure pushed and pulled the fabric in ways that got it noticed. After eighteen months with her now, Carson still watched her when she wasn't looking. As Carson's office manager, lover, and best friend, Jeanette understood the significance of an untagged raptor.

"Are you sure?" she asked, examining the neck and thighs.

"See for yourself," Carson said, pulling his scanner from the van.

Jeanette ran the scanner over the carcasses one at a time. "Untagged raptors!" Jeanette said, amazed. "That's supposed to be impossible."

"What's the reward?" Carson asked.

"Five thousand," Jeanette said.

"Each?" Carson asked.

"I'm not sure," Jeanette said. "No one's ever found a Visitor before. They might try to pay us one finder's fee for both." Jeanette paused, put a finger to her lips, and smiled slyly. "We could freeze one and turn it in later," she said.

Carson thought about it. "It won't work. They would want to know where it came from, and it's too easy to get tripped up when you start lying. Besides, the carcasses are covered in each other's blood. They're sure to type the blood to check against the gene database. We'd get caught for sure. Good idea, though."

"What's this?" Jeanette asked, pointing at the mound behind the carcasses.

Carson opened up both back doors, climbing in. Sally stood up, paws on the edge of the floor, sniffing the carcasses. Sally had sniffed a lot of dinosaurs but never a velociraptor.

"This is the jackpot," Carson said, throwing back a blanket.

"Eggs!" Jeanette exclaimed.

"Raptor eggs," Carson said. "And no one knows I have them."

"Nesting raptors?" Jeanette said, surprised. "In Florida?"

"Yeah, go figure," Carson said.

Jeanette climbed in, kneeling by the eggs, touching them. "They're heavy," Jeanette said. "And warm too."

"We need to keep them that way," Carson said. "You fix something up in the barn while I report our find. Those velociraptors are going south fast in this heat."

Carson went to the house to make the call. Carson's desk was an old door resting on two stacks of cinder blocks. Carson sat, pulling the computer keyboard closer, then surfed the Net to find the toll-free number for reporting off-reservation dinosaurs. Carson punched in the number and then waited in a phone queue for an operator.

"Dinosaur hotline, this is Lucille, how may I help you?"

Lucille said it so fast that Carson's mind was a second behind, and he paused while it caught up.

"I found a couple of untagged dinosaurs, and I want to claim the reward," Carson said.

"Yes, sir," Lucille said. "Please give me your name and address."

"Did you hear me?" Carson asked. "I found untagged dinosaurs and they're predators—velociraptor. I know there's a reward because I am looking at your website right now."

"I heard you, sir," Lucille said evenly. "We will need to verify your claim."

"Want me to bring them in?" Carson asked.

"That's not necessary," Lucille said. "If there is a preserve or a university near you, a ranger or a faculty member may be able to do an initial screening."

"Lucille, I catch dinosaurs for a living, and these are velociraptors. They don't need no verification. Just write me that check."

"We need to verify," Lucille insisted.

Unable to argue her out of it, Carson agreed to drive the carcasses to the Ocala Preserve for verification. Carson found Jeanette in the barn piling straw. Carson helped her transfer the eggs, covering them with six more inches of straw.

"I'll be back as soon as I can," Carson said, climbing back into his van.

"You're going now?" Jeanette asked. "Robby called, and he wants to know if you'll pay for the body damage to his van? That duck-bill you sent him after crushed the fender."

"The insurance doesn't cover that," Carson said, opening the van door. "Call the insurance company and tell them it was a hit and run, but the deductible comes out of Robby's fee, and tell him to watch where he parks his damn van."

Jeanette nodded. She was used to running the operation when Carson was out on calls. Just then the ground trembled, Jeanette reaching out, grabbing one of the van's mirrors to steady herself. A few seconds later, the trembling stopped.

"An earthquake in Florida?" Jeanette said.

"Weird," Carson said, eyes on the ground.

After a few seconds, Jeanette and Carson relaxed.

"Don't forget to bill Marty and Fanny Mills," Carson said, climbing in and closing the van door.

Jeanette leaned in the open window, kissing Carson. "Do you have to go right now?" she whispered.

"It's either that or throw the raptors in the fridge."

"Go," Jeanette said, pulling back out, her pouty frown even sexier than her smile.

The leaner and his friends were still on the porch when Carson drove past, the beer can pyramid a little taller now. The leaner flipped Carson off again.

Jeanette watched Carson until he was gone, then decided to check on the eggs one more time. If Carson could make the right connection, the eggs might be worth fifteen or even twenty thousand each. Sally was already in the barn, sniffing the pile of straw. Suddenly, Sally went rigid, the hair on her neck up. Following Sally's stare, Jeanette saw a patch of straw move.

5

Office of Security Science

After the discovery on the moon, we sent a team to the Yucatán and discovered similarly altered orgonic material. We have gathered and secured that material.

—Dr. Nick Paulson, classified report to the President

Present time
Office of Security Science
Washington, D.C.

Feet on an open desk drawer, hands behind his head, Nick Paulson stared at the ceiling, thinking about the good old days. Nick was a college professor once, teaching one section of Modern Physics fall and winter, and a section of Quantum Physics in the spring. Because Nick was a tenure-track faculty member, his lab took the bulk of his time, where three graduate students did all the grunt work, and Nick published two peer-reviewed articles a year. As Nick remembered it now, he'd had no worries when he was a professor. He loved research, the teaching came naturally, and his biggest concern was getting tenure—and he did not care about tenure. Today, leaning back in his chair, Nick was sure that teaching was the good life, because when he was a teacher, dinosaurs were still extinct.

Staring at his favorite stained ceiling tile, Nick thought back to the phone call that changed the course of his life. The local PBS station contacted the University of Chicago, looking for an expert to advise on a production called *The New Physics.* The department administrative assistant transferred the call to Nick, and Nick volunteered. Unfortunately, Nick proved good at explaining abstract concepts in everyday terms—so good that he became the narrator. The series won awards, and that led to more consulting, and more narration, on a wide variety of productions, including *Everyday Physics, Living Seas, The Evolution of Evolution,* and *Mind Science.* Ironically, his last production was *Time Enough for Time.*

Notoriety led to opportunities, and when former President McIntyre's science adviser succumbed to a sex scandal, Nick was offered the position. Back then, the role of the "science adviser" was to take complex concepts and put them in terms the president could understand. Nick was perfect for the position. Back then, science advisers did not sit on the cabinet, travel to the moon, jump forward and backwards in time, and did not get chased by dinosaurs. "Science adviser" stopped being an adviser when "past" and "present" lost their meaning.

Nick had planned on serving in the McIntyre administration for a single term, and then starting his own production company, using his connections in government and the entertainment industry. But when the present collided with the Cretaceous age and the world was time-quilted, the role of science adviser became a cabinet position, and Nick found himself in a maelstrom of the improbable.

Now that Nick was the director of the Office of Security Science, the president, the American public, and most of the world looked to him to manage an unstable time matrix—as if it could be managed. Sitting up, Nick turned to his monitor, where digital video of the moon dinosaur ran in a continuous loop. The video was classified, kept from the public to keep them content. Knowing the kinds of things he hid from the public made Nick wonder what other secrets were hidden from him by the CIA, NSA, and the DOD.

One of the many secrets hidden from Nick was responsible for putting a living dinosaur on the moon. Using DOD funding, scientists built a high-tech pyramid in Alaska to collect orgonic energy.

Orgonic energy was the secret power of the pyramids used for the preservation of pharaohs. The pyramid shape functioned to collect orgonic energy, with the focal point in the pyramid being the king's chamber. Egyptians labored for centuries to perfect pyramid construction, and ninety of their orgonic collectors still stood. But as the case with Leonardo's flying machine, the Egyptians were ahead of their time. The limestone pyramids could collect the energy, but the stone was a poor storage medium. The high-tech Alaska pyramid took the Egyptian orgonic collector to a level Egyptian engineers dreamed of but could never achieve using limestone. Acting as a charged capacitor, the Alaska pyramid began shifting the time waves still rippling across the planet, creating a convergence and opening passages in time–space that led Nick and his teams from the pyramid on the moon deep into the Mayan past pursuing ecoterrorists bent on destroying civilization by triggering another, larger Time Quilt. A nuclear explosion in the time–space tunnels ended the plan, sealing the tunnels—Nick thought.

Next to the monitor was a lead box with a leaded glass top. Inside was a sample of the material retrieved from the moon. Records of the Alaska pyramid project were lost when the site was destroyed, but Nick had been in the pyramid and knew this was that same material. What he did not know was what gave it the power to ignore the arrow of time. Looking back to the looping video, Nick was sure the struggling dinosaur was not trapped in the black material, but in the time matrix. The frenetic activity was impossible, even on the moon's one-sixth gravity. Tyrannosaurs were quick, but no dinosaur could move that fast, even when panicked.

Watching the tyrannosaur, Nick quickly concluded the dinosaur was alive in a different time flow than the one Nick was in, and the tyrannosaur's time flow was faster than the one Nick occupied. Nick was intrigued with the concept of variable time flow, speculating about a connection to explain variable speed of light (VSL). Interestingly, condensed matter influenced the speed of light, and transient dense matter produced by nuclear explosions created the time waves that swept the dinosaurs into the present. It was not too big a leap to connect VSL and variable time. Nick could even visualize a means of traveling into the future and past by jumping from one time flow to another. Unfortunately, all that had to wait until Nick could assess the threat the moon dinosaur represented.

A violent shaking broke Nick's reverie, his arms clutching the armrests tightly even before Nick could tell them to. With his feet still on the desk, Nick bounced on his bottom. Then the trembling stopped. Only after the earthquake was over did Nick remember that he should have left the building or found an archway to stand in.

Nick's phone rang. It was Kaylee Kemper, his administrative assistant.

"Dr. Paulson, Dr. Gah from the Ocala Dinosaur Preserve called about a man trying to claim the reward for an untagged dinosaur," Kaylee said.

"Did you feel the earthquake?" Nick asked.

"Yes, Dr. Paulson," Kaylee said. "I think it was stronger than the last one."

"Last one?" Nick asked.

"It happened when you were in Paris," Kaylee said. "There was one around Christmas too, I think. I barely felt that one."

Nick thought that was an unusual number of earthquakes for the region, but realized he did not know much about the geology of Washington, D.C. Were three earthquakes in six months unusual?

"What do you want to do about the man claiming the untagged dinosaur reward?" Kaylee asked.

The reward for untagged dinosaurs was a gimmick used by the Office of Security Science, and the Dinosaur Rangers, to reassure the public about dinosaur safety. The few tagless dinosaurs reported under the program turned out either to be frauds with their subcutaneous tags cut out, or unregistered dinosaurs that wandered away from a private reserve. There was no reward for pet dinosaurs or illegally bred dinosaurs.

"Another fraud?" Nick asked.

"No, that's why Dr. Gah called. He examined the carcasses, and they were untagged. He said there were no signs the tags were cut out."

"Carcasses?" Nick probed.

"The claimant had two of them," Kaylee confirmed. "Both velociraptors."

Nick sucked air through his teeth, thinking. Unconsciously, he jotted notes on yellow sticky pads. "They have to be fakes."

"You want me to tell them to deny the claim?"

Nick looked at the video loop of the twisting, turning tyrannosaur. Could there be a connection?

"Where's John Roberts?" Nick asked.

"Mr. Roberts is in Berlin for the International Conference on Dinosaur Management."

Nick hesitated, knowing he wanted to handle the call, but also knowing there would be consequences. Most troubling was the fact he would have to explain this to Elizabeth.

Nick and Elizabeth had been married for eight years now, but had known each other for a decade before that. Both career-oriented, they were perfect for each other in that they expected to come second to each other's job. Keeping her maiden name, Elizabeth Hawthorne was currently a Washington, D.C., lobbyist, and former chief of staff for President McIntyre. When the present collided with the Cretaceous past, President McIntyre ordered the use of nuclear weapons to try to reverse the catastrophe and bring back the world's missing cities and citizens, and send the dinosaurs back to the past. Instead, the massed detonations froze the dinosaurs in the present. That decision ensured that President McIntyre was a one-term President and ended Elizabeth's political career.

Nick was science adviser then, and a relationship with Elizabeth began that developed into love, then marriage, and now into the deep and abiding affection they had for each other. While they gave each other a lot of space to pursue their careers, Elizabeth had elicited a promise from Nick to let younger people do the fieldwork. Keeping that promise had been relatively easy, until now.

"Tell Dr. Gah I'm on my way and ask him to keep the man who brought the velociraptors there. I want to talk to him. And Kaylee, make arrangements to get me there."

"Commercial?" Kaylee asked. "Or are you in a hurry?"

"Get the jet," Nick said.

"Do you want me to call Ms. Hawthorne and tell her what you are doing?" Kaylee asked. "Or are you going to do it?"

"I'll be back before she knows I'm gone," Nick said.

"You better hope so," Kaylee said.

6

Hatching

Velociraptors were all claws and teeth. With thirty curved teeth, three-fingered clawed hands, and four-toed clawed feet, the meat-eating velociraptors evolved to be efficient killers.

—John Roberts, OSS, Director of Field Operations

Present time
Near Hillsdale, Florida

Carefully, Jeanette moved straw aside, revealing a gently rocking raptor egg. Pushing her nose into the straw, Sally sniffed suspiciously and then snorted. Picking up the egg, Jeanette turned it over. The egg stopped rocking. Examining it carefully, she found the surface unbroken.

"Maybe they move like this all the time?" Jeanette said, holding the egg close to Sally.

Sally pushed her nose against the egg in Jeanette's hand. The egg began rocking again. Surprised, Jeanette almost dropped it. Putting it down gently, Jeanette dug in the straw, checking the other eggs. One other was rocking. Then, from outside, came the shriek and whine of police sirens. Jeanette shoved the egg deep into the straw, hastily throwing more over the top.

"Stop moving," Jeanette whispered, gently patting the straw.

Sally was already at the door, frozen, listening to the sirens—they were close, but not too close. Stepping outside, Jeanette saw police lights at the farm down the road. Police rushed the front door, using a ram to bust inside. Like rats scurrying from a burning building, young men jumped out windows or bolted out the back door. Shocked by the number of men in the house, Jeanette watched in fascination as the cops gave chase. One fleeing man sprinted toward Dinosaur Wrangler property, two cops on his heel.

"Sally," Jeanette called.

Sally came close, putting her nose in Jeanette's cupped hand. Seeing the onrushing man, Sally stiffened, then huffed and barked.

"Good dog," Jeanette said.

The runner made it to the barbed-wire fence but the cops pulled him down before he could clear it. Relieved, Jeanette relaxed, scratching Sally's head. Jerked to his feet, the man made eye contact, glaring at Jeanette. Jeanette recognized him as one of the regulars at the farm next door.

"I'll get you for this, bitch!" he shouted.

"I didn't do anything!" Jeanette shouted back.

Now handcuffed, the man started another curse, but a cop slapped the man on the back of his head.

"Shut the hell up!" the cop said.

"It wasn't me!" Jeanette shouted again.

An hour later, another cop came to the door wearing a T-shirt with POLICE written in bright yellow. Jeanette recognized him as the county inspector who cited the neighbors for code violations. Jeanette talked to him through the closed door, Sally's nose pressed against the screen, sniffing the deputy, tail wagging.

"You're a cop?" Jeanette asked.

"Yeah," he said, holding open a leather badge holder, showing a gold star with a color outline of Florida in the middle. The words DEPUTY SHERIFF curved around the top of the central image, and LAKE COUNTY FLORIDA was written underneath. "I'm Deputy Wilson. I thought I better come over and explain."

Like most men who talked to Jeanette, he let his eyes wander whenever she looked aside, so she always kept eye contact. The long eye contact either intimidated men or was misinterpreted as interest. The police officer was taller than Jeanette, but not by much—maybe five foot ten. With black hair cut short in military style, delicate features, and small chin, he was a little too pretty for a man, especially a tough guy like a cop. He was close-shaved, showing no stubble.

"We were pretty sure we knew what was going on in the house but couldn't pry a warrant out of a judge. Then you called the county, and we kind of took advantage of it so we could get a closer look. I posed as the county inspector, but they wouldn't let me inside. It didn't matter. You could smell what was what from the outside."

"What was what?" Jeanette repeated, gently making fun of Deputy Wilson.

"They had a meth lab in the basement. Don't worry, a hazmat team is coming to clean it up.

"Glad I could help."

"So, are you alone?"

Jeanette glared at him.

"I'm just asking because a couple of those guys were making threats," Deputy Wilson added quickly. "They think you tipped us about the lab."

"Oh, great!"

"I told them you had nothing to do with it," Wilson said. "So I'm sure there's nothing to worry about. They're not getting out anytime soon anyway. There's at least two parole violations among those assholes, and one is a two-time loser. He'll be gone for life. Besides, with the lab confiscated, there's nothing to come back for."

"Except me," Jeanette said, surprised how scared she was.

"So, if you're alone out here, I could stop by once in a while. Just to make sure you're okay."

"This is my boyfriend's place," Jeanette said.

"Okay. That's good," Deputy Wilson said, not hiding his disappointment. "I'm sure nothing will happen but . . . I thought . . . Well, it's good you're not alone."

"Thanks for caring," Jeanette said.

"Here's my number, just in case," Deputy Wilson said.

His number was on the back of a napkin from Wendy's. Jeanette took the napkin, wishing she had a dollar for every phone number men had given her. Deputy Wilson walked to the road and then toward the police circus next door. He looked back twice. Jeanette waited until he was with the cops, and then she went to the steel building.

The straw pile was not moving. Sally sniffed the spot anyway.

"I think this is a good sign," Jeanette said.

Jeanette pushed her hand into the straw, feeling for the moving egg. Touching something slimy, she jerked her hand out, gasping and stepping back at the same time. Sally yelped, surprised by the sudden move. Waiting for her heart to recover, Jeanette gently brushed straw from the spot, slowly revealing a pink, wiggling baby raptor.

"This isn't good, Sally," Jeanette said.

Taking cues from Jeanette's body language and tone, Sally sniffed the raptor chick suspiciously.

Carefully, Jeanette scooped the chick from the straw, pulling its lower body from broken pieces of shell. It wiggled, its eyes closed.

"Carson's not going to like this," Jeanette said.

Then the chick's eyes opened, fixing on Jeanette. It was six inches long—Jeanette could crush the chick in one hand—yet she was afraid. Subconsciously, Jeanette knew what the chick would grow into and what raptors and their larger cousins ate—every living thing. The chick opened and closed its eyes, and then its mouth, Jeanette discovering baby raptors came ready to shred meat—it had teeth. Then Jeanette saw more movement in the straw. Brushing carefully, Jeanette uncovered another chick, peeking through a hole in its shell. Two more eggs were rocking.

"Sally, we've got a problem!" Jeanette said.

"Woof," Sally agreed.

7

Raid

These dinosaurs are hadrosaurs, but most people call them "duck-billed dinosaurs" because of their long flat snouts. They were one of the last dinosaurs to appear on the Earth, just before the age of dinosaurs came to an end. Duck-billed dinosaurs roamed the Earth in giant herds, and there were so many of them that people call them the cows of the Cretaceous. We think that duck-bills were likely the favored food of Tyrannosaurus rex.

—Nick Paulson, lecture to students of New James John Grade School, Portland, Oregon

Unknown Time
Neverland

They saw no guards, but skirted possible watch points. The humans rarely entered Inhuman territory, let alone raided the valley the Inhumans used as a corral. They counted on the security being light. Only Mel had actually seen the corral, so he led the way. Jacob brought up the rear, his eyes busy, his rifle ready.

Climbing down the box end of the canyon, the humans picked their way carefully, afraid of dislodging loose rock. Jacob climbed down with the others, knowing it was a bad idea but not willing to let the others down. As a rifleman, Jacob protected their backs. At the bottom, the humans hid among the rocks, looking for guards.

"So far, so good," Mel Williams whispered.

"Hell yeah!" Crazy Kramer said too loud.

Everyone shushed him.

"Hell yeah," Crazy Kramer whispered.

Now Willy Williams took the lead, keeping close to the canyon wall. The narrow end was rocky, but it quickly widened out into a small, lush valley. The herd was here, milling, grazing confidently, free of predators. A small waterfall poured from the rim, down to a lake along the east side of the canyon. The lake spilled out to form a marsh, streams running all the way to the valley outlet. At the far end of the valley were the stone pillars that kept the herd penned, and beyond that, lava rock that protected the valley from the carnivores like the *Albertosaurus, Deinonycus,* and *T. rex*. Smaller predators could navigate the lava forest, but the hadrosaurs in the valley were too big for them to hunt.

The Inhumans maintained a herd of about fifty hadrosaurs as a food reserve. The crested and duck-billed dinosaurs were semi-tame, despite the fact the Inhumans regularly culled the herd. Sprinkling the valley were the bleached bones of their kills. Ranging from the size of a small car to a bus, the bipedal hadrosaurs grazed in a loose herd, a third standing in marsh, sunk to their knees.

The hunters waited, letting Willy select the animal to kill.

"That one," Willy said, pointing.

Medium sized, the animal limped, a crust of blood on one knee. The humans had never hunted a hadrosaur before, since the only hadrosaurs near their home were in this valley. Wherever the Inhumans got the animals was not near human territory. Hadrosaurs did not mix with the herds the humans hunted. However, the duck-billed dinosaurs were bipedal, and that meant fast.

Following hand signals, the hunters spread out, staying low, moving slowly, creeping up on the limping hadrosaur. Periodically, one of the hadrosaurs would lift its head, watch the humans advance, and then put its head back down and eat, moving slowly away from the humans. The limping hadrosaur followed the same pattern, but moved more slowly, favoring its injured leg. With a signal from Willy, the humans all laid down, ferns and other low vegetation hiding them from the hadrosaurs. The herd stopped moving away, resuming the random milling. Occasionally, a juvenile would kick up its heels, prancing, splashing, and pawing up gobs of mud.

It was cool in the ferns, the ground moist, soaking through the ragged clothes that Jacob wore. Flies buzzed his head, and then a mosquito landed on the back of his hand. Cradling the rifle and needing to move slowly, it had a belly full of his blood before he freed a hand to squish it. *If I had to get sent back in time, why couldn't it be before mosquitoes evolved?* Jacob thought.

Hidden in the vegetation, the hunters switched to sound signals. A series of soft whistles from Willy put them in motion. Six hunters inched slowly through the ferns and canes, forming a semicircle around the limping hadrosaur. The others hung back, ready to pursue if needed. Light gusts from the open end of the valley kept their scent away from the hadrosaur until it was partially surrounded. Suddenly suspicious, the hadrosaur rose to its full height, rearing back on its legs, peering down into the vegetation. Alerted, others in the herd assumed the same position, all oriented toward the humans.

"Now!" Willy shouted.

Hunters erupted from the ferns, bows and spears launched. Reared back as it was, the hadrosaur had exposed its neck, and arrows and spears buried into its upper chest and neck. Ready with his rifle, Jacob tracked the screaming dinosaur, still rocked back, now clawing at its neck. The rest of the herd stampeded away from the attack toward the lake, splashing through the marsh. Too stupid, or too scared to run, the hadrosaur continued to stand tall, clawing its neck. It would run soon.

"Crazy!" Jacob called to Crazy Kramer who was reloading his spear thrower.

A huge grin on his face, Crazy partially turned, only half-aware of Jacob.

"Take out its knee!" Jacob yelled.

Confused, Crazy looked back and forth, Jacob frantically pointing at his own knee. Finally, understanding dawned. Just as the hadrosaur rocked back down, Crazy let fly, his spear burying in the wounded knee. Now the hadrosaur squealed from pain, or the unfairness of being singled out from the herd. Hopping on one leg, moving in a circle, more arrows and spears hitting home, and the hadrosaur went down. Willy raced forward, using his razor-sharp knife to slice deep into its neck, searching for the artery. Blood spurted and the hunt was over.

Not waiting for the hadrosaur to die, Willy and Mel went to work, using a boning knife to slice it from anus to sternum, and then reached in to pull out arms full of guts. The hadrosaur writhed in agony at first and then twitched and died. Other hunters sorted the intestines, packing some, then taking the liver and heart. Then they went to work, cutting ten-pound steaks and roasts from haunches, rump, and shoulders. Precision and pride were gone; the meticulously honed knives flew, chunks of meat tossed to men standing in two lines to take, wrap, and pack the meat. The bone saw remained in the pack, feeling there was no time to cut out ribs. When every man had all the meat he could carry, they left the rest. Half the animal was untouched, and it pained them to walk away.

Heavily laden, smeared with blood, they trooped in a long row down the valley. As a rifleman, Jacob carried less, his load closer to fifty pounds instead of the hundred pounds carried by most. Crazy Kramer carried two hundred pounds, walking easier than Jacob. They passed through the stone pillars built by the Inhumans to pen their herd in the valley, and into the volcanic terrain. Jacob had his best boots on, repaired many times, but some of the hunters wore moccasins, planning to hunt the jungles.

The passage through the rock was narrow, seldom trod, and the heavily laden men stumbled frequently. Hot and humid, with no time to stop for water, they hurried, the line stringing out with the slowest in the back. Positioned in the rear, Jacob watched the high points on either side and periodically turned to look behind—he saw nothing. It was late afternoon when they cleared the lava field and were into the cool of the leafy forest. Jacob backed up the last few yards between the lava field and the forest, eyes busy. Just as he stepped from the heat into the shade of the forest, he saw movement. Stopping in the shadow, Jacob studied an outcropping to his right. A lone Inhuman stood there, staring, not trying to hide. Its large eyes, noseless face, wide mouth showed no emotion that a human could read. Jacob stared back, feeling like he should shout an apology and explain that their families were starving, but humans and Inhumans did not communicate, could not communicate. Every contact so far had ended in murder. With no hope of explaining, Jacob turned and hurried away with his stolen meat.

8

Unlicensed

"Dangerous dinosaur" includes, but is not limited to, dinosaurs that are known to have a propensity, tendency, or disposition to attack unprovoked, cause injury, or otherwise endanger the safety of human beings or domestic animals. Any animal designated as a "dangerous dinosaur" must be licensed through the Office of Dinosaur Control.

—Federal Dinosaur Control Act, Section 47-3-320

Present Time
Ocala Dinosaur Preserve
Florida

Nick ran the scanner over the carcasses a third time—still no tag. The carcasses lay on stainless-steel countertops ready for dissection. One of the velociraptors was intact, with three holes in its chest. The other was partially shredded. Part of the Ocala Preserve complex, the dissection room's walls and floor were covered in white tiles. Two stainless-steel sinks were bolted to one wall. Over each island counter were pull-down hoses for hot and cold water and compressed air. The whole room could be hosed down or steam cleaned. The floor sloped toward the large drain in the middle. Banks of lights made the room as bright as an operating room.

"The tags go here, or here, or here," Dr. Norman Gah explained, pointing at the neck, thigh, and hips of the velociraptor Nick kept scanning. "Except the only velociraptors in the continental United States are in Texas and Louisiana, not Florida."

"They must be hobby velociraptors," Carmen Wynooski said.

Wynooski was a senior Dinosaur Ranger, the equivalent rank of captain in the army. Wynooski was five foot five, and 160 pounds. Little of it was fat. With a round face, sun-bleached hair in a ragged pixie haircut, brown eyes, and gray teeth, she looked like Nick's eighth-grade gym teacher, except not quite as attractive. With skin the color of the bottom of a tarnished copper pan, she was courting melanoma.

"Every bubble-riding day trader just has to have their own slice of Dinosauria," Wynooski continued. "And the bigger and badder, the better. These two velocies probably had their owners for lunch. We should start looking for some shredded designer jeans and a pile of bones."

"This is a male and a female pair," Dr. Gah said.

"They come that way," Wynooski said.

"Norman is suggesting a hobby farmer would not pick a male and female, since they will breed," Nick said.

"Of course they'll breed," Wynooski said. "Velocies hump like rabbits. What the hell do the yuppies care?"

Carmen was an excellent ranger, an organized and efficient administrator, and protective of her people, but she had enough confidence for two people, and it was annoying. Wynooski was always 100 percent sure, but only 50 percent right.

"Someone might buy a breeding pair, but it is unlikely," Dr. Gah said, pulling on plastic gloves and picking up a scalpel. "Let's see if we can find out where they came from."

Dr. Norman Gah was a small man of mixed race—Nick had no idea which races. Slightly Asian in appearance, he had pale skin, with eyebrows as thick and wild as his black hair. Both the eyebrows and hair were in need of combing. With a high forehead and gold-colored wire-rimmed glasses, he had a bit of a mad-scientist look about him.

"Where the hell else would they come from?" Wynooski asked, leaning against a sink, arms folded across her chest. She wore the cargo shorts version of the ranger uniform: green shirt, beige cargo shorts. "It had to be from around here somewhere. The damn things couldn't traipse cross-country without getting noticed, not to mention they'd kill everything that crossed their path."

Dr. Gah sliced the abdomen of the most intact velociraptor and then reached inside, feeling around. A mass of white intestines spilled out. Ignoring the intestines, Dr. Gah reached inside again, this time with his scalpel, working by touch, and then pulled out a shiny purplish mass—the stomach. When he sliced it open, liquid spilled out and lumps of gray meat.

Nick's eyes watered from the sour vomit smell, and he cupped his hand over his nose.

"Whee-ew!" Wynooski said. "Someone light a match."

Dr. Gah ignored Wynooski, sorting the lumps of meat and chunks of bone.

"Dog, I would say," Gah said, shoving a few pieces to one side. "Maybe some rabbit appetizer."

Dr. Gah shoved a soggy piece of fur to one side, a slimy mass with flecks of white.

"Let's see what's in the other stomach," Dr. Gah said.

Dr. Gah dug back inside, this time leaning over, nearly shoving his head into the cavity. Finally, he managed to pull out the velociraptor's second stomach. While he was opening it, more liquid spilled. Dr. Gah dug out gooey contents, spreading them on the stainless-steel surface.

"This is interesting," Dr. Gah said, leaning close, separating chunks from goo. After opening a drawer, Dr. Gah pulled out a pair of large tweezers. He dug into the goo and pulled out a small chunk. "This is a little piece of hollow bone. Do you know what has hollow bones?"

"Birds," Wynooski said confidently. "Those bastards are fast enough to snatch a hawk right out of the air."

"This isn't a bird bone," Dr. Gah said.

"Pterosaur," Nick said. "That's impossible."

"Can't be a pterosaur," Wynooski said. "Must be a bird. The only two pterosaur colonies on this continent are south of the border—

way south. You can't eat something you can't get to. It has to be a bird bone."

"Ranger, for the first twenty years of my professional life, all we knew about the Dinosauria came from fossilized bones. Often, chunks this size were all we had to work with. Trust me, this is a pterosaur bone."

Nick stood close, looking at the bone through his bifocals. Well outside his expertise, all he could tell was that it was hollow.

"Looks like some skin too," Dr. Gah said. "I'll send it to Washington to confirm, but eighty will get you only twenty that this membrane covered a wing."

"Where would these two get a pterosaur wing?" Wynooski asked. "KFC? Someone is playing a joke on you two."

"Untagged carnivores with pterosaur in their stomachs," Dr. Gah said, still poking in the intestine goo. "Velociraptors haven't eaten like that for sixty-five million years."

"You scientists just have to make everything so damn complicated," Wynooski complained. "The same yuppies that owned these velociraptors probably owned a pterosaur. When these velocies broke out of their pen, they had a little pterosaur snack before hitting the road. And that's the name of that tune."

"Look at this," Gah said, digging something out of the stomach goo. After picking it up with tweezers, he dropped it in a pan of water, swished it around, and then dried it off with a paper towel. Tossed in an empty stainless-steel bowl, it rattled like a rock. Before Gah could pass it to Dr. Paulson, Wynooski reached in and picked it up.

"Looks like plastic," Wynooski said. "Funny-looking stuff."

"It was in the stomach with the pterosaur," Gah said.

Dr. Paulson stepped over, looking into Wynooski's palm. "Drop that!" Paulson said, slapping her wrist.

"What the hell?" Wynooski said, the black bit falling to the floor.

Paulson picked the material up with tweezers and dropped it back in the bowl.

"Sorry, Carmen, but if this is what I think it is, you shouldn't handle it," Nick said.

Nick looked at the material, finding it hard to focus on. If this was the same material as on the moon, what was it doing in the stomach of a velociraptor with the remains of a pterosaur?

"Here's another piece," Gah said, still rooting around in the stomach contents. "That pterosaur might have had it in its gizzard."

"I want to meet the man who brought these in, and I want to meet him now," Nick said.

9

Brood

Observation of dinosaurs in the Houston Preserve confirmed that velociraptors lay their eggs in a spiral cluster, in a dug-out nest, and then cover the eggs with vegetation to keep the eggs warm. The velociraptors then guard the nest, night and day.

—*Dinosaur Facts,* Houston Preserve Brochure

Present Time
Near Hillsdale, Florida

"No, no, get back in there," Jeanette said, catching another chick tumbling down the pile of straw.

The straw pile was alive now with wriggling blue-skinned velociraptor chicks, kicking and flailing, trying to climb up out of the straw. With long whiplike tails, thin legs, and large heads, the chicks had trouble balancing, the straw giving way beneath them, or their heavy heads pulling them nose down. Tails and head high, the chicks kept trying to stand over and over.

Jeanette repeatedly covered them with straw, trying to keep them hidden, but the chicks would not cooperate. Making a hoarse mewing sound, they made so much noise, hiding them did no good anyway. Another chick slipped through the straw, sliding to the wood floor. Sally sniffed it, the chick continuing to mew, its beak open wide. Jeanette cupped it in two hands and put it back in the pile.

"This isn't working," Jeanette said.

Sally whined softly.

"Watch them, Sally," Jeanette said.

Stepping outside, Jeanette saw the sun coming up. It was dawn, and Carson had not returned.

"Carson, you owe me," Jeanette said.

Jeanette hurried to the house and got an old Mexican blanket: green plaid with fringe. It was Carson's, brought back from a trip to Matamoros. Jeanette had always hated the blanket. She took two old towels—the only kind Carson had—and returned to the barn. Sally was faithfully standing watch, her nose nearly touching one of the chicks.

Working the blanket under the chicks, Jeanette created a high-sided nest; she pulled chicks from the straw and put them in the blanket-lined nest. The blanket made a solid floor, and the chicks stayed put now but made even more noise. Piece by piece, Jeanette pulled the eggshells from the straw. All seven had hatched.

"Now what?" Jeanette said, the jaws of all seven mewing chicks open wide and pointed at her.

Sally whimpered, nuzzling Jeanette's hand.

Jeanette scratched the dog's ears. "You want breakfast, don't you?"

At the word "breakfast," Sally barked. Instantly, the chicks stopped mewing and all of them lay flat, eyes open, bodies motionless.

"Don't be scared," Jeanette said, reassuring the ugly brood. "Sally won't hurt you."

Slowly the chicks stirred, looking around.

"It's okay," Jeanette said, putting some cheer in her voice.

As if one, the chicks popped up and began mewing again.

"Stand guard," Jeanette ordered Sally.

Sally whined, as tired of the chicks as Jeanette was. Upon returning to the house, Jeanette went to the back porch, where they kept Sally's Purina Dog Chow. Built against the back wall of the house were shelves they used as a pantry. There were two cans of Alpo Prime Cuts on the shelf: one beef flavor, one chicken. Jeanette read the label. The first ingredient on the chicken Alpo can was water. There were also "poultry by-products." Carson was too cheap to buy Alpo for Sally regularly, but treated her to a can now and then. Sally loved it. Would velociraptor chicks?

Taking the two cans, Sally's bowl, a can opener, and a spoon, Jeanette went back to the barn. Sally was still on guard, but trotted over when she saw the bowl. The chicks erupted in loud mewing when they saw Jeanette. Ignoring them, Jeanette opened the can of beef Alpo and dumped it into Sally's bowl. Sally's nose was in the bowl before Jeanette had it on the ground. With Sally gobbling her breakfast, Jeanette opened the can of chicken Alpo.

Sniffing the contents, Jeanette turned up her nose. There was nothing chickenlike in the smell coming from the can. Whatever the smell, the chicks went wild, heads back, jaws open, mewing in their deep coarse way.

"Patience, you little brats," Jeanette said, scooping out a chunk.

The pieces were slimy and square. After tearing off a small chunk, Jeanette dropped it in an open mouth. With an audible series of snaps, the Alpo disappeared down a gullet, and the jaws came open again. Jeanette worked systematically, feeding small chunks to the chicks, trying to give each an equal amount. The chicks never stopped mewing between mouthfuls, but when the Alpo was gone, they settled down, mewing only occasionally. Finally, two flopped down, one with its head on the neck of the other. Jeanette noticed the chicks were pinkish now.

Her bowl licked clean, Sally sprawled in spilled straw, half asleep.

"You watch them," Jeanette said. "I have to run to the store."

Sally whimpered an objection but was too tired to get up.

Taking Carson's pickup truck, Jeanette drove past the house the police had raided. The front door was open. Jeanette made a mental note to walk over and close the door later. Right now, she had to get to the store and buy a case of Alpo.

10

Feast

When dinosaurs came to the present, we were finally able to answer the question that many of us have been asking since the beginning of recorded history. Dinosaurs taste like a gamey emu.

—Chef/owner, Dinosaur Café

Unknown Time
Neverland

The smell of barbecuing hadrosaur meat was intoxicating, putting the semi-starved Community in a party mood. Skinny children chased one another, roughhousing in ways they could not get away with on any other day. Too busy and too distracted, their parents ignored the misbehavior. Fragrant smoke rose from three pits where enough meat roasted to feed the entire Community. The pits were just outside the former Home Depot that served as the human fort. Pickets watched from the top of the earthen berm bordering the compound. The setting sun silhouetted guards on the berms, rifles on their hips or across shoulders providing a sense of security. On the other side of the berm, one hundred yards of cleared forest served as a killing field. Each day, older children armed with machetes patrolled the field, hacking and chopping the vegetation back, a never-ending war with nature.

Torches were lit as the shadows deepened. Mothers with children slung on their backs prepared bowls of roasted corn, potatoes, and yams taken from dwindling supplies. It was an extravagant meal, but few grumbled and none grumbled out loud. The reverend declared there would be a feast, so there would be a feast. At least in this, Jacob agreed with the reverend. There was little enough to celebrate in the dwindling Community.

Despite the rambunctious children, sprinkling of babies, and pregnant women, the Community was dying. Child mortality was high, one out of six women died in childbirth, and the hard work of farming and hunting made the men old beyond their years. The few humans who had lived to be old women and men helped as best they could, setting up tables, benches, and chairs, some too infirm even to do this much. Still, there were smiles all around this day, because today there was plenty.

The successful hunters would sit with Reverend at a special table facing the rest of the Community. Normally, the places on his left and right were reserved for his four wives, but today the wives shifted along the side tables to make room for the hunters. Despite having four wives, Reverend had no children of his own, but his wives, all widows, had ten children that he called his own.

Jacob carried chairs to the front, taking them from inside the former Home Depot, his wife, Leah, carrying another. Their two girls tagged along, one hanging on to Leah's apron, the other skipping ahead. Beatrice was six, and Bonnie three. Bea had her mother's curly brown hair, Bonnie taking after her father with straight hair so dark brown, it was almost black. Bea had her mother's delicate features, with a petite nose and a small mouth. It was early for Bonnie, but she might have been unlucky enough to get Jacob's large nose. Both girls wore their best clothes; sky blue dresses that hung below their knees. Leah fashioned the dresses from cloth she found in the ruins of the city. With the help of Grandma Reilly, Leah sewed her first dresses, giving them to the girls for Christmas. Few in the Community knew anything about sewing, so Grandma Reilly was passing the skill down so that it would not be lost when she died. Leah was her best student and had also crafted the loose dress that she wore under her apron. Made from kitchen curtains that Jacob found in a collapsed house, the light yellow dress with blue cornflowers was the envy of the other women in the sewing classes.

"What's wrong?" Leah asked as they put the chairs down and turned to go back for another load.

"What?" Jacob asked, pretending to look cheerful.

"I can tell something's not right," Leah said.

Husbands could seldom hide things from wives, and Leah was especially sensitive to guilty indicators—averted gazes, forced smiles, avoidance of topics.

"No one was hurt or killed, and you came back with enough meat to stretch our supplies until the herds come back," Leah said.

Six inches shorter than Jacob, Leah looked up at him, concern in her piercing blue eyes. Naturally curly brown hair hung to her shoulders, tied in back to keep it out of her eyes. Hard work countered some of the effects of childbirth on her body, so she was lean, having only a modicum of the middle age spread that came to women nearing forty. Tropical sun and heat leathered everyone despite wearing broad-brimmed hats. Deeply tanned, her face creased with smile lines, Leah studied him with genuine concern.

"Do you know what kind of meat that is?" Jacob asked.

"I didn't get a good look," Leah said.

"It's hadrosaur," Jacob said.

"Hadrosaur? Duck-bills?"

Saying nothing, Jacob let Leah work it out.

"Oh, no!" Leah said. "You stole meat from the Inhumans?"

"Rustled it right out of their canyon," Jacob said. "I couldn't talk Willy and Mel out of it. Believe me, I tried. The rest went along with the Williams brothers just like they do the reverend."

Glancing sideways, Leah checked to see if anyone was close enough to hear. Then she looked at Bonnie, who still clung to her apron. Two boys crawling on all fours under a table, knocking over chairs, absorbed her. Bea skipped ahead, almost back to the entrance to their fort.

"But everyone came back," Leah said, confused.

"We got away before they knew we were there, but I'm pretty sure one of them spotted us. Not that it matters. As far as they know, we're the only ones on the whole damn planet besides them."

"They'll do something," Leah said, biting her lower lip.

"Yeah," Jacob said, putting his arm around her shoulders and pulling her close.

Leah slipped an arm around his waist, leaning into him.

"Keep the girls close for the next few days," Jacob said. "Stay in the fort as much as you can."

"It's too hot," Leah said.

It was a complaint, not disagreement.

Reverend called everyone to dinner using the bell. Rescued from the ruins of a Catholic church, the bell had been scorched by one of the many fires that destroyed the city, but the brass bell polished up well. Mounted with a yoke and pillars, the bell could be turned with a big wheel mounted on one side. The bell rang for Sunday and Wednesday services, special events, and for emergencies. Generally, Jacob hated the sound of the bell, since the most common purpose was summoning the Community to church. A lifelong agnostic, Jacob participated in church for two reasons. First, because it was the only way to stay in the Community, and second because Leah was a true believer and Jacob loved Leah. Sitting in church, looking around during Reverend's long-winded prayers, Jacob caught the eye of many other skeptics, all just as cowed by the reverend as Jacob. If the Community were a democracy, the reverend might get voted out of office, but no one even dared hint of dissatisfaction. Banishment was the reverend's favorite punishment, and once cut off from the Community, there was no chance of surviving.

Taking a seat as far from the reverend as possible, Jacob waved at his girls, who beamed with pride that their daddy was sitting at the head table. Rising to his feet, the reverend did not need to ask for quiet. As though of one mind, the crowd quieted, only the few infants gurgling or whimpering. Church-trained, even the preschool children knew to be silent.

"God has blessed us," Reverend said.

"Amen," responded the crowd.

Jacob knew what was coming. Reverend was nothing if not predictable.

"I said, God has blessed us!" Reverend repeated.

"Amen," the crowd said with more enthusiasm.

"We can do better than that," Reverend said. *"God has blessed us!"* Reverend thundered.

"Amen!" the crowd shouted, some jumping to their feet.

"Wow!" Reverend said, patting his chest. "That nearly knocked me off my feet."

A few people chuckled.

"We are a thankful people, aren't we?" Reverend roared.

"Amen!" people shouted in affirmation.

"But we are a forgetful people," Reverend came back. "We are thankful now because we have plenty, but just yesterday some of you were doubting God. Weren't you? Don't deny it, you know who you are!"

Reverend slowly looked over the Community, most people avoiding eye contact. Reverend was all-powerful in the Community, doling out rations and supplies, deciding disputes, even approving or disapproving marriages. With a core of fanatic supporters, the reverend exercised total control.

"But that's okay," Reverend continued. "God forgives your doubt. God expects your doubt. God tolerates your doubt, but don't think for a second that God is happy with a bunch of backsliding doubters that forget about God's many mercies the first time they have an empty belly."

Jacob squirmed, knowing it had been weeks of empty bellies. Jacob also knew what the reverend would spew next.

"But I did not doubt. Did I?"

"No, Reverend," a few mumbled.

"I said, I did not doubt, did I?" the reverend thundered.

"No, Reverend," came the loud response.

"That's right. I am steadfast in my trust of God the almighty. God the father. God the creator. God our protector."

Now he paused, letting the guilt settle in.

"Because of that steadfastness, God has blessed us with this feast. So let us eat from the table that God has set, and tomorrow we will renew our commitment through a day of prayer."

Jacob moaned silently, making a note to bribe Larry Memphis to get assigned to guard duty. It would get him out of hours of sitting in silence. Now the reverend prayed a long flowery prayer composed of 50 percent praise of God and 50 percent self-aggrandizement. Then it was time to eat.

Joyous noise filled the clearing, plates passed, dishes clanking, friends and family talking and laughing. Plates were filled for the guards on the berm, older children running the plates across the clearing and up the berm to the guards and then racing back to their places. Jacob waved at his children again, happy to see them too busy eating to wave back. After cutting off a chunk of meat, Jacob forked it in his mouth, savoring the smoky crust, and then chewed, releasing the gamey taste. It was delicious. Two more bites and Jacob saw one of the guards waving both arms frantically. He was shouting, but nothing could be heard over the din. Another guard sprinted from his position on the berm toward the bell. Jacob stood, those on either side noticing, looking at him, and then at where he pointed. The din died quickly, the bell beginning to ring. A few seconds of frozen confusion, and then rifle fire from the berm. Then panic.

Men, women, and children collided as they rushed to find one another. Reverend shouted orders, but no one could hear him over the din. Then the ground shook, as if from an earthquake. Jacob knew what was coming, and now he rushed to Leah, who already had the children by the hand.

"Get them inside," Jacob said unnecessarily.

His rifle over his shoulder, Jacob surveyed the berm where the guards had gathered together, concentrating their fire. Suddenly, the guards broke, running down the berm pell-mell. Jacob ran to a point between the fort and the berm, families flowing past. Other riflemen came: one, two, four, six. Pitiful few for what was coming. Then Crazy Kramer joined them, holding a machete in one hand and a spear in the other.

"Bring it on!" Kramer shouted.

As if in response to Kramer, over the berm charged a triceratops. Jacob raised his rifle, but with the animal coming head-on, there was no target. A bullet could not pierce the huge bony collar, and with the massive head bobbing, hitting the snout or an eye was impossible. A rifleman next to Jacob fired, wasting a precious round.

Five more triceratops came over the berm at various spots, the ground shaking as the five-ton animals came on like living tanks. Tables and chairs were overturned, the precious foods trampled. The remains of a collapsed table fell into a cooking pit, flames erupting, a shower of sparks lighting the flow of panicked humans toward the fort. Charging triceratops closed from different angles, cutting off retreat. It was a coordinated attack by the triceratops, but how? Looking through the chaos, Jacob realized there was an Inhuman mounted on the back of the nearest triceratops. From his angle, Jacob could see the hairless head of another Inhuman mounted on a second. The Inhumans had not stampeded the triceratops through camp; they were riding them in.

"Come with me!" Jacob shouted in the middle of the maelstrom.

Pulling the other riflemen with him, Jacob angled them away from the triceratops now charging toward the entrance to the fort. Even with families still outside the building, the steel door was coming down. Jacob saw Reverend inside directing the closing.

"That one!" Jacob ordered. "Take out the rider. On my command!"

Rifles to their shoulders, the frightened men aimed as best they could. One man would have little chance of hitting the bouncing target, but concentrated, they might get lucky.

"Fire!" Jacob shouted.

It was a rippling broadside, but the rider toppled, the triceratops turning as the rider slid down its side. Confused, enraged, and wounded, the triceratops ran wild, sweeping its head, knocking everyone and everything from its path.

"All right!" Crazy Kramer bellowed, shaking his spear high above his head.

"Now that one!" Jacob said, pointing out another.

This triceratops Jacob saw was also bearing down on the steel door that was now nearly closed.

"Looky there!" Crazy Kramer shrieked. "Bring it on!"

Flickering light from the burning wreckage revealed Inhumans on top of the berm. Standing shoulder to shoulder, the Inhumans dotted the crest in a continuous line. More Inhumans crowded up behind those in the front row. This was not a simple punitive raid. The Inhumans had come in force.

The deafening crash of the triceratops hitting the door of the fort stunned everyone into silence. In the dim light, Jacob could see the door ajar. The triceratops was wedged between the frame and the twisted metal. The longest horn of the triceratops had actually pierced the steel.

The clicks, clucks, and guttural sounds of the Inhumans came from the top of the berm, and then as one the Inhumans charged.

"Fire at will!" Jacob yelled, as he shoved men into a line.

The riflemen aimed carefully, picking off Inhuman after Inhuman, but there were too many. The Inhumans were coming in overwhelming force and the riflemen could not do enough damage.

"Retreat!" Jacob ordered reluctantly.

Falling back, Jacob fired precious round after precious round. Crazy Kramer backed up next to him, yelling, "Bring it on!" over and over. Suddenly, Crazy Kramer brushed Jacob back with a meaty arm and then threw his spear past Jacob's face. Looking left, Jacob saw an Inhuman pierced through the chest, its large eyes wide in shock. Bleeding red, it collapsed, clutching at the shaft.

Looking to the fort, Jacob saw Inhumans at the door, urging the triceratops to back up. Torn metal cut into its side, and it shrieked and writhed its two tons. The Inhumans were gathering by the entrance to the fort, ready to rush inside. Crazy Kramer stepped forward, meeting an onrushing Inhuman, and with a mighty blow cut through the spear the Inhuman held up in a defensive move, burying his machete in the side of the Inhuman's head.

"Keep them off of me!" Jacob shouted.

"Bring it on!" Crazy Kramer said, shaking his bloody machete.

Taking aim, Jacob shot the triceratops still jammed in the door. The triceratops continued to struggle to get free, seemingly unaware that it was wounded. Jacob shot it again, and again, his third round killing an Inhuman. After his fourth shot, the triceratops dropped to its knees, its massive head sagging to the ground. Then it was still. Feeling he had done his best to protect his family, Jacob backed away, fishing for his remaining ammunition. He found two shells. He put one in the chamber. As he backed up, Jacob stumbled over a body. Looking around, Jacob saw a circle of Inhuman bodies around Crazy Kramer. Bleeding from a dozen wounds, Crazy swiped at another Inhuman, wobbling as he did.

"Let's go!" Jacob said to Crazy Kramer, pulling his arm.

"Bring it on," Crazy Kramer said, gasping for breath.

Hacking Inhumans to death was heavy work, and Crazy Kramer was exhausted. Backing up with Jacob, they moved toward the forest. Bodies littered the clearing; Inhuman and human. Triceratops rampaged up and down, destroying wells, gardens, sheds, tools, shelters, and stores. At the door to the fort, the Inhumans had created an opening large enough to crawl through, and now like a line of ants, were systematically squeezing past the dead triceratops and into the fort. Nearly running now, Jacob saw a triceratops turn their way.

"Run!" Jacob yelled.

With one last "Bring it on!" Crazy Kramer ran after Jacob.

11

Time Tunnel

Kenny Randall's original model predicting the intermix of the Cretaceous age and the modern age was a remarkable achievement. I regret that we have not been able to refine the model well enough to predict subsequent time disruptions.

—Dr. Emmett Puglisi, Office of Security Science

Present Time
Ocala, Florida

"Carson, where are you?" Jeanette demanded into her phone.

"In a Super Eight. The stingy bastards aren't too eager to cough up the reward."

"Tell them to send you a check and get back here," Jeanette said.

"I have to meet with the head guy or they won't give me the money. They're on their way over right now."

"You need to get back here!" Jeanette said. "You know that . . . that . . . stuff you left with me?"

"Not on the phone," Carson said quickly. "No one needs to know about my . . . my stuff but me and you."

"You need to get back here," Jeanette said. "Now."

"As soon as I get the reward, I'll hit the road."

There was a long silence.

"Just get back here before I max out your credit card on Alpo."

Jeanette hung up, leaving Carson puzzled. *Why the hell is Jeanette feeding Sally Alpo?* Carson thought. *It's not Christmas.*

A distant thumping developed into a roar. Carson pulled the curtains back, looking right and left. The roar nearly unbearable now, Carson went out onto the balcony. A helicopter cruised overhead, crossing the highway and hovering over the empty lot next to the Waffle House. The helicopter settled, kicking up dust and litter that blew across the highway toward the Super 8. An American flag was painted just behind the cockpit and another on the nose. Near the tail was USMC. The door opened, half folding up, and half folding down to make stairs. A marine in casual greens stepped out, followed by a man dressed in slacks and short-sleeved dress shirt. The civilian was tall, middle-aged, and lean. Two more stepped out, a beefy female ranger with hair shorter than Carson's, and a gnome with wild black hair, wearing long black pants and a white long-sleeve shirt. His armpits were wet.

Carson went down the stairs and out to the highway, waiting for the helicopter passengers to cross the road. Seeing the marines, Carson felt underdressed in his cargo shorts and short-sleeve khaki shirt. The name of his company was embroidered on front left, and the back was stenciled with the company's logo, a cowboy lassoing a *T. rex*.

"Carson Wills?" the lead man said, hand out.

"Yeah," Carson said, staring past him at the marine helicopter, two armed marine guards now posted on either side of the hatch. People streamed out of the Waffle House, carrying napkins and cups of coffee, staring. "When you said you were going to pick me up, I thought you meant with a car."

"I'm Nick Paulson. I need to know where you found those velociraptors."

"Nick Paulson?" Carson repeated, recognizing the name. "I told the rangers where I found them," Carson said, feeling in over his head.

"You weren't all that specific," the female ranger said, coming up next to Paulson. Over the ranger's ample left breast was a name tag that read C. WYNOOSKI. "Downright evasive is the way I heard it," Wynooski said.

"As I told your rangers, Ms. Wynooski, I killed them on the outskirts of Hillsdale," Carson said. "They were running loose on a farm."

"You caught and killed two velociraptors by yourself?" Wynooski asked.

"Yes, I did," Carson said.

"By yourself?" Wynooski repeated.

"By myself," Carson said emphatically. "I'm a professional."

"I'm a professional," Wynooski said. "You're a lucky amateur."

"Take us there," Paulson said, taking Carson by the arm and guiding him toward the helicopter.

"Pretty much killed them by myself," Carson said, wishing he had settled for selling the eggs.

"I need to see where you found them," Paulson said.

"I've got my van," Carson said.

"Leave the van," Nick said. "We'll bring you back here."

"I've got to check out by eleven or they'll charge me thirty-eight dollars for another day," Carson said, now across the road.

"I'll cover it," Paulson said, pushing Carson under the rotors and up the stairs into the helicopter.

Carson found himself buckled into a leather seat, watching Ocala disappear below him, worrying that his future was going bye-bye at the same time.

The marine pilots landed the helicopter on the Mills Ranch in an empty corral. The Millses came out onto their back deck, and then down the stairs. Fanny was in dark blue shorts, a sheer light blue T-shirt over a swimsuit top. Marty wore swim trunks and polo shirt with an alligator logo. Both wore flip-flops.

"Wow, Carson," Fanny said, hugging Carson in greeting. "You know how to make an entrance."

Fanny smelled of suntan lotion, but on Fanny it was exotic. Fanny released Carson. Her swimsuit was still damp, and now there were two wet spots on her shirt where her breasts had pressed against Carson.

"Who are your friends?" Marty asked.

"This is Nick Paulson, Ranger Wynooski, Dr. Gah, and a small sample of the U.S. Marine Corps," Carson said.

Fanny greeted each as warmly as she did Carson the first time they met, leaving Carson a little jealous.

"Nick Paulson?" Fanny said, taking Paulson's hand a second time and now holding it.

"Yeah, it's him," Carson said, stepping between them and breaking Fanny's grip. "If it's okay, I'd like to show them where I killed the velociraptors."

Carson started Fanny and Marty back toward their house.

"We'll go along," Marty said. "You might need our help again."

"We've got marines," Carson said. "Besides, I got the velociraptors already. There's no danger."

"We killed one of them," Fanny said.

"I meant we," Carson said. "You haven't seen any more, have you?"

"No," the Millses said at the same time.

"I'll just give them a walk-through, and then we'll be on our way," Carson said.

"They came in a helicopter!" Marty said. "We should at least give them lunch."

"We'll barbecue," Fanny said.

"I'll bring them to the house when we're done," Carson said. "You light the charcoal."

"It's a natural gas barbecue," Marty said.

"Of course," Carson said, shooing them toward the house.

Carson resisted patting Fanny on the fanny as she turned to go.

"They're nice folks, but it's best if the civilians stay out of the way," Carson said to Paulson's team.

"And just what branch of the service do the Dinosaur Wranglers belong to?" Ranger Wynooski asked, tapping the name embroidered into Carson's shirt.

"This way," Carson said, ignoring the obnoxious fat ranger.

Carson led them toward the dilapidated barn. Four marines accompanied them, wearing light combat gear and carrying M16s.

Paulson, Gah, and Wynooski carried daypacks. Carson stopped by the spot where the Millses killed the second velociraptor.

"I got one of them right here," Carson said.

Ranger Wynooski knelt, looking in the grass and sending up a cloud of flies with a wave of her hand.

"Quite a bit of blood. What did you shoot it with?"

"Shotgun," Carson said.

"The carcass looked like you put it through a meat grinder," Dr. Gah said.

"I shot it twice," Carson said.

"Right," Wynooski said. "Capturing it ever cross your mind? That's what I would have done."

"Rangers won't answer calls this far from a preserve," Carson said. "That's why they called me."

"We'd answer for velociraptors," Wynooski said. "That's for damn sure. And we wouldn't have to blow them to bits with shotguns either."

"I got the other one in here," Carson said, leading them through the opening in the wall.

Inside, everything was as Carson had left it. The nest was gone, the hay spread around. Two marines accompanied Carson's group into the barn.

"I shot it on the stairs and it fell down here," Carson said.

Dr. Gah squatted, studying the dirt where the blood had soaked in. Ants covered the spot.

"Was the velociraptor coming down the stairs?" Paulson asked.

"No, going up," Carson said.

"Was it in the barn when you came in?" Paulson asked.

"No . . . actually I'm not sure," Carson said, thinking back. "When I first came through here, the barn looked empty. I was searching for the velociraptors when I heard the first one. It might have been hiding. Back in there, maybe."

Carson pointed toward the collapsed end of the barn. The jumble of beams and boards created dark hollows.

Paulson pulled a flashlight from a side pocket of his backpack, peering into the crevices, systematically working along the back wall away from the opening to the far corner.

"I said I got them," Carson said.

"They were male and female," Paulson said. "They may have nested."

Carson said nothing, concentrating on not looking guilty.

"This looks like it goes pretty far back," Paulson said.

Dr. Gah knelt next to him, and then Wynooski knelt, who was surprisingly flexible for a woman of her size.

"It can't go too far," Wynooski said, "the wall ends right there. If it goes more than five feet, you'd be outside again."

"I don't see daylight," Dr. Gah said.

"You come out in a shadow on the other side, that's why," Wynooski said.

"You know that, or you think that?" Dr. Gah asked.

"Has to be," Wynooski said. "What else would explain it? Here, I'll crawl in and show you."

"Ma'am, don't do that," one of the marines said, stepping forward.

Lieutenant Sam Weller was in charge of the detail, their orders to protect Nick Paulson. Now Weller squatted next to Paulson.

"We'll confirm it's secure. Kelton, crawl in there and make sure there's nothing hiding. Snead, check outside and see where it comes out."

A marine barely old enough to shave came forward, getting ready to crawl through the opening.

"I can see from here it doesn't go anywhere," Kelton said.

Kelton started forward, ducking under a broken beam. Inching forward, rifle in his arms, he did not get far.

"It ends right here," Kelton said, his voice strangely muffled. "It's kind of funny. I can't really touch the end, but I'm stuck."

To Carson it looked like the marine had room to spare.

"All right, get out of there," Weller said.

Snead came back from outside, reporting that he could not find an opening. With Kelton back out of the hole, Wynooski stood.

"I could have told you that went nowhere. That's barely big enough for a velociraptor anyway."

Wynooski wandered off, looking around the interior and then going up the stairs. A marine followed her. Gah and Paulson continued to stare into the opening. Gah had his own flashlight out now. Carson stayed with Paulson and Gah, preferring anyone's company to Wynooski's.

"What do you see?" Paulson asked.

"I can't see anything past those boards there," Gah said, using his flashlight like a pointer. "The light just kind of goes nowhere."

Paulson crawled into the opening, holding his flashlight in one hand. He did an awkward three-point crawl, moving a little at a time. Lieutenant Weller watched without concern.

"It kind of widens out," Paulson said in a muffled voice. "Is this a sewer pipe?"

Then Paulson disappeared into the dark.

"Where'd you go?" Gah asked, getting down on his knees and leaning in the opening.

Gah crawled into the hole, and soon he was gone too. Surprised, Lieutenant Weller squatted, using his own light to look inside.

"Dr. Paulson? Dr. Gah? Where are you?"

No answer. Carson looked but could not see anyone. Weller got down, crawling into the opening. His polished boots were still sticking out when he stopped. Then he backed out in a hurry.

"Something's not right. They're gone. They're not in there."

"Who's not in where?" Wynooski asked, coming back down the stairs.

"Kelton, Sampson, stay here," Weller ordered the other two marines. "Snead, come with me."

Weller ran outside to check the perimeter. Wynooski knelt by Carson.

"What happened?" Wynooski asked.

"Dr. Paulson and Dr. Gah crawled in there and now there's no sign of them."

"What the hell are you talking about?" Wynooski shone her light in the opening. "There must be a side passage."

Wynooski crawled into the opening. Carson turned away as her large khaki-covered bottom rocked back and forth and then disappeared like the others.

"I knew it," Wynooski said, her muffled voice coming from the blackness.

"Knew what?" Carson asked, and then repeated it, shouting.

Wynooski was gone. Cursing, Carson crawled into the opening, not afraid of the dark, but of running into Wynooski's big ass.

"I wouldn't do that, sir," Kelton said.

Kelton's muffled voice sounded like it was coming from a long distance off and strangely low pitched. Carson paused, looked back, seeing Kelton saying something he could not hear. Small and distant, it was as if Carson were looking through the wrong side of a pair of binoculars. Kelton's lips were silently voicing something. Carson crawled a few more feet, felt the surface change, and then felt his stomach flutter. Carson stopped crawling, but his forward motion continued. Then he was falling.

12

Strange Journey

Alice laughed. "There's no use trying," she said, "one can't believe impossible things."

"I daresay you haven't had much practice," said the Queen. "When I was your age, I always did it for half-an-hour a day. Why, sometimes I've believed as many as six impossible things before breakfast."

—Lewis Carroll, *Through the Looking-Glass*

Unknown Time
Unknown Place

Carson tumbled down a rocky slope, shoulders, knees, elbows, and hands scraped and bruised as he flailed, trying to break his fall. Ranger Wynooski's ample bottom finally stopped the tumble.

"Oof," Wynooski said. "I knew you were going to do that."

Quickly rolling away, Carson sat up on a spongy surface under a leafy canopy. Low on the horizon, the sun punched through holes in the canopy, the rays warm on Carson's skin.

"Where the hell are we?" Carson asked, looking around.

The open farmland, paddocks, and house were gone. Instead they stood amongst tall, ugly palms, the ground clear except for patches of ferns, the spongy ground thick with decaying vegetation. The humid air smelled of decay, lacking the manure accent that characterized the Mills Ranch. Paulson and Gah stood a short distance away, by a palm tree in a patch of ferns nearly head high.

"We're on the Mills Ranch," Wynooski said with confidence. "Where else could we be?"

"But it was afternoon," Carson said. "And what's with all this?"

Carson indicated the leafy vegetation that looked more like the Everglades than a central Florida farm.

"Obviously, the Mills have a garden," Wynooski said, now sounding a little uncertain.

Ignoring her, Carson moved closer to Paulson and Gah.

"What is this?" Carson asked.

"It's a cycad," Paulson said, showing Carson the leaf of the tree they were standing by, misunderstanding Carson's question.

The leaf looked like a comb, with fine green teeth.

"Not the palm tree!" Carson said. "I'm talking about all of this!"

"It's not a palm tree," Dr. Gah said, arching thick black eyebrows.

"It's a cycad," Paulson repeated. "See, the fronds grow out of the top, then die off creating a layer, and then more grow out, and layer by layer it forms what looks like a tree."

"Where are we?" Carson demanded, ignoring the lecture on the characteristics of cycads.

Paulson took Carson by the shoulders, looking him straight in the eye. "Mr. Wills, I am sure you know that the dinosaurs you captured had to come from somewhere. I believe that we have gone to where they come from."

"He murdered them, he didn't capture them," Wynooski said, walking closer so she could butt in.

"What? But they come from thousands of years ago," Carson stammered.

"Millions, actually," Dr. Gah said, infuriatingly calm.

"At least sixty-five million years ago," Paulson said. "Although we can't be sure from the cycads, since they survived to the modern age."

"What?" Carson said, using his standard reflexive response.

"The Dinosaur Wrangler isn't an expert on dinosaurs!" Wynooski said, mocking Carson. "What a surprise."

"It's hard to explain," Paulson said, "but ever since the Time Quilt that brought the dinosaurs to our present, we have been connected to the Cretaceous period. This is probably where your velociraptors came from."

Carson looked around with new interest. "Velociraptors? Here?" Carson asked, now nervous.

"If this is the Cretaceous period," Paulson said cautiously, "then yes. We would need to see some local fauna to confirm the era."

"Screw that!" Carson said, eyes darting to movement when the slight breeze rustled leaves. "How do we get back?"

"The way we came, of course," Wynooski said, jerking a thumb over her shoulder.

Carson looked back up the hill he had tumbled down. It was loose rock, and steep. Near the top was a dark depression.

"Let's go," Carson said, scrambling up the steep hill.

Carson's efforts sent rocks and dirt tumbling down, the others backing out of the way of the small avalanche, waving away dust. Every time Carson made progress, he would find himself sliding back down. The opening remained maddeningly out of his reach.

"Give me a shove!" Carson yelled, wiping dirty sweat from his eyes.

"You'll never get there that way," Wynooski said, hands on her hips. "The way to do this is to find a way up there and then down that path to where we came out."

Carson backed down the slope, studying the opening toward the top. He hated it, but Wynooski was right. There was a path from the top of the cliff down to the cave.

"Okay, let's do that!" Carson said, starting left, and then seeing no path, turning right—no path either way. "Which way?" Carson asked.

Now everyone looked right and left.

"Left," Paulson said finally.

"I was just going to say that," Wynooski said, taking the lead.

Frustrated with how calm the others were, Carson fell in behind, eyes busy, expecting velociraptors at any second.

"Dr. Paulson?" Carson asked as they pushed through the vegetation. "Are you sure this is the past? That tree looks like an oak tree."

"Angiosperms developed late in the Cretaceous period. There should be maples, oaks, and even walnut trees in this period," Paulson said, his voice drifting off, staring at the tree that stood a short distance away.

"And if there are velociraptors, there will be other predators?" Carson asked.

"Yes," Paulson said. "But you have to remember that like our own ecosystem, predators occupy the top of a food chain that is shaped like a pyramid. Most of Dinosauria are herbivores."

"Yes, but I believe thirty-five percent of Cretaceous dinosaurs were carnivores," Gah the gnome added, taking away the small bit of comfort Paulson had created.

"What?" Carson said.

"In this period, the pyramid has a flat top," Gah said, as if it were an interesting bit of trivia. "That means that the flora and fauna supported a higher percentage of carnivores than is possible in our era. It's probably because of the high oxygen content."

Gah inhaled deeply several times.

"Notice how much energy you have," Gah said. "This atmosphere has fifty percent more oxygen than our own. With that kind of oxygen content, even I could run a marathon. The oxygen is what made the enormous size of Cretaceous dinosaurs possible and bigger prey means more, and bigger, predators."

"What?" Carson repeated, thinking of the implications.

"Calm down," Paulson said, breathing a little faster as they began climbing up a gentle slope. "That number includes omnivores that eat everything and scavengers that eat carrion. Most of the rest of that number is made up of small predators like *Troodon* or *Dromiceiominus*."

"Never heard of them," Carson said. "How small is small?"

"*Dromiceiominus* was no more than twelve feet long or so," Paulson said.

"Walk faster," Carson said.

Wynooski led them through a grove of the ugly palm trees and uphill past more familiar-looking trees—maybe maples. The hill was steep, but here the loose rock was patched together in places where vegetation had taken root. It was steep but climbable. Carson could see the crest of the hill and began looking to his right for a route back to the cave.

"Nick, look at this," Gah said, squatting on the slope.

Paulson stopped, walking back down to where Gah knelt.

"Let's go, let's go," Carson said. "Remember that little talk we just had about killer dinosaurs?"

"Killer dinosaurs," Wynooski repeated. "I'm not familiar with that classification. Is that a system you professional dinosaur wranglers use?"

"Yeah, killer dinosaurs are in the class 'run like hell.'"

The gnome and Paulson were still kneeling, looking at something. Carson walked over. They were examining a small patch of grass.

"Let's keep moving," Carson said.

"Mr. Wills, this is grass!" Gah said.

"Yeah, I know. I've got a yard full of it, and you can have all of it if you get yourself up that slope."

"You don't understand," Gah said. "We believe we are in the Mesozoic era, but grass does not evolve until the Cenozoic era."

"I thought we were in the Cretaceous era?" Nick said. "Are there *T. rexes* and raptors in the Mesozoic or Cenozoic eras?" Carson asked hopefully.

"The Cretaceous period is part of the Mesozoic era," Gah said patiently. "Because of your velociraptors, and the cyads, we thought we were in the late epoch of the Cretaceous period in the Mesozoic era. The presence of well-developed grasses suggests at the very least the Paleocene epoch of the Tertiary period of the Cenozoic era. Grass is supposed to have evolved fifty-five million years ago, not earlier."

"Not necessarily," Paulson cut in. "There are some discoveries of fossilized grass in coprolites, and that placed grass evolution at sixty-five million years ago."

"Coprolites?" Carson asked.

"Fossilized dinosaur shit," Gah said to Carson. Then to Nick he said, "I thought the only nonvascular plants the coprolites contained were rice and bamboo."

"No, I'm quite sure there was evidence of grass phytoliths."

"Wow, this is interesting," Carson said. "Let's finish this discussion at a Starbucks. I'll buy the first Vanilla Latte."

"Well, look at this!" Wynooski said.

Wynooski waved them over to where she stood, leaning toward the hill, her left leg bent, her right extended because of the steep slope.

"What now?" Carson asked.

"Can't you see?" Wynooski said, tapping a big rock. "It's concrete."

Gah and Paulson worked across the slope to look at Wynooski's find.

"Starbucks. I'm buying. What else do you want?" Carson said, trying to entice the eggheads. "I'll pay for Venti size."

"She's right," Paulson said.

"Okay, okay, it's concrete," Carson said. "Let's talk about what it means when we're sipping that espresso."

"It means I was right," Wynooski declared. "We are still on the Mills Ranch."

"No, the vegetation confirms the rough time period," Paulson said. "This just means that we weren't the first ones to be transported to this time and place. Or at least not the first thing."

"It would also explain grasses showing up sporadically in the fossil record ten million years before they should have evolved," Gah said.

"Perhaps Cenozoic grasses evolved from the modern grasses sent back by the Time Quilt?" Paulson said. "But if so, then when did the modern grass evolve? It creates a time paradox."

Frustrated, Carson sat on the slope, shaking his head, mumbling, "Biscotti? Anyone want some biscotti?"

"If this is from the original Time Quilt, there should be more than this," Gah said, slapping the concrete. "If there is concrete, there are people—were people. We should try to identify where this came from. Atlanta? New York?"

"We should try to get the hell out of here!" Carson said.

Then the ground shook, pebbles bouncing out of place. Everyone froze, even Wynooski silent. More vibrations and more loose material slid past them. Locating the direction of the vibrations, they all looked uphill. Over the crest of the hill appeared the head of a carnivore, and it was much bigger than twelve feet long.

"Tyrannosaur?" Gah asked, leaning back so that he could see up the hill, but then tilting his head down to look through the distance portion of his bifocals.

"Probably," Paulson said.

"Run," Carson said.

"I was just going to say that," Wynooski said, turning and running downhill faster than a fat woman should be able.

13

Elizabeth

ELIZABETH HAWTHORNE: *I was one of those in the Fox Valley building housing the orgonic pyramid when the three nuclear devices detonated. The black ripples that spread out ahead of the blast wave converged on our building and transported us to the moon and back in time. Later, we escaped from the moon, back to the time before the nuclear bombs went off, and removed one.*
SENATOR SCOT WILHITE: *If I understand your testimony, you were able to remove one nuclear device, and take it with you into the orgonic collector—pyramid—so that when the other two devices detonated, you, and the others with you, were killed? At least a version of you was?*

—Testimony before the Senate Committee on Security Affairs

Present Time
Office of Grayson, Weinert & Goldfarb
Washington, D.C.

"Kaylee Kemper is on your line," Elizabeth's assistant said.

Kaylee was Nick Paulson's administrative assistant at the Office of Strategic Science. Elizabeth sighed with relief, her concern at not hearing from Nick quickly changing to anger. Frequently, Nick traveled, and would be gone like this for days, or even weeks at a time, but he always called if delayed. This time he had been gone three days, and Elizabeth had not heard from him. Her sixth message to his cell was, "Call me or else."

"Nick better have a good excuse," Elizabeth said in greeting.

"Ms. Hawthorne, Dr. Paulson has disappeared," Kaylee said.

Kaylee had never pulled a prank or told a joke in Elizabeth's experience, and deference and hierarchy were deeply ingrained in the woman. Nick was always "Dr. Paulson," and Elizabeth was always "Ms. Hawthorne." Kaylee was telling the truth, and her tone conveyed concern.

"What's happened?" Elizabeth asked.

Elizabeth was prepared for any answer, because she had been with Nick Paulson through the unimaginable. Before they were married, Nick and Elizabeth had inadvertently been sent through time and space to the moon, and into the Mayan past. Because of her marriage to the director of the OSS, Elizabeth knew more than the average citizen about the distortions in the time–space continuum that had changed the world. She also knew the real reason behind the nuclear explosions in Alaska and California. The public was told it was terrorism, and it was, but what the public was never told was how close the terrorists had come to destroying the world. The ecoterrorists' plan had been to shred the space–time continuum, intermixing the past and the modern so completely that civilization would be impossible. Highways, phone systems, Internet, sewage, industry, and government would be gone, pieces distributed through the eons, leaving nothing but a few fragments in the present. Essentially, finishing the job that started with the original Time Quilt. Nick and his teams had stopped the terrorists, but had paid a price in doing it. So when Kaylee said that Nick was gone, Elizabeth was prepared for anything and everything.

"Ms. Hawthorne, I am only an administrative assistant—" Kaylee said.

"What happened?" Elizabeth demanded, cutting her off.

As Nick's administrative assistant, Kaylee made Nick's travel arrangements, took minutes in meetings, transcribed notes, and filed sensitive documents. Kaylee was also the biggest gossip in the OSS. If she knew anything, she was dying to tell someone, even someone without security clearance.

"He went to Florida to confirm a claim for two Visitors," Kaylee said. "That's all I know, and I shouldn't have even told you that much."

Elizabeth knew that "Visitors" were untagged dinosaurs. Nick offered a reward, believing that Visitors might be the leading indicator of new holes in space–time. Nick hoped he would never pay the reward.

"Visitors?" Elizabeth probed.

"The Visitors were two velociraptors," Kaylee said in a conspiratorial tone.

"No," Elizabeth said, genuinely surprised.

"They were both dead, but Dr. Paulson went to the site where they were killed. Dr. Paulson took a marine escort just to be safe, but somehow when they got to the site, Dr. Paulson, Dr. Gah, one of the rangers, and the man who found the velociraptors just disappeared."

Elizabeth got a sick feeling when she heard the words "just disappeared." In a world where dinosaurs lived side by side with human beings and millions of people had suddenly vanished one night, "disappeared" sounded ominous.

"It's been three days, Ms. Hawthorne. It's not like Dr. Paulson to not check in. He always checks his e-mail and calls me. I can't remember him going a day without contacting me, even when he was on vacation."

Elizabeth knew that was true. She and Nick had gone to Cancún, and Nick had spent half the time on his phone doing e-mail. If Elizabeth had not been doing the same thing, it would have been a sore point.

"Where's John?" Elizabeth asked.

John Roberts directed Field Investigations for the Office of Security Science. Once, John led an OSS team into the past and ended up getting pursued by juvenile tyrannosaurs through time and space, clear to the moon.

"Mr. Roberts was in Berlin for the Association of Professional Dinosaur Managers meeting. I spoke with his assistant, and he is on his way back now. He's flying directly to Florida."

"I'll call John," Elizabeth said.

"Ms. Hawthorne . . ." Kaylee began.

"And I will let you know anything as soon as I know it," Elizabeth assured her.

Taking her cell phone, Elizabeth selected the directory and then pushed R. Then she scrolled down to JOHN ROBERTS. When she selected the name, two phone numbers came up. Elizabeth chose his personal cell number.

"Hello, Elizabeth," John answered.

"What happened to Nick?" Elizabeth asked.

"I don't know," John said. "He was following a lead on a couple of Visitors, and now no one knows where he is."

"I know that much," Elizabeth said. "What aren't you telling me?"

"Nothing," John said. "I'm on my way to the last place he was seen. What I'm hearing makes no sense."

"Doesn't it?" Elizabeth said.

"Well, it couldn't be that," John said.

"Was he investigating a pyramid?"

"It was on a farm," John said. "There is nothing in the report about a pyramid or any kind of orgonic energy collector."

"No one just disappears," Elizabeth said.

"Funny thing for you to say, after what you went through. Let me investigate before you jump to conclusions."

"What do you know about the person who turned in the Visitors?" Elizabeth asked.

"He worked for one of those businesses helping citizens handle their pet dinosaurs."

"Does he have terrorist connections?" Elizabeth asked. "Is he an animal rights activist?"

"Nothing like that," John said. "As far as we can tell, he's just what he seems. He's gone too, you know?"

"Yes, I heard."

"Elizabeth, I'll be at the farm where Nick disappeared tomorrow morning. I promise to call you if I find anything."

"Call me if you don't find anything."

"I will," John promised.

14

Family

I've seen 'em. That's what I'm saying. I've seen 'em. Dinosaurs popping up all over the damn place. It's the government, I'm saying. They're loosing those dinosaurs to scare people, so we'll beg them to protect us. And how will they protect us? By taking away more of our rights, that's how.

—Caller to Cat Bellow's *Radio Rebel* show

Present Time
Near Hillsdale, Florida

Jeanette pounded the last nail into the box she built to hold the chicks. She had nailed eight 2 x 6 boards into two simple boxes, using scrap to make braces to hold one box on top of the other. Jeanette was proud of the simple structure. The box ended up eight feet by eight feet because that was the size of the boards she found behind the barn.

"Pretty good," Jeanette declared, putting the hammer back into Carson's tool belt.

Jeanette had had to cut new holes in the belt to get it to fit around her waist, and that would irritate Carson. Carson jealously guarded his tools, and Jeanette took great pleasure in modifying his tool belt and then using the tools. Wearing an old yellow tank top with tears and paint stains, a pair of old tattered shorts, and the tool belt, Jeanette looked like Daisy Mae of Dogpatch.

Sally got up, coming to sniff the box. Jeanette spread a layer of fresh straw in the bottom, and then began transferring the velociraptor chicks. Most were asleep, huddled in a pile, comforted by each other's warmth. Picking one chick up in each hand, Jeanette gently lifted them up and down as she moved them, weighing them.

"They're getting big," Jeanette said to Sally.

Sally nuzzled one of the chicks. Eyes open, the chick chirped softly, only half awake. Still stuffed from the morning's Alpo breakfast, the chicks were only half conscious. Putting one down, Jeanette studied the other. The chicks had lost some of their purplish color, their skin now blotchy with gray patches. The chick's head still seemed disproportionately large to Jeanette, but the body was bigger and the legs longer. Jeanette stroked the chick several times, then drew her hand down the length of the chick's tail. The chick let out several satisfied pants as she did. Examining the velociraptor's hands, Jeanette felt the taut skin that stretched over the three fingers. Each finger ended in a small claw that was covered with skin. Jeanette noticed the tip of the claw protruding farther from the skin covering than just yesterday. Looking at the feet, Jeanette found one of the claws much larger than the others, and most of its tip was exposed. Gently putting the chick in the new enclosure, Jeanette finished transferring the remaining chicks.

"Time to name them, Sally," Jeanette said. "We need seven names. Let's see. Snow White had seven dwarfs. Happy, Sneezy, Doc, Bashful, Grumpy, Sleepy, and Dopey. Yeah, I think that's all of the names." Looking at the sleeping chicks, Jeanette said "I couldn't name one of them Dopey. That would be cruel. What else has seven names? Santa has eight or nine reindeer. Dasher, Dancer, Prancer, Cupid . . . A velociraptor named Cupid? I don't think so."

Kneeling, Jeanette leaned on the edge of the box, watching the velociraptor chicks sleep. Occasionally, each chick would let out a small sigh or soft peep. Jeanette noticed the voices of the chicks were different. Larger chicks had deeper tones than the smaller chicks.

"Do, Re, Mi, Fa, So, La, Ti," Jeanette sang. "That's seven names."

Sally leaned over the edge of the box, Jeanette scratching her head. After hand-feeding the chicks for days, Jeanette knew them intimately.

"You are Do," Jeanette said. "You are next largest, so you are Re, and you are Mi."

As she pronounced the names, Jeanette's pitch changed, just as it did in the scale. "Ti" was said with the highest pitch.

"Sleep tight, Do, Re, Me, Fa, So, La, Ti," Jeanette said, virtually singing the names.

As she returned to the office, one of Jeanette's phones rang. It was the Dinosaur Wrangler phone.

"Dinosaur Wrangler, how can we help you?" Jeanette said mechanically.

"This is Maury Dillman calling from the Super Eight in Ocala? I am trying to reach Carson Wills?"

"Aren't we all," Jeanette said.

"Excuse me?" Dillman said.

"I'm Mr. Wills's executive assistant. What do you need from Mr. Wills?" Jeanette asked.

"Well, we have not seen Mr. Wills since he checked in, but he does not seem to be using his room. He has not checked out, and his van has not moved since he parked it."

"You haven't seen Mr. Wills at all?"

"Not since he flew away in the helicopter," Dillman said.

"Helicopter?" Jeanette probed.

"Yes, the marines took him away."

Jeanette gasped. People were supposed to turn in Visitors, not get arrested for it. And why would the marines be involved?

"Should we continue to keep the room for Mr. Wills?" Dillman asked.

"You're still charging his card for the room?" Jeanette asked.

"Yes, Mr. Wills has not checked out."

"It's a company card," Jeanette said. "Stop charging today. Mr. Wills is no longer staying there."

"His luggage is still in the room."

"I'll send someone to collect it," Jeanette said.

"And the van? It can't be parked here if he is not a guest."

"The van will be picked up too."

"If you send someone before noon, we will not charge for today," Dillman said, sounding magnanimous.

Hanging up on Dillman, Jeanette called Lymon Norris, one of the men who worked for the Dinosaur Wrangler company.

"Lymon, how are you doing with that *Monoclonius*?"

"Not so good," Lymon said. "I got it back in the pen, but then it broke out the other side. It's a wood corral. Can you believe it? These dumb sonsofbitches built a wood corral for a fucking *Mono*. You think Carson could come on out and lend me a hand?"

"Can't," Jeanette said. "He's still in Ocala. Do the best you can."

Jeanette called Robby Bryson next.

"Robby, are you free to make a run to Ocala?"

"Will be in about an hour or so. Just finishing up on that call about the oviraptor."

"Was it a raptor?" Jeanette asked.

"Nah. It was an emu. No bull. It came off a farm that leases animals for TV shows, commercials, and shit like that."

"It's still five-hundred-dollar minimum," Jeanette reminded Robby.

Robby had a soft heart and had been known to discount for old women and pretty girls. Jeanette was convinced that if she brushed up against Robby and followed up with a smile, Robby would kill for her.

"I told them," Robby said. "They're not happy, but they'll pay."

"When you get done, run over to the Super Eight in Ocala. Pick up Carson's suitcase and the van. There's a spare key under the back bumper. Get someone to go with you to drive it."

"My cousin might go with me, but he won't do it for free," Robby said.

"Fifty dollars," Jeanette said.

"Yeah, he'll go for fifty. Where's Carson?"

"Into something," Jeanette said.

"Something big?"

"He better be," Jeanette said.

"Come again?" Robby said.

"Just bring the van back. Get Carson's suitcase too, and don't forget to check Carson out of his room."

"Seriously, Jeanette, where the hell is Carson?"

"God only knows," Jeanette said.

Sally jumped up, stiffening, pointing at the door.

"I've got to go," Jeanette said.

A shadow appeared on the screen door, and then came three hard raps. Jeanette stiffened, suspicious. Virtually all the Dinosaur Wrangler business came over the phone. Rarely, an unhappy customer would visit the office, but there had been no recent complaints. With grumpy customers, Carson handled the women and Jeanette the men. Jeanette waited behind the desk, one arm dangling toward a wooden box on the floor. The box held a few files and at the bottom, a revolver.

"Come," Jeanette said.

A young man stepped in. He wore beige Dockers and a light blue polo shirt and sandals. His hair was black, his nose small, even delicate. It took Jeanette a second to recognize him.

"Officer Wilson," Jeanette said, standing. "This can't be good."

"No, it's good," he said nervously.

Officer Wilson's eyes quickly scanned Jeanette, from her stained short-shorts to her tool belt to the tank top with tears that turned it into a peekaboo shirt. Not expecting visitors, Jeanette had not bothered with a bra. Officer Wilson was having trouble keeping his eyes on her face.

"I just came by to update you and see if you needed anything," Officer Wilson said.

"Are you working undercover?" Jeanette asked, putting her hands on her hips.

"No, I'm off duty. I was passing by and I thought I would stop in and make sure everything is okay."

"You live near here?" Jeanette asked.

"Not right near here," Officer Wilson said, "but it's not that far out of my way."

"Well, thanks, Officer Wilson, I appreciate your concern."

Worried that if she put her body in motion, it would be too much for Officer Wilson, Jeanette held still, her hands still on her hips.

"Les," Officer Wilson said. "My name is Les."

"Les," Jeanette said.

"Are you fixing something?" Officer Wilson said, using the tool belt as an excuse to scan her body again.

"I'm all done," Jeanette said.

"So, you run the office, and do the repairs, and everything? What about your boyfriend?" Les said, looking around.

"He's out on a job," Jeanette said. "You said something about an update?"

"Oh, yeah, everything's fine. I'm sure there's no problem, but I thought you should know that a couple of the guys we arrested have a pretty sharp lawyer. He's making a big deal out of the fact I impersonated a code inspector. It's a bogus argument. I don't think a judge will buy it."

"What would it mean if a judge did buy it?" Jeanette asked.

"It's not going to happen, but if it did, it might mean some of the evidence would be kicked."

"And that would mean?" Jeanette probed.

"Well, it could mean the charges would have to be dropped."

"And they would be released?" Jeanette asked.

"It won't happen," Les said.

Jeanette shook her head in disbelief. The mess next door had nothing to do with her, but somehow she was being drawn into the middle of it.

"Officer Wilson . . . Les, maybe you should give me your phone number again. I lost your napkin."

"Yeah, sure," Les said, frantically searching pockets for a piece of paper.

Jeanette bent over, taking a yellow pad and pen from the box on the floor. Les gawked as she bent and then stood again. Distracted, Les only managed to take the pad and pen from Jeanette after two tries. Les wrote his number and then wrote it a second time underneath in clearer handwriting.

"If you need me for anything, please call," Les said. "Anything."

"I'll keep the number," Jeanette said, sticking it to a bulletin board already papered with a blizzard of scraps.

"Anything," Les repeated.

Jeanette could not help but smile at the nervous policeman. When she did, revealing the gap in her teeth, Les beamed.

15

Strangers

T. rex *is an almost perfect killing machine. With large feet and powerful legs, it can reach speeds of up to 35 mph on open ground. Its massive jaws are so powerful, it could bite through the frill of a triceratops. As we have seen in the preserves, the only animal a* T. rex *has to fear is another* T. rex.

—John Roberts, OSS, Director of Field Operations

Unknown Time
Neverland

Jacob and Crazy Kramer ran until they could not run anymore, and then climbed a tree to spend the night. Once in the forest, the Community had scattered, disappearing in deep shadows. It was hours since Jacob had seen anyone other than Crazy. Worried about his family, Jacob could only hope they had found a haven. Night in the forest was bad, but the dawn energized the carnivores, which were very efficient eating machines.

Impatient to find his family, Jacob climbed down when there was barely enough light to see.

"Damn, what a night," Crazy said, dropping out of the tree and landing with a loud thud. Covered in dried blood—some of it his own—a strip of cloth tied around his head to keep his hair out of his eyes, and wielding a machete, Crazy Kramer was the stuff of nightmares.

"So, where do you think everyone else is?" Crazy asked.

"Shhhh!" Jacob said.

Crazy Kramer was a mixed blessing. Strong and fearless, Crazy was the man to have next to you in a fight. Unfortunately, Crazy was also dumb and reckless.

"Right," Crazy said, his voice barely above a whisper. "Where to?"

"The rendezvous," Jacob said.

"Right," Crazy said in his near whisper.

As fanatical as the reverend was, he also had a sensible streak and planned for contingencies. If catastrophe befell the Community, they were to find their way to an old church in the ruins of the city. This church was one of the few buildings that had not collapsed when they came to the land of dinosaurs, and had not burned in one of the subsequent fires. The church was a survivor, like the people of the Community, and that made the building special to most, but the church held special significance to the reverend. The reverend's father had been pastor of the church.

Leading the way, his rifle always ready, Jacob walked carefully through the forest, avoiding open areas. Keeping a westerly direction, he watched for landmarks to guide him to the church, where he hoped his family was waiting. The problem was that it was years since Jacob had been to the church, and between the fires, earthquakes, and ever-expanding forest, less and less of the city could be found. Only the reverend, who did an annual pilgrimage, would be certain of the way.

Jacob tried to stay vigilant, but thoughts of Leah and his girls kept intruding. Where were they? Were they trying to find their way through the forest to the rendezvous just like Jacob, but without a rifle or even Crazy Kramer for protection? Because of his worrying, Jacob missed the first sounds of trouble.

"You hear that?" Crazy Kramer asked.

Jacob stopped, listening. Something was coming.

"Hide," Jacob said.

Jacob and Crazy hid behind a clump of small trees, peering through leaves. Whatever was coming was coming fast, and coming right for them. Now the vibrations in the ground confirmed Jacob's expectation. A predator was running down its prey. Jacob and Crazy hunkered down as the vibrations and noise signaled the nearest approach. Then bursting from the underbrush came four humans—humans Jacob had never seen before. In the lead was a young man, followed by a short bent man, then a fat woman, and finally a middle-aged man. All wore new-looking clothes, no beards, and were fat by Community standards. Exhausted, the shorter man stumbled, falling, tripping the woman, who fell on top of him, her mass swallowing him. The man in the rear paused, helping them to their feet. The young man in the front hesitated, and then ran back, helping drag the woman off the man underneath.

"Funny," Crazy Kramer said.

Then a tyrannosaur hit the trees the strangers had run between, bending but not breaking them. Jacob knew this tyrannosaur and the pack it ran with. It was small by tyrannosaur standards, but particularly tenacious. The tyrannosaur screeched angrily, then backed up, looking for a way around. Now on their feet, the humans were moving again, but more slowly, the small man limping, helped along by the younger man. Exhausted, and too slow to outrun even a small tyrannosaur, they were doomed. Frustrated, the tyrannosaur bulldozed between the trees, getting back on their trail. Now only steps ahead, the strangers had a minute to live.

Jacob stepped out of hiding, lifted the rifle, aimed carefully, and shot the tyrannosaur in the neck. Reflexively, the tyrannosaur jerked its head, snapping in Jacob's direction, stopping his forward motion. Jacob waved one arm, shouting.

"All right," Crazy said, stepping from his hiding place. "What's the plan?"

"Distract him," Jacob said.

"All right. Bring it on," Crazy said, shaking his machete.

Momentarily confused with prey in two directions, the tyrannosaur paused, screeching at both. Jacob saw blood streaming from its neck, but doubted it was a killing wound. Stopping a tyrannosaur with a single round from a .30-06 would be like stopping a dump truck with a BB gun. With the tyrannosaur distracted, the strangers crawled into hiding. Jacob continued to shout and wave, Crazy Kramer even louder, and with only one set of prey in sight, the tyrannosaur made its decision. With powerful long strides, the tyrannosaur was nearly on them before Jacob and Crazy could run. Dodging around trees, rocks, and anything that would slow the tyrannosaur, they ran pell-mell through the forest. Persistent, the tyrannosaur continued pursuit, even though the humans would be little more than a snack. Tiring, Jacob was ready to use his last bullet, hoping for a lucky killing shot, but then they broke into a clearing where a small herd of ankylosaurs grazed. Heads up, already alert, they stampeded when the humans and the tyrannosaur burst from the forest. Jacob and Crazy veered back into the forest, leaving the ankylosaurs to deal with the tyrannosaur. As the two men were turning back the way they had come, the sounds of the resulting fight slowly faded until the forest was silent again.

They found the strangers near where they had left them, the old man sitting, leg up, one shoe off, rubbing a swollen ankle. The fat woman knelt next to him, loosening the ties on his shoe. The younger man and the middle-aged man stood, facing them, both watching Crazy warily.

"He's harmless," Jacob said, jerking his head toward Crazy. "Who are you?"

"Nick Paulson," the middle-aged man said.

"Never mind that," the younger man said. "Who the hell are you, and how do we get out of this nightmare?"

"Get out?" Jacob said. "There is no way out."

16

John Roberts

I lost a friend to the Time Quilt, and that's probably why I work for the OSS. My friend Cubby was killed when President McIntyre ordered the nuclear strike on the Portland Time Quilt. McIntyre's "hair of the dog" treatment did nothing more than cost me a friend.

—John Roberts, OSS, Director of Field Operations, quoted in the *Washington Times* series, "Remember When 'When' Meant Something?"

Present Time
Hillsdale, Florida

With Fanny Mills hanging on one arm, and her husband on his other side, John Roberts walked to the barn where Nick Paulson had supposedly disappeared. Marines still guarded the site, not knowing what else to do. John flashed his ID at everyone who gave him a questioning look. Dressed in jeans and a yellow polo shirt, John looked like a civilian who'd wandered in off the street. Instead, he was the director of Field Operations for the Office of Security Science.

John was enjoying Fanny's attention, glad that Rosa could not see him. John and Rosa had met on a mission for the OSS that nearly killed both of them. Being chased by a tyrannosaur, nearly killed in a nuclear explosion, and escaping from Mayan Indians with human sacrifice on their mind had a way of bringing people together. Rosa and John married two months after helping to stop terrorists bent on ripping the time line to shreds. With Rosa's first pregnancy, she requested a reassignment from Area 51, where she piloted black bag aircraft like the Aurora spaceplane. At the end of her enlistment period, Rosa resigned, and now flew commercial, with Washington, D.C., as her home base. With two children at home, and parents who both traveled for a living, the Robertses managed to mesh schedules well enough so one parent was home most of the time. While the arrangement did interfere with their love life, it made being together all the sweeter. So, feeling a bit of guilt at Fanny's touch, John gently disengaged as they approached the marines guarding the barn.

"This is as far as you can go," John said, pulling free.

"It's our barn," Fanny said, pouting a little.

"I know," John said. "But until we find out what happened to our missing people, we need to make sure it doesn't happen to anyone else."

"We understand," Marty said, putting his arm around his wife. "Fanny just isn't used to having this many people around without a party erupting."

"When we get this settled, I'll bring my wife over to meet you," John said.

"Just tell me how you like your steaks," Marty said, smiling.

"Wine or margaritas?" Fanny asked.

"Margaritas," Marty said. "My wife's name is Rosa."

"Excellent," Marty said.

Marty and Fanny seemed so genuine that John made a mental note to talk to Rosa about meeting the Millses. She would like them.

"This way, sir," Lieutenant Weller said.

Weller walked John to a dilapidated barn, bent, and entered through a hole in the wall. Inside, work lights had been strung, extension cords running everywhere. The lieutenant walked to two powerful work lights on stands, and turned them on. The lights illuminated a portion of the collapsed wall.

"They crawled in there," Lieutenant Weller said, squatting and pointing.

John squatted too, seeing nothing but collapsed boards and a dark crevice. "There's no place to go," John said.

"Yes, sir, but that's where they went," Lieutenant Weller said. "There is one strange thing. Notice the light?"

John looked again, slowly realizing that work lights should penetrate farther than they did. Without speaking, Lieutenant Weller passed John a flashlight. John pointed it in the opening, but the dark crevice did not get any brighter.

"Weird," John said.

"Yes, sir," the lieutenant said.

John got up, searching the barn until he found a loose board. Using it as a probe, he poked in the opening. The farther he pushed, the more resistance he felt, but he never hit anything solid.

"Anything on the outside?" John asked.

"Nothing," the lieutenant said. "We even dug down six feet."

Other marines drifted closer, listening.

"Ever seen anything like this?" the marine asked.

"Not exactly," John said evasively.

John wasn't sure what he was looking at, but he had once entered a pyramid in the Yucatán and popped out on the moon. After that, nothing would surprise him.

"Have you got a rope?" John asked.

"You gonna try crawling in?" Lieutenant Weller asked.

"Yeah."

"It's been done. I tried it myself."

"I still have to try," John said.

A marine brought a coil of nylon rope and a climbing harness, helping John in and cinching it tight. Then a marine attached the rope with a carabiner to a ring on the back of the harness.

"You're good to go," the marine said, slapping him on the shoulder.

With two marines feeding the rope, John got down on all fours and crawled into the opening. Moving slowly, John paused every few inches, looking and listening. He heard nothing and saw nothing except a fuzzy darkness. A few more inches, and he felt resistance. Reaching out, John found he could barely extend his arm in front of him. It was like pushing his arm through Jell-O. Pushing hard now, John found he could not move even though he had not reached anything solid. Feeling a slight fluttering sensation in his stomach, John recognized it from his previous time-traveling experiences. Suddenly, he was jerked backwards and dragged out by his harness.

"Sir, sir? Are you all right? Can you hear me?" Lieutenant Weller was shouting at John.

"What?" John said stupidly. "Yes, of course I am all right. Why did you pull me out?"

"You weren't responding. We left you in as long as we dared."

"How long was I in there?"

"Thirty minutes," Lieutenant Weller said.

"What time is it?" John asked.

"Four twenty-five," Lieutenant Weller said.

John looked at his watch. By his watch, it wasn't even four yet.

"What's going on?" Lieutenant Weller asked.

"I don't know," John said honestly.

Looking at the faces of the marines, John knew they needed more from him than an "I don't know."

"There's a tunnel there, but for some reason, only some people can pass through it. Until I can figure out how to get through the tunnel, we can't go after Dr. Paulson and the others."

Appreciating the honesty, the marines nodded with respect. Taking off the harness, John looked back at the opening. Four people made it through that tunnel. Why could they, but not John? Like John, Nick Paulson had been through time to the past and the future, but the other three people with Dr. Paulson had not, thus eliminating one possibility. However, all four of them had examined a potential Visitor. John decided it was time to look at the Visitors since they were the only common denominator. Then the ground began to shake.

Everyone froze, ready to run if the earthquake threatened to bring the old barn down. The structure creaked, and dust and hay fell from the ceiling and the loft. Then the earthquake was over. Others relaxed, but John stood still, his mind racing. As one of the few people on the planet who had experienced the full ramifications of the Time Quilt, he suspected the earthquakes, the mysterious time-bending tunnel, and Dr. Paulson's disappearance were connected. But how?

Leaving the barn, John took out his cell phone and started to call Elizabeth Hawthorne, but then stopped. What would he tell her that she did not already know? Nick had crawled into a passage that was now gone, or impassable, and might never be passable again. Until it was, Nick could not get back, and John could not go after him. Eventually, John called Elizabeth, even though he had no understanding of what was going on or how to stop it.

17

Patrol

The horse must rank high as one of man's best friends. They provided transport for us for hundreds of years. They are also rather beautiful animals with a sense of humor. Fortunes have been made and lost on horses and some have become legends, such as that earthy little fighter Seabiscuit. In times of war, a man and horse together became the cavalry.

—Animal Kingdom

Present Time
Orlando, Florida

As a girl, Kris Conyers had been a tomboy, hunting and fishing with her father and brothers, the dresses that her mother insisted on buying gathering dust in her closet. Kris could tie a fly but not braid her own hair. She could adjust the air–fuel mixture on an outboard by ear, but could not remember if it was baking soda or baking powder that went into cookie dough—not that she made cookies. Now grown up, Kris was still a tomboy, with her hair cut short so she did not have to worry about braiding it or fixing it in any way except brushing it. More important, short hair fit better into her helmet. Kris Conyers was a member of the Orlando Mounted Patrol.

Kris had followed her father into the Orlando Police force, making a slight detour. Six months ago, Kris earned one of the rare openings on the Mounted Patrol. One of only eight mounted officers, Kris loved the duty, quickly bonding with her mount, a Thoroughbred bay named Torino. A former racehorse, Torino had been donated to the unit when the owners could not find a buyer. Too slow to earn his keep on the track, and a gelding so he was useless as a stud, Torino got his second chance with the Mounted Patrol. Torino's personality made him a natural for police work. In simulations, Torino quickly learned to stay calm when guns were fired, when he was hit with objects, and when sprayed with liquid. Most important, when faced with screaming, angry people, Torino kept his head, taking guidance from his rider.

Today, Kris and Torino were working a rock concert. The Orlando police were present in a show of force to head off potential problems. Orlando was the fifth tour stop for Bust-a-Cap, Twisted Gerbil, and Poppa's Kum. Hundreds of groupies followed the bands on the tour, cleaning out local food banks like locusts do a cornfield, camping under overpasses, and urinating and defecating where convenient. Worse, these particular groups attracted gangs, and Kris had already seen tats for the Jamaican Posse, MS-13, and most worrisome, Jacksonville City Boys. Not that the Jacksonville City Boys were any worse than local gangs, but gangs were as territorial as alligators. You could not encroach on a gang's territory and not expect to get bit.

For the concert duty, Morgan Nara partnered with Kris, riding a big filly named Tess. A hand taller than Torino, Tess was tall, thick-chested, and kid-tested. The only filly in the police stable, Tess nevertheless ruled, using her size to intimidate the geldings. Like his mount, Nara was big. A result of his Samoan, Japanese, and Irish mix, Nara's size was half the battle with most pimps, dealers, abusers, thieves, drunks, and thugs. Only gangbangers took Nara's size as a challenge. The Asian and Hispanic gangbangers were generally smaller men, and always had more to prove, seeing Nara much the same way Sir Edmund Hillary looked at Everest—he just had to take it on. Kris had more luck confronting gangbangers, but often ran into machismo issues, the fragile egos of the males easily pricked. However, Kris was getting good at male ego management, and mothered them, taking the "bitch," "cunt," and "dyke" references without reaction, all the while giving them firm, clear direction with just enough wiggle room for face saving. If Kris had a dollar for every middle finger she had seen, she could retire, buy Torino and a ranch, and ride off into the sunset.

Torino and Tess did most of the crowd management. If a crowd started to coalesce into a mob, the officers would use the mass of the horses to break up the clumps of people, isolating the ringleaders, forcing the others to think for themselves. As individuals, even gang-bangers could be reasonable and even moral, but in a gang, they suspended moral reasoning, letting stronger personalities make decisions for them. Unfortunately, in gangs, the sociopaths tended to be the charismatic leaders.

Starting the concert at 7 P.M. was part of the agreement with the promoter. The earlier time cut down on the drinking/using/smoking time before the concert, and then the concert ended with enough time for the concertgoers to make other plans, dispersing through the city to favorite bars or hangouts or, better yet, going home. The audience would be 70 percent young-adult male, and dispersion was essential to prevent friction, because friction caused sparks, and sparks fires. Extra buses would be ready, getting people out of the area as fast as possible. More police would arrive just before the end of the concert to create an intimidating presence.

The crowd was queuing up into four security lines, passing under an awning, putting bags on a table to be searched by security guards. Two police officers stood just behind the security guards, lending their authority. Garbage cans stood near the lines, slowly filling with water bottles, beer bottles, cigarette butts, and joints. Guns would get screened out, but the crack, meth, and PCP would get through. Kris hoped those would stay hidden until well after the concert.

The crowd was well mannered, the gangbangers clumped, self-absorbed, competing for attention. Even from a distance, Kris could pick out the leaders, seeing the subtle deference of the others, and she marked them. Control the leaders, and you controlled the gang. Torino snorted as they passed through a sweet cloud of marijuana smoke.

Kris ignored the joints hidden in cupped hands, guilty-looking boys and girls turning away, blending into the crowd, giggling as they moved toward the security lines. With a last couple of puffs, the butts were tossed into the cans. The potheads did not worry Kris. Let them smoke their joints, giggle through the concert, and return home short a few more brain cells. The other users would be the problem.

They finished their latest pass, using the corner of the block as one end of their patrol line. As far as Kris could see down the street, young people were flowing toward the concert venue. A city bus disgorged another thirty, mostly men, most pierced and tattooed, heads shaved or hair cut in bizarre patterns and colored neon orange or green.

"Give it another half hour and nuke the theater and watch the crime rate plummet," Nara said. "I might be able to let my kids play in the park again."

"They're all somebody's baby," Kris said.

"There but by the grace of God go my kids," Nara said, turning Tess with just a light touch of the reins.

Torino turned just as easily; then with a gentle nudge from the heels of Kris's black boots, they started back through the throng. Torino stepped on a sewer grate without flinching at the clang. The horses were trained for urban surfaces, something Torino never encountered in his short racing career. Kris's radio crackled from where it hung on her belt; then she heard the code "Be advised, ten-ninety-one C" followed by an address near their location. A unit responded, taking the call.

"Ten-ninety-one C?" Kris repeated, racking her brain for the code.

"Injured animal," Nara said, looking puzzled. "Usually it's a dog hit by a car. Sometimes a cat, but they tend to get squished up pretty good so you don't get many cat calls. I once answered a ten-ninety-one C, and it was a ten-foot python run over by a bus."

"Not a lot of dogs around here," Kris said, indicating the office buildings and stores lining the streets. "Or snakes."

"Lots of apartments above some of those shops," Nara said, nodding vaguely down the street. "Probably someone's Lhasa apso got out and had a close encounter with an SUV."

"Nara, you're overdue for sensitivity training."

"Not to worry. I can fake sensitivity better than any bitch, wetback, or fag on the force."

"Damn, Nara. Watch your mouth. Buy me a beer after the shift or I report what you just said to the watch commander. As bitches go, she's particularly sensitive."

A commotion ahead caught their attention. People were running, colliding, clearing out of the street in front of the theater.

"What the—?" Nara said.

Kris and Nara nudged their mounts toward the commotion, the leading edge now reaching them. Then, far ahead, a dinosaur stumbled into the street, squealed, struggling to get its balance.

"Ten ninety-one C my ass," Nara said.

"What is it?" Kris said, wondering out loud.

The dinosaur was wide bodied, with a potbelly. Its neck was long and thin, tapering to a small head. It was skidding on all four legs, trying to get traction. The back legs were much larger than the front. The dinosaur was the color of ripe eggplant, with white striping reminiscent of a badger. Kris had never seen anything like it.

"Who the hell cares what it is?" Nara said. "All I need to know is if the damn thing eats cop?"

Neither knew if it was a carnivore. As post-Quilt officers, they had undergone training that did include a unit on dinosaurs, but nothing like this had been covered. Kris's equestrian training had nothing on managing dinosaurs, although the horses had been crowd trained. Horses were trained to bump up against people—barrels simulated human bodies—driving them back. This dinosaur was bigger than a person but smaller than a horse, leaving Kris wondering if Torino's training was ingrained enough to handle a dinosaur.

Running men and women flowed past Torino and Tess, dispersing into any and every open door in the buildings lining the streets. Those closest to the scrambling dinosaur parted like the Red Sea, leaving a lane leading straight to Kris and Nara. Then another dinosaur slid into the street, followed by another—four, five, six of the striped animals piled up, clearly panicked. The first dinosaur squealed frustration, snapping at its brothers and sisters, who kept it off balance.

"What the hell is going on?" Nara said.

"It's a damn stampede," Kris said.

The first striped dinosaur regained its balance, then reared back, lifting its front two legs off the ground; extended its long, fat tail; and charged through the parting crowd, front legs barely off the ground. One by one, the other dinosaurs got traction and followed the lead dinosaur toward Kris and Nara. Young people pushed, shoved, tripped, and trampled one another, getting out of the way.

"We have to stop them before someone gets killed," Kris said.

"How?" Nara asked.

"Down the alley," Kris said, pointing to a space between buildings. "It dead-ends behind the theater."

Without waiting for a reply, Kris kicked Torino into a trot, closing quickly on the dinosaurs. Never having seen a human or a horse, the lead dinosaur slowed almost immediately, eyeing the two-headed thing coming at it. Kris yelled and whistled, waving one arm. Tess came up on Torino's right flank, Nara's booming shout loud enough to be heard over pounding hooves. It was a game of chicken, and the lead Stripy broke, turning left into the alley, the others following. Pulling up, Kris slowed Torino, Tess moving ahead.

"Don't get too close!" Kris yelled.

Nara pulled Tess sharply right and gave the herd of dinosaurs room, letting them flow into the alley, encouraging stragglers in the same direction. Then Kris noticed the last few Stripys twisting their long necks, looking back where they had come from. Kris caught the head move and pulled up, stopping Torino. Nara missed the warning sign and charged along the flank of the last of the herd, encouraging them down the alley.

"Wait!" Kris yelled.

It was too late. Screams from scattered concertgoers announced the arrival of another dinosaur. This one Kris recognized. It was a *T. rex* or a close cousin. As allosaurs went, this one was small, only three times the size of Torino. Tess sensed the danger before Nara spotted the *T. rex*. Unable to arrest her momentum, Tess veered away, almost tossing Nara with the unexpected move. Jerking on the reins, Nara tried to stop Tess's turn, but managed only to hang on. Too late, Nara saw the *T. rex*.

With its meal disappearing down an alley, the *T. rex* ignored the small humans running for their lives, instead going for the full meal. With giant steps, the *T. rex* covered the ground to Nara and Tess with surprising speed. With its small arms pulled up to its chest and its jaws opened wide, the *T. rex* lunged for Tess. Nara rolled off his mount just as the *T. rex* clamped down on Tess's neck. Hung up on one stirrup, Nara dangled as Tess was briefly lifted from her feet. The horse's momentum twisted the *T. rex*'s head, but its grip held. Tess screamed, kicking and bucking as blood spurted from her neck. With a jerk of its head, the *T. rex* broke Tess's neck. Nara kicked free of the stirrup and hit the ground, tried to get to his feet, and then collapsed again, clutching his left leg.

Torino danced nervously as the *T. rex* tore a chunk of meat from Tess's neck. Splashed with blood, Nara used his good leg to inch away from the *T. rex*.

"Easy, Torino," Kris said, studying the scene. "Let's go."

Kicking Torino into a run, Kris kept a firm grasp on the reins, fighting Torino, whose instincts told him they were going the wrong way. Like the warhorses of the Crusaders, Torino sensed the courage of his rider and drew on it. Horse and rider ran toward trouble.

Nara saw them coming and crawled faster, trying to get some distance away from the feasting *T. rex*. Protective of its meal, the *T. rex* hunched, a bloody strip of hide hanging from its jaws, eyes on the approaching horse and rider. Afraid of triggering an attack, Kris reined Torino in, the horse wide eyed and on the edge of panic. Tess's blood flowed into the street, giving the humid air a metallic smell. The *T. rex* roared a warning, putting one giant three-toed foot on Tess's neck.

Approaching Nara, Kris pulled her foot from the stirrup. She would never be able to lift Nara, who had eighty pounds on her.

"Grab the stirrup!" Kris yelled, pulling up next to the injured officer.

The *T. rex* lunged, snapping its jaws, then roared another warning, a mist of blood coating horse and rider. Torino jumped and danced, eyes wide, turning, wanting to run. Kris talked to the horse, soothing, praising him for his courage. When Torino settled down for a second, Nara grabbed the stirrup, stuck his hand through, and then clamped his other hand down, holding on tight.

"Easy, boy," Kris said, nudging Torino forward.

Kris held Torino's head in tight, fighting Torino's desperate need to run. If Torino took off, the stirrup would be pulled from Nara's grip. Dragging along the ground, Nara winced, his injured leg stretched out behind. Foot by foot, Kris dragged Nara clear, not stopping until they were two blocks away. Nara finally released his grip, lying flat in the street, breathing hard.

"I can't take anymore," Nara said, rocking from side to side.

Kris looked back at the *T. rex,* which was now ripping entrails from Tess's belly, snapping them up with jerking motions of its head, then rearing back, using gravity to help get the intestines down its gullet. Tess's blood flowed along the curb, a red river disappearing into a storm drain. A distant siren reminded Kris that the problem was not over. Getting on her radio, she warned the incoming officers, advising the dispatcher of the situation. Then began a series of calls from the chain of command as each layer refused to believe Kris's report.

As she explained, and reexplained, police cars arrived without sirens, blocking the street at either end of the block. A fire engine and a ladder truck helped fill in the gaps. Meanwhile, the Stripys milled in the blind alley by the theater, occasionally peeking out but ducking back down the alley when they spotted the *T. rex*. EMTs arrived, hauling Nara off on a stretcher, and Kris led Torino back behind the wall of police cars.

"It won't do," Kris said as she passed between the cars making up the blockade. "Look at the size of that mother."

Crouched behind the cars, officers looked nervously at the *T. rex* and then at their nine-millimeter pistols.

"This is nuts," one of the officers said.

Kris waited behind the line, stroking Torino's muzzle. Increasing distance from the blood and the *T. rex* was a tonic for the horse. Torino shivered, pranced a few steps, and then settled down. Looking back down the street, Kris could see that the *T. rex* was halfway through its meal, although Kris had no idea how much horse a *T. rex* could eat.

"Let's get you out of here before that tyrannosaur decides it wants seconds on horse," Kris said, leading Torino down the street.

"Oh no, there are people down there," an officer said.

Kris turned, looking back down the street. The concertgoers had scattered, but now Kris could see that many had hidden, and were now peeking out from behind parked cars, corners of buildings, and doorways. With no rescue coming, and the *T. rex* gorging on horse, Kris could see those hidden calculating their chances of getting away.

"Don't do it!" one of the officers said from behind his squad car.

"He's going for it," another officer said.

Kris spotted four young people hiding behind a car, one of them leaning around the back bumper, watching the *T. rex* and then looking down the block to the police barricade. Kris could see him estimating the distance, his speed, and the likelihood the *T. rex* would chase him. Looking at the *T. rex*, Kris could see that the best parts of Tess were gone, the carcass gutted, the haunches devoid of meat. The *T. rex* was gnawing bone and licking blood now. Then one of the officers stood, shouting down the street.

"Get down! Don't do it!" he shouted.

Unable to make out the words, the man behind the car took the policeman's call as encouragement and bolted. Kris estimated the young man was eighteen or nineteen, his hair cut in a Mohawk and then segmented with each section a different color of the neon rainbow. Heavily pierced, with rings and chains hanging from his lips, nose, and cheeks, he jingled as he ran. Adrenaline powered, he was fast, but not fast enough. As soon as the *T. rex* caught the movement, it gave chase, catching its prey in six steps. With a muffled scream, the young man's head and chest disappeared in the bloody maw, the scream cut off as *T. rex* chomped down. Crunching bone, the *T. rex* pulverized the body, then tilted its head back and swallowed its meal.

"Let's shoot," an officer said. "Can we shoot?"

"Hold your fire!" three or four voices ordered. "There are people down there."

"Stay hidden!" someone near the center of the police line said through a bullhorn. "Do not try and run. Help is on the way."

Kris looked at the array of weapons along the line. Pistols and shotguns, for the most part, the heavy weapons in transit. Some of the officers were wearing bulletproof vests as if the *T. rex* would return fire. Kris doubted the body armor would stop teeth and claws.

"He's after the others!" an officer called.

The *T. rex* had spotted the others hiding behind the car, and now flushed them, two men and a woman running back toward the theater. Hesitating just a second as it tracked multiple targets, the *T. rex* moved, snapping up the young woman, who was chomped in half, and then swallowed one half at a time. Then the *T. rex* was after the other two.

Kris jumped up on Torino, jerked his head around and worked between the police car barricade, and then kicked the horse into a gallop. Pulling her pistol, she fired into the air, violating department policy. The crack of the pistol brought the *T. rex*'s head around, arresting his charge, allowing the two men he was chasing to make the safety of the police line at the other end of the block. Seeing Torino, the *T. rex* smacked its jaws and charged. With only half a plan in mind, Kris continued straight for the *T. rex*, the gap closing rapidly.

Torino tensed, seeing the monster coming. The *T. rex* was fast, and Kris calculated it would be close. With a jerk of the reins, Kris turned Torino down the alley where the Stripys cowered. Hugging a wall, she drove Torino forward, the Stripys clearing a path. Then she fired three quick rounds. The Stripys panicked, stampeding. The small herd reached the open end of the alley, just as the *T. rex* arrived, crashing into the predator and knocking it from its feet. Squeals from the terrified Stripys mixed with the surprised bellow of the *T. rex*. Kris followed the Stripys out, mixing with the fleeing herd.

Coming out of the alley, Kris followed the Stripeys down the street toward the theater. The *T. rex* was up, giving chase, and it took no urging to keep Torino in a run. Instead, Kris reined him in to keep him from getting ahead of the herd. The Stripys butted and banged into one another, but feared the horse, giving Torino room.

Kris urged Torino into the middle of the fleeing herd, as the Stripy leader turned in toward the theater, running back toward wherever they had come from. Kris stayed with the herd, determined to keep a few Stripys between Torino and the *T. rex*. Glancing back, Kris saw the *T. rex* make the turn, losing ground, and then picking up speed and closing fast.

Ahead Kris saw that the glass front of the theater had been shattered, and the Stripys were running though the opening. Afraid of getting trapped inside the theater on a horse, with nowhere to maneuver, Kris started to pull up, but if she did, there would be nothing between her and the *T. rex*. Guessing her chances were better in the theater, Kris stayed with the herd, concocting a vague plan to separate from the herd somewhere inside.

Mounted on Torino, Kris followed the herd inside into dim light, down a wide hallway, and then through a demolished wall, and then blackness. Disoriented, she hung on, letting Torino's instincts guide the horse. Vaguely aware of the Stripys still around them, Kris feared collision and a fall where she would be trampled, or eaten by the *T. rex*. Then it was bright daylight, and Kris found herself in a meadow, the Stripys running as a pack. With a touch of the reins, Kris separated from the herd, kicked Torino hard, and leaned over his neck. Torino flew like the racehorse he used to be, putting distance between him and the Stripy pack. A pitiful scream told Kris the *T. rex* had another kill, but she did not slow until she reached a clump of trees. Looking back, she saw the distant *T. rex* was busy ripping a Stripy to shreds, the rest of the Stripy herd gone. Behind the lunching *T. rex,* the terrain rose, a steeply sloping hill that cut off the view in that direction. The only variation was a *V*-shaped cleft in the hill.

"We must have come out of that opening," Kris said to Torino.

The cleft was wide at its mouth but narrowed quickly and ended with a deep shadow. Looking at the position of the sun, and then at the valley shadow, Kris realized it wasn't possible for a shadow to fall in that spot. With the sun high, that cleft in the hill should have been lit, end to end. Kris was disoriented. It had been evening, but now it was midday. The city was gone, the landscape unfamiliar. Most of the valley she had ridden Torino through was filled with ferns, thick succulent plants, and horsetails. Stumpy palm trees sprinkled the tree line, larger palms behind that. There were no buildings visible in any direction. Sensing her discomfort, Torino shuddered and pranced a few steps, still blowing hard from the run.

"Where are we?" Kris asked.

In answer, the *T. rex* bellowed from down the valley. Approaching the kill was another *T. rex,* this one larger than the one that killed Tess. The two supercarnivores faced off over the Stripy carcass.

"Let's get the hell out of here," Kris said, directing Torino away from the fighting behemoths.

She rode Torino through terrain that alternated between thick stands of the strange palms and meadows. Occasionally, she would hear something moving through the forest, and would kick Torino into a run. Finally, she broke out into a large meadow with a large mound near the far end.

"Let's get up there and get a look around," she said.

As Kris Conyers and Torino trotted toward the hill, Inhuman eyes watched from hiding.

18

The Lost

The end of the human race will be that it will eventually die of civilization.

—Ralph Waldo Emerson

Unknown Time
Unknown Place

Only one of the strangers looked civilized, with a clean-shaved face but ragged clothes. He carried a rifle casually in one hand. The other man was bigger, and wild looking with a bushy beard and head hair that blended together seamlessly. A strip of cloth was tied around his head, and his clothes were bloody rags. The big man's eyes were wide, his mouth hanging open, his pink tongue running across his lower lip. He carried a machete that he slapped rhythmically against his thigh. Dried blood marked where the man had repeatedly wiped the machete on his leg.

"You're the people who saved us?" Nick asked, directing the question at the clean-shaven man.

"For now," the clean-shaven man replied.

"Yeah, for now!" the wild man said, shaking the machete.

"I'm Nick Paulson," Nick said, offering his hand.

"Jacob," the clean-shaven man said. "And this is Cra— Mike Kramer."

"Crazy Kramer," the wild man said, shaking his machete again.

"He won't hurt anyone," Jacob said.

"Like hell I won't," Crazy said.

"Crazy, knock if off!" Jacob said. "He's okay, really."

Nick introduced the others. Carson nodded a hello but then drifted farther from the one called Crazy Kramer, eyes on the machete.

"Where did you come from?" Jacob asked, his face taut, as if he was afraid of the answer.

"From Florida," Nick said.

Jacob's eyes grew wide, his face threatening to break into a smile. "Is it like this?" Jacob asked.

"It's subtropical, if that's what you mean," Wynooski said.

"That's not what he's asking," Nick said. "It's like it was before you came here."

Now Jacob smiled, then leaned his head back and whooped.

"Yeah!" Crazy Kramer said, shaking his machete above his head. "Bring it on."

"The world is there, Crazy," Jacob said, grabbing Crazy by the shoulders. "Don't you remember what it was like? No, you were too young. But we can go home. You will love it there."

"Bring it on!" Crazy Kramer said.

Then Jacob turned back toward the others, and Carson stepped forward and simultaneously they both asked, "How do we get there?"

"How did you get here?" Jacob asked.

"Crawled through a damn hole," Carson said. "What about you?"

"There was a flash, then everything shook, and then we were here, city and all," Jacob said. "For a long time, we never knew whether the rest of the world went somewhere else or whether we were the ones who went somewhere. We finally figured it out from the stars. They're all different."

"You went some-when," Nick said. "Big chunks of the planet's surface were displaced into the past. Based on the Dinosauria that came to our present, we theorized that most of the time displacement moved pieces of our present into the Cretaceous past. Although, we've had some bits and pieces of other time periods showing up in the present. Actually, some from the quite recent past."

"We have?" Carson asked, surprised. "How recent?"

"He's talking about that herd of indricotheres that came down out of Canada," Wynooski said.

"I can't talk about it," Nick said.

"You have dinosaurs there? Is it like this?" Jacob asked.

"Indricotheres are not dinosaurs, they are mammals," Wynooski said.

"All of the dinosaurs and formerly extinct mammals are on preserves," Nick said, restoring Jacob's hope. "Dinosaurs are controlled and managed."

Jacob looked at Wynooski's uniform and patch and the logo on Carson's shirt. "You *manage* dinosaurs?" Jacob asked, incredulous.

"I manage them," Wynooski said. "He's a pretender."

"I clean up their messes," Carson said, jerking his head toward Wynooski.

"I direct the Office of Security Science," Nick Paulson said, stepping in to stop the squabbling. "This is Dr. Gah. He's a paleobiologist."

The old man stayed on the ground, rubbing his ankle, but waved.

"Are there others here?" Nick asked.

"Yes, I think so. We lived in a Community but we were attacked last night. We're on our way to find the others."

"Attacked?" Carson asked, glancing about nervously. "By like a *T. rex* or something?"

"A whole mob of stinking *rex*es," Crazy Kramer said. "Took our kill, and all I got was a taste." Kramer sucked on his finger.

"That was earlier, Crazy," Jacob said. "Last night, the Inhumans attacked our Community. They drove us out of our homes and burned everything. In the fight, I got separated from my wife and daughters. They're out here somewhere, if they're still alive. I'm trying to find them."

Nick could see the pain in Jacob's eyes. "Inhumans?" Nick asked. "You mean dinosaurs?"

"No. The Inhumans are . . . are people, but not like us."

"They're animals," Crazy said. "And they bleed real good." Crazy held out his machete, twisting it back and forth, showing the dried blood.

"What do you mean, not like us?" Gah asked, trying to get to his feet.

Carson helped Gah up, supporting him with an arm around his shoulders. "Let's talk about this at home," Carson said. "Which way is that damn tunnel?"

"Can we go home, really?" Jacob asked.

"Sure, of course," Carson said, looking at Paulson. "We did the Alice in Wonderland thing to get here. We just go back through the rabbit hole to get home."

"It's possible," Nick said, but held back what he was thinking.

To Carson, returning home was as simple as crawling through the hole they had come through. But Nick remembered that only some people who crawled into the Alice hole actually passed through. Getting back the way they had come was not necessarily a sure thing for Carson, Nick, and Norman, and it was even less certain for Jacob and his people.

"I say we go back to the hole, crawl through, and then figure out the best way to find your family," Carson said.

"I can't leave without my family," Jacob said. "There are probably others too. We're all supposed to meet at the rendezvous point. That's where we're headed."

"Okay, we crawl back through the hole, and then you guys come back with an army of armed marines and rescue Jacob's family. Doesn't that make more sense than us wandering around with just one rifle between us?"

"The rifle's empty," Jacob said. "I used the last bullet on that tyrannosaur."

"Empty?" Carson said, his voice loud. "Then let's crawl through the hole and get some more ammo. I've got everything we need in my van back at the Super Eight."

"You still have Super Eights?" Jacob asked nostalgically.

"Super Eight?" Crazy said, suddenly interested. "Super duper!"

"It's a motel," Carson said. "Soft beds, warm showers—you could use one. Help me get back to that hole, and I'll take you there."

"We stick together," Nick said, taking charge. "First let's find the rendezvous point and see if Jacob's family is there. Then we'll figure out how to get out of here. Carmen, do you think you can find that tunnel we came through again?"

"Of course," Wynooski said. Wynooski's confidence meant nothing, since she was confident about everything. Still, she was a ranger, and she had been promoted for some sort of competence.

"Thank you, thank you," Jacob repeated. "My children were born here. They don't know what the real world is like."

With Crazy in the lead, hacking at anything in reach with his machete, they followed the pair, passing through thinning ranks of cycads that were twenty and thirty feet tall.

"We're going the wrong way," Carson grumbled as they walked.

The sun was past the zenith and the day warm but not unbearable. Jacob and Crazy's clothes were ragged, Crazy's pants cut off at the knees, and Jacob wearing his long. Crazy wore crude leather sandals and Jacob tattered running shoes that looked like they would fall apart at any moment. Crazy was cocoa colored, although not African-American, just deeply tanned. Jacob's face was nearly as dark, but glimpses through rips in his clothes showed much lighter skin. Both men had old scars and fresh cuts and bruises. Both looked like they worked and lived a hard outdoor life.

Nick the scientist was fascinated by the world he was walking through. Bits and pieces of it had turned up in his present, but this was more than just a sample; this was a functioning ecosystem. Much of the flora and fauna displaced to the modern age had died, simply because of being displaced into incompatible latitudes. What could be saved was on preserves, most of these in southern climates, although cooler regions like the U.S. Pacific Northwest supported a preserve. Here, in the Cretaceous past, Nick could experience a fully functioning ecosystem and see species that did not make it to the present.

Nick was also a realist and understood the danger. There was no guarantee they could return to the present, and the present held everything he was familiar with and everything he loved. Elizabeth was there. He had almost lost Elizabeth before, and that taught him how much he loved her. He only hoped he could get back before she knew he was gone.

They walked for hours, Gah limiting their pace because of his twisted ankle. Carson was impatient, but attentive too, stopping at one point and retrieving a broken limb, then directing Crazy to use the machete to shave it into a walking stick. Gah made better time after that, Carson's impatience diminishing proportionally. They stopped briefly for rests, all of them hungry but no one with food. Eventually they came to a stream, stopping for water.

"Who knows what nasty little buggies are swimming in this," Carson said between drinks.

"Obviously it's fine," Wynooski said, indicating Jacob and Crazy. "They drink it and they're alive."

"Yeah, we can drink it," Jacob said. "But there used to be a lot more of us."

Carson spit out his last mouthful.

The sun was getting low when they broke into a long open valley.

"We need to get to the other side," Jacob said. "It's dangerous to be in the open, but it would take us another day to work our way around."

"Nothing but a machete and a rifle-shaped club for weapons," Carson said. "I vote for the long way."

"We would have to spend an extra night in the forest," Jacob said.

"I vote we cross," Carson said.

The others agreed with Carson's second vote, and they left the tree line, heading into the low growth of the valley. Picking the shortest path across, they walked quickly, eyes busy, everyone alert. Crazy took the lead again, and Jacob took the rear, carrying his empty rifle like it was loaded. Everyone kept their eyes on the setting sun, calculating their chances of reaching the far side before dark. The sun was low when they approached a large mound in the valley.

"What's that?" Crazy said, pointing with his machete.

Nick looked to see something climbing the mound. Then it reached the top, the sun creating a silhouetted figure. It was a person on a horse.

"A Cretaceous horse?" Gah said, shielding his eyes.

"It's a cowboy," Carson said.

"What's a cowboy?" Crazy asked.

19

Gathering Storm

Nothing in this world can take the place of persistence. Talent will not; nothing is more common than unsuccessful people with talent. Genius will not; unrewarded genius is almost a proverb. Education will not; the world is full of educated derelicts. Persistence and determination alone are omnipotent. The slogan "press on" has solved and always will solve the problems of the human race.

—Calvin Coolidge

Present Time
Orlando, Florida

John Roberts stepped through shattered glass that once was the front wall of the theater. Based on reports, the dinosaur herd, the *T. rex,* and the police officer had stampeded through the front glass, down a hall, and through the back wall into the green room, and then disappeared. The green room was just a small back room with high windows, looking out through security wire. That room was filled with wreckage, but no dinosaurs, no police officer, and no horse. What interested John was the back wall of the room. Most of it was plastered with concert posters, as were the other intact walls in the room. The top layer of posters was for groups called Twisted Gerbil and Poppa's Kum. The lead singer in Twisted Gerbil was shown biting the head off a gerbil, blood running down his chin. Three men and two women dressed in S & M leather and chains played penis-shaped guitars in the Poppa's Kum posters. Posters were layered over posters, a decade's history of performances. However, there was something different about the back wall.

Staring, John found it hard to focus on the posters. His eyes struggling to focus, the wall briefly became clear and then blurry again. Detail and definition were elusive, the poster-covered wall was solid looking but difficult to see. Gingerly, John touched the wall. The concrete blocks under the posters felt spongy.

John stepped back, still having trouble fixing his focus on the wall. Police had searched inside and out of the theater, but no one could find any dinosaurs or their missing officer. That was especially strange, but there was also weirdness to the wall, just like the passage under the back wall of the Millses' barn. John concluded that like the space where Nick had disappeared, the passage in time had opened and then closed again—although not completely closed. As in the Millses' barn, the more time John spent near the wall, the stranger he felt.

"You feel anything?" John asked the man next to him.

"Yeah, like a fool," Mike Stott said. "I can't find a herd of dinosaurs in an empty theater."

Nearly a foot shorter than John, Mike was thick, from his short, broad neck to his tree-trunk legs. Thick lips, cone-shaped head shaved free of hair, Mike resembled a bullet. Mike was John's second in command in the loose structure of the Field Operations unit of the Office of Strategic Science.

"You don't feel nauseated or light-headed?"

"Light-headed? You mean lightbulb-headed?" Mike said, rubbing his scalp. "Is that a bald joke?"

"Never mind," John said.

They returned through the wreckage to the outside, to find anxious cops waiting. The injured Mounted Patrol officer was in surgery, the injured concertgoers dispersed to emergency rooms. Identifying the young woman who was eaten would be difficult until the men who were with her contacted the police to report her missing. John dodged a dozen questions until his phone rang. It was Elizabeth.

"What happened in Orlando?" Elizabeth Hawthorne asked.

"Give me a break, Elizabeth," John said. "I just got here."

"They're showing it on the news, John," Elizabeth said. "They said there was a tyrannosaur running through the streets and that it ate a couple of people, a horse, and a policeman."

"I can't confirm any of that," John said.

"I can see you," Elizabeth said.

John and Mike looked up at a television news helicopter with a big number *2* painted on it, hovering high above. John waved.

"Is this connected to what happened to Nick?"

It had been a month since Nick disappeared, Elizabeth calling daily for an update. Hesitating, John fumbled for an answer.

"It is, isn't it?" Elizabeth said, answering her own question.

"I'll be in Washington tonight," John said. "I'm going to go through Nick's files again in the morning. The president has named me acting director of the OSS. I'll have a new level of security clearance. There might be something there I haven't had access to before now."

"I'll meet you at his office," Elizabeth said.

"I can handle it," John said.

"I'm coming," Elizabeth stated firmly.

John gave up, agreeing to meet at Nick's office at nine. The Office of Security Science was located between the Office of Unified Communication and the Department of Small and Local Business Development. Down the block were the Office of Victim Services and the Pretrial Services Agency. John had no idea of what any of the other agencies did, but then he doubted any of the hundreds of government employees on the block understood what the Office of Security Science did.

Elizabeth was waiting outside. John took her through security and to the third floor. Kaylee Kemper was waiting. Barely five feet tall, Kaylee exuded energy, never completely still, some body part always in motion. Now, her brown eyes were busy, looking John and Elizabeth over. Relaxing near Kaylee was impossible since she radiated tension like enriched uranium. Short brown hair, a pixie face, and delicate hands gave her a childlike persona, although the forty-year-old face had the age-appropriate lines and wrinkles around the mouth and eyes.

"I've been named acting director," John said, deciding on a preemptive strike.

"So I was told," Kaylee said coldly. "Until you find Dr. Paulson. You do want to find him, Acting Director?"

John ignored Kaylee's jab.

"Hello, Ms. Hawthorne," Kaylee said politely.

Kaylee was fiercely loyal to Nick Paulson, and like a dog whose longtime master finally married, Kaylee never attached to John, the newcomer. Kaylee also blamed John for Nick's disappearance, since John was the field operative, and felt Nick had been doing John's job. John's elevation to director further strained their relationship.

"I'm so glad you came to help," Kaylee said to Elizabeth. "Dr. Paulson has never been out of the office this long without contacting me."

"I'm worried too," Elizabeth said. "We're going to do everything we can to find him."

"It's about time someone did something," Kaylee said, glaring at John.

"Is his office unlocked?" John asked.

"Of course," Kaylee said with a chill. "I'll lock the door when you leave."

"I'll need a key," John said.

"You're moving into Dr. Paulson's office?" Kaylee said, scowling. "He's missing, not dead."

"I'll be working from my office, but I don't want to ask you to open the door every time I need to get inside."

"I don't mind," Kaylee said, dismissing John's request for a key.

After a hug from Elizabeth and another cold glare at John, Nick's administrative assistant left them at Nick's office door.

"She doesn't like you," Elizabeth said.

"She won't be happy until Nick is back and I'm the one who has disappeared," John said.

Nick's office was semi-neat. The desktop was cluttered, but the bookshelves that covered every available wall space were neat, and ordered by topic. Nick's computer sat on the short arm of Nick's *L*-shaped desk. John sat in Nick's executive chair, rolling to the keyboard and starting up the computer. Elizabeth leafed through the papers on the desk. With his elevation to director, John would have access to all security levels. Previously, John had had access to virtually all Nick's files, since he knew Nick's password, but he hoped there was still something he had missed.

"Nick really needs another password," John said.

"Is it still Elizabeth thirteen?" Elizabeth asked.

"Elizabeth fifteen," John said. "The IT fascists force us to change passwords twice a year, so Nick just changes the number."

Pushing papers aside, Elizabeth found yellow sticky notes stuck to the desk. "These are interesting," Elizabeth said. "These say 'Visitor,' 'velociraptor,' 'Ocala Preserve,' 'carcasses' with a big question mark next to it, and then this one says 'jet.' "

"Yeah, I told you about that," John said, looking at time stamps on Nick's files. "That's what took Nick to Florida. Some guy showed up at the Ocala Preserve with two dead velociraptors."

"One of those private dinosaur managers," Elizabeth said.

"Yeah. He disappeared with Nick through the back wall of a barn. When I crawled in the hole, I could feel some sort of time distortion. To me it felt like seconds had passed, but the marines told me it was minutes. Whatever the conditions were that allowed Nick to get through have changed."

"Take me there," Elizabeth said.

"There's no point," John said. "Nobody has been able to get through that hole in the wall since Nick."

"So how does it connect to what happened in Orlando?"

"Same kind of weirdness. A tyrannosaur and a herd of dinosaurs popped out of nowhere and disappeared back to wherever they came from. Believe it or not, they seemed to have come right out of a wall. It had the same kind of weird properties as the hole on the farm where Nick was investigating."

"Time distortion?" Elizabeth asked.

"Something," John said. "Being there made me sick to my stomach. Elizabeth, I am about to show you what Nick was looking at just before he left for Florida. I'm breaking federal law, so my professional life is in your hands. Swear you won't share this."

"I used to be chief of staff to a president," said Elizabeth.

"Swear," John said.

"Cross my heart and hope to die," Elizabeth said.

John clicked on the file, and the video loop of the moon dinosaur ran.

"Where is that?" Elizabeth asked, leaning over John, pressing against his back and head.

"The moon," John said.

"What? The pyramid on the moon blew up. I was there."

"This is the wreckage," John said. "The dinosaur is still there, even now. Before the astronauts left, they set up a camera. It sends secure data bursts every six hours. This tyrannosaur is still on the moon, still stuck like this."

"But what does it mean?" Elizabeth asked.

"I don't know, and before you ask, I don't have any idea about whether it connects to Nick's disappearance or not." Returning to the computer, John searched through other recently opened files.

"What's this?" Elizabeth asked.

John ignored her, finding a file marked "Mission Harsh Mistress." John got the literary reference, and sure enough, the file held reports on the mission to the moon. John knew most of the OSS secrets but not all, and now searched documents for something he did not know. Virtually all the recent files related to the dinosaur trapped in the folds of time on the moon, and the strange material collected in the surrounding area. After the moon mission, Nick had asked John to send a team to the Yucatán to collect any similar material in the vicinity of the pyramid destroyed there.

"It's funny stuff," Elizabeth said. "It refracts light in an odd way."

John looked up to see Elizabeth holding a strange-looking chunk of black plastic. A small lead box sat open on the desk.

"Don't touch that," John said, taking the lead box and holding it out, so she could drop it in. Once in, John closed and latched the lid. "I think that's what they found on the moon," John said.

"Is it radioactive?" Elizabeth asked, looking at her hands.

"No, but Nick had it in a lead box, so let's not touch it."

"It looks like it came from the interior of the moon pyramid," Elizabeth said, once again leaning over John.

They read files together for an hour, and then Elizabeth stood, stretched her back, and went to Nick's leather couch, lying down. "John, I want to see where Nick disappeared," Elizabeth said.

"There's nothing to see," John insisted.

"Then there's no reason for me not to go," Elizabeth said. "I won't be convinced that we can't get him back until I see for myself."

"I haven't given up," John said.

"It's been a month, John," Elizabeth said. "I want to visit the place where Nick was last seen."

"There is nothing to see," John said. "We've secured the site with marines. I'll check with them and see if anything has changed."

"Call me," Elizabeth insisted.

"I won't stop looking," John said.

"All right," Elizabeth said, knowing she was running out of patience.

20

Big Chicks

The velociraptor is a bipedal carnivore with a long, stiffened tail and can be distinguished from other dromaeosaurids by its long and low skull, with an upturned snout. It [bears] a relatively large, sickle-shaped claw. . . . This enlarged claw, up to 67 millimeters (2.6 in) . . . is a predatory device, used to tear into the prey, delivering a fatal blow.

—www.velociraptors.info

Present Time
Near Hillsdale, Florida

Nearly three months old, the velociraptor chicks were the size of turkeys, with razor-sharp claws on fingers and toes. Most of the purple coloring was gone, replaced by dull greens, mixed with patches and streaks of brown and gray. The chicks looked like they were wearing army camouflage. By now, all of them easily hopped over the box wall Jeanette had built, only Ti still struggling a bit, sometimes teetering on the wall before she had the confidence to hop off. Do, the biggest chick, was the first to leap out. Coming into the barn one morning with Sally, Jeanette found Do waiting for her, hopping up and down, snapping at the food bowls she carried.

Now, all the chicks hopped out to wander the barn, chasing mice, cockroaches, and occasional birds. They were excellent hunters, and occasionally caught a mouse and killed it, but they never ate their kills. If the food did not come from Jeanette, it was not considered food by the chicks. Graduating from Alpo, the chicks now ate chicken, fish, beef, and occasional lamb—whatever was cheapest. Watching the chicks, Jeanette was struck by two qualities. First, the chicks coordinated hunting to an uncanny degree. If Re chased a mouse into a pile of hay, Me, Fa, and So would circle the pile, stationed an equal distance apart, and then freeze, holding as still as a cat stalking a bird. Then Re would plunge into the pile, flushing the mouse into the waiting claws of another chick.

Even more surprising than the coordinated hunting was the submission of the chicks to Jeanette and Sally. The chicks were highly sensitive to Jeanette's and Sally's moods, responding instantly to a bark or whimper from Sally, or a command from Jeanette. Despite their ugliness, Jeanette found herself attracted to the little carnivores, even knowing she could not keep them. Getting caught with seven unlicensed velociraptors meant jail and fines. Besides, these chicks represented thirty, forty, or even fifty thousand dollars to the right buyer. Maybe more, since they were tame enough to be hand-fed. If Carson ever returned, he would either butcher them or sell them. Watching Me chase a fly around the barn, Jeanette smiled and cheered Me on as she would a kitten.

The fly got away, so Jeanette got the fishing pole from the corner. The pole had a rubber mouse dangling from the end of it; now she held it above Me, who jumped for the mouse, Jeanette jerking it out of Me's reach. The other chicks came running, jumping and snapping at the mouse. Sally barked at their antics, but it was a playful bark, and the chicks ignored Sally. Walking slowly, Jeanette led the flock around the barn, teasing them with the mouse, careful to keep it out of their reach. The chicks enjoyed the game, hopping, snapping, landing on one another, and making their hoarse *awk-awk* sound. The game ended when Jeanette tossed a handful of dry dog food onto the floor and put the pole away. Jeanette stood by the door, watching the chicks scramble for the treats. Sally whimpered softly, watching the chicks eat her dog food, but did not join the fray.

"What are we going to do with them?" Jeanette asked.

Jeanette's phone buzzed, and she took it from the holster on her belt. There was an e-mail response from someone selling a cargo van—Jeanette was negotiating the purchase of another truck. With Carson gone, Jeanette ran the Dinosaur Wrangler business now, dispatching their trucks, doing the billing, reception, and hiring two more wranglers. One hire was to replace Carson—Nate Simpson, Robby Bryson's cousin—and another to handle the increased business. Doris Melton was the newest wrangler, and the first female. Business was booming, with four or five calls a day about dinosaurs running loose. Jeanette was raking in more cash in a week than she and Carson had previously earned in a month. Between the growing business and raising the velociraptors, Jeanette had little time to think about Carson and where he had gone. She called the Ocala Preserve every day, and every day she got the same response: "Mr. Wills is assisting with a dinosaur retrieval. I will tell him you called as soon as he returns. No, there is no way to contact him at this time."

They never said Carson was dead, but Jeanette assumed it. Carson would never work for the government, the military, or any group that made him get up early in the morning or go to bed before 2 a.m. If they had arrested him, Carson would have called and told Jeanette to get rid of the eggs. No, Jeanette was sure something bad had happened to Carson. As the months went by, Jeanette became the face of the Dinosaur Wrangler company, and spent her nights alone.

Angry chicken clucks and the sound of footsteps panicked Jeanette.

"Hide," she said sharply.

Instantly, the chicks fled in every direction. The door opened before Jeanette could reach it, and a man leaned inside. He was wearing sandals, dark blue board shorts, and a Florida Marlins T-shirt.

"Les, what are you doing here?" Jeanette asked, trying not to look worried.

Deputy Les Wilson smiled, showing his perfect teeth. Les Wilson had dropped in regularly, talking to Jeanette, flirting with her. Since he had never met Carson, Les assumed Jeanette had made up a boyfriend to discourage unwanted attention. Ever since puberty, Jeanette had received more attention from men than ten average women, and mostly it annoyed her. She wasn't above using her body to manipulate men, but had come to hate the constant looks, whistles, lewd comments, and leering of men who undressed her with their eyes. She had reacted to Les Wilson the same way at first, but there was a boyish sincerity to Les that won her over.

"I got bored and asked myself if I could do anything I wanted to do today, what would it be? So I'm here."

"That's a good line," Jeanette said.

"Thanks. I worked on it all night because I couldn't sleep. I kept thinking about you."

"Wow, a twofer. Did you pull these off the Internet?"

"I'm insulted. I'm not just some dumb flatfoot."

"What's a flatfoot?" Jeanette asked, looping her arm through Les's and leaning gently against him. Les sighed involuntarily, letting Jeanette turn him toward the door.

"A flatfoot? That's a cop."

"Oh, I've never heard that," Jeanette lied.

For total control over men, Jeanette mixed just a hint of dumb blonde with light physical touch.

"Flatfoot, dick, five-oh, Barney, bear, bull, fuzz, narc, pig. We get called lots of things."

Jeanette pushed Les out the door, looking back over her shoulder—no chicks in sight.

"Dick?" Jeanette said. "Why do they call you guys dicks?" Jeanette giggled, finishing off Les Wilson's self-control.

"I think it comes from Dick Tracy, or maybe Fearless Fosdick," Les said, realizing Jeanette was not interested and just teasing.

Jeanette walked Les to the office, then sat on the edge of the desk while Les leaned against the wall. Les was the anti-Carson in many ways. Handsome but not rugged-looking, neat, reliable, tender, mainstream, and undoubtedly brave. Carson was good-looking if you liked country boys, sloppy, unreliable, unpredictable, reckless and antisocial, or at least socially indifferent. The most striking difference between Carson and Les was in their attitudes toward Jeanette. Carson took Jeanette for granted, but Les worshipped her. Sleeping alone for a month made being worshipped feel good.

Jeanette wore a pink polo shirt with the Dinosaur Wrangler logo embroidered over her left breast, jean shorts, and pink flip-flops.

"No tool belt today?" Les asked.

"It's an office day," Jeanette said, scooting back on the desk, then crossing her legs. Jeanette smiled, pushed her short brown hair back off her forehead, knowing it would tumble back down. Then she let the tip of her tongue play with the small gap in her front teeth.

"Any chance you could take a couple of hours off?" Les asked. "We could run over to the lake for a swim."

"What would my boyfriend think?" Jeanette asked.

"You sure you've got a boyfriend?" Les asked.

"Yeah."

"How come I never see him?"

"He's working with the government on something," Jeanette said.

"He wouldn't want you sitting around here all the time having no fun, would he?"

"Yeah, he would," Jeanette said. "Besides, someone's got to run the business while he's gone."

"Just two hours," Les pleaded.

Jeanette wavered. Calls came in sporadically, and the answering service could handle any that came while she was gone. All the wranglers had assignments that would take them a few hours to handle, and each had two or three calls stacked on top of those. Jeanette looked at the clock.

"I suppose I could do an early lunch," Jeanette said. "Did you bring any food?"

"Beer," Les said.

In that way, Les was just like Carson.

"I'll make a couple of sandwiches and grab my suit," Jeanette said.

"All right," Les said, as excited as if she had agreed to go to bed with him.

Jeanette made a chicken salad out of chicken chunks she had cut up for the chicks, and then spread it on bread. She threw in a bag of chips and two bottles of water. In the bedroom, Jeanette took off her clothes, grabbed her one-piece swimsuit and stepped into it, pulling it up. She looked in the mirror and then took pity on Les. Pulling the suit down, she picked out a two-piece, put it on, and then stood in front of the mirror. Carson had picked the suit, giving it to Jeanette for her birthday. It covered enough, but barely enough.

Les earned this, Jeanette thought.

Putting on a silver beach cover-up, Jeanette stepped into gray flip-flops, picked up the beach bag with her towel and the lunch, and left with Les.

Les was attentive, opening the door to his pickup for her, and then jogging around to get in the driver's side. Sally watched them go, unconcerned, and then walked slowly to the barn door, flopping down in front of it.

The lake was only fifteen minutes away and not crowded. A few moms sat in lawn chairs, their children splashing in shallow water. They walked away from the families, gaining a little privacy. Les had a blanket, and they spread it on the grass.

"Swim first?" Les said.

"First?" Jeanette asked suspiciously.

"Before we eat!" Les said.

"Oh. Sure."

Jeanette pulled off her cover-up, and Les gawked. Until now, her clothes had camouflaged her body. Fighting to take his eyes away, Les stripped off his shirt and kicked off his sandals. Les was always so clean-shaven that Jeanette wondered whether he actually had body hair. There was chest hair, but not much. He wasn't as hairy as Carson, and that was okay with Jeanette. Taking Les's hand, Jeanette pulled him toward the water.

"Let's go," she said, and they ran into the lake.

Like most men, Les was a playful show-off and Jeanette let him perform. Les swam, dived, splashed, and picked Jeanette up and tossed her. They played like kids for a while, and then swam, Les demonstrating different strokes, and then floated next to each other, talking. After half an hour, Jeanette's fingertips were puckered and they got out, drying, and then lying on the blanket. Drinking cold beer from the cooler, they ate the sandwiches and munched on chips, Les talking about police work, Jeanette telling him stories about runaway dinosaurs.

"Seems like there are more and more loose dinosaurs turning up," Les said.

"Yeah," Jeanette said. "I guess they suspended the reward for Visitor dinosaurs. They had to pay too many claims. Our company's put in for ten claims for our customers. We get a share of the reward."

"Any of them predators—you know, dangerous dinosaurs?" Les asked.

"Not really," Jeanette said. "Mostly vegetarians, except for a couple of egg stealers."

"So, nothing like what happened in Orlando," Les said.

"Was there really a tyrannosaur loose?" Jeanette asked. "The Dinosaur Rangers deny it. Seems impossible to me."

"It was a tyrannosaur," Les said, rolling up on his side, leaning on an elbow. "It ate a police horse."

"Seriously?"

"Yeah."

"What happened to it? Did they shoot it? Some people say the police killed the tyrannosaur and then took it away so people wouldn't know."

"No, it wasn't shot. That's the weird part. They never found it. They couldn't find the herd it was chasing either."

"That doesn't sound good," Jeanette said, thinking of the implications. "All these dinosaurs popping up. Are we heading toward another Time Quilt?"

"They say we aren't," Les assured her. "If anything, it might be just a little leakage through time."

"That's good," Jeanette said, thinking about Carson's velociraptors.

Les rolled onto his back, so Jeanette rolled up on her side so she could see his body. Les was fit, with little body fat. He did not have a full six-pack, but there were hints along his abdomen. Jeanette ran her finger from his belly button to his rib cage. Then she leaned over and kissed him lightly on the lips.

"I have to get back to work," Jeanette said, sitting up as his arms reached for her.

"Now?" Les whined.

"I'm in charge while Carson is gone," Jeanette said, pulling on her cover-up.

"Wait, there's something I need to tell you," Les said. "Those guys who were running the meth lab in the place next to yours? The case got kicked. The judge didn't like me pretending to be a code enforcement officer. He said it queered the evidence, and they tossed it. All of it. The case went poof with it."

"When are they getting out?" Jeanette asked.

"They're out," Les admitted, sitting up. "That's why I thought I'd hang around with you for a while."

Jeanette appreciated Les's offer, but she could not have a cop around with a barn full of illegal velociraptors. "I'll be fine," Jeanette said, not really certain.

Les apologized all the way back to the ranch, and then left reluctantly, making Jeanette promise over and over again to call if she had any concerns. Touched by his guilt and his concern, Jeanette kissed him again, and then sent Les off.

Jeanette checked the revolver in the box on the office floor, making sure it was loaded, and then took lunch to the chicks. Opening the door, she noted no chicks in sight. Jeanette sang "Do, Re, Me, Fa, So, La, Ti," and chicks came running from hiding places, *awk*ing and hopping, jumping up at the food bowls. Jeanette put the bowls down and marveled at how fast the chicks were growing.

"I think they're bigger than they were this morning," Jeanette said to Sally.

Three calls about loose dinosaurs came in that afternoon, and

Jeanette assigned the retrievals to her wranglers, although none would be able to respond until the next day. Doris had been slightly injured by a triceratops, but had single-handedly managed to use a cattle prod to force the monster into a corral with an electric perimeter. Unfortunately, no one had claimed the triceratops, and the owner of the corral wanted it removed. Jeanette told Doris to collect her fee and then call the Dinosaur Rangers to collect the triceratops.

After feeding the velociraptors dinner, Jeanette played with them, then closed them in the barn and sat in the office, drinking iced tea, watching the light fade from the sky. Sally was lying in front of the screen door, sleeping. This was the time of day when Jeanette missed Carson the most, since work and the velociraptors kept her busy during the day. Evenings and nights were when she thought of Carson. Tonight, however, she felt guilty, because she was not thinking about Carson; she was thinking about Les, and the thrill she got when she kissed him.

"Carson, you better get home soon," she said, blaming him for her feelings.

Sally stirred at Carson's name, sitting up and barking at something in the dark. Jeanette's hand dropped to her side, feeling the box on the floor next to her, and the gun resting on top. Sally settled down again, but Jeanette continued to finger the gun, watching the dark.

21

Confidential

Kaylee Kemper is reliable, helpful, and attentive to her responsibilities. Given the confidential nature of the material that she comes in contact with, I particularly value her discretion.

—Performance review for Kaylee Kemper
by Nick Paulson, Supervisor

Present Time
Washington, D.C.

"Kaylee, it's Elizabeth."

"Hello, Ms. Hawthorne," Kaylee Kemper said. "I'm sorry to say there isn't any news today. I'm so discouraged."

"I'm not just discouraged, I'm fed up," Elizabeth said. "I'm going to do something."

"What?"

"I'm going to look for Nick," Elizabeth said.

"But where? No one seems to know where he's gone." Kaylee was whispering now, as if she were entering into a conspiracy.

"That's where you can help me," Elizabeth said.

"Me? How?"

Instinctively, Elizabeth dropped her voice to a near whisper. "To find Nick, I need to start somewhere. John told me he disappeared from a farm, or a ranch, in Florida, but he won't tell me exactly where it is."

"I can't tell you that," Kaylee said.

"I don't want you to break any laws," Elizabeth said.

"It's not that," Kaylee said. "I'd go to prison for Dr. Paulson. I just don't know the exact address. I know it's near Ocala, but that's all. Dr. Gah called me from the preserve about the velociraptors, but all he said was that some man calling himself the Dinosaur Wrangler brought in two Visitors."

"Dinosaur Wrangler," Elizabeth repeated.

"That won't help, Ms. Hawthorne. The Dinosaur Wrangler person disappeared with Dr. Paulson."

"I suppose," Elizabeth said, thinking. "Thanks for your help."

"If I find anything out, I'll call you," Kaylee said.

Hanging up, Elizabeth opened her laptop, and then she typed "Dinosaur Wrangler" into a search engine.

22

The Big One

Evolution from sentience to partial-sapience or full-sapience requires billions of years, and not all species succeed in reaching it.

—scienceray.com/philosophy-of-science

Unknown Time
Unknown Place

The cowboy waited for them on the hill. By the time they reached the top, Nick realized the mounted rider was a police officer. Her badge and shoulder patch identified her as part of the Orlando Police force.

"Boy, am I glad to see you," she said, walking toward them, pulling her horse along by the reins.

"Were you sent to find us?" Carson asked, hope rising.

"Find you? No. I have no idea where I am. Don't you?"

"Hell no," Carson said.

"We've passed through a time junction connecting our present with the Cretaceous past," Nick explained.

"Did you crawl through a pipe?" Carson asked.

"On a horse?" the officer said.

"Horse?" Crazy Kramer said, eyes wide, reaching out to gently touch the horse's neck.

"Nick Paulson," Nick said, offering his hand.

Exchanging names, Officer Kris Conyers took off her helmet, wiping sweat from her brow. She wore her hair short, with bangs swept across her forehead. She had large eyes, slightly almond shaped, her face an oval that narrowed to a pointy chin. A mole marked the jawline on the left side of her face.

"Dr. Paulson of the OSS?" Conyers asked. "Well, that can't be good if you're stuck here."

"We're not stuck," Carson said. "We're going back the way we came as soon as we find his family."

"Yeah!" Crazy Kramer added, shaking his machete.

Conyers looked sympathetically at Jacob and suspiciously at Crazy Kramer. "I'll be glad to help, but I can't get Torino back through a pipe, if that's what you came through."

"Where is your entry point?" Nick asked.

"Back down the valley," Conyers said, pointing. "I didn't get a good look at it, because I was running from a *T. rex* at the time. We came out of a little valley or ravine, or something. It was dark until just before we came out. I can find it easily enough by backtracking the trail."

"A blind man could follow that trail," Wynooski said. "I could find it easy."

"There's a *T. rex* back down your trail?" Carson said. "I say we crawl through the pipe and screw your friend Flicka."

Officer Conyers stepped in front of Carson, inches from his face. "That horse saved my life, and a lot of other people's lives," Conyers said, her nostrils flaring, her cheeks reddening. "If the horse doesn't go, then I don't go."

"Suits me," Carson said.

"We'll resolve this later," Nick said, trying to push between Carson and the officer. "The first priority is to find Jacob's family and any other survivors."

"Survivors?" Officer Conyers asked.

"There were thousands at one time," Jacob said. "But disease, fires, earthquakes, fighting, famine—all the worst parts of the Bible—killed most of us. Others left to find a better place to live. There were two hundred and thirty-eight of us still alive when we got attacked."

"Attacked?" Conyers said.

"Look, Roy, we don't have time to fill you in on everything you missed," Carson said.

"I'll explain as we walk," Nick said.

With a final glare at Carson, Conyers agreed to go along.

"Maybe he better ride," Conyers offered, pointing at Gah.

Gah's ankle was swollen, and his limp slowed them down. They helped Gah up into the saddle, Conyers adjusting the stirrups for the injured man. She had two water bottles in a saddlebag and passed those around. The bottles were drained. On top of the hill, Nick looked around while there was still light, Jacob next to him, Wynooski on the other side.

"That's where we need to go," Jacob said.

"Strange-looking formations," Wynooski said.

The horizon was a series of low green hills split by taller brown and gray spires. Finally Nick recognized what it was—the ruins of a city.

"That's Portland," Jacob said. "There's even less left than the last time I saw it. We've been having a lot of earthquakes. I think they brought down more buildings."

"Looks like some of your survivors," Conyers said, pointing down the valley behind them.

Everyone turned, looking into the shadow-filled valley.

"Bring it on!" Crazy Kramer shouted, waving his machete.

"We've got to go," Jacob said, pulling Crazy Kramer down the hill, away from the advancing group.

"Why?" Conyers asked, pulling Torino after the others.

"They're Inhumans," Jacob said.

"What does that mean?" Conyers said.

"It means get your ass in gear, Hopalong," Carson said, passing Conyers.

"They're people, but not like us. They evolved from a different biological root than we did," Nick said, coming alongside the bewildered officer.

"Oh, Torino, what have I gotten us into?" Conyers said.

They hurried off the hill across the valley to the tree line. Pausing just inside, hidden in shadows, they watched for anyone or anything following.

"They had to see us up there," Dr. Gah said.

"They saw us!" Wynooski said flatly. "A blind man could see us standing on top of that hill. I knew it was a bad idea to climb up there."

"You didn't say anything," Carson pointed out.

"I'm not the one in charge," Wynooski said.

They worked their way through the forest, the horse a mixed blessing. With Torino carrying Gah, they could move faster, but the horse could not squeeze through tight spaces. They walked until everyone was staggering and tripping in the dark, finally resting in a small clearing. The only food they had were energy bars that Officer Conyers had in her saddlebag, which they split up, satisfying no one. They had refilled the empty water bottles at a stream, but split seven ways, there was not much to go around. Everyone was hot, thirsty, and hungry, except Torino, who happily munched juicy ferns. As people started to fall asleep, Nick suggested taking turns watching. Nick volunteered to take the first watch.

Nick watched the shadows for a while, but soon turned his gaze to the sky, seeing more stars than he ever had in his own time period. The pollution-free Cretaceous heavens were stunningly beautiful, but disquieting at the same time. Nick could not recognize a single constellation. Nick knew stars moved. Edmond Halley had discovered this when comparing his astronomical observations to Greek star charts and finding that Sirius, Arcturus, and Aldebaran had shifted position, although just slightly. Looking at the Cretaceous sky, Nick could not pick out a familiar star, fragment of a constellation, or what the ancients called the "wandering stars," which were planets.

"We started renaming the constellations," Jacob said, as if reading Nick's mind. "See that near circle over there? That's Ezekiel's Wheel. The vee-shaped clump over there is Noah's Ark, and that box shape is the Ark of the Covenant."

"All your constellations have biblical names," Nick said.

"The names have to be approved by Reverend. He's the head of our Community."

Nick looked at Jacob, judging his feelings about this Reverend. "It's a religious community?" Nick probed.

"It's the only Community," Jacob said. "Don't repeat this, but I wouldn't live there if I had any choice, but my wife's a believer, and even if she agreed to leave, how could I take care of my wife and kids out here? We don't have any choice of where to live. No one has a choice. You live in the Community, or you don't live at all. If you don't obey, you get expelled—and that's a death sentence."

"If we find your people, will they come with us?" Nick asked.

"Why wouldn't they?" Jacob asked. "It's a chance to be safe again."

"Even in the modern age, people drop out and form their own communities," Nick said. "The religious are particularly prone to doing this. The Amish have lived separate from the world into the modern age, but if they could have a world of their own without the temptations of modern conveniences, wouldn't they take it? Then there were the Branch Davidians and Heaven's Gate. They were willing to die to live separate from the world."

Jacob lay flat, looking at the sky, thinking. "I don't know if the reverend survived the attack last night," he said. "Maybe he didn't. Maybe there won't be a problem."

"Maybe you do what the hell's best for your family and stop letting this Reverend guy boss you around," Wynooski said.

"It's not that easy," Jacob said, staring at the sky again.

"It sure as hell is," Wynooski said.

They lay quiet then, Nick finishing his turn on watch, and then nudging Wynooski, who grumbled, "I wasn't sleeping," as she woke up. Nick slept poorly, as did most of the others, only Carson seeming to fall into a deep sleep. As the sky began to lighten, they were all awake, waiting for enough light to walk by.

Nick's attention returned to the sky. He wondered about Polaris, the polestar of his age. Polaris was actually three stars, a bright giant and two companions that lined up with Earth's north pole. Nick wondered if Polaris's three stars would be close enough in this age to be seen as one, or as three separate stars? Then Nick saw a shimmering light he thought was a planet, maybe Venus, low on the horizon. Searching for other planets, he spotted a bright light coming over the trees, trailing a bright smudge. Puzzled, Nick studied the strange star. Suddenly, he sat up.

"How could I be so stupid?" Nick said suddenly. "I know where we are. I mean when we are."

"Who cares," Carson mumbled, still half asleep.

"How long has that star been in the sky?" Nick asked Jacob.

"Long time, I guess. We used to see it in the night sky, but now it's a daystar. It's been getting a lot brighter lately, so you can usually see it during daytime. The reverend calls it the Fire of God. He says it's the same fire that wouldn't consume the burning bush that God used to speak to Moses."

"Has anyone in your Community been tracking it?" Nick asked.

"Tracking it? No, not really. I don't know if anyone would know how. The reverend has been telling us it's going to bring a new age and that everything is going to change when the light comes."

"He's right about that," Nick said. "I think we are on the brink of the K–T event—the end of the Cretaceous era."

Only Dr. Gah understood, sitting up, looking aghast.

"What are you talking about?" Carson asked, now fully awake.

"The K–T event is what ended the age of dinosaurs. That light in the sky is an asteroid the size of Mount Everest, and it is going to impact the Earth near where the Yucatán is in our present. That explains the earthquakes and the time junctions. They're all because of the coming impact."

Nick looked around, seeing that they only half understood.

"The impact of that comet is going to kill nearly every living thing on this planet," Nick said.

"It's the big one?" Carson asked.

"Yes," Nick said.

"Of course it's the big one," Wynooski said.

"When?" Conyers asked.

Nick looked at the bright glow. "Soon," Nick said. "Very soon."

"Yes, I would say soon," Wynooski said.

"Then maybe we better get the hell out of here," Carson said.

23

Taking Charge

JEANETTE JOHNS: *Is there any news today about Carson Wills?*

SHIRLEY NICHOLS *(receptionist, Ocala Dinosaur Preserve)*: *No, Mr. Wills has not returned yet; however, as I have told you repeatedly, I will call you when I know when he will return.*

JEANETTE JOHNS: *I'll call you tomorrow.*

Present Time
Near Hillsdale, Florida

After dinner, Jeanette played with the chicks, teasing them with the fishing-pole mouse and then playing tug-of-war with a knotted rope. Then she sat on the front porch with Sally, enjoying the evening, watching the house next door for signs of activity. The sun was just touching the horizon when a car came down the road. Sally stiffened, and Jeanette stood, positioned near the door so she could bolt inside for the gun. The SUV was new and nothing like the cars that had been parked next door when the meth lab was running. The car pulled up and a woman got out. She was tall and pretty, with red hair hanging to her shoulders. Jeanette thought the woman, in her forties, was a little old to wear her hair that long, but it looked good on her and it wasn't Jeanette's business if the woman tried to look younger than she was. Dressed in a long-sleeved, cream-colored cotton shirt with the sleeves rolled up, and cargo pants with zip-off legs, she had a taste for expensive-casual clothes.

"This can't be good," Jeanette said to Sally.

"Is this the Dinosaur Wrangler?" the woman asked.

"You found us," Jeanette said. "If one is running loose, we round 'em up."

"My name is Elizabeth Hawthorne. Nick Paulson is my husband. He was with someone from this business investigating two Visitor velociraptors when they disappeared."

"Disappeared? Carson disappeared?"

"Maybe we better talk," Hawthorne said.

"Yeah, maybe we better, Ms. Hawthorne."

"I'm Elizabeth."

They sat in the office, drinking iced tea, the ceiling fan stirring the air, Jeanette listening to the story of how Carson and others disappeared. Elizabeth Hawthorne explained the situation clearly, in simple terms, and in a linear fashion. Obviously a brilliant woman, she was not condescending, and Jeanette warmed to her.

"I know that Nick and Mr. Wills went back to the place where Mr. Wills found the velociraptors, but I'm not sure where it is. I want to go there to look for myself."

"I have the address," Jeanette said, going to the computer and opening the call file, scrolling back three months. She found the record. "It's not far. Let's go together. I want to find Carson too. It's high time he got back and did his share of the work."

"There might be marines guarding the place," Elizabeth said. "They won't want to let us in."

"If the marines are men, I can handle them," Jeanette said.

Suddenly, Sally jumped up, giving a sharp bark. The screen door was yanked open, torn partially from its hinges. An aluminum baseball bat smashed the computer monitor. Throwing herself back, Jeanette tumbled out of her chair. Rolling onto her knees, Jeanette scrambled for the gun in the box. The baseball bat whistled down, smashing the box. Jeanette jumped back, saving her hand as Sally attacked, giving Jeanette and Elizabeth time to escape. Sally's yelp and squealing broke Jeanette's heart, but there was nothing she could do.

"Who are they?" Elizabeth asked as they ran through the kitchen and out onto the back porch.

"There were two?" Jeanette asked, having seen only the swinging bat. "Drug dealers."

Footsteps behind them drove them off the porch.

"This way," Jeanette said, pulling Elizabeth toward the barn.

The men behind were closing on them when they reached the door, getting inside and pulling it closed. The men immediately pulled on it, jerking repeatedly, making it impossible for Jeanette to latch it.

"Is there another way out?" Elizabeth asked, finding a light switch and turning it on.

"Yes, but we'll never make it," Jeanette said. "I can't hold them."

Elizabeth took a hammer from the workbench, backing up.

"Stop there," Jeanette said, and then released the door, the men nearly falling to the ground as the door suddenly flew open. Grabbing a screwdriver, Jeanette stood in front of Elizabeth.

Two men stepped in. Jeanette recognized one as the man that the cops had dragged off her fence. With long blond hair, three-day growth of beard, wild blue eyes, and wearing a denim shirt with cut-off sleeves, he carried the baseball bat, now slapping it in his palm. His denim shirt was unbuttoned, and Jeanette saw a dagger-through-a-heart tattoo in the middle of his chest and a pistol shoved in the waist of his jeans.

The second man was taller, with a shaven head and a tattoo of a dragon on his scalp. He had Elvis sideburns that seemingly sprang out of nowhere, since his head was bald. He wore a muscle T-shirt with a skull on it, and dirty cargo shorts. Dark sunglasses hid his eyes. He had a knife in a sheath on his belt. Both had the nervous energy of heavy users.

"Damn, I thought we were going to have to share, amigo," the one with the baseball bat said. "Looks like we're taking turns instead."

The big one snorted, then smiled, showing the bad teeth of a meth addict. "Dibs on the redhead," Amigo said.

"Suits me," the other said, still slapping the bat.

The men advanced slowly, expecting the women to bolt.

"Stay still," Jeanette said, reaching behind her to hold Elizabeth's hand. "Let me sing you a song," Jeanette said.

"What the hell?" the bat man said.

"Do, Re, Me Fa, So, La, Ti," Jeanette sang.

Amigo laughed, showing his rotten teeth. Then his smile faded as velociraptors crept out of dark spaces and from under piles of straw. Heads low, tails straight, mouths open showing sharp teeth, they spread out, taking positions around the men, Do on one side of Jeanette and La on the other.

"What the hell?" the bat man said, looking around. "Those are some ugly chickens."

"They're raptors," Jeanette said.

"Raptors?" Amigo repeated, understanding finally cutting through the drug fog.

"Little bastards," the bat man said. "What? You expect us to be scared of some pissant dinosaurs?"

"You should be," Jeanette said.

"Well, batter up!" the man with the bat said, taking a swinging stance.

Stepping toward Ti, the littlest raptor, he swung hard enough to bat the turkey-sized velociraptor into the loft. Ti dodged, the bat swishing through empty space, the man with the bat stumbling as he missed. Re leapt from behind, slashing with his toe claws, slicing through his pant leg and deep into the calf. Screaming, the man collapsed to one knee, using the bat as a crutch. Amigo fumbled for his knife as Do and Ti attacked, leaping waist high, slashing with toe claws, bouncing off the ample stomach, landing on their feet, and running out of range of the slashing knife.

Jeanette entered the fray, running forward and kicking the bat man in the side, knocking the wind out of him. Now he dropped the bat, going down on both knees, reaching for the gun in his belt, one hand flat on the floor. Jeanette drove the screwdriver through his hand hard enough to stick to the floor. Screaming, he jerked his hand up, pulling the screwdriver free. Coming up onto his knees, he gingerly touched the handle of the screwdriver, eyes wild with fear. Velociraptors attacked from all sides now, slashing and biting, opening wounds in his belly, chest, arms, and legs. La cut a deep slice across the right side of his neck, and he slapped a hand to the wound to stem the flow. Three more slashing attacks and he collapsed to the ground, curling into a protective ball.

Swiping wildly with his knife, Amigo caught Do in midair, knocking the biggest velociraptor down, opening a gash in his side. Instantly, Do was up and attacking again. Panicky now, Amigo slashed and spun, finally turning on Jeanette.

"Call them off!" Amigo yelled, lunging.

Then Elizabeth was there, swinging the hammer, hitting Amigo in the back of the head. Surprisingly, he did not go down. Instead, his arms went limp, and he staggered in a circle, as if looking for who had hit him. Velociraptors struck over and over, slicing him, finally bringing him down.

"Hide!" Jeanette yelled.

This time the velociraptors hesitated, looking at Jeanette and then at the prostrate men.

"Hide," Jeanette repeated.

Reluctantly, the velociraptors ran to hiding places.

"Help me drag them outside," Jeanette said, taking the gun and knife.

"What? Why?" Elizabeth Hawthorne said, frozen, looking for the velociraptors.

"They won't hurt you," Jeanette said.

Moving slowly at first, Elizabeth gained courage, coming to help Jeanette. With each woman taking an arm, they dragged the unconscious men outside. Both men were bleeding badly.

"Where did those velociraptors come from? How can you control them?" Elizabeth asked.

"Later. I've got to feed them."

Jeanette ran to the kitchen, coming back with two bowls of chopped fish. She took the bowls into the barn and then called the chicks, who ate greedily.

"I don't want them to think of people as food," Jeanette explained, checking the unconscious men.

"Good thinking," Elizabeth said, keeping well away from the feeding predators.

Working on the men, Elizabeth used one man's belt as a tourniquet, stemming the blood loss from the badly gashed leg of the bat-swinging thug.

"It's cut to the bone," Elizabeth said. "This one could bleed to death."

"Yeah. That would be too bad, wouldn't it?" Jeanette said.

Elizabeth looked at Jeanette with concerned green eyes, Jeanette regretting the black humor.

"No one can know about the velociraptors," Jeanette said.

"Why?" Elizabeth asked. "How do we explain this?"

"I cut them with this," Jeanette said, holding up Amigo's knife.

"Jeanette," Elizabeth said doubtfully.

"We'll call an ambulance to take them to a hospital," Jeanette said. "I know a cop we can call. He's a friend."

Sally came limping up, whimpering. She flinched when Jeanette touched her, checking for injuries.

"She's not bleeding," Jeanette said, "at least on the outside. Good dog, Sally. Good dog."

"Call for help," Elizabeth said.

"Give me a chance to get the chicks home," Jeanette said. "We can take them to where Carson and Dr. Paulson disappeared. That's where they came from in the first place. When Carson found the velociraptors, they were protecting a nest. He brought the eggs here before he turned the carcasses in. Maybe if we take them back where he found them, they can go home. If we don't, they'll be killed for what they did here."

Jeanette studied Elizabeth's face. Clearly conflicted, Jeanette tried pushing her over the edge. "They saved your life," Jeanette said. "Help me save theirs."

"They'll turn on you," Elizabeth said. "Their instincts will take over, and they'll kill you."

Jeanette stroked Sally's head, soothing the hurting dog. "Give me the chance to get them home," Jeanette said. "That's all I ask."

"They'll never believe you did this," Elizabeth said, falling in line.

"As long as they're men, they'll believe me," Jeanette said.

Jeanette called Les first, giving him a head start, and then the ambulance. Then Jeanette called the chicks from the barn, and she and Sally herded them into the back of Elizabeth's SUV. They parked the SUV behind the house.

Les made it to the ranch first, lights flashing and siren blaring, his white patrol car bouncing recklessly down the unpaved road. Les pulled to a stop a few yards from where the men lay. Jeanette had never seen Les in his patrol uniform, and he looked impressive. The uniform included a black shirt with a patch on his shoulder, his gold badge on his left chest, his name tag over that, and gray pants. A wide black belt held his radio, cuffs, Mace, and gun.

"Are you all right?" Les asked, pulling his weapon and holding it on the prostrate men.

"They're unconscious," Jeanette said. "I cut them pretty bad." Jeanette held up the hunting knife from Amigo's belt.

Les looked from the knife to the two bleeding men. "You're kidding?" Les said, looking at Jeanette in a whole new way.

"They were high," Jeanette said. "And Sally helped."

"Me too," Elizabeth injected, holding up a kitchen knife.

"Wow," Les said, struggling for words. "They picked on the wrong damn chicks," he said, trying to be funny.

Jeanette and Elizabeth exchanged looks, and then smiled at Les, accepting the praise. Les cuffed Amigo and then used a cable tie to secure the bat man. Les took both wallets.

"Yeah, this is them," Les said, wiping blood from both faces and comparing driver's license photos. "The big guy is Rodney Dalton. That pile of hamburger is Sean McCord."

The ambulance arrived with two more patrol cars. The sheriff followed shortly, taking charge. Strapped to gurneys, Dalton and McCord were whisked away, bags of fluid feeding into their arms. Jeanette and Elizabeth spent hours repeating the story over and over, careful to stay together so they kept their stories straight. Like Les, the sheriff and his deputies were astonished by the number of cuts on Dalton and McCord, but all the questions were designed to make the case against the meth dealers. The only awkward moment was when the sheriff squatted inside the barn, looking at footprints.

"You have chickens?" the sheriff asked.

"Yes," Jeanette said. "They scattered all over."

The sheriff looked at the footprints, measuring the size with his fingers.

"A couple of turkeys too," Jeanette added.

Satisfied, the sheriff stood, looked at the gun, hammer, and bloody screwdriver now secured in ziplock bags, and announced they were done. Les lingered, and it was after midnight when Jeanette finally convinced him not to spend the night. A hug and a kiss on the cheek finally satisfied him, and the deputy left reluctantly, making Jeanette promise to call him in the morning.

Jeanette brought the chicks back to the barn, feeding them, petting and praising each one individually. Elizabeth stood to one side with Sally, watching Jeanette with her chicks. Elizabeth was wary, like she feared they would turn on her at any moment.

"We have to go before Dalton and McCord wake up," Jeanette said. "The sheriff will be back when he hears their story. The Mills Ranch isn't far from here. We can be there in an hour."

They agreed to sleep until near dawn, timing their arrival at the Mills Ranch for sunup. Before they slept, Elizabeth followed Jeanette around while she gathered supplies, including two rifles, the revolver from the office file box, ammunition, water, granola bars, fruit snacks, flashlights, spare batteries, and walkie-talkies. Jeanette stuffed the supplies in two packs. Most of the space in the packs was reserved for ziplock bags filled with either Alpo or Purina Dog Chow.

"We're just going to take a look," Elizabeth said, looking at the packs full of supplies.

"I bet those were Carson's last words," Jeanette said.

Elizabeth slept on the couch until Jeanette woke her. While sleep-drunk, Elizabeth made coffee, and Jeanette and Sally woke the chicks and loaded them in the back of the SUV. Elizabeth drove, she and Jeanette sipping coffee out of insulated mugs with Dinosaur Wrangler logos. Everything Jeanette brought had Dinosaur Wrangler logos—the two packs had patches, Jeanette's shirt was embroidered with the logo, and her shorts had the logo on the back right pocket. Sally slept in the back with the chicks, the juvenile velociraptors snuggled against the golden retriever. Amazingly quiet, the chicks took turns looking out the windows, or over the seats at Jeanette and Elizabeth. Elizabeth flinched each time a velociraptor snout appeared by her shoulder.

"They won't hurt you," Jeanette reassured Elizabeth.

"They hurt Dalton and McCord," Elizabeth said.

"Only because they were going to hurt me," Jeanette said. "They don't like people who don't like me."

"We're friends, right?" Elizabeth asked, smiling.

Jeanette laughed.

They pulled off the road just past the entrance to the Mills Ranch. A Hummer parked in a field was the only obvious military presence. Nothing had happened at the site since Dr. Paulson and Carson disappeared, so there was nothing to guard. They unloaded Sally and the chicks, the velociraptors taking their cues from Jeanette, moving stealthily.

"Carson found the velociraptors in an old barn," Jeanette said as they climbed a fence and then crept through a pasture.

The sun was coming up, giving just enough light to see. Two tents were pitched in a corral. Jeanette could see a soldier sitting in the driver's seat of the Hummer, white earbuds in his ears. Jeanette led the way, Elizabeth, Sally and the chicks following in a line. After climbing through a wooden fence, they stayed away from the modern house at one end of the property, keeping close to a small boarded-up house at the far end. Behind the old house they found a barn that was partially collapsed. Interior lights made cracks in the barn walls glow.

"In there," Elizabeth whispered.

They followed cables through an opening in the wall and inside. Lights hung from wires, although the only lights turned on were work lights aimed at the collapsed wall. Devices hung from the ceiling and sat around the opening. Poles were buried in the ground with wires running down hollow centers. The chicks sniffed the equipment and then spread out, sniffing everything else in the barn. Sally limped to the center of the barn and then lay down so she could watch every creature, in every corner of the barn.

"It's like they know they're home," Jeanette whispered, watching the chicks poke around.

"Look at the way the lights are pointed," Elizabeth said.

The work lights stood on stands, and all were pointed at the same spot. Mounted on a tripod between the lights was a video camera. Jeanette squatted, looking into the mess at that end of the barn.

"I don't see anything," Jeanette said.

"How can it be so dark with all of these lights?" Elizabeth asked.

"Do?" Jeanette called in her deepest voice.

Do came trotting from under the stairs. Jeanette looked at the crusted wound in his side. It looked superficial and did not seem to bother Do.

"What's in there?" Jeanette asked, leaning forward, pointing and staring.

Do followed the point, bent low, and hissed softly. Then he trotted forward, disappearing into the dark. Jeanette waited. Do did not return.

"Do?" Jeanette called after a few minutes.

They waited ten more minutes, but Do did not return. Re and La came and squatted next to Jeanette and Elizabeth, staring into the dark space. Elizabeth inched away from La.

"That may be the place," Elizabeth said after a while. "Would . . . Do come back if he could?"

"I think so," Jeanette said. "We're his family."

"Then it may be a one-way trip," Elizabeth said. "If we go in, we can't come back."

Then Do trotted out of the hole, *awk*ed at Jeanette, and bobbed his head.

"Well?" Elizabeth said. "What does that mean?"

"It means it is time for the chicks to go home," Jeanette said.

"Time to find Nick," Elizabeth said, taking out her cell phone. After punching in numbers, she waited and then said, "John, it's Elizabeth. I'm going to look for Nick." Elizabeth put her phone in her pack, put the pack on, and said, "Let's go bail our men out of whatever jam they've gotten themselves into."

"Do, Re, Me, Fa, So, La, Ti," Jeanette sang. "Sally."

Do led the way into the opening. Jeanette came next, and then Elizabeth, the chicks crowded around, pushing up against the women. Sally came last, whimpering into the unknown.

24

Quasi-Time

The Egyptians understood that orgonic energy negates the laws of entropy; therefore, they built tombs in the shape of orgone collectors, and used that energy to preserve the bodies of their pharaohs. The Egyptians saw the ability of orgonic energy to inhibit decay as proof that orgone is a living energy.

—Nick Paulson, Ph.D., "Executive Summary: Form and Energy Relationships" (Classified Top Secret: NOFORN, Not Releasable to Foreign Nationals)

Present Time
Washington, D.C.

John met regularly with Nick's staff and continued to search Nick's records, looking for anything useful. The Office of Strategic Science was decentralized, using a network of scientists connected through the PresNet, a proprietary ultra-high-quality Internet. Primarily a data-gathering and -sifting organization, the staff in the OSS were mostly young Ph.D.'s or graduate interns who spent their days collating information, searching for patterns and anomalies, and then feeding summaries to Nick—now John. Too monotonous for the best minds in the country, Nick kept cutting-edge scientists involved through the PresNet, special grants, and access to bleeding-edge technology. More intriguing to the science and technology movers and shakers, and what really kept them working for the OSS, was being the first to know about anomalies like the moon tyrannosaur. Two decades of scientific surprises had made membership in PresNet prestigious and competitive.

John sent a PresNet alert out on the network shortly after Nick disappeared. Dozens of messages came back, asking for more information and suggesting tests to be done. John complied with all requests, sending staff to the Mills Ranch to take radiation readings, including gamma ray spectral readings, to search with ground-penetrating radar, and to gather soil samples from the Mills Ranch based on a grid pattern designed by physicists in Louisiana. Others requested access to Landsat photos from the U.S. Geological Survey, bringing in cameras that could record images outside the human range, including infrared and ultraviolet, and getting access to navy data on LFA (Low-Frequency Active Sonar) in use at the time of Nick's disappearance. None of the tests or observations had generated helpful information.

There were so many questions about physical details of the site, most asking if the collapsed portion of the barn formed a pyramid, that John posted photographs of the barn and ranch from every conceivable angle and then had an intern create three-dimensional models of the barn that could be accessed online. When a sharp-eyed scientist noticed that one of the photos of the ranch house included Fanny Mills in a bikini on her deck, requests poured in for more photos of Fanny.

At the site, John installed a dozen different kinds of instruments to measure everything requested, including electrical resistance of the soil, gamma radiation, humidity, infrared radiation, and geological tremors. Instrument data was periodically downloaded to a database and accessible by anyone on the PresNet. Finally, John set up a high-definition camera that could be remotely operated by PresNet members for real-time inspection.

Increasingly frustrated by the lack of progress, John sifted through the PresNet traffic, looking for anything helpful. The e-mail had a dozen threads, some of it seemingly unrelated, the scientists bogged down in minutiae. One thread concerned the lack of sodium-24 and manganese-56 radioisotopes in the soil samples, another discussed the proportions of sodium and manganese atoms present in the soil around the Mills barn. There was an exchange of mathematical mod-

els too, which were impenetrable to John. If any of these could help to find Nick, John could not see how.

One thread dealt with the moon tyrannosaur, and most of it was mathematical modeling. John had traveled through a time tunnel from a Yucatán pyramid to the moon and back, so he knew it was possible that there was a connection between the moon tyrannosaur and what had happened to Nick, but what the connection was, he could not see. Eight years ago, ecoterrorists had used the orgonic energy collected by pyramids to manipulate time waves, and create tunnels through time and space. However, the orgonic-energy-collecting pyramids had been destroyed. Besides, the tunnels the pyramids had created had been two-way. Through the mazes in the pyramids, you could travel to and from sites distant in both geography and chronometry, although the passages were complex. If Nick had crawled into a time tunnel on the Mills ranch, the tunnel was unlike what was created by the pyramids. This tunnel was either selective in who or what could travel through it, or it was a variable phenomenon, coming and going. Also, Nick and the people with him had not returned, suggesting that they either could not return, or that they were dead or injured. The dinosaurs that appeared in Orlando were able to return to wherever they had come from, and to take a policewoman and a horse with them, suggesting that it might be a different phenomenon than the one on the Mills Ranch. Since then, no one else had managed to pass through the storeroom in the Orlando theater. After three months and no problems, John had allowed the theater to repair and rebuild.

John skipped the equations, and did not bother downloading models he could never understand. Scanning the commentaries that came with the models, John picked up repeated references to "quasi-time," which he took to refer to the conditions that held the moon dinosaur. Since the dinosaur did not age, exhaust, or suffer from the moon vacuum, it could not exist in time, as we know it. Since it moved and seemed to have some perception of its surroundings, including the astronauts who found it, it experienced some form of time. The fact that it was impervious to the vacuum conditions on the

moon meant it was likely that it was not actually on the moon, but instead somewhere on Earth, in some time period other than the present. All modern tyrannosaurs were accounted for, thus ruling out a present-day source. Therefore, the scientists in that track referred to the "time state" of the moon tyrannosaur as "quasi-time," speculating it would help explain VSL (variable speed of light). Until reading this post, John did not know that the speed of light varied, having learned in school that it was a constant. Remembering his experience after crawling into the opening on the Mills Ranch made John think the quasi-time idea had merit. There was something different about the time flow in that opening.

The physicists speculating about quasi-time were condensed-matter physicists, a booming branch of physics ever since the transient dense matter created by nuclear explosions was found to create the time waves that coalesced with devastating effects. John found promise in this line of thinking, since he found it easy to connect Nick's disappearance, and his experiences traveling through time and space, to what the astronauts found on the moon. Most puzzling was the sudden appearance of these new time junctions. The transient dense matter created by testing fusion bombs caused the original time quilting, and the ecoterrorists used orgonic energy to redirect the time waves. But what was powering this new phenomenon?

After logging on to a discussion site on the PresNet, John sent out a request.

> FROM: JOHN ROBERTS, OSS. WHAT IS THE POWER SOURCE FOR THE CURRENT TIME JUNCTIONS? WE KNOW OF NO ORGONIC ENERGY SOURCES AND NO CONTEMPORARY NUCLEAR TESTING.

A minute later, the responses started coming in.

> FROM: MAE TANG, U OF MINN. POWER SOURCE NEED NOT BE IN THE PRESENT.

FROM: LEE PINTER, U OF BC. ORGONIC ENERGY IS INSUFFICIENT TO SUPPORT TIME JUNCTIONS. WITH THE LAST EVENT THE ORGONIC ENERGY INFLUENCED BLACK RIPPLES FROM FUSION EXPLOSIONS, IT DID NOT CREATE THE TIME DISRUPTIONS.

FROM: KARL KRUEGER, BATTELLE LABS. ORIGINAL TIME QUILT ACCOUNTS FOR ONLY 86% OF ENERGY RELEASED BY FISSION EXPLOSIONS. THE REMAINING ENERGY MAY ACCOUNT FOR THE CURRENT TIME JUNCTIONS.

FROM: J. MARTIN KAHN, TCU. INSUFFICIENT ^{24}NA AND ^{56}MN CONFIRM NO SIGNIFICANT NEUTRON-INDUCED ACTIVITY.

FROM: LINCOLN PENN, U OF MISS. KARL, CHECK YOUR CALCULATIONS. I FIND SUFFICIENT ENERGY FOR STABLE TIME JUNCTIONS. TRANSIENT JUNCTIONS MAY BE POSSIBLE.

John jumped in.

FROM: JOHN ROBERTS, OSS. IS THERE SUFFICIENT RESIDUAL ENERGY FROM FISSION TESTING TO SUPPORT ONE-WAY JUNCTIONS?

FROM: LINCOLN PENN, U OF MISS. NO. WHILE THE RESIDUAL ENERGY WOULD PROVIDE FOR A BASE TIME MATRIX, IT IS INSUFFICIENT TO OPEN JUNCTIONS REGARDLESS. DIRECTIONALITY IS NOT INFLUENCED BY THE AVAILABLE POWER.

HOW MUCH ADDITIONAL ENERGY IS NEEDED FOR STABLE, BIDIRECTIONAL TIME MATRICES?

John asked.

There was a long pause now, and John imagined scientists sitting in offices and labs scribbling on pads, typing into computers, and pounding on calculators, estimating the energy needs.

FROM: KARL KRUEGER, BATTELLE LABS. DR. ROBERTS, YOUR QUESTION GOES RIGHT TO THE HEART OF THE FUNDAMENTAL PROBLEM IN MODELING THE ORIGINAL TIME QUILTING AND SUBSEQUENT EVENTS. IN ORDER FOR MODELS TO SUFFICIENTLY PREDICT DENSE MATTER TIME WAVES, ASTEROID IMPACTS ON EARTH MUST BE INCLUDED IN THE MODELS. A SINGLE ASTEROID IMPACT ALONE CAN BE ONE THOUSAND TIMES THE EXPLOSIVE POWER OF ALL NUCLEAR WEAPONS ON EARTH, OR MORE. TO SPECIFICALLY ANSWER YOUR QUESTION, IT TAKES A MINIMUM OF 10.4 MEGATONS TO CONDENSE MATTER TO THE POINT OF CREATING A TIME WAVE. HOWEVER, SUCH A WAVE WOULD BE INSUFFICIENT TO ALLOW EVEN A MOSQUITO TO PASS THROUGH TIME. THE HARMONIC CONVERGENCE OF MORE THAN NEARLY 100 FUSION EXPLOSIONS COMBINED WITH TIME WAVES PRODUCED BY NATURAL AND EXTRATERRESTRIAL SOURCES, COMBINED TO ACCOUNT FOR THE ORIGINAL TIME QUILT. THE ORGONIC COLLECTING MATERIAL LINING THE ALASKAN PYRAMID, AND THE FORM OF THE ALASKAN PYRAMID (AND THE YUCATÁN PYRAMID?) FUNCTIONED TO STABILIZE AND HOLD OPEN TIME JUNCTIONS PRODUCED BY THE TIME RIPPLES. (OTHERS WILL DISPUTE THIS, BUT THIS IS WHAT I BELIEVE.) HOWEVER, WITH THE DESTRUCTION OF THE PYRAMIDS, AND DR. PAULSON'S REFUSAL TO RELEASE DATA ON THE ORGONIC COLLECTING MATERIAL, WE ARE LIMITED TO SPECULATION. PLEASE RELEASE SAMPLES OF THE ORGONIC MATERIAL.

FROM: LINCOLN PENN, U OF MISS. I CONCUR. RELEASE DATA AND SAMPLES OF ORGONIC MATERIAL.

Other scientists wrote in also demanding the material. Until that moment, John had had no idea that Nick embargoed the samples collected in the Yucatán and those on the moon. Turning to Nick's computer, John searched files, finding the records of the mission to the moon. In the file he found more video, and a database detailing the quantities of material collected, including the size, shape, and mass of each piece, and then current location. All the samples were in Florida, stored at NASA at a facility called the University of Florida Physics Extension. Digging deeper, John discovered that the Physics Extension was in Lake County, Florida, near Hillsdale, where the Mills had their ranch.

"Sonofabitch," John muttered.

Then remembering the material in the lead box on Nick's desk, John shoved papers aside to find it, and looked through the glass at the unassuming black material. Elizabeth had handled the material, but it had no physical effect that she reported. John pulled out his phone to call Elizabeth and then spotted the small symbol telling him he had a voice message. The call log told him it was from Elizabeth. John called his voice mail.

"John, it's Elizabeth. I'm going to look for Nick."

"No, you didn't," John said, his hands already on the keyboard.

John accessed the hard drive with the video recordings from the Mills Ranch. Checking the time that the message came in, John ran the recording to when Elizabeth called and clicked on Play. Immediately, John saw Elizabeth's back. She was there with another person. Even from behind, John could tell it was a young woman. Then the two of them crawled forward with a dog and other animals. John reran the image, looking at the animals. They were velociraptors.

"What the hell is going on?" John said, watching Elizabeth rub shoulders with the vicious killers and then disappear.

25

Strangers in a Strange Land

A varying speed of light contradicts Einstein's theory of relativity, and would undermine much of traditional physics. But some physicists believe it would elegantly explain puzzling cosmological phenomena. . . .

—Eugenie Samuel Reich

Sixty-five Million Years Ago
Unknown Place

Elizabeth, Jeanette, Sally, and the velociraptors tumbled down a rocky slope, finding themselves in an alien landscape. As in Florida, there were palm trees, ferns, and low-lying shrubs, but the landscape was more arid, the palm trees not really palm trees, the shrubs like nothing they had seen. It certainly was not the farmland around the Mills Ranch. Gone were the barn, the ranch house, and the old boarded-up house and every other sign of civilization. Years before, Elizabeth had traveled through a pyramid and emerged on the moon in a similar way, so she had expected the unexpected when she crawled into the hole. But this was a new experience for Jeanette, and she was bewildered.

"Is this what happened to Carson?" Jeanette asked, looking around wide-eyed. "Did he come here?"

"Probably," Elizabeth said. "Let's look for signs."

Studying the ground, the women circled out from their landing point. Following their cue, Sally sniffed along behind Jeanette, the chicks spreading out, equidistant from one another, forming a perimeter.

"Here," Jeanette said.

Elizabeth found her pointing at what could be a footprint.

"This has to be them," Jeanette declared.

"I suppose so," Elizabeth said, knowing something of the contortions time and space had been put through since the original Time Quilt.

Looking at the footprint from all angles, they decided on the direction it was going and started the same way. The chicks skipped about happily, sniffing, making their weird *awk*ing noises, turning their heads with quick jerks at every real and imagined movement and sound. Dense foliage made following the trail difficult, since the trail was not a path, only torn leaves, broken branches, and faint impressions in the soil. They stopped frequently, circling, making sure they were going the right direction. Elizabeth led with Jeanette right behind. Sally limped along at Jeanette's heels, and the chicks fell into a line behind Sally. The chicks stayed close, and when the vegetation was particularly dense, the chicks tightened up, nose to tail.

Finding occasional footprints, mashed leaves, and broken leaf stems, they moved parallel to the hill they had tumbled down.

"Where do you think they were going?" Jeanette asked.

"No idea," Elizabeth said. "Knowing Nick, he was probably chasing some prehistoric butterfly. What about Carson?"

"If he stayed here voluntarily, a lot of money changed hands."

They paused for water, both sweating through their long-sleeved shirts. Jeanette wore shorts, but Elizabeth had long pants with zip-off legs. While it was hot, Elizabeth found she had a lot of energy, her breathing shallow and under control. When they stopped to drink and check Sally and Do, Elizabeth zipped off the legs of her pants and stowed them in her pack.

"Nice legs," Jeanette said, watching Elizabeth pull off the bottom half of her pants' legs.

"Used to be," Elizabeth said. "A bit too much cellulite now."

"No, they're still nice," Jeanette said seriously.

Elizabeth smiled, enjoying the compliment.

"I hope my legs look that good when I'm your age," Jeanette said.

"Let's go," Elizabeth said, losing the good feeling.

Each woman carried a rifle, the pistol in Jeanette's pack. At first Elizabeth carried the weapon at the ready, but soon put it across her shoulders, hooking her wrists on the weapon to rest her arms. Jeanette carried the rifle over her shoulder by the strap, frequently shifting it from side to side.

After a long hike, they drank more and Jeanette pulled the tail of her shirt out of her pants, unbuttoned the bottom, and then hiked her shirt up and tied it just below her bust. Just as hot, Elizabeth wanted to do the same but hesitated. Jeanette was a beautiful young woman with no body fat. Her belly was flat, her waist tiny, and her breasts large. Elizabeth felt like she was hiking with Jungle Barbie. Reluctantly, Elizabeth did the same to her shirt, and now they were walking with bare midriffs.

"This isn't good," Jeanette said after a time, squatting.

Elizabeth knelt next to her and instantly eight curious animals surrounded them. Do leaned against Elizabeth as he sniffed the ground in front of Jeanette. Elizabeth gave an involuntary shudder, Do briefly looking at her, then going back to his sniffing. While the velociraptors had trampled much of the footprints, Elizabeth could see the large three-toed track of a large predator.

"*T. rex*?" Jeanette asked.

"Maybe," Elizabeth said. "Or something just as nasty."

"Poor Carson," Jeanette said.

"There's no blood," Elizabeth pointed out.

Looking hopeful, Jeanette stood, searching around, and then began following the trail again. Elizabeth and Sally fell in behind, but the velociraptors stayed, sniffing the predator tracks. Then Jeanette sang, "Do, Re, Me, Fa, So, La, Ti," and the velociraptors came running, lining up and following like ducklings do the mama duck.

The trail was easy to follow now, since it was made by a dinosaur ten times the size of a human. They watched for branches where the humans had split off, but they found none for a long distance, and then the trail became confused. They circled, the chicks immediately sniffing the tracks of the predator, suddenly getting excited and *awk*-ing loudly. Jeanette and Elizabeth found the chicks huddled in a circle around a few drops of dried blood.

"Oh no," Jeanette said.

"Keep looking," Elizabeth said. "That doesn't tell the whole story."

They found a diverging trail that was too small for the dinosaur and had renewed hope. They followed this trail now, thankful for every step where they did not find more blood. As they walked, they realized the trail changed at some point. Now there were cut branches lining the trail where before branches had been only broken or bent. Hesitating, they discussed whether they were following the right trail. Deciding to follow the trail until there was evidence they were on the wrong track, they moved on. It was wider now with a lot of cut branches, and they moved faster, eating as they walked, sipping from their bottles without slowing down. Eventually they came to a clearing, where they paused. The trail led into a valley devoid of trees. Leaving the protection of the trees unnerved them, and they stood, resting, thinking.

"I say we go," Jeanette said after a time.

Elizabeth liked Jeanette, although they were very different. Jeanette exploited her body and looks, while Elizabeth tried to professionalize hers, refusing to be sexualized. Elizabeth could not know what forces had led Jeanette down her path, but she was an intelligent, courageous woman, and Elizabeth was beginning to think of her as a friend.

"We didn't come this far to give up now," Elizabeth said.

They plunged into the meadow, with the chicks trailing, heads down, nearly touching the tail of the chick ahead of them. The trail led directly toward a mound in the middle of the valley, Elizabeth thinking that they should climb it and look around. Then Elizabeth nearly crashed into Jeanette, who had stopped suddenly.

"I think we came to the wrong place," Jeanette said softly.

Elizabeth stepped up beside her. Coming across the meadow were six figures, but they were not human. Wearing loincloths and leggings, the six carried spears and packs that were secured with leather straps that crisscrossed their chests. They were hairless, with copper-colored skin. The nose and chin merged together into a single facial feature. The eyes were huge, at least double the size of a human's. Their feet were wrapped in leather strips, each of three toes wrapped separately, large toe claws exposed. The hands were three-fingered, with short, curled claws.

The figures came on aggressively, shoulder to shoulder. Jeanette and Elizabeth readied their weapons, Elizabeth working a shell into the chamber, Jeanette cocking the semiautomatic rifle. Now the figures slowed, as if they had seen rifles before. Still they came on.

"Do, Re, Me, Fa, So, La, Ti," Jeanette sang.

The velociraptors came from behind the women, fanning out, heads held high, studying the approaching creatures. Noses in the air, the velociraptors sniffed, then *awk*ed loudly and dropped into attack positions. The figures stopped, bringing their spears down, holding them with two hands and hunching. The creatures exchanged sounds that resembled Chinese, with a wide range of pitch. The exchange was animated, maybe even heated. The conversation ended, and one of the creatures on the left end separated, taking a curved path as if to flank the women.

"Do! Me!" Jeanette said sharply, the two velociraptors separating, stalking the creature.

The creature stopped, and moved slowly back to its companions. The velociraptors tracked him every step of the way, bodies low, eyes fixed on their target.

"Good Do!" Jeanette said. "Good Me."

The creatures exchanged more unintelligible speech, and then slowly backed up, eyes on the velociraptors. Sally barked for good measure, although her tail was wagging.

"Good chicks," Jeanette said.

"Good chicks," Elizabeth echoed. "Very good chicks."

26

Preacher Man

Civilization is social order promoting cultural creation. Four elements constitute it: economic provision, political organization, moral traditions and the pursuit of knowledge and the arts. It begins where chaos and insecurity end. For when fear is overcome, curiosity and constructiveness are free, and man passes by natural impulse towards the understanding and embellishment of life.

—Will Durant

Sixty-five Million Years Ago
Unknown Place

The signs of ruined civilization were everywhere now. Crushed rusted cars poking from green clumps, the broken stump of a light pole, chunks of concrete and asphalt, broken glass, and neatly spaced mounds of rubble that had once been city blocks. Mother Nature had won this round, what had been a thriving city now unrecognizable.

"The church isn't too far," Jacob said. "Reverend's father was the pastor. The way Reverend tells the story, he was a teenager when God punished the world. When the reverend and a couple of his friends found out that Portland was taken away, they went looking for it because that's where their homes were. They didn't know the land was full of dinosaurs when they started, and they almost got themselves eaten. But they persisted and finally Reverend found Portland. He said right after God's punishment of the world, Portland was like a shimmering mirage. Reverend said that the city kind of came and went like it was here but then wasn't really here."

Nick thought about the moon dinosaur, trapped in some kind of inter-time. Portland might have experienced a transient version of what happened on the moon.

"Reverend left his friends to try and get to his home in Portland. Reverend says Portland was like a vision from God and he followed it. Even though the city was under God's punishment, God was calling to Reverend to go with the sinners, and preach repentance. When Reverend found his way to his vision, he could see people in the city begging for his help, but no matter what he did, he could not get inside. Then he learned the lesson God was teaching him. It was not by the reverend's power that he would get into the city, it was only through God that he could enter. Once Reverend realized that, and prayed to God to forgive him for his self-centeredness, there was a bright flash and he was in Portland."

Nick knew the "flash" was likely the detonation of dozens of nuclear warheads ordered by President McIntyre. Acting with incomplete understanding, President McIntyre rashly ordered a nuclear strike on the Portland Time Quilt, believing it would reverse the quilting and bring back the missing cities, including a portion of Atlanta, where the First Lady had disappeared. Instead, the nuclear detonations froze the displaced time segments in place. The First Lady and millions of people around the world were never recovered. What Nick did not know until now was that Portland had survived that blast. There had been no fusion explosions in modern Oregon where Portland had been, and Portland made it into the past untouched, so the detonations either took place in another time line, or in inter-time, or quasi-time as some of the scientists on the PresNet called it.

"The reverend found his father, but his father was killed a short time later in a food riot. The church was running a feeding program, and a mob ransacked it. It got real bad for a while. It seems people get uncivilized real fast when times get tough. I was single back then and tried to get to my mom and dad, but they lived in Salem and there wasn't any Salem any longer, just a dinosaur-infested forest. They turned the Rose Garden—Portland's basketball arena—into a public shelter, and I lived there for a while but there were too many people and not enough food. I finally holed up with some friends in a basement on the north end of the city. I did some things to survive I'm not too proud of, but I never killed anyone. Things got bad, really bad."

Nick let Jacob collect his thoughts. Everyone was walking close to Jacob, listening. Even Torino seemed interested, keeping close. Only Crazy Kramer was in a world of his own, walking out front, mumbling, slashing randomly with his machete.

"When we first jumped here, a lot of the buildings collapsed and many of the ones still standing just weren't safe to live in. Electricity and water were gone. No phones, light, television, cell phones, or Internet. There was no way to find out what had happened to the rest of the world. Only Reverend claimed to know the truth, and as he told it, Portland was selected for God's punishment.

"There was mass hysteria and a lot of suicides. It was so bad for a while that you couldn't walk close to a tall building because someone might land on you. Eventually people banded together in groups to help each other survive. That helped some, but then groups started fighting other groups. I once saw a fight over canned food found in a basement. Fifty men and women went at it with bats, pipes and knives. It was the most horrible thing I'd seen. I've seen worse since. One side finally won, and they chased down the losers and beat them to death. That wasn't the only time that happened, either."

Jacob stopped, looking around, trying to make sense out of the fern-covered rubble.

"Crazy, that way!" he shouted, pointing.

Crazy Kramer had ranged ahead, and now came back a hundred yards, leading between a thick stand of modern-looking firs and a giant pile of bricks with a cycad growing out of the middle.

"There were five of us living together then in the basement of an old house. We kept the location secret and went out only at night, foraging through the houses in the neighborhood, looking for food.

Even five years after it happened, you could still find canned and dried food if you looked hard enough. After eight years, if you could find it, it wasn't any good.

"We were eating dogs, cats, rabbits, and rats when I first heard the reverend walking through the streets preaching. He told us that what happened was God's punishment. It was the Tower of Babel all over again. My friends and I pretty much ignored him until the big fire burned us out. We waded into the river and survived by floating in the shallows. The heat was so bad, I had to keep dunking my head to keep from frying my brains. Even then I still got first-degree burns on my face. The fire jumped the river and pretty much destroyed anything you could live in except the reverend's father's church. That was another sign to the reverend. By then, the only place you could get food was from one of the big organized groups, and one religious nut or another ran all of them."

Jacob paused, looking at the newcomers.

"I'm not offending anyone, am I?" Jacob asked, clearly worried.

"We're not offended," Nick assured him.

Relieved, Jacob continued his history. "The world was so topsy-turvy that it made even the craziest religion seem rational. Since I had heard the reverend preaching from our basement, I picked the devil I knew and joined up. I met my wife there, and the reverend let us marry. If it wasn't for Leah and the girls, I'd find another basement and go it alone."

"Take cover," Crazy Kramer said in what passed for a hushed tone.

Everyone hid, Conyers leading Torino behind a lush mound, helping Gah off the horse. Nick peeked out to see two figures hurrying toward them, down the same path they had been walking. The man and a woman moved confidently but quickly.

"Betty! Lincoln!" Jacob called, stepping out and waving at them.

Startled, the two stopped, stared, and then ran to Jacob, taking turns hugging him.

Talking all at once, they greeted one another, praised God for their deliverance, and then started hugging and praising all over again when Crazy Kramer wandered up. The happy reunion ended abruptly when Nick and the others stepped out of hiding and Lincoln and Betty saw strangers for the first time in eight years.

"Betty and Lincoln Brown, meet Dr. Nick Paulson," Jacob said.

"Oh, praise God," Betty said, coming straight for Nick, arms wide. Then Conyers led Torino out of hiding, and Betty changed directions, forgetting about Nick's hug, and walked straight to the horse, wrapping her arms around Torino's neck.

"It's a roan," Betty said. "A Thoroughbred?"

"Yes. He had a short career on the track."

"God bless you," Betty said, still hugging Torino.

Lincoln finally pried her off Torino, and there were introductions all around. Frustrated, Carson took the lead, naming everyone in the group to speed things up.

"You're police?" Lincoln said, looking at Conyers and Wynooski, then closely at the front of Carson's shirt.

"She's the police, I'm the ranger, and he's a pretender," Wynooski said.

"I see," Lincoln said, not really understanding.

"We need to keep moving," Carson said.

"We're almost there," Lincoln said. "It's not far now."

"Have you seen any others?" Jacob asked. "Leah and my girls?"

They had not, but then they explained that they had hidden for a long time under a log, Inhumans running past their hiding spot twice. Then Betty and Lincoln had Nick explain where they had come from, excited that the world they had left behind was still somewhere.

"Maybe God's banishment is coming to an end," Lincoln said.

"The reverend was right," Betty said. "He told us if we remained faithful and obedient, that God would redeem us."

Nick saw Jacob turn his head and roll his eyes.

"My sister and mother lived in Missoula," Betty said. "Are they still there?"

"Missoula was untouched," Nick assured her.

"What about Seattle?" Lincoln asked. "I have cousins there, but the rest of my family was in Portland."

"The Time Quilt triggered a tidal wave and there was some damage along the waterfront areas, but if they lived in the hills, or inland, they should be okay."

"One lived near Green Lake," Lincoln said.

"That area did fine," Nick said. "You do understand that it has been eighteen years since the Time Quilt? People move, they get sick, some of them may have died."

Nick's caution had no impact, and Betty and Lincoln peppered them with questions about other cities and other countries, and then finally asked the question Nick was waiting for.

"Can we get back the way you came?"

"Sure we can," Carson cut in. "But the horse can't. I vote we go anyway and leave Trigger here."

"We can't leave the horse," Betty said, horrified by Carson's suggestion.

"Then stay with the damn horse," Carson said, "but the rest of us are getting out."

"Don't curse, young man," Betty said. "The reverend teaches us that Jesus Christ and an unbridled tongue cannot live in fellowship."

Carson slapped his hand to his forehead, drawing it down his face, stretching his skin. "Now I know how Alice felt," Carson said. "Well, Tweedledee and Tweedledum, can we just keep moving?"

"Let's go," Nick said, trying to keep the peace. Nick fixed Carson with a stare and shook his head, silently scolding him.

"What?" Carson said, helping Gah back up on Torino.

"Asshole," Conyers whispered to Carson, making sure Gah was secure.

"What?" Carson said again. "You care what these Jim Jones Kool-Aid drinkers think?"

Not waiting for an answer, Carson double-timed it to catch up with Crazy Kramer, borrowing the machete, hacking violently for a few minutes, and then handing it back.

They picked their way through overgrown ruins, to what had once been a freeway. Large sections of cracked but unbroken concrete remained, and lane markings were still visible in some sections. A rusted steel guardrail still ran down the center; a streetlight bent in half kissed the ground. Most of the other streetlights were merely stumps, or completely gone. A short distance to their right was an overpass, the center collapsed, leaving a gaping hole. Straight ahead were hills, thick with cycads. Sprinkled in between were black trunks, the remains of what had been the original vegetation. In one place, Nick could see a section of brick wall, split by a rotting snag. On top of a nearby hill was a cell phone tower, vines covering the lower third.

"This way," Jacob said, Crazy Kramer and Carson already leading.

Turning left, they followed the road, keeping the hills to their right. Littered with debris, the flat road was nevertheless easier to negotiate than the forest, or the ruins of the city. As they came around the curve, Crazy Kramer gave a whoop.

"It's still there," Jacob said.

"Praise God," Betty and Lincoln said.

Soon Nick could see a church sitting on a hill, the only intact building he had seen. A cross stood on the steeple that was the apex of the wedge-shaped building. Stained glass panels were set high in the walls, generous amounts of clear glass ran along the near side.

"I see someone," Betty said.

Nick saw a figure waving from the corner of the building. Soon others appeared, waving, one looking through binoculars and then passing them around so that others could see.

"Hurry," Jacob said, picking up the pace and passing Carson and Crazy Kramer.

"Finally, someone's getting religion on this hurry thing," Carson said.

An old landslide blocked the road to the church in one place, the group detouring to a path cut through downed and burned firs. The last stretch up the hill was through a burned neighborhood, the houses barely recognizable through the ferns and cycads that grew from their ashes. A steel fence blocked the entrance to the church, where dozens of people peeked through gaps in the steel, excited, smiling, shouting greetings.

Only when they were almost to the gate did it swing open, four men pushing it open, letting the small group in, and then pulling it closed, locking the gate with three large steel bolts. Inside, four more men stood with rifles ready, not smiling. Nick ignored them for now, letting Jacob, Betty, Lincoln, and Crazy Kramer enjoy their homecoming. Almost immediately, the attention turned to Torino, the crowd surrounding the nervous horse and the police officer, looking at them as if they were ghosts. Gah slid off, hobbling out of the way.

"Have the police come for us?" an old woman asked, looking at Conyers and then at Wynooski. "Does that say Orlando? Like in Florida?"

"We'll explain later," Jacob said. "What about Leah? Beatrice and Bonnie?"

"They're here," two or three said at the same time.

Suddenly the people quieted and the crowd parted, a big man in a black suit, white shirt, but no tie coming through, flanked by men with rifles. Wearing aviator sunglasses, his black hair slicked down and combed straight back, he suddenly broke from a grim expression into a lopsided smile.

"Brother Jacob, Brother Kramer, Brother Lincoln, Sister Betty, you are as welcome a sight as the prodigal son."

Hugging them individually, only Jacob did not hug back.

"What do we have here?" Reverend said, looking briefly at Nick and the others, and then lingering on Conyers in her uniform, and then Wynooski in hers, before finally walking slowly to Torino.

"It's a sign, isn't it, Reverend?" Betty said, those in the crowd mumbling agreement.

"A sign? Yes, but is it from God or Satan?"

"It's from Florida," Carson blurted out.

The reverend turned on him, the lopsided smile fading. "Do you presume to know God's will?" Reverend demanded.

"I presume to know Wills's will," Carson said.

Confused, and not used to backtalk, the reverend settled into a malevolent stare, struggling to understand Carson's remark.

"His name is Carson Wills," Wynooski explained. "That was his feeble attempt at humor."

"Is there a doctor here?" Nick asked. "My friend here hurt his ankle."

"We no longer rely on the human healers," Reverend explained. "True healing comes only from God."

"How's that working out?" Carson asked. "The way I heard it, your flock gets smaller every year."

One of the reverend's bodyguards stepped forward, pointing his rifle at Carson's belly. Reverend put a hand on the bodyguard's chest, holding him back.

"Those who confess their sin are healed; those who cling to their sin reap what they have sown," Reverend said.

"Faith healing is a myth," Wynooski asserted. "Show me someone who claims to be healed by faith, and I'll show you a liar."

Even Carson understood Wynooski had gone too far, inching away as the reverend turned on her.

"I'm just stating facts," Wynooski said.

"Every person here today survived famine, epidemic, rampaging animals, and war because God is in their lives." Reverend's cheeks were red, his voice deep, his words carefully measured.

"That's not important right now," Nick said, immediately regretting his words. "What I mean is that we need to find a way to get you and your people back to the modern age. You know about the asteroid, right?"

Nick saw blank looks from everyone, including the reverend.

"The light in the sky," Nick said, seeing Jacob pointing. Looking up, Nick saw the glow of the asteroid in the blue sky. "Yes, that," Nick said.

"That is the Fire of God," Preacher explained. "It is a harbinger of change. God is pleased with us, his faithful, and his fire brings a message."

"It's not fire," Nick said carefully. "It is an asteroid called the Chicxulub impactor. The impact of that asteroid triggers the Cretaceous–Tertiary mass extinction. Seventy percent of the animal life on this planet is going to be destroyed."

"Cretaceous?" Reverend probed.

"Cretaceous period," Nick explained. "You are sixty-five million years in the past. That asteroid ends the age of the dinosaurs."

Reverend smiled, showing his amusement to his followers. "Sir," Reverend said patiently, "the Earth was created ten thousand years ago, as was the entire universe. We could not possibly be sixty-five million years in the past, since nothing existed sixty-five million years ago."

"Oh, brother," Carson mumbled, walking away, shaking his head. "We're all gonna die."

"Reverend, we need to talk," Nick said.

27

Village of the Damned

Most educated people are aware that we are the outcome of nearly 4 billion years of Darwinian selection, but many tend to think that humans are somehow the culmination. Our sun, however, is less than halfway through its lifespan. It will not be humans who watch the sun's demise, 6 billion years from now. Any creatures that then exist will be as different from us as we are from bacteria or amoebae.

—Sir Martin Rees, Astronomer Royal

Sixty-five Million Years Ago
Unknown Place

Jeanette insisted on calling them aliens, although Elizabeth thought that impossible. Too primitive to have traveled to another planet, that could only mean that she and Jeanette had traveled to their planet, but that seemed equally unlikely. Besides, Elizabeth had experienced the time–space distortions caused by dense matter before, and felt them again traveling to here. Whatever the creatures were, they were from Earth in some time period or place. More important, they were afraid of the velociraptors and kept their distance.

"Are they going to just stand there?" Jeanette asked after a while. "Maybe they'll run if I shoot one of them."

Jeanette raised the rifle to her shoulder, the aliens hunching in anticipation.

"Don't shoot," Elizabeth said, gently pushing the barrel down.

"Shooting won't scare them away. They seem to know what a gun is. If they were afraid of getting shot, they would have run by now."

"Really?" Jeanette said, and then aimed over the aliens' heads and fired.

The creatures flinched but did not move.

"Yeah, they do know what a gun is," Jeanette said. "There're only six of them. Let's shoot them so we can get going."

"Jeanette, do you really want to kill them in cold blood?" Elizabeth asked, surprised by Jeanette's callousness.

"Why not? If we really are in the past, then they've been dead for millions of years. It's kind of like shooting a corpse."

"No, it's not," Elizabeth said, not as certain as she sounded.

"There's nothing like those things back where we came from," Jeanette argued. "They have to be one of Darwin's dead ends." Jeanette was an intelligent woman, but used superior abilities in a twisted way.

"Let's leave and see what happens," Elizabeth said.

"Might as well," Jeanette said. "We can always shoot them later."

With the velociraptors orbiting Jeanette, and Sally trailing, the women angled away from the creatures. Jeanette's aliens watched, letting the women arc around them and then following, keeping a hundred yards behind. Elizabeth led now, directing Jeanette toward the hill in the meadow. The creatures kept their distance but followed. The velociraptors slowly lost interest in the aliens, although every once in a while, one would look behind, see the creatures following, and *awk* a warning at the group. Reaching the hill, Jeanette and Elizabeth climbed it, the creatures stopping at the bottom. The sun low on the horizon, Elizabeth estimated how long it would take to get from the hill to the forest.

"We should sleep here for the night," Elizabeth said.

"It's a defensible position," Jeanette said. "We can pick them off as they come up the hill."

"Were you in combat?" Elizabeth asked.

"Every day since puberty," Jeanette said, pointing at her breasts.

"I had a smaller version of your problem," Elizabeth said.

They took turns watching the creatures that remained at the bottom of the hill. When it was Elizabeth's turn, there was still enough light to see one of the creatures detach, crossing the valley and disappearing into the trees on the east side. Night fell, Jeanette feeding Sally and the velociraptors. Elizabeth and Jeanette ate as the moon rose and then settled in for the night.

In the eastern glow of the rising sun, they could see they were now surrounded. More of the creatures came during the night, circling the hill; however, none of the creatures climbed the hill in the dark. On the south side, Jeanette and Elizabeth found a large clump of the creatures, and in the still morning air, they could hear their strange language. Like a mumbled song, it was melodious, peppered with clicks, and incomprehensible. With the rising sun, the creatures' camp came to life with a fire and the smell of roasting meat. Finishing breakfast, one of the creatures separated, taking a few steps up the hill and shouting unintelligibly.

"Go to hell!" Jeanette shouted back.

The creature started up the hill.

"Do, Re, Me, Fa, So, La, Ti," Jeanette sang.

Velociraptors fanned out on either side of Jeanette and Elizabeth. While still afraid of the ruthless predators, Elizabeth nevertheless welcomed their presence, reaching down and patting one next to her—Me, she thought. Sally shoved in between Jeanette and Elizabeth, giving a hearty *woof.* Me awked his own warning.

"Good chick," Elizabeth said, still patting the velociraptor.

Me hissed. Elizabeth was pretty sure the hiss was aimed at the creature climbing the hill, but took her hand back just in case.

At the halfway point up the hill, the creature stopped, large eyes looking at the velociraptor picket line, the taut gray skin on its face registering nothing recognizable by a human. Turning, the creature called back down to the others.

"I'll shoot him," Jeanette said. "It'll discourage the others."

"No," Elizabeth said. "He may be coming to talk."

"You speak alien?" Jeanette asked.

"Maybe he speaks English," Elizabeth suggested.

Now the creature started walking around the hill, keeping his distance from the women and velociraptors.

"Fa, So," Jeanette sang out.

Two velociraptors separated from the others, staying with the creature, walking along the side of the hill. As they did, the creatures below erupted in their singsong speech, huddling together and then pointing at the women. The creature on the hill stopped, walking back to his starting point, Fa and So keeping between him and the women. Giving up, the creature retreated down the hill to the others.

"I love the velociraptors," Elizabeth said.

"I wonder why they're so afraid?" Jeanette asked.

"You saw what your velociraptors did to those two men on your farm," Elizabeth said, "and they're only half grown."

"Yeah, but that mob of aliens could easily take this hill," Jeanette said. "The chicks would slow them down, but couldn't stop them."

"Between the velociraptors and the guns, we would kill many of them," Elizabeth said. "Maybe they care as much about their lives as we do about ours."

The discussion below ended, and now the alien who had walked up the hill came forward again, held his spear high, and then dropped it. Turning sideways, he made an unmistakable motion, indicating he wanted Elizabeth and Jeanette to come down the hill.

"Hell no!" Jeanette shouted.

The creature repeated the motion.

"He doesn't understand," Elizabeth said.

"Hell no!" Jeanette repeated, louder.

The creature said something to the others below, and they separated into two groups, creating a lane and then dropped their spears and got down on their knees. The lead creature repeated the "come this way" motion.

"Don't fall for it," Jeanette said. "Men always worship us until they get what they want."

"This isn't about sex," Elizabeth said.

"If they're male, it's about sex," Jeanette asserted.

Not able to disagree, Elizabeth took another approach. "What choice do we have? We're trapped on this hill. We don't know where Carson and Nick are, and we can't follow them with those creatures blocking the trail."

"We have the guns," Jeanette said.

"I don't think they mean us any harm," Elizabeth said. "They might know where Nick and Carson are."

"Not that we can ask them," Jeanette said.

Jeanette walked the perimeter of the hill, looking for options, finally giving up.

"If one of them pinches my ass, I'll kill them all," Jeanette said.

"Agreed," Elizabeth said.

They came down slowly, the chicks forming a perimeter, heads low, tense. The creatures backed away, giving them plenty of space. Picking up his spear carefully, the lead creature put it across his shoulders, the others following suit. Staying ten yards ahead, the creature led them across the meadow, the others falling in behind, primarily interested in the velociraptors and the dog, not the women.

Reaching the edge of the forest, they found a well-worn trail, the chicks tightening up the formation, still protective of Jeanette but more tolerant of the creatures following close behind.

Elizabeth studied the creatures. They were humanlike in many ways, walking on two legs and with two arms. They wore loincloths over leggings, and most wore bundles strapped to their backs with leather straps that crisscrossed their chests. Their three-fingered hands were dexterous, and they manipulated even small items with ease. Their feet looked awkward, with three large toes like the velociraptors, and very little heel or ball. Wrapped in leather strips, the creatures protected their feet as humans did, suggesting their feet were sensitive. Their shoulders were narrower than a human's, their chests strangely bowed, as if overinflated. Strangest of all were their eyes. Large, and set in a face that sloped so that the nose and jaw seemed to merge into one snout, the eyes were green with vertical slits. The body was hairless, not even eyebrows, the eyes protected by a bone ridge.

Their tools and weapons were Stone Age but made of an odd material. Spearheads were shiny and black, resembling plastic. If it was flint, it was smoother than any handmade spear tip she had ever seen. Their knives were made of the same black substance and carried in leather sheaths. The creatures' water bags were the stomachs of an animal, leather stoppers used as corks. They wore no necklaces, bracelets, or anything that looked like a totem. Their bodies were unmarked, lacking tattoos or paint.

"They're male," Jeanette said, nudging Elizabeth.

One creature had stepped to the side, lifted his loincloth, and was urinating. The appendage was male enough, although the penis was longer and slimmer. Elizabeth could not see any testicles.

"Watch your ass," Jeanette said.

Wiping the sweat from her forehead, Elizabeth spotted a glowing object in the sky. As she stared at it, a creature stepped nearer, pointing at the bright dot with the middle finger of the three on its right hand, and said something more song than sentence.

"I don't understand," Elizabeth said.

When it stepped closer, Sally growled, and the creature jumped back, startled. Two velociraptors trotted to Sally's side, heads low, hissing at the creature. Its taut gray face registered fear, and the creature backed away, eyes on the animals.

"Good chicks," Elizabeth said. "Good dog."

As they walked, the trail became wider and well trodden, smaller paths connecting to it like tributaries feeding a river. It was well maintained, with ferns, succulents, trees, and limbs hacked back from the path, so that nothing brushed Elizabeth's arms or legs. More of the creatures appeared, coming out of hiding places, holding spears or wooden swords, staring at the human women and the orbiting velociraptors. The odds were rapidly changing.

"I don't like this," Jeanette said. "Now I'll have to reload twice before I can kill them all."

"They're just curious," Elizabeth said. "I'd stare at us if I was them too."

"The chicks are getting nervous," Jeanette said.

One of the velociraptors snapped, just missing the leg of a creature that drifted too near. Other chicks hissed, the creatures giving the women and their velociraptors more room. The chicks calmed down but stayed wary. Panting hard, and limping noticeably, Sally kept pace, wasting no energy on barking.

They came out of the forest to the narrow end of a *V*-shaped valley. Nestled up against a steep rocky hillside was a village. Huge sharpened poles surrounded the village. Looking like overgrown pick-up sticks, the poles were buried in the earth at one end, the sharpened ends pointing outward. There was plenty of space for people and small animals to pass between the poles. Seeing the size and number of poles, Elizabeth easily imagined the animals the villagers defended against.

Passing between poles, they entered the village and were immediately surrounded by creatures, male and female (four nipples but no external mammary glands), young and old. Sooty and smelling of cooking fires, the women pushed in front of the men, staring and pointing at the velociraptors, shooing children away, snatching up toddlers and taking them into huts. The toddlers were potbellied to the point of making Elizabeth wonder how they could stand without falling over. With deeply curved backs, the toddlers held their shoulders back, counterbalancing the protruding stomachs. The men were lean, the women plumper, but not fat. Like the men, the women wore loincloths and leggings. Also like the men, the women were hairless.

Huts were made of woven mats over wooden frames. Cooking fires sprinkled the village, with fewer fires than huts, suggesting shared fires and collective cooking. Strips of meat hung over a smoky fire, the strips impaled on miniature versions of the giant poles surrounding the village. A clay pot sealed with a leather cap sat in front of a hut, and bags made of leather, or intestines, hung from a pole mounted near the roofline of the hut. A *Monoclonius* stood between huts, wearing a harness, a huge travois stretched out behind. Seven feet tall at the shoulder, the armored quadruped had a bony neck collar, one long snout horn, and smaller horns over each eye. Instead of a mouth, the *Monoclonius* had a beak, now munching a mouth full of green stalks.

"Look," Jeanette said, pointing between two huts.

There a triceratops sat, rigged with a harness and saddle.

"Domesticated?" Elizabeth said, amazed.

"I don't see Carson or anyone," Jeanette said. "This is a waste of time."

Jeanette let her rifle fall from her shoulder and whispered something to the chicks, pulling them in closer, heads dropping low, hissing. Terrified alien women pulled back, men stepping forward, spears pointed at the chicks.

"Let me talk to them," Elizabeth said.

"Might as well," Jeanette said. "There's no way we can shoot our way out of here.

"Calm the velociraptors down," Elizabeth said.

"No," Jeanette said. "Talk fast."

The huts were rectangular, most the size of a two-car garage, but they walked straight through the village, past another feeding *Monoclonius,* to the largest structure, a long house, two stories tall, made of the same woven mats and wooden poles. Two carved tree stumps marked the entrance, more mats hanging between them, hiding the opening. These mats were green, not like the brown of the dried mats on other buildings. The carvings in the stumps were fresh, showing leaves and trees, but odd, stylized trees with puffy tops and impossibly thin trunks.

The group stopped, the crowd whispering and pointing at the velociraptors, Sally, and the human women, but mostly at the velociraptors.

"We mean you no harm," Elizabeth said slowly, exaggerating each syllable.

The creatures stared, interested, strange cat eyes unblinking.

"We're looking for our friends," Elizabeth said.

More unblinking stares.

"Try saying it louder," Jeanette said.

"I know it's stupid, but we have to try something," Elizabeth said.

Then one of the creatures leaned forward, looking at Elizabeth's pack. Sally growled a warning, and two raptor chicks lunged and snapped. Elizabeth twisted, trying to see what the creature was looking at.

"The patch? Are you looking at the patch?" Elizabeth said.

Carefully, the creature reached out, pointing a long, clawed finger, touching the patch.

"Easy, Sally," Elizabeth said. "Easy, chicks."

Elizabeth took off her pack, then tore the patch free from the pack, handing it to the creature, which took it gingerly, eyes on Sally and the chicks. Patch in hand, the creature retreated to the others, all of them examining the image of the *T. rex* and the cowboy lassoing it.

"What the hell do they want with our logo?" Jeanette asked.

More creatures appeared, coming through the mats hiding the entrance to the building they were standing in front of. Staring at the velociraptors, the newly arrived creatures ignored Elizabeth as she continued to talk at them. Abruptly, they spoke to one another, animated, their combined voices sounding like a dysfunctional choir. Soon the patch was the center of attention, then the velociraptor chicks, then Sally, and then the creatures pointed at Jeanette and Elizabeth. The discussion was vehement, individual creatures leaning forward to get the floor, then leaning back when their argument was finished. After a long, discordant discussion, one of the aliens stood tall, the others lowering their heads, backing away. Turning to Elizabeth, Jeanette, Sally, and the velociraptors, the creature spoke for a minute, its speech a song to human ears, and then it stopped and stepped back and sideways, bending, and motioning them inside.

"Why the hell should we?" Jeanette asked. "If the boys are in there, he can just bring them out."

"They don't understand," Elizabeth said.

"They'll understand a bullet," Jeanette said.

"Jeanette, they aren't threatening us. They are inviting us into their home."

"That's not a home," Jeanette said. "It's the biggest building in the village. For all you know, it's a prison."

"Or a palace, or a temple," Elizabeth said. "The only way to know is to step through that door."

"The chicks go with me, or I don't go in," Jeanette said.

"Absolutely," Elizabeth said. "I love the chicks."

Elizabeth and Sally went first, Jeanette and the velociraptors right behind. It took seconds for their eyes to adapt to an interior that was one big room with a dirt floor. Built against the side of the hill, the far side of the room was the wide mouth of a cave. Ten feet high and thirty feet wide, the cave entrance was an irregular oval. A few woven mats lay in front of the opening. Looking into the cave, Elizabeth expected blackness, but instead she saw weird vegetation and the dandelion trees like those carved on the posts outside the hut. The hill was backlit by a soft glow, like the rising sun.

"It's like looking through a window," Jeanette said.

"It's an opening," Elizabeth said. "Like the one that brought us here."

"But where the hell is that?" Jeanette asked. "I've never seen trees like those."

Then Do trotted forward and into the cave scene.

"No!" Jeanette shouted, quickly drowned out by the musical shrieking of the creatures.

28

Rescue Team

According to Einstein's special theory of relativity, our lives pass more slowly if we travel close to the speed of light. He has also shown that we live longer if we go and live in an intense gravitational field. Einstein has thus opened up the future and shown that it is possible to slow down time.

—John Baruch

Present Day
Lake County, Florida

John Roberts waited impatiently in the lobby of the University of Florida, Physics Extension. After showing his badge to a receptionist, an office manager, a faculty member, a division chair, and a unit supervisor, John was asked to wait. John was just about done waiting. Nick Paulson had disappeared; Elizabeth Hawthorne, was gone, as well as others; Visitors were appearing and disappearing; and the damn earth was shaking. The world did not have time for John to be standing in a waiting room.

"This way, Mr. Roberts," a young woman said.

Dressed in a lab coat, the short-haired blonde had a noticeable Southern drawl. Her name tag identified her as Dr. Webb, but she looked like a teenager. Controlling his temper, John followed her to an elevator, where she used a key to take them down three floors. When the door opened, she motioned him forward but remained in the elevator. Stepping out, John found his hand feeling along his belt for the sidearm that wasn't there. Dr. Webb smiled as the doors closed, leaving John alone.

White material lined the hallway, floor, ceiling, and walls. Shiny and smooth, it looked like plastic but felt like rock. Canister lights, recessed into the ceiling, lit the corridor intermittently. A door at the far end was open. More curious than angry now, John walked the length of the corridor, passing four side doors made of the same white material. None of the doors had handles or visible locks. The door at the end opened into a domed room, where even the bins lining the wall lacked sharp angles or edges. Everything looked like it was molded out of plastic. Workstations filled the center of the room, each piece of equipment connected to a computer. Hanging from the ceiling near one section of the curving wall was a large monitor. Under the monitor, sitting on a white desk, was Emmett Puglisi.

Friends since Nick Paulson sent them on a mission through time and space, John and Rosa had helped Emmett stop a Mayan priest from cutting Emmett's wife's heart out. A white scar still marked Carrollee Chen-Slater-Puglisi's chest where the priest had made an incision.

"Shouldn't you be in Hawaii?" John asked, not as surprised at seeing Emmett as he should be.

"Carrollee and her mother are watching the kids," Emmett said. "I'm on temporary loan to the OSS."

There was some gray in Emmett's brown beard and on his temples, his scalp well into male-pattern baldness. He was middle-aged pudgy, average in height, with brown eyes and a kind-looking face, almost cherubic. With a little less hair, he would look right at home in monk's robes.

"Carrollee let you work for Nick again?" John asked.

"I'm on a short leash," Emmett said. "I have to call home three times a day. How's Rosa?" Emmett asked.

"Unaware of what I'm doing," John said. "She and the kids are happier this way."

"Is she still flying the Aurora?"

The Aurora was the secret spaceplane that Rosa had once copiloted from Earth to Freedom Station in orbit.

"Commercial," John said. "None of that Area Fifty-one technology. How did Nick lure you back?"

"With this," Emmett said, tapping a key on the keyboard next to him.

The moon tyrannosaur appeared, writhing in its endless struggle.

"I've seen the video," John said.

"This is live," Emmett said. "The astronauts set up a camera before they left, and it's still operating. We have hundreds of hours of that juvenile tyrannosaur fighting to get free from whatever is holding it. Nick thinks that might be the tyrannosaur that followed you and Robert Ripman out of the Yucatán past. There were two, but you killed one on the moon. This one was still in the passages when the nuclear bomb destroyed the pyramid and the time passages connecting the pyramids."

"How could it live so long?" John asked, amazed at the resolution of the image broadcast from the moon.

"How can it live in a vacuum at all?" Emmett asked. "It couldn't. It isn't in space–time as we know it."

"Quasi-time," John said.

"You could call it that. It really isn't time as we understand it at all. The space–time that we exist in is unidirectional. The arrow of time is a constant, and we move from the present to the future—never to the past. This tyrannosaur exists in space–time that lacks the arrow of time."

"Could a nuclear explosion rip away that time arrow thing?" John asked.

"Not by itself," Emmett said. "But through an interaction with orgonic energy, black ripples, and other forces that we've released? Who knows?"

"Isn't this outside your field?" John asked, remembering Emmett as an astrophysicist and instrumental in extending Kenny Randall's model predicting the Time Quilt into space to include the moon effect.

"This isn't anyone's field," Emmett said. "I've been working on form–energy interactions since we made it out of that pyramid. Mostly math modeling—that's all Carrollee will let me do. The engineers that built this isolation lab used the results of that research."

"Isolation lab?" John probed.

"We're still interested in orgonic energy," Emmett said. "But it's strictly defensive research and purely theoretical. No one here is trying to manipulate time and space, so there's nothing here that accounts for what happened to Nick."

"Emmett, this lab is ground zero for whatever the hell is going on," John said. "You are just miles from a ranch where Visitor velociraptors showed up. Orlando had a Visitor tyrannosaur loose in the streets, not to mention that herd it was hunting."

"Brachylophosaurs," Emmett said.

"Whatever," John said impatiently. "And what about the earthquakes? In Florida?"

"Earth tremors," Emmett corrected. "And they're not just in Florida. Mostly, though."

"Emmett, it isn't just Nick that's disappeared, it's Elizabeth too."

"Elizabeth Hawthorne?" Emmett asked, hearing it for the first time.

"She went after Nick and disappeared through the same passage in the same way. But when I tried to get through, I couldn't, no matter how hard I tried."

"Nick and Elizabeth, but not you?" Emmett said. "That kills one of my theories. I hypothesized that any of the survivors of the destruction of the orgonic-collecting pyramids might carry a residue allowing them to pass through a space–time barrier."

"There's another problem with your theory," John said. "Elizabeth went through the passage with another woman who had nothing to do with our jaunt through the time tunnels."

"That's disappointing," Emmett said.

"Maybe not," John said. "When they went through the passage, they had velociraptors with them."

"What? You're kidding."

"Little ones. A flock of them. Those velociraptors had to be Visitors. Maybe whatever let them pass through that tunnel rubbed off onto Elizabeth."

"That or there's something about the velociraptors that modifies the time–space around them."

"There's something else," John said. "When I tried crawling into the passage where Nick disappeared, something weird happened. It felt like I was in the passage for seconds, but when I got out, it had been minutes."

"Interesting. Differential time flow?" Emmett said, thinking out loud. "So the planet has experienced time displacement, quasi-time, and now differential time."

John waited, but Emmett was lost in his own head, thinking, weighing probabilities, trying to put it all together.

"Could it have anything to do with this?" John asked, pulling out the lead box with the sample brought back from the moon. "Elizabeth was handling this the night before she went into the passage."

Emmett was thoughtful, stroking his closely cropped beard. "Might," he said finally. "Maybe."

Emmett turned to the keyboard behind him, and soon a new image replaced the moon dinosaur. The video was from the moon mission and shot from a helmet camera, the struggling tyrannosaur in the background. Center screen, an astronaut reached out with a long-handled pair of tongs. The tongs held black material. When it touched the smooth surface, the material blended with it.

"Is that stuff in the tongs, this?" John asked, holding up the lead box.

"Yes. Somehow the orgonic energy interacted with the nuclear explosion, altering the properties of the material."

"If we made a spear out of this stuff, could I stab that tyrannosaur?"

"What?" Emmett asked. "Why?"

"Never mind," John said. "I'm going to try going through that passage again, but this time with this." John said, tapping the box.

"It could be a one-way trip," Emmett said.

"The Visitors came and went," John said.

"There may be reasons for that," Emmett said. "We don't know the conditions on the other side. The environmental conditions could have prepared the Visitors to pass through, but those same conditions may not affect you in the same way. Nick and Elizabeth haven't returned."

"It doesn't matter," John said. "I'm going."

"What would Rosa think?" Emmett asked.

"She's not going to know," John said. "She would just worry."

"What can I do to help?" Emmett asked.

"I need more of this," John said, opening the box.

Twelve hours later, John was back on the Mills Ranch, with six marines. Fanny passed out cold bottles of Evian water and Godiva chocolate bars while Marty shook each marine's hand.

"It's a brave thing you're doing," Marty said, over and over.

"You can't have enough water," Fanny said, "and here's something for a little extra energy when you need it," handing out the cold chocolates. "I froze them so they'll keep for a while."

"Thank you, ma'am," the marines replied, furtively checking out Fanny, who wore white short-shorts with a pink spaghetti-strap tank top.

"Thank you," John said, taking his water and chocolate bar. "We need to go, Lieutenant."

Lieutenant Sam Weller called his squad to order, and they walked to the collapsed barn. Lining up inside, Weller ordered his sergeant to come last. Weller would lead, and John would follow the lieutenant.

"Each of you take one of these," John said, passing out sealed plastic bags. Inside each clear bag was a chunk of the material returned from the moon.

"Lucky charm?" Kelton asked.

"It's your ticket home," John said. "Don't lose it."

Without another word, the marines tucked their bags into pockets, closing and buttoning the flaps. Each marine also carried a pack, and a belt with water, radio, and ammunition clips. The marines wore tropical camouflage, the lightest fabric issued. None of the marines wore body armor, since it was engineered to stop lead projectiles, not six-inch, razor-sharp teeth.

"Let's see if it works," Weller said, duck-walking forward to the collapsed end of the barn. Pausing briefly, Weller looked in the opening, then got down on his hands and knees and crawled forward, disappearing into the dark. Not waiting, John followed him into the unknown.

29

The Reverend

Then God said, "Let us make man in our image, after our likeness; and let them have dominion over the fish of the sea, and over the birds of the air, and over the cattle, and over all the earth, and over every creeping thing that creeps upon the earth."

—Genesis 1:26

Sixty-five Million Years Ago
Community Sanctuary

"This was my father's office," the reverend said, sitting behind the desk, leaning back in a dirty executive chair.

A thick layer of dust covered the desk, bookcases, side chairs, desk, and table lamp. Upholstered in cracked green leather, the chairs were a set. Nick sat in one, looking up high on the wall behind the reverend, where cracked stained-glass windows strained the midday sun.

"He was a preacher's preacher," Reverend continued. "A great man and a man of God, as all great men are."

Reverend paused, waiting for an argument. Nick smiled.

"When God punished us for our sins and sent the dinosaurs to torment us, the people in my father's congregation were spared because of his faithfulness. It was the world that took my father, leaving God's work undone."

"The world?" Nick asked.

"Murdered. Killed by a mob for the food he would have given them willingly. They took him before he fulfilled his mission. The day

I buried him, I knew my calling—to finish the work God called my father to do."

"I know you helped a lot of people. Fed women and children and gave them protection."

"God did all that," the reverend said dismissively. "I was only his hands."

Nick liked most religious people. In his experience, they were gentle folks, worked hard, paid taxes, gave generously to charities and their church, and volunteered in their communities. Through their churches, or para-church organizations, they fed the poor, sheltered the homeless, and cared for the sick. Society was better off because of religion, and if religion did not exist, Nick would invent it to fill the resulting void. Overwhelmingly good citizens, they were nevertheless taken for granted by government and mocked by the media. However, Nick did not like all religious people he knew, and the worst of that lot were the manipulators, who took advantage of goodhearted people by exploiting their generous natures and lining their own pockets from the offering plate. Listening to Reverend, Nick found it hard to classify the dark-haired preacher, but the more he talked, the more Nick believed he was sincere in his beliefs, just woefully, and dangerously, wrong.

"Reverend, with all due respect, what the world experienced eighteen years ago was a disruption of time and space as a result of the explosion of fusion bombs in the fifties and sixties. It wasn't God's punishment that brought the dinosaurs back to the world, it was men's stupidity."

"What's the difference?" Reverend asked, spreading his arms wide and smiling. "God often uses man to punish man."

Even knowing it was useless, Nick pressed on. "What you see in the sky isn't a sign from God, or any kind of holy fire; it is an asteroid and it is going to hit the planet and kill just about everything on it. You and your people will not survive. We know this because it already happened. We call it the K–T event, and the resulting mass extinction of dinosaurs made it possible for mammals to dominate the planet, and for humans to evolve."

"Listen to you," Reverend said, losing some of his smile. "You insist on propping up the theory of evolution when the evidence for creation is all around you."

"Evidence?" Nick said.

"Evolutionists like you insist that dinosaurs and people never lived side by side, yet here we are."

"But we're here only because of an accident," Nick said.

"God is no accident," Reverend said.

Sinking in the quicksand of Reverend's convoluted thinking, Nick slogged his way toward solid ground. "You can't survive what is coming," Nick said.

"Not without God's help," Reverend said. "But we have survived worse with God's help." Again, the reverend spread his arms, indicating the existence of his father's church as proof of God's intervention.

"You haven't survived anything like what's coming," Nick said.

"Dr. Paulson, your God is too small. Try kneeling before the God of the universe."

"I'm agnostic," Nick said, "but I respect your beliefs and would fight for your right to believe anything you wish. Reverend, I am telling you the truth, if you stay here, you and anyone who stays with you will die. If you want to continue to worship your god, you need to let me try to help you get back to our present."

Reverend leaned forward, putting his hands flat on the desk. The old chair squeaked as he rocked forward. A condescending smile on his lips, Reverend said, "God is the path to salvation, in this world and the next."

"Reverend, a rock ten kilometers in diameter is going to hit the Earth and leave a crater one hundred and eighty kilometers in diameter. The resulting explosion will be the equivalent of one hundred million megatons. That is ten thousand times the explosive power of all the nuclear weapons on the planet."

"There are no nuclear weapons on the planet," Reverend said, his smile back.

"You're making jokes?" Nick asked indignantly. "When that space rock hits, it will vaporize the surface layer of the Earth and pulverize bedrock. The resulting acoustic wave will make the whole planet ring. Earth's surface will ripple, dormant volcanoes will explode into life, and active volcanoes will erupt like nothing ever seen. Every crack in the mantle will seep magma, rivers of lava will flow like water. Ejecta will rain from the skies and the blast wave will level every tree and building. If you survive that, you'll find yourself engulfed in a firestorm that will sweep the continent. Particulates will circle the globe for decades, and that will be the end of summer for years. If by some miracle you live through the initial destruction, you will starve to death."

"By some miracle," Reverend said, jumping on the phrase. "Exactly."

Knowing it was useless, Nick changed tactics. "God gave us free will," Nick said.

"Free to sin, free to repent," Reverend said.

"Let me talk to your people and let them make their own choice."

Reverend paused, his smile shrinking slightly; then the smile faded away. "Of course you can talk to them," Reverend said. "This isn't a prison, Dr. Paulson. These people are here by choice. I know you think I'm some sort of puppet master, controlling their lives, but what little control I have is because they gave their lives over to God and God has put them in my hands."

Nick sensed the man's sincerity, but knew also his sincerity would get them all killed.

"Do you read the Bible, Dr. Paulson?"

"I read it in college."

"In the first chapter of Philippians, Paul writes something that may shock you. I know it shocked me when I read it. He says, 'Some preach Christ out of envy and rivalry, but others out of goodwill. The latter do so in love and the former out of selfish ambition. But what does it matter? The important thing is that in every way, whether from false motives or true, Christ is preached.' So you see, Dr. Paulson, ultimately my motives don't matter. I am preaching Christ to people who need to hear Christ's message."

"I don't doubt your sincerity," Nick said. "But I am just as sincere as you are, Reverend. That asteroid will destroy your Community."

"If it is God's will."

"If God's will is inevitable, then it is God's will," Nick said.

Reverend lowered his eyes, then slowly leaned back and sighed deeply. "Are you a prophet of God or Satan?" Reverend asked, and then held up his hand, stopping Nick's answer. "Don't answer. You'll only deny there are spiritual forces at work, and if you don't believe in God and Satan, you would be deaf to both voices."

"I am speaking truth, doesn't that mean I speak for God?" Nick said.

"Whether what you say is true or not, some killer space rock, no matter how big, is any match for the God who created the universe. If God wills it, God can save us."

"We can save ourselves," Nick said. "At least we can try."

"Or we can trust God," Reverend said.

"No offense, but I plan on giving God a hand in saving me."

Reverend smiled and then chuckled. "God helps those who help themselves, eh?" Reverend said. "Did you know that's not from the Bible? Ben Franklin said it, but no one remembers that. In truth, the opposite is true. God helps the helpless, and you don't get much more helpless than a group of pampered people suddenly dropped into a forest teeming with killer beasts. Yet here we are."

"But you're not thriving, you're just barely surviving, and there are fewer of you every year. This used to be a city with half a million people in it. Where have they gone?"

Looking genuinely sad, Reverend's eyes moistened, and he cleared his throat before speaking. "Most of the buildings collapsed when we came here," Reverend said, then cleared his throat again. "I can still hear the people inside begging for help. We helped those we could, but day by day we heard fewer cries for help, and then finally none. Then came the fires and plague and fighting—wars, really. Man's sinful nature reared its ugly head, and the desperate killed the desperate, the strong the weak, the weak the weaker. Starvation took many, disease and exposure many more, and then there were the beasts. We had guns, but they are big and fast and hard to kill. I saved what people I could, and other men and women did God's work too, but Satan was loose in the land and many fell to temptation. Then the demons came."

"Demons?" Nick asked.

"Beasts in the guise of man," Reverend said.

"What your people call Inhumans?"

"The same," Reverend said. "They massacred the People of Martha who were farming a piece of land to the north. I took a hundred warriors to help them, but it was too late. The demons killed everyone: men, women, children. I even saw an infant dead in her mother's arms."

"Did you try talking to them?" Nick asked.

"Talk to animals? I'm not Doctor Doolittle," Reverend said, finishing with a forced smile. "We wasted so much ammunition on the big beasts that we did not have enough for the demons. We killed many of them, yet they would not stop coming, them and their beasts."

"Their beasts?" Nick said.

"Yes, the beasts have beasts," Reverend said. "That is why I know they are demons, because they command the other beasts."

"They've domesticated dinosaurs?" Nick asked.

Frowning, Reverend leaned forward again, spreading his hands on the desktop and then sighing. "Dr. Paulson, don't go down that road. The Inhumans aren't people, they aren't cute, they aren't like us in any way that you can imagine. God gave man dominion over the beasts, not them. The power they have over the great beasts must come from Satan because it does not come from God."

Reverend stopped suddenly, eyes now bright, seeing something that Nick could not.

"Of course," Reverend said, excited. "It makes sense now. That space rock that you think will destroy us was sent by God, but not to destroy God's faithful, it was sent to destroy Satan's minions."

"Reverend, that asteroid is not going to discriminate," Nick said, but he had lost the reverend.

Sitting tall now, his fixed smile back, confidence swelling, Reverend resumed his megalomaniacal persona. "Can't you see the way your truth and my truth came together to give us God's truth?" Reverend said, excited. "Some had speculated that the fire in the sky was an asteroid, but I knew God would not save us only to kill us. And I could not understand why God would tolerate the continued persecution of his people at the hands of demons. You brought me the answer, Dr. Paulson. God is coming to the aid of believers."

Nick wanted to ask why God would not just sweep the Inhumans away, why God would use a blunt instrument like an asteroid, and why God would wait so long to destroy the Inhumans, but there was no chance. Reverend was a true believer. Retreating so deep into his worldview, there was no way to drag him back to reality.

"Reverend, we have little time. My friends and I need to find a way home. I'm willing to take any of your people who want to come with me."

"Of course," Reverend said, now brimming with confidence. "You can ask, but will they follow you?"

They found the Community celebrating, the horse and police officer the center of attention. Never having seen a real horse, children cautiously approached, touched Torino's flank, and then scooted back, bragging to the others about their courage. Officer Conyers supervised, protecting her mount from rambunctious children and the children from any sudden moves Torino would make. The horse, however, munched happily on handfuls of grass, gathered by children.

Dr. Gah sat on the remains of a picnic table, leg stretched out, surrounded by middle-aged men and women and a few young adults, answering their questions about the world they had been ripped away from eighteen years ago. Carson Wills had his own worshippers: young women, mostly, with young men at the back of his circle, listening intently as Carson described his life in Florida. From the few snatches Nick heard, Carson's life amounted to capturing rogue dinosaurs, driving fast cars, listening to rock music, drinking copious amounts of beer, and living with his hot girlfriend. Nick hoped Carson had the sense to stop talking as the reverend approached.

Ranger Wynooski stood in her own group, scolding the adults. "Look at these children," Wynooski said. "They're nothing but skin and bones. You folks aren't looking much better. You need to put some meat on these kids."

A big woman, and overweight, Wynooski was average in modern America, and the people of Reverend's Community were thin, even emaciated, but tough from years of hard work. Every mouthful was hard earned, the calories it took to extract the food from the land little less than the food itself. Obesity was a luxury none could afford.

Jacob was holding his wife, Leah, their children bouncing around, hanging on the pant leg of their father, or trying to wedge between their parents. Seeing Jacob holding Leah, Nick thought of Elizabeth and punished himself for not spending enough time holding her.

"Listen, people," Reverend said.

The crowd quieted quickly, even the children who knew not to interrupt the reverend.

"Dr. Paulson believes that the light in the sky that I have called God's fire, is actually an asteroid—a big rock. He believes it will hit the planet and kill every one of us and almost everything else on the planet. He says our only hope is to follow him and he will take us back to where he came from."

A hundred silent people listened attentively.

"Was that a fair representation of your message?" Reverend asked.

"Two things," Nick said. "I know the asteroid will hit the Earth because it already has hit the Earth. You are living in Earth's past and we have documented evidence that when that asteroid hits, it will kill every one of you. Second, I will try to get you back home, but there is no guarantee. The only thing I know for sure is that if you are here when that asteroid hits, you will die."

"Thank you for your concern," Reverend said. "What Dr. Paulson is not telling you is that while we were speaking I had a revelation. I came to understand the purpose of the coming of the asteroid. Dr. Paulson's killer rock is not for us, but for the demons that command the great beasts. Let me assure you that we have been faithful and obedient ministers of the Word. God is not going to kill us; God is going to protect us. I believe Dr. Paulson when he says that the space rock will kill many creatures including the demons, but God is not going to kill us too. That would make no sense. Why kill what you have saved? God's plan isn't to kill us; it is to free us from the Inhumans. When the demons are gone, God will usher in a new age, and this will be a New Earth and we will be his New People.

"You are free to make your choice. You may go with Dr. Paulson and find your way back to the sinful world that God rescued us from, or stay here and build that New Earth and populate it with our children, not demons. Like Joshua, I say as for me and my house, we will serve the Lord!"

Silent men and women bowed heads, avoiding eye contact with Reverend. He had saved them, and kept them alive through the tribulation, as many saw it. Abandoning Reverend would be hard, and given the conversations Nick had overheard, most of them wanted to get home for the creature comforts they missed, not remain for some spiritual purpose.

"Look!" a teenager shouted, pointing down the hill at the broken highway that curved out of sight.

Hurrying with the others, Nick kept close to the reverend, the flock parting like the Red Sea to make room for their leader. Men, women, and children pressed against a chain-link fence marking the back of the property line. Nick followed the reverend into a gap, then grabbed a piece of fence for himself. The hill dropped off sharply just beyond the fence, giving a view down the valley. Coming down the road were a dozen figures.

"Inhumans," someone whispered, others picking up the fear, embellishing. "Must be fifty of them."

"You wanted to talk to them," Reverend said to Nick. "Here's your chance."

30

President

> *Time warps, time bubbles, variable speed of light, wormholes, time quilts, black ripples, black holes, quasi-time—when it comes to understanding the physics of time, we have just managed to put our toe in the ocean.*
>
> **—Emmett Puglisi, Ph.D., e-mail to President Brown**

Present Time
Washington, D.C.

Wilamina Brown never set out to become President of the United States, and even now she was ambivalent about the job, and it was a job to Willa, not a joy. When President Pearl finished his second term, the party turned to her to be the standard bearer. With the reconstruction and economic recovery from the Time Quilt, and the nuclear attacks in Alaska and near Los Angeles well under way, Willa knew it would be nearly impossible for her party to keep the presidency for a third term. Complacency was the curse of the public, and the opposition was promising a shiny new candidate with a gilded tongue and movie star wife. Two years out, polls showed Willa running only competitively with the California governor. Loath to see the progress of the Pearl administration undone, Willa entered the primaries, ate hundreds of chicken dinners, shook hands with thousands of people she did not know, and put up with yellow journalists administering pop quizzes masquerading as interviews. As a black female, Willa pulled from disparate groups, including some traditionally voting for her opponent, and eked out a victory.

While Willa held the presidency for her party, the Senate flipped, and once again government was divided. With liberal use of her veto power, and occasional filibusters, Willa managed to keep the country on an even economic keel, but the constant fight with the loyal opposition drained Willa. And now Dr. Paulson had disappeared, and dinosaurs were popping up in places where they should not be. Willa's science adviser was not as much help as Willa wished, but then Willa was asking her adviser to explain the unexplainable. Willa missed her director of the Office of Security Science, and wasn't sure where to turn. The economic progress would be all for naught if the planet came apart in another time-twisting catastrophe.

Sipping tea, President Brown sat in her private study, just off the Oval Office. Papers cluttered her desk, spread out and layered across the surface, an idiosyncratic horizontal filing system. Less system, and more memory cures, Willa forbade her executive assistant from touching the desktop, although she could scour the Oval Office to her heart's content. Strictly ceremonial, Willa greeted important visitors in the Oval Office, or posed there for pictures, but worked in her study, the same space used for sexual trysts by an earlier administration.

Taking her cup, she walked through the Oval Office and looked out onto the Rose Garden. An overcast summer day, it was unusually cool for summer in Washington, and that worried her. Every unusual event worried her, since it was seemingly random events that presaged the Time Quilt catastrophe. For a century, odd events had been recorded, and ignored, since they did not fit into orthodox physics. Continuing into the modern age, the odd and unexplainable were relegated to the pages of supermarket tabloids and ignored by the mainstream press. Unexplainable events like fish falling from the sky, people bursting into flame, people drowning in the desert, people suddenly disappearing and appearing, and other oddities were finally recognized for what they were—harbingers of doom. Recognized too late to stop it, the disaster happened, civilization was shredded, and humanity met dinosaurs face-to-face. Unknown to the public was the extent of the damage to the time stream, and the mission of the OSS to monitor and, if possible, manage time itself.

Cool summers might not be a symptom of more trouble, but what of the odd pattern of earthquakes? What of the Visitor dinosaurs? And most troubling of all, Dr. Paulson's disappearance. Something was going on, but what? Her chief of staff's familiar tap interrupted her.

"A Dr. Puglisi from the OSS is calling. I think you should speak with him."

Major Lund grew up in a military family, but was the only son not to serve. Instead, Lund drove himself through school, graduating from college a year early, then earning a Harvard MBA. A learned man, Lund loved books and all knowledge, but when Willa asked him why he never became a university professor, he said, "If you teach, you have to go where the jobs are. With an MBA, you can live anywhere you want." A friend of Willa's since working on Pearl's Senate campaign, Lund rose in power, becoming a key player in the Pearl administration but remaining in the background. When Willa asked him to run her campaign, he surprised her by agreeing. They were even closer friends now.

"Put him on," Willa said, afraid of what she would hear.

Lund punched a remote control, a hidden television rising out of a credenza. Willa took her usual chair, Lund on the couch to her left. Coming to life, the screen showed Dr. Puglisi looking around the Oval Office.

"What can I do for you?" Willa asked.

"John Roberts was here, and he said something that got me thinking," Puglisi said, pausing to collect his thoughts. "He's trying to follow Dr. Paulson now."

"I know," Willa said. "Mr. Roberts succeeded in going through the same passage as Dr. Paulson. At least as far as we know. What did Mr. Roberts say to you?"

"He believed the material recovered from the moon was the key to passing through the time passage like Dr. Paulson. I now believe he was right. The material, or at least contact with it, seems to be the key."

"Because of its unusual properties?" Lund asked.

"Exactly," Puglisi said. "The differential time flow between the entrance and terminus may be the barrier. Somehow the material recovered on the moon exists in a state that is time neutral and that empowers the traveler to make the transition between time flows."

"You know I am understanding only part of this," Willa said honestly.

"Yes, Madam President," Puglisi said. "I don't understand much of it myself, but I do understand this: We know that the region, and especially Florida, is experiencing an unusual series of tremors. After meeting with John, I mapped the quakes using longitude, latitude, and then added Richter strength and duration of the quakes and found a pattern. The quakes spiral out from this lab. That material we recovered is the epicenter for whatever is happening."

"Exactly what is happening?" Willa asked.

"Honestly," Puglisi said, staring intently from the screen, "I don't know, but the quakes are increasing in strength and decreasing in spacing. We need to do something and do it quick, before it is too late."

"Too late for what?" Lund asked, frustrated by the vagueness.

"I don't know, but earthquakes are part of it," Puglisi said.

"I assure you that I am as concerned as you are, but what can we do?" Willa asked.

"That black material is acting like a giant magnet, attracting something. I suggest we get rid of it before it pulls whatever is at the other end to us."

"Get rid of it? You mean burn it? Blow it up?"

"I don't think that would work," Puglisi said. "The force it is projecting could be released, intensified, or transformed. Better to stick with the devil we know."

"Then what?" Willa asked.

"Pack it all up and send it into space," Puglisi said.

"We'll lose the strategic value of the material," Willa said, thinking through the consequences. "That is a lot to give up."

"It's not just about Nick and Elizabeth," Emmett said. "Whatever has ripped open these time passages isn't just affecting time and space, it is also altering time flow. The time ripples that created the Time Quilt came from nuclear explosions in the thirty- to one-hundred-megaton range. Those bombs did not have the megatonnage to alter time, and it took a convergence of ripples through time to cause the Time Quilt. What's causing this new phenomenon is exponentially more powerful than anything any nation has detonated."

"That's not possible," Willa said, anxiety growing. "Unless these tunnels connect to the future?"

"Not with velociraptors and tyrannosaurs popping out," Emmett said.

"Then what?" Willa asked.

"I did some calculations, and I think I might know what's anchoring this," Emmett said. "It's the K–T event. An asteroid strike that kills eighty-five percent of the animal life on the planet."

"It killed the dinosaurs," Willa said.

"And more," Emmett said. "Dinosaurs, pterosaurs, marine reptiles, ammonites, many plants, even forms of plankton were eliminated or devastated."

"You think that destruction could bleed through to the present?" Willa asked.

"I think the connections we've found are the larger time fractures, but that there are many more that could rupture as the K–T event approaches."

"Approaches in the past," Willa said.

"I know it's confusing. The time effects ripple out on both sides of any event. We're experiencing the before ripples, and after the strike, we'll suffer the after ripples unless we can minimize the effect."

"But it has already happened," Willa said.

"Yes, but we've only experienced the time ripples, the full waves have not hit yet. Normally, they would ripple out through all of time, but I believe that the orgonic material that we have been collecting is altering time–space, creating a path of least resistance leading right to our present. Specifically to Florida."

Willa understood, grasping the potential disaster. Florida was heavily populated and loaded with tourists year-round. There had already been an incident in Orlando, and if the energy from an asteroid strike bled through into present-day Orlando, the death toll could be staggering.

"Your plan is to get rid of this orgonic material?" Willa asked.

"Since the orgonic material is acting like a magnet, yes."

"To space?"

"Off the planet, yes. Let the energy released dissipate in space."

"I suppose we must," Willa said, accepting the idea.

"There's a problem, though. If we move the material, we may shift the time tunnels that have been created. I don't know if once created they are fixed, or transient based on proximity to the orgonic material."

"I see," Willa said. "You're saying that the passage that our people passed through may dissipate if we send the orgonic matter into space."

"Yes."

Willa did not hesitate. "Wait as long as you safely can, then move the material. I can't risk losing a city or even a state to save one or two people."

"There is a way that will make it possible to wait to the last minute," Emmett said.

"How?"

"With a little help from Area Fifty-one."

31

New World

For about 250 years, our species has been known as Homo sapiens, a scientific name in Latin that means "wise man." Given the havoc humans are wreaking on natural systems, putting ourselves and so many other living things in peril, we don't deserve this name contends Julian Cribb, an Australian science writer . . .

—Wynne Perry, Live Science

Sixty-five Million Years Ago
Inhuman Village

"No, wait!" Elizabeth shouted, pulling Jeanette back.

Jeanette was about to follow Do through the opening into the weird world on the other side.

"You don't know where that goes," Elizabeth said. "You don't even know if you can breathe there."

"Do can," Jeanette said.

Elizabeth looked to see Do trotting in the distance, his head showing above tall waving grasses with green stalks and golden tassels. Tracking something, Do was moving away at an angle.

"Maybe that's where the boys went," Jeanette said. "That's why they brought us here."

Doubtful, Elizabeth turned to the lead creature, still uneasy with their weird catlike eyes. "Our friends, they went through there?" Elizabeth asked slowly, walking her fingers across her hand toward the opening, the best gesture she could think of. "People like us went there?" Elizabeth pointed to herself and Jeanette, and then at the opening, repeating the walking gesture.

Still agitated by Do's run into the opening, the creatures sang to one another, two or three mimicking Elizabeth's finger gesture.

"I'm going," Jeanette said. "I can't see Do anymore, and Carson might be in there."

"Wait," Elizabeth said.

Velociraptor chicks inched forward, searching for Do, heads high, tails low, emitting soft *awk*s.

"No, Fa," Jeanette said. "Stay, So. Stay, La."

"Woof," Sally said, reinforcing Jeanette's command, her nose almost inside the cave opening.

"Our friends, did they go in there?" Elizabeth repeated, gesturing with her fingers.

After a few singsong exchanges, the lead creature looked directly at Elizabeth, bowed his head, and then used two of his three long fingers and made the walking motion right toward the cave entrance.

"Look, he's telling you that's where Carson and your guy are," Jeanette said.

"Maybe," Elizabeth said, unsure of what the creature was communicating.

"Re, Me, Fa, So, La, Ti, we're going," Jeanette sang out, rifle ready.

"We'll be back," Elizabeth said to the creature just as Jeanette stepped into the opening, surrounded by velociraptors.

"This is a bad idea," Elizabeth said to Sally, and then followed Jeanette.

"Woof," Sally said, and limped through the cave opening.

32
Communication

Whorf coined what was once called the Sapir–Whorf hypothesis, which is more properly referred to as the Whorf hypothesis. This states that language is not simply a way of voicing ideas, but is the very thing that shapes those ideas. One cannot think outside the confines of their language. The result of this process is many different world views by speakers of different languages.

—Amy Stafford

Sixty-five Million Years Ago
Community Church Refuge

"I'll talk to them," Nick volunteered, looking down at the approaching band of Inhumans.

"Please don't," Reverend said. "I feel like I pressured you into this, and I did not mean to. I spoke rashly. Don't do it because of what I said."

"Reverend, I want to do this," Nick said. "Look at them! They're a sentient species evolving on a parallel course with us."

"Actually, they predate us by sixty-three million years," Gah said, joining the conversation.

"At least sixty-three million years," Wynooski said.

Sighing loudly, the reverend said, "You're speaking nonsense. The theory of evolution is a distraction, created by Satan. It is a false trail to lead you into the wilderness of sin, and it has worked beautifully since the very first day Mr. Darwin was led astray. Now Satan has his hooks deep into your souls. Listen to your heart, not your clouded mind. Those are demons down there, and to speak to them is to speak to the devil."

"Kind of ironic the way these evolution-deniers end up back in time before their kind actually evolved," Wynooski said, as if Reverend and his people could not hear her.

"Everyone who believed in evolution got killed!" someone in the crowd shouted.

"They didn't die because they believed in evolution," Wynooski said. "You are talking nonsense."

Rumbling with angry disagreement, the crowd became restless, surging forward.

"Wynooski, have you ever had a thought you didn't express?" Carson asked.

"Ranger, this isn't helping," Nick said.

" 'So God created man in his own image, in the image of God he created him; male and female he created them'," Reverend said in his deep booming voice, quieting the crowd. "Genesis 1:27 says 'man' was created in the image of God," he thundered, "and that is not man!" Reverend finished with a dramatic sweep of his arm, pointing down the hill. Amens erupted, rallying to the side of their leader. Jacob and his family stood at the rear, holding one another, concerned.

" 'Let us make man in our image, in our likeness, and let them rule over the fish of the sea and the birds of the air, over the livestock, over all the earth, and over all the creatures that move along the ground'," Reverend boomed. "Every creature that moves along the ground, no exceptions, and those things marching on God's sanctuary will bow before God and man or they will suffer God's wrath."

The vehemence of Reverend's words frightened everyone into silence, even Wynooski. Gently, Nick tried to reason with Reverend.

"They are coming here for a reason," Nick said. "Maybe sent by Satan but maybe brought by God for his purpose. There is only one way to know their reason for coming here, and that is to talk with them. Let me meet with them. If they kill me, then you'll know they came for war. If they let me live, maybe I can find out what they want."

Reverend hesitated. In Nick's short experience with the reverend, he found the man swung between reasoned caring and irrational religious fervor like a clock pendulum.

"Might as well talk," Carson said. "They've got us cut off anyway."

Members of the Community were looking over the edge and toward the gate, where armed men stood with rifles poking through the wrought-iron fence.

"We're surrounded," one of the men at the gate said.

Still red-faced, Reverend slowly got control of himself, considering the options—there were few. Talking or fighting were the obvious choices, and talking did not rule out fighting.

"Speak with them if you must," Reverend said.

"Thank you," Nick said. "Norm, keep things together while I'm gone."

Gah, sitting against the wall of the church, waved. Now Nick looked at Wynooski and Carson Wills. He wanted someone to go with him, but Wynooski was a know-it-all who could not keep her mouth shut, and the Dinosaur Wrangler would not volunteer unless his life depended on it.

"Let me go with you," Officer Conyers said, leading Torino forward.

"I'll be going with Dr. Paulson," Wynooski said, butting in.

"I'll take Officer Conyers," Nick said. "The horse might impress them."

"Then you should ride," Conyers said, indicating the stirrup.

"I don't know how to ride," Nick said.

"Just sit on him," Conyers said. "I'll lead him."

"I can ride," Wynooski said.

Ignoring Wynooski, Nick let Conyers guide his foot into the stirrup and then gave his bottom a shove, helping him onto Torino. Nick had not ridden a horse since eighth grade, and he hated it then. His eighth-grade mount had refused all Nick's commands, going wherever it wanted to go, and it wanted to go to the barn. So far, Torino was different, standing patiently, waiting for direction.

"Okay, let's go," Nick said, hanging on to the saddle horn.

Conyers led Torino to the gate, waiting while the chains were removed and the gate opened. Three Inhumans waited down the road, several more stood farther back. Nick found them fascinating creatures, with grayish green skin, large eyes, and three-fingered hands. Their weapons meant they were tool-users, so clearly intelligent, but evolving from a different root than humans. Gently rocking on Torino, Nick studied the Inhumans and, as they got closer, their tools. Nick was shocked. The tips of their spears and the shafts of their knives were made of the same orgonic material found on the moon.

Leading Torino, Conyers stopped a few yards from the creatures, the Inhumans more interested in Torino than in Nick or Conyers. Engrossed, Nick looked down at them from his perch, appearing imperious. Finally, one of the creatures broke the silence, its voice like a xylophone played softly.

"Got that?" Conyers said, smiling, one hand holding the reins, one hand on the butt of her gun.

"Help me down," Nick said.

Moving slowly, Nick slid down the side of the horse, trying not to look awkward, but failing.

"I don't understand," Nick said, approaching slowly, hands open.

One of the creatures separated and came forward a few steps, mimicking the open-hands gesture.

"I mean you no harm," Nick said, stopping a few feet away from the Inhuman.

The large eyes stared blankly, blinking once, twice, showing no understanding.

"What are they?" Officer Conyers asked. "Can they even understand us?"

"Not our verbal language," Nick said.

"Do you know sign language?" Conyers asked.

"It's up to them," Nick said. "They came to us."

The Inhuman watched the exchange between Conyers and Nick intently, making no more sense out of the human language than Nick could theirs. Now the Inhuman opened the palms of his three-fingered hands, slowly folding one hand into a pointing finger, and then slowly raised his arm, pointing into the sky. Following the point, Nick saw the oncoming asteroid.

"The asteroid?" Nick said. "You mean the asteroid?"

Its facial skin taut, the Inhuman showed nothing resembling an emotion. Thin lips on its snout did not, or could not, curl into a smile or a frown, and without eyebrows, there was nothing to arch. If there were emotional cues, they were too subtle for Nick to discern.

Now the Inhuman slowly lowered himself into a squat, brushing a broken piece of asphalt clean, then untying a leather pouch hanging from its belt. One by one, the Inhuman extracted stones of different sizes. Putting the largest down first, the Inhuman arranged the other stones around the first. When finished, there were five stones arranged around the larger stone. Then the Inhuman repeated its point at the asteroid, then took the claw of one finger and scratched a line past the larger stone, directly to the third stone from the center.

"I can't believe it," Nick said.

"What?" Conyers asked.

"They know about the asteroid and they know it's going to hit Earth."

Watching the humans talk, the Inhuman waited patiently.

"The sun," Nick said, pointing at the larger rock. "Mars, Earth, Venus, Jupiter, and Saturn," Nick said, pointing at each rock in turn. "They know all the planets visible to the naked eye."

"If they have been watching the sky, they couldn't miss that," Conyers said, pointing to at the asteroid. "Is it just me or is that asteroid brighter?"

"We don't have much time," Nick said.

Nick looked around, finding a small piece of crumbled asphalt. Taking it, he looked the Inhuman straight in the face, and then held up the piece, pointing at the glowing dot in the sky. Then Nick put the piece on the line scratched by the Inhuman, and dragged it along the line, tapping it against the third rock from the sun. In response, the Inhuman spread his arms wide, opening his palms, and then turned to the Inhumans behind him, singing a few sentences. When he did, a cacophony erupted among the others, sounding like a prepubescent boys' chorus.

Now the Inhuman extended its arm, bowed slightly, took a step back, and motioned down the road. Unsure he understood, Nick simply stared. The Inhuman repeated the motion.

"He wants us to go with him," Conyers said.

"It looks that way," Nick said. "But why?"

"Something to do with the asteroid?" Conyers offered. "He brought those pebbles to show us something."

Intensely curious, Nick longed to go with the creatures, but there was not enough time. The asteroid would strike soon, and they did not want to be on the planet when it hit. Nick shook his head no, and then pointed back up the road at the gate where the humans waited.

The Inhuman repeated the "come with me" motion, and again Nick refused. Still showing no emotion, the Inhuman dug deeper into his pouch, to pull out something and hand it to Nick. It was a Dinosaur Wrangler patch.

"Get Carson down here," Nick said.

Conyers swung up into the saddle, galloping the short distance to the gate, yelling for Carson. Reluctantly, Carson came through the gate, arguing with Officer Conyers, who finally convinced him to walk down the road. Staying close to Torino and Conyers, Carson came to Nick, eyes on the Inhumans, looking like he would run at the slightest suspicious movement.

"What's this about?" Carson asked.

"This," Nick said, handing him the patch.

Unconsciously, Carson touched the logo embroidered on his breast and then the patch. "It's one of mine," Carson said. "Where did it come from?"

"He had it," Nick said, indicating the Inhuman.

"But how?"

"Did you take anyone else to the Mills Ranch?"

"Handled it myself," Carson said, clearly puzzled.

"So no one else from your business knew about the Mills Ranch?" Nick asked.

"Just Jeanette. She handles the calls."

"Would she come looking for you?" Nick asked.

"Jeanette? It couldn't be," Carson said. He agonized, rocking back and forth, looking up, then down, and then screwing up his courage. "Where did that thing get this?" Carson asked.

"There's only one way to find out," Nick said.

Seemingly interested, even perceptive, the Inhuman had watched the humans talk, its unreadable face moving slightly back and forth as each human spoke. As Nick and Carson looked at the Inhuman, it repeated its bow and arm motion, indicating they were to follow. Nick raised an open hand saying "Wait," then walked with Carson and Conyers, still mounted, back to the gate. Inside Reverend waited.

"They know about the asteroid that is going to hit the Earth," Nick said, loudly enough that the crowd could hear.

"Of course they do, it's brighter than the moon," Wynooski said.

"Somehow they've plotted its course and know the asteroid will intersect the Earth, and for some reason they want us to go with them. I think it's related to the coming asteroid, but other than that your guess is as good as mine. They also have one of Carson's Dinosaur Wrangler patches. We don't know where they got it, but I'm going to go with them to find out. The rest of you need to find your way out of here. Officer Conyers can lead you back to where she came through. Can you find your way back?"

"If someone can get me back to the hill where we met up, I can find it from there," the officer said.

"Jacob?" Nick called. "Will you take them back to the hill?"

"What about the Inhumans?" Jacob asked, his wife and daughters pressed against him.

"Bring it on," Crazy Kramer said, shaking his machete as he came to stand by Jacob.

"If we go with them, I think they'll let you go," Nick said, realizing that the compound was deathly quiet, all listening intently.

Accepting the responsibility, Jacob started forward, but his petite wife pulled him back.

"Reverend, what should we do?" Leah Lewinski shouted.

Others called out to the reverend, looking for direction.

"Can we really go home?" someone asked.

Reverend looked at the ground, shaking his head in disappointment, then stood erect and pulled off his sunglasses dramatically, dark eyes sweeping the crowd. "This is your home," Reverend said. "This land is your home, not their home," indicating the Inhumans. "It is true that you might be able to go back to the world with these people, but ask yourself why? God brought you here. If God wants you to return, he will send you home."

Guilty looks spread through the crowd, everyone avoiding the reverend's eyes.

"We have come to a choice-point," Reverend continued. "I have decided to go with the demons, to confront them with the power of God, to turn them from their ways and to save their souls if they have any. I ask that the rest of you remain here, praying without ceasing for our enemies and that I succeed. I promise you that I will return, and we will be a Community once more."

Nick waited a respectful few seconds to speak, but Wynooski did not.

"What a lot of hooey," Wynooski said.

"Ranger, that's enough," Nick said before she could do more damage. "That asteroid," Nick said, pointing at the sky, "is going to strike the Earth very soon, and it will kill everything bigger than a cockroach. The only chance for your Community to survive is to go with Officer Conyers and try to find your way back to the present."

"Exactly," Wynooski said.

"That's your choice," Reverend said. "God, or the world."

Silence followed, then the crowd began to murmur, and soon debate broke out, people taking sides, families squabbling, couples arguing. Jacob and Leah talked quietly to one side, Jacob doing most of the talking, Leah most of the listening. Finally, Jacob and his family pushed through the milling crowd to Nick.

"We're going back," Jacob said.

"Bring it on," Crazy Kramer said, coming to stand with Jacob.

"I guess Crazy is going with us," Jacob said.

Now the Community began an agonizing split, as choices were made.

"So be it," Reverend said suddenly. "If God is not tugging at your heart, then you must go."

More arguing erupted, more families and friends split, some parents arguing over their children. In the end, half the Community, about a hundred people, had decided to go back to the world they had come from. The parting was painful, those staying begging the others to stay, those going pleading for their friends and family to leave with them. Nick noticed that more of the families with children decided to go, although several families elected to stay behind. Reverend talked with his bodyguards, giving instructions. Then, Reverend hugged each of his four wives in turn. Nick realized all would wait for the reverend.

Clearly hurting from losing half his flock, Reverend looked grim, as sure that those leaving would regret it as Nick was that those staying would die. To his credit, Reverend did not preach again to the leavers, and reluctantly, Nick did not try to persuade those deciding to stay. Honestly, he was not sure that those leaving could escape anyway. A quick look at the growing dot in the sky told Nick that if they did not leave soon, no one would make it.

"Give us some guns or something," Carson said, pleading with Reverend.

"We'll be safe," Nick said, trying to reassure Carson.

"We'll be safer with guns," Carson said.

Reverend turned to his bodyguards, asking for their pistols. Nick declined a gun, but Carson and Reverend took revolvers. Both checked to see if they were loaded.

"Spare ammo?" Carson asked.

Reluctantly, the guards gave Carson a handful of cartridges. Reverend accepted some too, but declined more when offered. Now the guards argued with Reverend, begging to accompany him. Reverend refused, however, asking his bodyguards to protect his wives until he could return.

Puzzled by the number of humans coming from the compound, the Inhumans backed up. Nick, Reverend, and Carson separated from the column. Jacob, Conyers leading Torino with Gah in the saddle, and Crazy Kramer were at the head of the column, waiting for the Inhumans to clear out of the way.

Several Inhumans came up the road, weapons ready, unsure of what was happening. Looking past Nick and the others, they chirped and chimed, gesticulating and pointing.

"It's Crazy," Reverend said. "He is a fierce warrior."

"Jacob," Nick said. "Hide Crazy in the crowd."

Reluctantly, and noisily, Crazy Kramer relented, working his way back in the column. The Inhumans settled down but continued to argue. Finally, the argument was settled, and the leader made the "come with me" gesture. Nick and the others moved forward, the Inhumans parting, letting them through. Jacob's column held back, letting the Inhumans march away. Behind them, those remaining closed the gates of the church compound, watching friends and family march away.

As Nick rounded the corner, he was shocked to see dozens of armed Inhumans. There were many more than seen from the compound.

"Does this look like they came in peace?" Reverend asked.

It did not. Nick realized the hatred between the humans and Inhumans was deep and wide. With Inhumans in front and behind, they followed the ruined highway, curving around the hill, toward the unknown. Looking back, Nick saw the column of humans come off the hill, turning the other direction, Gah mounted on Torino, waving good-bye. Some of the Inhumans saw the humans leaving and sang out dismay, shaking weapons, only to be shouted down by other Inhumans with voices resembling muffled police sirens. Reluctantly, the recalcitrant Inhumans fell silent, many throwing hate-filled looks at the fleeing humans. Seeing the reaction, Nick finally discerned one of their emotions. It was hatred. Then the ground shook.

33

Marines

The Marines I have seen around the world have the cleanest bodies, the filthiest minds, the highest morale, and the lowest morals of any group of animals I have ever seen. Thank God for the United States Marine Corps!

—Eleanor Roosevelt

Sixty-five Million Years Ago
Unknown Place

John tumbled into Lieutenant Weller, who was on his knees, trying to get to his feet. Five more marines tumbled down the slope, quickly getting up, weapons ready.

"What the hell?" Sergeant Kwan said, looking around at the strange landscape. "That's a trip."

"Check the radios," Weller said. "Snead, Kelton, look for signs. Let's make sure we're in the right place."

"Right time too," John said.

Snead and Kelton found tracks immediately.

"This can't be good," Kelton said, squatting and pointing.

"Form a perimeter," Weller ordered when the marines all drifted over to see.

John and Weller went to Kelton and Snead, careful where they stepped.

"These tracks here and here are human," Kelton said. "There are five or six different people. These here are raptor tracks. A lot of them."

"Juveniles," Snead said. "But if the young'uns are here, the mama and papa won't be far away."

"You find any full-sized tracks?" John asked.

Both marines scouted around, finding nothing.

"Those raptors may not be hostile," John said. "The two women who entered last night had velociraptors with them."

"With them?" Weller asked. "You mean chasing them?"

"No, just with them," John said. "Like pets."

"No way," Snead said.

"Bull," Kelton said.

"It's true," John said. "So don't assume every velociraptor is hostile."

"What!" Kelton said. "So if we run into a velociraptor, we're supposed to check for dog tags?"

"Sir, you can't be serious," Snead whined. "Lieutenant, it's shoot on sight, right?"

"Shoot the big ones," Weller said.

"And the little ones?" Snead asked.

"Make sure no one's got the damn thing on a leash and then kill it," Weller said. "Let's move."

The sun was high, the day hot, the marines grateful for the light uniforms. Kelton and Snead were good trackers, but this trail was well trod and John could have followed it. They moved quickly, overconfident in their weapons. Hunting dinosaurs was illegal, so none of the marines in the patrol had experience bringing down one of the monsters. Deer hunting did not prepare one for tons of rampaging predator. John could have chosen Dinosaur Rangers, but they were trained to manage dinosaurs, not kill them. That attitude had cost lives on a previous expedition, so this time John was betting his life on marines.

A mile down the trail, the marines moved faster, the trail clear, any danger seeming less imminent. There was no doubt they were in the right place and time, but nothing made sense to John. Why were there stable holes in time without orgonic pyramids? Why was there a *T. rex* frozen in time on the moon, and why were velociraptors following Elizabeth Hawthorne around?

"Problem, sir," Snead said from the lead.

Lieutenant Weller put up a fist and the marines spread out, wary, ready for action. John followed Weller to Snead, who squatted, pointing.

"Predator," Weller said. "*T. rex.*"

"Not a *T. rex,*" John said, "but we don't want to meet it."

"They did," Kelton said, pointing at more tracks. "It came down that slope over there. They took off running that way."

Bent over, Snead walked the trail, studying it.

"The *T. rex,* or whatever it is, ripped up the trail, but the women and the velociraptors were walking," Snead said. Snead walked farther, looking for more signs. "Not a lot of blood," Snead said.

"Easy to say if it's not yours," Kelton said.

"If someone got eaten, there would be a lot more blood," Snead said.

"Not necessarily," John said. "They can eat you whole. Two bites max."

"Nice," Snead said.

"Follow the trail," Weller said.

Fear of being eaten slowed the pace, the marines now wary, even edgy. Having seen friends killed and eaten, John was on edge too, his dinosaur rifle ready. Specially designed for twenty-foot predators weighing seven tons, the gun could punch a hole the size of a tin can. Even then, with a diffused nervous system and a tiny brain, a superpredator was virtually impossible to kill quickly.

"This is interesting," Kelton said, again squatting, then getting up and walking south, and up a slight rise to a clump of trees and then back.

John joined Weller, Kelton, and Snead, studying the trail.

"They got chased to here, but then the *rex* stopped and then ran up into those trees," Kelton said. "There's some blood here and up that way. It's probably from the *rex,* since there aren't any human tracks by the blood over there, just *rex* tracks."

"Okay, we follow the original tracks," John said.

"Good call, sir," Snead said. "I wasn't too keen on tracking a wounded *T. rex*."

Fear of the superpredator returning drove the marines, and they picked up their pace, moving faster, covering more ground. John drank regularly, careful to stay hydrated but conserve his water. Watching the sun, John began to worry they would be spending the night. Then Kelton and Snead suddenly split up, the others taking a knee, resting, rifles ready.

"Could a *T. rex* sneak up on someone?" Sergeant Kwan asked. "I heard those mothers cause an earthquake with each step."

"If the ground's soft, they can get pretty close before you know they're there," John said. "They're fast too, at least for a short distance. They can outrun a human."

"That's enough, sir," Sergeant Kwan said. "If we see one, we're screwed. That's all you've got to say! *S-c-r-e-w-e-d*."

"The people we're following ran into something and they're still alive," John said. "That's why there's a trail."

"There's more tracks here, sir," Kelton said.

John joined the lieutenant and the trackers.

"Two more people came from that way and then they all headed out this way," Snead said. "The women and those velociraptors went the same way."

"If they're all together, it'll be a lot easier," Weller said.

"Let's find them before it gets dark," John said.

"Feel that?" Sergeant Kwan asked.

Everyone held still.

"I get nothing," Washburne said. "What about you, Sam?"

The lanky marine looked about nervously. Privates Washburne and Tafua were buddies, keeping close, protecting each other's backs. Where Toby Washburne was a lanky-looking cowboy with a slight drawl, Afa Tafua was a big Samoan who smiled a lot but said little. The Samoan shook his head.

"We're getting nothing, Sarge," Washburne said.

Everyone held their breaths, reaching out with their senses. John felt nothing.

"Let's move," Weller said after a minute.

Now they moved stealthily, alert.

"There it is again," Kwan said.

All stopped, waiting. They were in a grove of the strange-looking palm trees, and they could not see far in any direction. The rustling of leaves was the only sound. Then John felt a vibration.

"I felt it," Washburne and Tafua said simultaneously.

"Yeah," Weller said. "Is this a good defensive position, Mr. Roberts?"

"We don't know if it's hunting us," John said. "It could be passing by. Let's keep moving. We might lose it."

"Let's go," Weller said.

Like a patrol in a hostile urban area, tense marines moved quickly but carefully, guns covering every angle.

"It's still coming," Kwan said.

All the marines agreed. They were right, John knew, based on past experience. He also knew something the others had not picked up on. There was more than one vibration.

"Freeze," Weller said.

Something big was coming through the trees.

"Take cover."

Quickly, the marines hid behind trees, a fallen log, a rock pile, and bushes. The large animal coming through the trees was bipedal, with a huge head and tiny arms. Behind the leader, John glimpsed more of the same predators—tyrannosaurs.

"We're screwed," Kelton whispered from behind a tree.

Weller silenced him with a look, the other marines ready to shoot him. Seemingly unaware of the human presence, or uninterested, the leader led the other predators slowly through the trees, the animals moving in two parallel lines. Walking slowly, heads high, tails low, the predators did not seem to be hunting, just walking.

Smaller than most tyrannosaurs John had seen, they might be female, juveniles, or cousins, like *Albertosaurus.* John estimated the leader weighed three tons. Size mattered in Dinosauria. If you were going to make your living hunting triceratops, you needed to be gigantic yourself. From a human perspective, however, it mattered little if the predator was three tons or six. Then the dinosaurs froze, heads high and tilted—listening. John heard it too. It was a very human sound. The sound of gunfire.

34

Delivery

Don't even get me started on black bag spending. Our government's got more secret missions, projects, weapons, aircraft, spaceships, and bases than any of your TV-addled brains can imagine.

—Cat Bellow, host of *Radio Rebel*

Present Time
Dryden Flight Research Center
Edwards Air Force Base

"Why us?" Mike Watson asked, puzzled by the emergency mission.

Watson, Sarasa Chandra, and Rick Maven sat at a round table with a coffee-ringed top, in a small briefing room. Called in on short notice by Deputy Flight Director Connie West, they were more than a little curious. West had started at NASA as an aeronautical engineer and repeatedly applied for astronaut training. When her propensity for motion sickness doomed her to dirt-side, she discovered her administrative gifts, quickly rising in the NASA ranks. Sick with envy at every launch, West was nevertheless respected by the flight crews for her attention to detail. While she frustrated crews with zealous caution, no ships or crews had been lost under her watch. Her penchant for safety made it all the more puzzling that Watson's moon team was now being asked to fly again on unprecedented short notice.

"It's about the material that you collected on the moon," West said.

"The crazy it-can-pass-through-solids black crap?" Rick Maven asked. "Yes, I remember it well. It was spread all around a crater right next to a dancing *Tyrannosaurus rex*."

West's patience, even with smart-ass astronauts, was another of her gifts. In her mid-forties, West wore her hair long, like a younger woman. Gray hairs in her red hair were noticeable, but she disdained dye, committed to going natural. Married twenty years to an insurance executive, the last of her three boys was in the Naval Academy, and a PROUD NAVY MOM sticker was plastered to the bumper of her Ford. Fit, petite, and looking like the middle-aged cheerleader that she was, she was all business when on duty, and friendly and even flirtatious when not. She was all business now.

"Yes, the material that you collected," West said in her usual executive tone. "We have been instructed to get it off the planet."

"We just brought it to the planet," Chandra Sarasa said. Chandra's black eyes were bright with curiosity, not fear. The moon mission was her first, and to get the draw for a second mission so soon was a dream come true.

"The order came from the executive branch," West said.

"It's radioactive, isn't it?" Maven asked. "Or poisonous."

"You know it's not radioactive," West said. "And no one is going to ingest or inhale whatever it is. It is being delivered in sealed containers."

"So, we're taking it back to the moon?" Chandra asked.

"It's going into the sun," West said.

"It's radioactive," Maven repeated.

"It's not radioactive," West said, keeping her calm demeanor.

"Why us?" Watson repeated.

"Security," West said. "You already know about the special properties of the material."

"But if it's in sealed containers, what difference does it make?" Watson asked.

"A new team would ask too many questions that could not be answered," West said. "You, on the other hand, already know too much. It's either kill you, or use you."

"Well, then, I'm good to go," Maven said.

"We launch in three weeks," West said.

"Three weeks?" Maven said. "That's impossible."

"Launch what?" Watson asked. "There's nothing on a pad."

"Your ship will be going up out of Area Fifty-one," West said.

Chandra, Watson, and Maven exchanged looks.

"They have launch facilities?" Maven asked.

"You'll be going up in an Aurora," West said.

"What's an Aurora?" Chandra asked.

"It's a hypersonic spaceplane that doesn't exist," Maven said. "So our government assures us."

"The program was shut down," Watson said. "The Aurora was mothballed."

"It's being prepped as we speak," West said. "We're bringing in a pilot to take you up. Captain Watson will copilot the flight, and Chandra and Maven will babysit the cargo and then attach it to a Payload Assist Module booster we're sending up out of Vandenberg. Then we send it on its way to the sun, and in three years the problem is solved.

"Chandra and Maven, you will spend most of the next three weeks in EVA training, and learning the mating and diagnostic procedures for the PAM booster. Captain Watson will be in the Aurora simulator, getting a refresher course."

"Captain, you've flown an Aurora?" Maven asked.

"All simulated," Watson said.

"That's why we're bringing in an experienced pilot," West said. "She's taken an Aurora to orbit six times."

"Who is the pilot?" Chandra asked.

"Rosa Perez-Roberts," West said.

35

Stranger and Stranger

SENATOR MALLORY: *Are you asking this committee to believe that connections—or tunnels, if you will—allowed you and others to travel to the past and future and even to another celestial body—the moon?*

NICK PAULSON: *Yes, sir, that is correct.*

—Closed-door testimony before the Senate Armed Services Committee

Unknown Time
Unknown Place

The exotic perfume of the strange land was Elizabeth's first sensation.

"It smells wonderful," Elizabeth said.

"Like a candle store," Jeanette said.

Velociraptors spread out, disappearing into the tall golden grass. Sally sneezed and then set about sniffing the ground, circling. Elizabeth took another deep lungful, and then wrapped her arms around her chest.

"It's cool," Elizabeth said.

"A lot cooler than where we were," Jeanette agreed. "We're wet from sweat too."

Elizabeth found herself breathing deeply, as if she had been running.

"Not a lot of oxygen," Jeanette said. "I feel kind of light-headed."

"I feel funny too," Elizabeth said. She bounced on her toes and then jumped higher and higher. "The gravity's not right," Elizabeth said. "I feel like Supergirl."

"The pack isn't as heavy either," Jeanette said.

Jeanette copied the moves, jumping higher than Elizabeth. Watching Jeanette bounce with her blouse tied up under her breasts, Elizabeth was a bit jealous and glad that Nick was not there to watch.

"Where are we?" Jeanette asked, landing on her toes to absorb the shock.

"Maybe we should go back?" Elizabeth suggested.

"We'll be okay," Jeanette said, breathing hard. "We've got to find Do and the boys."

Looking up, Elizabeth saw the blue sky had a pinkish tinge. A thin overcast smeared across the sky, filtering the sun. Oddly, the sun looked smaller, like the size of a baseball. Using the sun's position to orient, Elizabeth could see a mountain range to the east, dominated by one gigantic peak twice the height of the peaks on either side. Golden-tipped grasses ran north to the horizon, a hill topped with the puffy-headed dandelion trees stood to the west, and a little south of it was a larger hill where the golden-tipped grass was patchy, broken by reddish earth and gray rocks. Behind them was a rocky hill, looking like a pile of rubble. Caves pockmarked the hill, the one they emerged from dark. Looking closely, Elizabeth could see shapes moving on the other side, but the creatures made no move to follow them through.

"Do!" Jeanette called over and over, gasping for breath between calls.

"Jeanette, maybe we should look around before we make a lot of noise," Elizabeth said.

"There's nothing here," Jeanette said. "I can see a mile in all directions, except for that way," pointing at the nearest hill.

As if on cue, a large animal lumbered over the nearest hill. Bulky like an elephant, with four stumpy legs, the creature had the long neck of a giraffe that ended in a horse-shaped head. Two large eyes on short fat stalks took up the top third of the head, the snout ending in long buckteeth that overlapped fleshy lips. With pinkish skin, the animal looked flushed but stood calmly, looking down at the humans, its eyes moving back and forth on its stalks as if the animal was trying to get an angle on the humans that made optical sense. To her left, Elizabeth saw Jeanette raise her rifle.

"Don't shoot," Elizabeth said. "Not yet."

"Do, Re, Me, Fa, So, La, Ti," Jeanette sang.

Grasses rustled, velociraptors emerging then spreading out, heads high, looking over the grass at the creature on the hill.

"Where's Do?" Jeanette wondered out loud.

Its eyestalks finally at rest, the creature continued to study the humans and their animals. After another minute, the eyestalks shifted, then the head turned, the animal looking at the puffy trees.

"Elizabeth," Jeanette said. "The trees are leaving."

Jeanette was right. What they had thought were trees were moving slowly over the hill where they had stood, and down the other side. The creature turned, revealing a stumpy pink tail, following the trees in a slow-motion chase. A little while later, the trees and the creature were gone over the hill.

"That's just too creepy," Jeanette said.

"Let's climb the big hill and see if we can find any sign of Nick and Carson," Elizabeth said.

"And Do," Jeanette added.

The grass varied in height but most stood waist- to chest-high, the green stalks resilient, bending when pushed aside and then springing back. The well-mannered grasses were evenly spaced and easy to walk through. Even stepping on the stalks bent them, but did not break them. The golden tops were cone-shaped clusters of grains covered in yellow down. Fine yellow dust fell from the clusters when the grass was disturbed.

"Do," Jeanette called as they walked.

Elizabeth did not bother chiding Jeanette. She was genuinely concerned for Do, although Elizabeth noticed Jeanette did not call her boyfriend's name, just Do's. At the base of the hill, they paused, catching their breath. Walking was easy, but still Elizabeth was breathing like she had been running. Feeling nauseated, her head aching, Elizabeth bent, putting her hands on her knees. Jeanette leaned back, hands on her hips, eyes closed. Elizabeth had skied Aspen once, getting altitude sickness on the first day. This felt like that day, only it came on more quickly and with less exertion.

"If we make the top of this hill, that's about as far as I can go," Elizabeth said.

"Yeah," Jeanette said. "The boys wouldn't stay here if there was a way out. Those aliens suckered us into coming here."

Too nauseated to argue, Elizabeth climbed the hill, one slow step after another. Head pounding, Elizabeth focused on the climb, placing each foot carefully. Jeanette gave up calling for Do, walking with her hands on her hips. Reaching the top they were sweating, breathing hard, and pressing their temples to stop the throbbing.

"I'm going to puke," Jeanette said, looking for a good spot.

The hilltop was bare, the crown made up of red earth broken by protruding gray rocks. Sitting on a boulder-sized rock, Elizabeth rested, trying to ignore the headache. Sally was just as winded, lying down next to the boulder, panting and drooling. The velociraptors showed the least effect, spreading out across the crown, forming a picket line.

"Did you train them to do that?" Elizabeth asked.

"I trained them to chase a rubber mouse on a string," Jeanette said. "They started doing this kind of stuff right after they hatched."

"They think you're their mother," Elizabeth said.

"I guess I am," Jeanette said.

The headache subsiding a bit, Elizabeth stood, scanning the landscape. The giraffe-necked creature had caught one of the trees and had it on the ground, one foot on its trunk, ripping off the yellow fronds making up its puffy-looking top. Both creatures were silent, one eating, the other apparently dying. In the distance, Elizabeth saw clumps of puff trees here and there, and miles of the golden grasses. In the far distance, Elizabeth thought she could see patches of purple shapes resembling bushes or trees, but it would be a long walk to be sure. There were no animal trails in any direction, but the springy grass would hide animal travel.

"There's nothing here," Elizabeth said. "I wouldn't even know which way to walk."

"That way, maybe," Jeanette said, coming to stand next to her. "There's a lake or something."

Following Jeanette's point to the north, Elizabeth found the silver smudge, outlined with more of the yellow puff tree creatures.

"I don't know if I could walk that far," Elizabeth said, still breathing deeply.

"Do!" Jeanette screeched.

Do came running up the hill, something squirming in his jaws. Jeanette embraced the predator, stroking its head.

"Where have you been?" she said. "I was worried."

Taut skin and beaks were not made for expression, but Do bounced excitedly, then spit his bundle at Jeanette's feet. The other velociraptors crowded around, interested in the find. Pushing through the throng, Sally sniffed the bundle. The little brown fur ball bled pinkish blood from lacerations in its side. Slowly, it uncurled, revealing a head and tail. The head was feline, the tail long, whiplike, and ending in a bony knob. Long legs unfolded, with five-toed and -clawed feet. Orange stripes created flamelike shapes running from around the eyes back along its head. Black lips opened to reveal double rows of pointed teeth. The creature whimpered, clearly suffering. Large green eyes open wide, it stared in terror at the creatures surrounding it.

"It's a kitten," Jeanette said.

"That's no cat!" Elizabeth said.

"I mean it's a baby," Jeanette said.

"Quick, get rid of it," Elizabeth said.

"What?" Jeanette said, eyes flashing. "Do hurt it. We can't just dump it."

"We've got to," Elizabeth said. "That's something's baby."

Elizabeth stood, looking back where Do had come up the hill. Elizabeth saw nothing but grasses in all directions. A light breeze made gentle ripples. Then Elizabeth froze, seeing a ripple of grass moving against the ripples produced by the breeze. The contrary ripple moved slowly, inexorably toward the hill.

"Get your gun," Elizabeth said.

Alerted by Elizabeth's tone, velociraptors trotted to the edge, sensing the danger. Do in the middle, the velociraptors stood frozen, eyes on the waving grasses. Jeanette joined them, the kitten nestled in the crook of her arm.

"Jeanette, you're getting blood on your clothes," Elizabeth said.

"It's hurt," Jeanette said.

"There," Elizabeth said, pointing. "See the way that grass moves."

"That may be nothing," Jeanette said, but watched the anomalous movement approach the hill.

Near the base of the rise where the grass began to thin, the ripple stopped, the grass resuming normal movement.

"What do you think?" Jeanette asked, eyes on the spot.

Perfectly still, the velociraptors watched expectantly. Sally squeezed between Jeanette and Elizabeth, giving a soft *woof.*

"I think you should shoot," Elizabeth said.

"Seriously?" Jeanette asked. "Shoot the grass?"

"Yes," Elizabeth said.

Shrugging, Jeanette gently set the kitten on the ground, then lifted her rifle, aimed, and fired. At the report, dozens of golden shapes erupted from the grasses a mile in all directions, rising into the air. Many trailed long tails, forked at the end, and some were surprisingly large—big enough to lift a golden retriever, or maybe a person. Most rose on batlike wings, but others had small bodics and long bird wings. Shocked, the women watched the creatures climb and circle. They were still looking up when the attack came from below.

36

Unfrozen

I am tired of all this sort of thing called science here. . . . We have spent millions in that sort of thing in the last few years, and it is time it should be stopped.

—Simon Cameron, U.S. Senator, on the Smithsonian Institution, 1861

Present Time
Lake County, Florida

Emmett Puglisi sat on the edge of his desk, feet on his desk chair, running his fingers through his thinning hair and listening to his mother-in-law, Grandma Chen, scold him.

"None of her sisters' husbands run around the world like you do. I thought you quit that dinosaur-hunting job. Why aren't you here with your wife and children?"

"I told you, Grandma, I'm not looking for dinosaurs," Emmett explained for the third time. "All I do is mathematical modeling."

"So they don't have chalkboards in Hawaii?" Grandma Chen asked.

Emmett could picture his mother-in-law, sitting on the stool in Emmett and Carrollee's kitchen, wearing a tropical shirt over shorts, her legs a deep Hawaiian tan, her gray hair in a tight bun, her mouth just as tight, her brow knitted, part of a permanent disapproving scowl. Grandma Chen was half Chinese and 100 percent committed to meddling in the lives of her children. All five of the Chen children were successful by any standards—doctors, lawyers, scientists—but that did not stop her from driving them and their spouses even further, and from shaping the futures of her nine grandchildren.

"I don't use a chalkboard, I use a computer," Emmett said, regretting it immediately.

"So, they don't have computers in Hawaii? You got one in your office. I know, I saw it."

"It takes a special computer," Emmett explained, wanting to tell her to stay out of his office. "Let me speak to Carrollee," Emmett said.

"When you coming home?" Grandma Chen demanded.

"Soon," Emmett said. "Let me talk to Carrollee."

Grandma Chen started to say something, but Carrollee interrupted, arguing briefly with her mother and then wresting the phone away.

"Grandma sends her best," Carrollee said.

"Thank God you got the phone," Emmett said.

Now Emmett pictured his pretty wife sitting on the same stool. Carrollee Puglisi was a short, pretty woman with a peculiar sense of style. Carrollee always coordinated what she wore, from shoes to clothes to hair bows and sunglasses. If she wore white, everything she wore was white. If she decided to wear tropical print clothes, her shirt and pants would have flowers, her shoes would complement, as would her hat, and there would be a fresh flower in her hair. Carrollee had a collection of watches in various colors and styles, so that even her watch would match. While she had a lot of clothes—two closets full—her taste was stylish, not expensive, and Emmett loved her for it, not in spite of it. Carrollee's tastes also dictated what she purchased for their children, and they wore the outfits enthusiastically when younger, then stoically as they grew. Now in middle school, Emma was developing a style of her own, often clashing with Carrollee. Lee resisted the color coordination by mixing and not matching the clothes his mother purchased for him.

"Grandma loves you," Carrollee said.

"Yeah, she loves the hell out of me," Emmett said.

Carrollee laughed. Grandma Chen was well meaning but relentless. "How are things going?" Carrollee asked.

Carrollee knew Emmett was working for the Office of Security Science again. Both of them had worked for Nick Paulson in the past, and both had gone into the field, traveling to the past, and to the moon on one mission. Carrollee had a scar on her chest, where a Mayan priest had started to cut out her living heart, stopped by Emmett's and John Roberts's timely arrival. Because of that shared history, Carrollee also knew that Emmett had to be careful about what he shared on a public phone.

"Things are complicated," Emmett said. "It would be easier if Nick were around to help."

"Nick's gone?" Carrollee asked, puzzled. Carrollee knew Nick had personally asked Emmett to come back and help with whatever problem he was having.

"Yeah, disappeared on me," Emmett said.

Carrollee paused, frustrated with Emmett's roundabout talk. "Like we did before?" Carrollee asked.

"Exactly."

"I see," Carrollee said. "You're not going after him, are you? You promised."

"John's gone to get him, but I haven't heard from him since," Emmett said. "Elizabeth went too."

"Elizabeth Hawthorne?" Carrollee asked. "How did she get mixed up in this?"

"Can't say," Emmett said. "You know how she is. Just like before, she kind of took things into her own hands."

Carrollee was silent, and Emmett knew she was worrying through the implications of what he had told her. The planet had been devastated once by time disruption, and she and Emmett had helped avert an even bigger catastrophe.

"I have a model that may explain it," Emmett said. "I think I found the anchor for the event. It's sixty-five million years in the making."

It took Carrollee a few seconds to grasp what Emmett was saying. "That strikes me as odd," Carrollee said.

"Exactly," Emmett said.

"Come home," Carrollee said.

"Can't. I'm working on something that might help."

"I'll come to you," Carrollee said.

"Make it a family reunion on the mainland," Emmett said.

"That bad?" Carrollee asked.

"Potentially," Emmett said. "Better safe than sorry." A buzzer went off behind Emmett. "Just a minute," Emmett said to Carrollee, and put the receiver down.

Emmett called the video feed from the moon and fed it to the big monitor. Shocked, he ran the recording back and then watched it happen from the beginning. The recording began with the writhing juvenile tyrannosaur, in its endless struggle. After a few seconds, the tyrannosaur began moving faster and faster, jerking violently from side to side, and then suddenly it stumbled across the moon's surface. Now free from the quasi-time that trapped it, it felt the effects of vacuum. While the dinosaur was staggering a few steps toward the camera, its eyes bulged and its chest heaved, swelling, but without air pressure to fill the lungs, the chest eventually collapsed, a spray of blood erupting from the open jaws, droplets spattering the camera. Next, one eye exploded, then the other, then the dinosaur collapsed, twitching, kicking up moon dust. Then it died. Emmett hurried back to his desk and the phone.

"Changed my mind," Emmett said. "Don't fly."

There was a long silence.

"Is it too late?" Carrollee asked finally.

"It's too close to call," Emmett said. "You're probably fine. I'm sure you're fine. Hawaii is a long way from Florida."

"I see," Carrollee said.

"I love you," Emmett said.

"I love you too," Carrollee said.

"Tell Emma and Lee I love them," Emmett said.

"I will," Carrollee said. "What about Grandma Chen?"

"I love you," Emmett said.

37

Safari

In the eighteenth and nineteenth centuries, Western explorers wandered the globe and brought back fantastic tales of people living off the land, like animals. . . . At first, those people were considered ignorant savages . . . less than human. But philosophers such as Jean-Jacques Rousseau, great thinkers who had not actually ever seen one of these "primitive people," took the opposite view. The "savages," they contended, were regular humans with souls, but they were more innocent, more natural, more what nature intended than citizens of the modern world.

—Meredith F. Small, Cornell University

Sixty-five Million Years Ago
Unknown Place

Walking through a primeval forest, wearing sunglasses, and dressed all in black, Reverend looked like Johnny Cash on safari. Despite wearing a suit in brutally hot weather, the reverend kept up even at the Inhumans' brisk pace, and did it without sweating. Moving easily, Reverend walked next to Nick, Carson Wills following, keeping close to Nick and the reverend and as far from the Inhumans as possible.

"I admit you surprised me," Nick said. "I thought you would put more pressure on people to stay."

"Conversion by the sword never worked," Reverend said. "Come freely to God, or do not come at all. Give joyfully, or keep your grudging gifts. Serve with all your heart, or serve yourself alone."

"That sounds like a sermon," Nick said.

"I preached it last month," Reverend said, chuckling.

Nick laughed. Despite their vast differences, Nick liked Reverend. His tunnel vision was going to kill half his congregation, but the man was sincere in believing he was saving the ones he had talked into staying behind, and unlike other messianic leaders, Reverend was ready to make the same bet with his own life.

"Why did you come with me?" Nick asked. "You could have stayed at the church with your wives."

"Because I am on a mission for God," Reverend said. "Those Inhumans did not come for you; they came for me. They could not know you were with us, so they must have been coming to find me. I think God has been working on their hearts, opening them to his word. I will preach that word."

"But you don't speak their language," Nick pointed out.

"On the day of Pentecost, the disciples of Christ were given the gift of tongues. God will make it possible for me to preach the good news."

"If the Inhumans came for you, why did they bring that patch?"

Reverend shrugged. "To entice me? It does not matter. All will be revealed."

"Anybody notice anything strange?" Carson asked suddenly.

Nick looked back, and then around. Something was different, but he could not put his finger on it.

"There aren't as many of them as there used to be," Carson said.

Nick realized Carson was right. At least half their troop was gone. Not knowing their customs, Nick was unsure if the behavior was unusual.

The strange safari kept up its quick pace for over two hours, Nick finding himself on a narrow trail leading through a dense copse. Once through, they came to a large meadow, a village three hundred yards from the tree line, protected by sharpened poles. Older children ran from the village, staring, pointing, following along, their large eyes blinking rapidly as if a sign of excitement. As they passed through the poles, smaller children and women with babies crowded close. The women pointed at Reverend, huddling and whispering sounds like someone playing a child's xylophone.

Fascinated, Nick studied their clothes—minimal—their construction, the arrangement of the huts, the large structure they were being led to, and their tools and weapons, some of which were made out of the black orgonic-collecting material. Curiosity overcoming him, Nick stopped, Reverend stopping next to him, Carson right behind. The crowd hushed, the xylophone sound fading away. Now Nick stepped toward a woman with an orgonic blade in her hand. Warriors rushed Nick, brandishing spears, one of which had an orgonic spearhead.

Reverend pulled Nick back. "Dr. Paulson, that is not a good idea," Reverend said.

"What the hell were you thinking?" Carson asked.

"Do you see that black knife she is holding?" Nick said. "That material came from the future."

"Excuse me, but didn't we just leave a wreck of a city full of modern crap?" Carson asked.

"Yes, but that substance came from a classified project developed after the Time Quilt that sent Portland to this time period. It shouldn't be here."

"Who cares?" Carson asked. "Let's get Jeanette and get out of here."

"What kind of project?" Reverend asked.

Still surrounded by warriors, the Inhumans let them talk, seemingly interested.

"It's classified," Nick said.

"Classified," Reverend repeated. "How many of our leaders have used that to cover a multitude of sins."

"All I can say is that that material lined the inside of a special structure," Nick said. "That structure was destroyed."

"So how did it get here?" Reverend asked.

"Jeanette, remember," Carson said. "We're here to find Jeanette."

The Inhuman with the pouch full of pebbles came close, listening.

Nick then pointed at the knife on his belt. "Where did you get that?" Nick asked.

The large eyes stared at Nick, and then followed his point to the knife. Looking back at Nick for a second, the Inhuman then took the knife from his belt and handed it to Nick. Warriors stiffened, pointing their spears at Nick. Nick felt the flat of the black blade. It was firmer than the original material, and holding up the knife, Nick pointed it in all directions, saying "Where? Where? Where?" Finishing, he carefully handed the knife back.

"It looked like you were blessing the knife," Reverend said.

"It's the best I could do," Nick said.

"Did you forget about the asteroid?" Carson asked, pointing up.

Even in the bright sunlight, the onrushing asteroid could be clearly seen. The Inhuman stared at Nick, his expressionless face revealing nothing. Then he said something to the other Inhumans, and motioned Nick and the others to follow. Turning away from the building they were approaching, the Inhuman led them between two huts, to a path leading up a hill. Well worn, the path was easy to walk, and they climbed quickly, until they were breathing hard.

"Why are we doing this?" Carson complained, but kept close.

At the top they found a depression filled with debris. Large and small stones lay everywhere, grass growing from cracks in the rocks. They walked among waist-high stones.

"These were quarried," Reverend said, touching the grooved surface of a stone. "It's too rough for power equipment. Someone cut this with hand tools."

"Mayans," Nick said. "It's possible these came from a Mayan pyramid."

"Then how did they get here?" Reverend asked. "Like we did?"

"Not exactly," Nick said.

Walking farther, Nick came to circular depression twenty feet across filled with sandy material. Nick dragged a foot, seeing the gray sand turn dark. Scooping up a handful, Nick sifted it through his fingers, finding small chips of the orgonic material.

"What happened?" Reverend asked.

"The Time Quilt that brought you here was caused by a convergence of time waves created by nuclear testing. That convergence not only threw you into the past, but it also dragged pieces of the Cretaceous period into the present. After that catastrophe, we built a mathematical model to simulate and track the time waves, and found they were dissipating. With a freeze on nuclear testing, our predictions were that time and space would return to stability. Then, a decade after the catastrophe, a group of terrorists discovered a way to manipulate time waves using orgonic collectors. It's complicated, but these black fragments are part of what's left of a kind of capacitor that stored the energy. We used a nuclear weapon to destroy the structures used to manipulate time. It looks like some of it blew out here and showered their village. Now I'm convinced that the Time Quilt did more damage to time and space than we realized. It seems to have left cracks and weak spots that have been ripped open by the impact of that asteroid."

"But the asteroid hasn't hit yet," Carson said.

"When it hits, it will condense matter, creating a transient black hole. That dark matter sends out time ripples through time, both forward and back."

"My explanation is so much simpler," Reverend said. "God wrought all this."

"And this?" Nick said, holding up a chunk of orgonic material the size of his thumbnail.

"If that is the tool God used to accomplish his purpose, that does not make God any less the workman," Reverend said.

"I just love all this science crapology, but let's get Jeanette and get the hell out of here," Carson said.

"Carson's right," Nick said. "We don't have much time."

Sensing they were finished, the Inhuman led them back down the hill into the village. Even more villagers had gathered, and again Reverend took most of the attention. Faces expressionless, the Inhumans' body language screamed fear and loathing of Reverend.

Six Inhumans waited shoulder to shoulder at the entrance of a large hut built up against the side of the hill. All of them stared malevolently at the reverend. Even Carson noticed.

"Reverend, you're as popular as the plague around here," Carson said.

"For every one of my flock they took, we took ten of theirs," Reverend said.

"Were they ever friendly?" Nick asked.

"Perhaps," Reverend said, "but I never knew them then. The war was going on before I saw my first Inhuman, and that one was being roasted on a spit."

"You ate one?" Carson asked. "That's cannibalism."

"They're animals," Reverend said, "and no, I never ate one. They are unclean."

"They build villages," Nick said.

"We didn't know that," Reverend said, looking past the people at the structures and the tame dinosaurs. "We saw only demons throwing spears. Look at them. You can see why humans feared them."

"So you ate them?" Carson asked again, incredulous.

"They ate our people too," Reverend said. "I've held services when all there was to bury were gnawed bones."

"They may see us as animals too," Nick said.

"But we're not," Reverend said. "We were created in God's image by God for this world, the world created by God."

"They may believe the same thing," Nick said.

"Then they are deluded," Reverend said.

"Then why are you here?" Nick asked.

Reverend frowned, momentarily lost about what to say. Then he smiled, took off his sunglasses, and said, "I don't know why God brought me here, but he will give me a sign and then I will know."

The musical background that was their speech was rising. Nick realized the crowd was agitated, surging. A warrior jabbed at Reverend, who held his ground, not flinching. Seemingly unperturbed, Reverend put his sunglasses back on. Another large-eyed creature jumped forward, poking Reverend with his spear, this time stinging Reverend in the side, but not hard enough to pierce. Again, Reverend held his ground, acting as if nothing had happened. As that warrior danced backwards, another stepped forward and lunged with his spear. Suddenly, Carson grabbed the spear, yanking it forward and sideways past Reverend, the warrior stumbling. Carson ripped it from the creature's grip and then broke the spear over his knee, throwing the pieces to the side.

"Knock it off!" Carson yelled. "Is everyone crazy but me? Where the hell is Jeanette?"

"Easy, Carson," Nick said, afraid the anxiety had pushed Carson over the edge.

The musical speech died, the Inhumans now intent on Carson.

"Why did I do that?" Carson said, stricken. "Crap. Do you think that was bad?"

The Inhuman whose spear was broken got up slowly, big eyes on Carson, and then backed into the crowd. Surrounded by others, he was the center of attention, other warriors crowding around. Now the Inhumans standing in front of the building conferred, alternating between huddled conversation and glances at the humans. Finally, they parted, revealing a door covered with a flap, and motioned the humans inside.

"Is that good or bad?" Carson asked.

"We're in God's hands," Reverend said.

"I don't do the church thing, Reverend. Is that good or bad?" Carson asked.

"You can wait here," Nick said, moving to the opening with Reverend right behind.

"Forget that," Carson said, keeping close.

Inside, Nick found himself facing a large opening that looked out onto a bizarre landscape of waving, golden grasses and strange trees.

"It's another conjunction," Nick said.

Reverend took off his sunglasses, stepping close to the opening. "It's beautiful," Reverend said.

"Where is that?" Carson asked. "Is that this time or is it our time?"

"It's not like anything in our time," Nick said. "It could be another time, but I've never seen anything like those trees in the fossil record. It could be another dimension."

Now one of the Inhumans stepped forward and held up the Dinosaur Wrangler patch. Then he held out his left hand flat, and then used two of his three-clawed fingers to do a walking motion toward the opening.

"No, no, no," Carson moaned. "Tell me she didn't."

"Afraid so," Nick said. "Wherever and whenever that is, that's where we need to go next."

38

Attack

The fact is that velociraptor attack is the third leading cause of death among the Community. Only disease and Inhumans kill more of my people.

—Reverend to Nick Paulson

Unknown Time
Unknown Place

Do attacked before Elizabeth and Jeanette sensed the danger. Me, Fa, and Ti launched as well, angling left and right. Re, So, and La held their ground, heads low, legs bunched. Nearly as slow as the human women, Sally snapped her jaws shut in surprise at the response of the velociraptors.

Leaping out of the golden-topped grasses was a feline creature built like an emaciated lion, but with long bony legs that lifted it above the grasses. Covered with brown fur and marked with yellowish flame-shaped coloration around the neck, the creature bounded up the hill, mouth open in a silent roar, revealing a double row of needle teeth.

Do leapt, meeting the attacking creature in midair, feetfirst, toe claws extended. As quick as Do, the feline creature twisted, Do striking its shoulder and bouncing off. The creature swiped at Do with an oversized clawed paw, missing, but then switched its tail, clubbing Do with the large knob on the tip.

Fa and Ti struck next, toe claws drawing blood, raking the sides of the creature. Large square jaws snapping left and then right, the creature spun, keeping the attacking velociraptors in sight. Now Re, So, and La joined the melee, jumping high and long, striking the creature's haunches. Attacked from all sides, the creature spun, snapping jaws, swiping at the velociraptors with wide paws, and whipping its tail club. Smart and quick, Jeanette's chicks darted in and out, gashing and nipping, and then jumping out of range. The velociraptors were quick, but so was the creature, and chicks were clubbed and slashed. Despite their injuries, the chicks kept attacking. Suddenly, the creature bunched, then leapt high, disappearing into the grass, pink gashes in its brown fur.

Jeanette and Elizabeth had their rifles at their shoulders, but had no shot with the velociraptors jumping and bouncing in and out, attacking and then chasing the creature away. Tenacious, the velociraptors followed the creature into the grass.

"Do, Re, Me, Fa, So, La, Ti," Jeanette sang out.

The velociraptors did not return.

"Put the kitten down," Elizabeth said.

"My velociraptors might kill it," Jeanette said.

"That thing was after the kitten," Elizabeth said. "It could come back."

"I'll put it over there," Jeanette said. She walked to a large boulder with a crevice at its base and put the kitten in the crevice. "You'll be safe here," Jeanette said.

"Let's go," Elizabeth said. "The velociraptors can catch up."

Jeanette called for them again, but then reluctantly followed Elizabeth down the hill, pausing for one look back for her chicks.

"Elizabeth, you better look at this," Jeanette said, lingering at the top of the hill.

Reluctantly, Elizabeth walked back up the hill.

"Ripples," Jeanette said, pointing.

A half dozen ripples in the sea of golden grass were converging on the hill where they stood. Looking closer, Jeanette realized there were even more smaller ripples moving away from the larger ripples.

"It's like an ocean," Elizabeth said. "The grass is full of animals."

"We walked through it," Jeanette said.

"We still have to get back," Elizabeth said.

Turning to look for their exit, Elizabeth had just enough time to scream.

"Jeanette!"

Elizabeth shoved Jeanette aside, the pair tripping over each other and falling. With a snarl, Sally charged. The golden retriever was bowled over but managed to sink her teeth into the shoulder of the creature, three times her weight. Twisting violently, Sally broke free and then lunged. The feline raked Sally's right side and then tore off her left ear. Sally squealed but continued the fight.

Jeanette was up, rifle ready, trying to shoot the creature. "I can't get a shot!" Jeanette shouted.

Velociraptors raced over the hill, joining the fight. Ti, Fa, and Me slashed at the creature that was killing Sally, ripping its haunches, and clamped powerful jaws on bony legs. Pink blood flowed, and then like the other feline, it broke free and bounded down the hill, leaving bloody footsteps. This time the velociraptors did not give chase. Jeanette shot the creature just as it reached the beginning of the tall grass at the bottom. It collapsed, violently flopping and twisting. Then, whimpering, it crawled deeper into the grass. Just before it disappeared, Jeanette shot it again.

Going to Sally, Jeanette squatted next to her dog. Sally's left ear was gone, along with most of the flesh from that side of Sally's head. Blood flowed from deep gashes in her side, and a chunk of flesh had been torn from her shoulder. Ti, Fa, and Me alternated between licking Sally's wounds and their own. Sally seemed impervious to their attentions but whimpered when Jeanette stroked her head.

"Good dog," Jeanette said, voice quivering. "Good dog."

Tears running, Jeanette shrugged off her pack, dumping the contents and finding the first aid kit. Soaking a cotton swab with alcohol, she dabbed a bleeding wound. Sally whined. Jeanette hesitated, unsure whether to keep treating the dog.

Elizabeth looked at the spreading pool of blood and knew there was no hope. "Jeanette, there's nothing we can do for her," Elizabeth said.

Still holding the cotton ball, Jeanette was frozen with indecision. Sally's breathing quickened, and she whined constantly now. Ti, Fa, and Me stopped the attentions, hovering but not touching the suffering dog.

"Will you do it?" Jeanette asked.

"Yes," Elizabeth said, knowing it would be hard.

Gently, Jeanette stroked Sally's head one more time, then bent and kissed her forehead. Then she stood, and began walking away. "Ti, Fa, Me, come," Jeanette said.

Ti and Fa came at once, but Me hesitated, giving Sally one last lick. Then Me trotted after Jeanette.

Quickly, so she wouldn't have to think about it, Elizabeth shot Sally in the head, her own eyes tearing. As Elizabeth turned away, Ti, Fa, and Me trotted back to Sally, sniffing and nudging her. Elizabeth froze, worried the velociraptors would blame her for Sally's death. After another couple of nudges, the velociraptors trotted back to where Jeanette sat, crying.

"She saved my life," Jeanette said.

Elizabeth sat close, unsure of what to say.

"You saved me too," Jeanette said, pulling Elizabeth close, hugging her.

Re, So, and Do came over the hill, nursing wounds, Do collapsing every few yards, and then resuming the climb. Re and So stayed with Do, resting when he rested, licking their own wounds. Jeanette jumped up and ran for the first aid kit and then hurried to Do. Carefully, Jeanette cleaned Do's wounds, the velociraptor's breaths quick and shallow.

The rest of the velociraptors formed a circle around Jeanette and Do, lying down and licking their wounds. Elizabeth walked from velociraptor to velociraptor, checking the severity of their wounds. Ti was hurt the worst, but Elizabeth dared not touch the wound, since the velociraptor watched her intently when she leaned in to get a better look. Elizabeth read warning in Ti's green eyes. There was blood on Ti's snout, and the chick licked it, still looking at her.

Elizabeth took off her pack and dug out dog food and water, feeding and watering each of the velociraptors. They ate greedily. Elizabeth then put a pile of food in front of Do, but he did not eat.

"He's hurt bad," Jeanette said.

Do was bleeding in several places, but the worst wound was on his belly. Elizabeth could see intestines bulging from the gash.

"I don't know that we can help him," Elizabeth said.

"I can't lose another one," Jeanette said, lifting Do's head and scooting underneath, so his head rested in her lap.

Elizabeth had never been comfortable with the velociraptors. To her, the little horrors were vicious killers, different from the tyrannosaurs only in size, and in some ways worse. Velociraptors were intelligent, stealthy hunters, who coordinated their killing. Because Jeanette and Sally had been there since their birth, they accepted them as part of the pack, but Elizabeth was a latecomer. Elizabeth never felt more than tolerated, and if she put Do down, the others might not respond the same way as they did to Sally's death.

Looking down the hill, Elizabeth saw the dead feline's body disappear into the grass. Ripples in the grass showed converging scavengers, followed by hissing and snapping. Occasionally Elizabeth glimpsed fur, alligator tails, and horns. Checking the other direction, Elizabeth saw nothing, but was certain one or more of the felines was waiting in the grass.

"We've got to get away from the kitten," Elizabeth said.

"I can't leave him," Jeanette said.

"Carry him," Elizabeth said, taking charge.

Elizabeth sorted through the remains of Jeanette's pack, taking food, ammunition, and a flashlight, then offered more water to the velociraptors. Then Elizabeth cut holes in the bottom of the pack and slit the sides. She and Jeanette gently slipped Do into the pack, his legs dangling. The chick emitted a high-pitched moan. Carefully, Elizabeth lifted the pack with Do in it, freezing when Do made a soft *awk* sound and the other velociraptors oriented toward Elizabeth, heads down.

"Good chicks," Elizabeth said, helping Jeanette on with the pack. "Good Do."

Do *awk*ed again, but then rested his head on Jeanette's shoulder. Now on her back, Jeanette realized how big the chicks had gotten.

"Can you carry him?" Elizabeth asked.

"I'll do it," Jeanette said, wiping away a tear and leaving a smear of Do's blood under her eye.

Handing Jeanette her rifle, Elizabeth scouted down both sides of the hill, seeing nothing, and knowing that seeing nothing meant nothing.

"Let's move quickly," Elizabeth said.

"We should bury Sally," Jeanette said halfheartedly.

"Think about Do," Elizabeth said.

They started down the hill, the exit from this world nearly a mile through a grass sea that hid the feline predators and a myriad of unknown creatures. Reaching the bottom of the rocky hill, they were about to plunge into the grass when Jeanette reached out, grabbing Elizabeth's arm.

"Someone's coming," Jeanette said.

In the distance, Elizabeth saw three figures, and she could swear one of them was wearing a suit.

39

Pickup

Just what does it require to get into Low Earth Orbit? . . . First, you need something that can push, pull, drag, or carry a given mass and volume about 150 kilometers up with a net velocity of at least 7,814 m/s tangent to the curve of the Earth. The height is needed to get out of most of the drag in the air, which is noticeable at the needed speeds to stay in orbit. The velocity is what is needed to stay in orbit at that altitude.

—James V. H. Hill, Ph.D.

Present Time
Groom Lake, Nevada

Mike Watson, Sarasa Chandra, and Rick Maven sat around a table with Aurora pilot Rosa Perez-Roberts. Dr. Emmett Puglisi participated from Florida, his image projected on a wall screen in one of Area 51's conference rooms. Like much of Area 51, the facilities and furnishings were spartan, the lion's share of resources going to black bag projects like the SR-91 Aurora, a hypersonic aircraft capable of flying a payload into orbit, returning to Earth, and landing on a normal runway. There were other aircraft on-site, but Mike Watson and his flight crew were kept well away from those hangars. Even Rosa Perez-Roberts, who had flown the Aurora to orbit several times, was kept on a short leash.

"So, any idea what's in those other hangars?" Maven asked Rosa Perez-Roberts one day after finishing simulator training.

Rick Maven was single, and fancied himself a ladies' man. At five-foot-ten, with a medium build, cropped brown hair, and a face that projected boyish innocence, he was generally liked by women. Perez-Roberts was married, however, and married in the way that mattered. Perez-Roberts's husband worked for the OSS, doing something with dinosaurs, but Perez-Roberts was a bit vague about his exact job.

"It's been a few years, but I know what used to be in that hangar over there," Perez-Roberts said.

Rosa Perez-Roberts was taller than average, maybe five feet five, with short brown hair and brown eyes. Nearing forty, she was entering middle-age an attractive woman who kept herself fit. Her Hispanic heritage showed in her light brown skin and brown eyes so dark, they could be black. Recalled from work as a commercial pilot, Perez-Roberts was very professional, without being overly formal. She was easy to relax around, and Watson was comfortable with her from the first day they met.

"What's in it?" Maven asked.

"Can't say, but it could fly circles around the Aurora," Perez-Roberts said.

"Really?" Maven said, exaggerating surprise. "Then you must be talking about the Pumpkin Seed," he said, smiling. "External combustion pulse detonation engines that push that ship to thirty-eight thousand miles per hour in the atmosphere."

Perez-Roberts smiled and said, "Damn Internet."

When Puglisi came on the screen, Perez-Roberts and Puglisi exchanged friendly greetings. The Puglisi and the Roberts families were friends. Perez-Roberts was a bit vague about the reason for that friendship too, since the Puglisis lived in Hawaii, and Perez-Roberts in Alexandria, Virginia. As far as Watson could discern, sometime in the past, the two families had worked together on a project that was as secret as the one Watson now found himself involved with.

"How are Carrollee and the kids?" Perez-Roberts asked.

"Doing well," Puglisi said. "How about yours?"

"They're with Grandma," Perez-Roberts said. "They're being spoiled."

"Does John know you're flying the Aurora again?" Puglisi asked.

"No, and you're not going to tell him," Perez-Roberts said. "Do you know where John is and why I can't get hold of him?"

Puglisi looked uncomfortable, and changed the subject. "We're all set on this end," Puglisi said. "Is the Aurora flight ready?"

"Took her suborbital, and she behaved like the lady she is," Perez-Roberts said. "They are finishing the inspection and systems checks as we speak."

The checkout flight was Watson's first actual flight in an Aurora, and it was every bit the gut-checking ride that the simulator put pilots through.

"Commander Watson, how about your assembly team?" Puglisi asked.

"Maven and Chandra are ready to go," Watson said. "Mating the capsules and the PAM booster is pretty simple."

"Obviously it's easy," Maven said. "I can do it."

"Then we need to go as soon as possible," Puglisi said. "Conditions are changing rapidly, and we need to get this material off planet as soon as possible."

"When you say 'conditions,' just what are you referring to?" Watson asked. "Is there a risk to the mission?"

"Honestly, I don't know, but I don't see how this could impact the mission. Put simply, we have a minor connection with a different time period—kind of a microversion of what happened with the Time Quilt."

Everyone stiffened now, hearing details they did not know.

"What is different this time is that there is a time differential between this time period and the time period on the other side," Puglisi explained. "Time on the other side is running slower than on this side. So a day over there could be a month here. What has changed is that the differential is changing. The two time rates are coming together. Soon the flow of time in that time period will match the flow of time in this period."

"Wouldn't that be a good thing?" Chandra asked.

"I don't know, is it?" Puglisi said.

"You're asking us?" Maven said. "I'm barely smart enough to connect a PAM booster to a couple of capsules."

"The point is that this is new territory for us," Puglisi said. "Until this event, as far as I knew, time was a constant. So, it could be that whatever caused the differences in the rate of time is dissipating, and time is resuming its normal state. Or, it could be that this is a countdown to something catastrophic."

"I'll go with the former," Maven said.

"You believe that the material we recovered on the moon has something to do with this effect on time?" Watson asked.

"Getting it off the planet is a precaution," Puglisi said. "Something we need to do soon."

"We're ready," Watson said. "Let's get it done."

"Very good," Puglisi said. "Then we'll launch tonight. We'll meet you at Cape Canaveral with the cargo."

The oldest member of the team, Watson had been an astronaut for nearly twenty years, and gray for the last five. Balding like Puglisi, he kept his hair short, barely different from shaving his head. Shorter than average, with a barrel chest and thick arms and legs, Watson was an ex–fighter pilot turned astronaut. Watson had had more flight time than any active astronaut, and in all his experience, he had never seen a mission like this one. NASA normally overtrained its crews, had overtrained backup crews, and in some cases, overtrained third crews. NASA also went over launch vehicles with a fine-toothed comb, replacing even functioning parts if there was even a suspicion a part might function below optimum. With this mission, there was minimal training, only one crew, and a launch vehicle that had to be pulled from mothballs and reconditioned in less than three weeks. That suggested urgency to Watson, and that Puglisi was genuinely concerned about what would happen if the two time periods ever matched.

Even though retired, the Aurora could be flown only at night. The first leg of the flight plan was suborbital. The Aurora would take off from Area 51, fly sixty-two miles into the sky, and then drop back down and land in Florida. The flight would take fifty minutes. After picking up the cargo, they would fly into orbit, deliver the cargo, and then return to California, again landing at night.

They ate dinner together in a dining room with an old wooden table and metal folding chairs. While the furniture consisted of Goodwill rejects, the food was good: garden salad, chicken and steak, potatoes or rice, broccoli or carrots, and apple pie or raspberry sherbet for dessert. No wine, since they were flying, they drank soft drinks and coffee. After dinner, most of them napped or wrote messages for family, which would be screened by censors and then sent.

Mike Watson e-mailed his wife, assuring her that he would be home soon, since the mission was essentially a one-night mission. Twice before, he had taken classified cargos to orbit, so his wife was relaxed about the mission. Watson, on the other hand, was nervous. Not about the mission, but about Puglisi's countdown.

Built for hypersonic flight, the Aurora had a torpedo-shaped nose that widened out into a delta wing configuration, and twin tails. Dull black in color, the skin converted heat to electricity, partially powering the craft, and at the same time absorbing electromagnetic energy, thus making it invisible to radar. Watson climbed into the cockpit, taking the second seat. Configured to reduce drag, the pilot seats were tandem. Watson's instruments would mirror Perez-Roberts's displays, and he had his own stick. The Aurora was fly-by-wire, as were most modern jets. Watson was used to flying ships with essentially radio signals, but the thought of the computer controlling the ship even when they were flying on "manual" still unnerved him.

Maven and Chandra were loaded into the cargo bay, Chandra essentially sitting between Maven's legs. Also married, Chandra was as immune to Maven's flirting as Perez-Roberts was, and ignored his suggestive comments as she was helped into her seat. Once airborne, no one would have a window, since windows created drag. Instead, video displays provided an external view, although Perez-Roberts had a retractable periscope that she could use to line the airplane up with the runway. They would take off with no runway lights, the Aurora not even equipped with wing or tail markers.

"Let's run the checklist," Perez-Roberts said, Watson picking up his one important duty.

While they worked through the list, the ground crew buttoned up the cockpit hatch, covered the Aurora with a tarp, and then removed the chocks, pulling the ship to launch position with a small yellow tractor. Invisible to Watson were other preparations, including radar scans of surrounding airspace, security patrols of the perimeter, and sweeping of the mile-long runway. High above the site, a Crystal Seven satellite stood guard, ready to destroy any snooping satellites that moved into position over Area 51.

Finishing the preflight checklist, Perez-Roberts fired up the engines, which sounded something like normal jet engines, although instead of a rapid burn, the propulsion consisted of a series of detonations just behind the plane, driving the ship with shock waves. With the engines warmed up, Perez-Roberts requested clearance, and was given permission immediately. Then they were moving.

All of the crew were experienced, either as astronauts, pilots, or both, so they were used to violent acceleration, and accelerate they did. Perez-Roberts took them vertical as soon as she cleared the runway, giving the Aurora just enough time to reconfigure her wings and then giving her full throttle, the pulse detonations more distinct as the ship climbed. Eventually the sound of the engines changed, the Aurora switching to onboard fuel, since the oxygen-poor atmosphere starved the engines. It was smoother flying than a rocket launch, and Watson watched his external monitor, the clear sky growing blacker, the stars brighter, until they were white-hot pinpoints in the black of space. Then, the engines cut off. They continued to rise, becoming weightless. Watson ignored the fluttery feeling while scanning instruments, as Perez-Roberts let the ship reach apogee and then slip back to begin free fall.

The plan was to bring the ship in dead-stick, using the Aurora's lifting body design, and land unnoticed at Cape Canaveral. Once refueled, and the cargo in the hold, they would be off before the public knew they were there. The string-of-pearls contrail left by the Aurora's pulse detonation engines, the only evidence of its existence.

Coming in under computer control, the Aurora was as stable as a shuttle, and they touched down softly. Without jet engines to reverse, and undersized brakes, they needed most of a mile to stop the Aurora. Trucks raced out of the darkness, the Aurora partially covered by tarps to camouflage its shape. Crew from Area 51, flown out ahead, opened the cargo hatch, Maven and Chandra supervising the loading of the canisters.

"We didn't bring this much crap back from the moon," Maven said over the intercom.

Seeing the canisters on the monitor, Watson agreed. One canister would hold all the material returned from Flamsteed crater. Curious, but not surprised, Watson had guessed they were getting only as much of the story as they needed to do the mission.

Tanker trucks replenished the fuel tanks, including the internal oxygen tanks. Other technicians looked over the skin of the Aurora for any pit or blemish. Two orbital flights in less than two hours were unprecedented, although within specifications. Running internal diagnostics, Watson and Perez-Roberts checked all systems, and then updated guidance data. With only fifty minutes on the ground, they were buttoned up and ready to go.

"Now it gets real," Maven said over the intercom.

"Stand by," Perez-Roberts said as the tractor disengaged and she checked the Aurora's alignment.

Takeoff permission came, and they were roaring down the runway again. Flying out over the ocean, they turned nearly vertical and shot into the air. Even with only two previous flights in the Aurora, Watson could feel a difference in the performance of the Aurora. Scanning the instruments, Watson found no lit warning indicators, no warning messages, and heard no warning buzzers—but something was different.

"Rosa, everything nominal?" he asked.

"I feel it," she said.

Perez-Roberts said nothing more, since they were switching to internal oxygen, and the pulse detonations increased in power and frequency. They shot into orbit, g-forces pressing them deep into their seats, pressurized flight suits inflating to keep them conscious. Watson continued to watch for warning indicators, and then he saw the anomaly—it had to be an error. Through the vibrations and g-forces, Watson watched the anomalous readings, becoming more puzzled with each minute. Then the engines shut down, and they were in orbit. Shutting down flight systems, Watson and Perez-Roberts set the Aurora up for orbital flight.

"Look at the fuel usage," Watson said.

"It's a false reading," Perez-Roberts said. "It has to be."

"Maven, Chandra," Watson said. "Check the readings on those tanks back there."

"We're already doing it," Chandra said.

"We're getting the same reading," Maven said. "Unless you want me to unscrew a cap and measure it with a stick, everything says these tanks are nearly full."

Sitting behind Rosa, Watson could not see her face, but she had to be as surprised as he was.

"We used only ten percent of our fuel," Perez-Roberts said.

"A little more," Watson said, "but not much."

"That's impossible," Perez-Roberts said, struggling to understand how they could reach orbit and have nearly full tanks. "Just what is in those cylinders?"

"It's like nothing I've ever seen," Watson said.

"No one's seen anything like it," Maven said, "and the sooner we get rid of it, the better."

"I'm going to have to contact Houston," Perez-Roberts said, "because we've got a problem."

"Problem?" Maven asked.

"Too much fuel," Perez-Roberts said.

"Isn't having too much fuel like having too much cake?" Maven asked. "A good kind of problem?"

"Usually, yes," Perez-Roberts said. "But there are no simulations for landing an Aurora with nearly full tanks. There would be no conceivable reason for doing such a thing. Who would pick up liquid oxygen and hydrogen in orbit and return it to Earth?"

"Let Groom Lake and Houston sort it out," Watson said. "In the meantime, we're sixty-seven minutes from rendezvous with the PAM. Let's be sure we're ready to send this stuff on its way."

"Send it way, way away," Maven said.

40

Reunion

Our Sun is about 4.6 billion years old, and Earth is just slightly younger, at 4.5 billion years old. The first, most basic cells are thought to have formed on our planet about 3.8 billion years ago, although the Homo *genus, to which humans belong, did not appear until about 2.5 million years ago. And modern humans are only about 200,000 years old. For more than 80 percent of the Sun's existence, life has existed in some form on Earth. It seems the timescales of biology and astrophysics have favorably aligned in our case. According to the anthropic argument, this coincidence means that Earth, and its life, are unique.*

—Clara Moskowitz

Unknown Time
Unknown Place

"It's half gravity," Nick said, bouncing, remembering his time on the moon.

"Why would Jeanette come here?" Carson asked. "This is some weird damn place."

Reverend was silent, looking at the sky, then running his hands across the golden-topped grasses. "It's an unspoiled land," Reverend said. "God has prepared this for us."

"Reverend, this isn't what you think it is," Nick said. "Look at the sun. It's the size of a grapefruit. Feel the gravity? It's half of Earth's. Take a deep breath. The air is thin. There's enough oxygen to breathe, but it's the equivalent of standing in La Paz, in the Andes. Or even higher. It would take some time to acclimatize to air this thin, if you can at all. Put all of that together, and what does it tell you?"

"It tells me we need to find Jeanette and get the hell out of here," Carson said.

"God's creation never ceases to amaze," Reverend said.

"Reverend, this isn't Earth," Nick said.

Even with his eyes hidden by sunglasses, the Reverend showed surprise on his face.

"Not Earth?" Carson asked. "What the hell does that mean?"

"My best guess is that it's Mars," Nick said.

"Mars?" Carson said, looking around with fresh eyes. "Shouldn't there be canals and stuff?"

"Mars is a dead world," Reverend said. "Not a lush garden."

"This isn't the Mars of our time," Nick said. "We jumped sixty-five million years into the past to find you. This may be another sixty-five million years in the past or more. Mars wasn't always a dead world. It once had seas and an atmosphere."

"Mars," Reverend said, taking in the implications. "Why would God open Mars to us?"

Nick sighed. Reverend's universe was deocentric, or more accurately, Reverend-centric.

"Look over there," Carson said suddenly.

Following his point, Nick saw figures on a hill.

"Jeanette!" Carson began calling, over and over.

The figures ignored Carson's yelling. Nick could see they were both women and both wore shorts and shirts pulled up and tied, leaving a bare midriff. Both women also carried rifles, coming better prepared than Nick had. They both wore packs, but there was something strange about the pack worn by one of the women. Nick looked over the landscape, seeing nothing dangerous.

"Let's go get them," Nick said.

Carson led the way, hurrying through the grass. Nick followed, with Reverend taking his own path, walking with his arms wide, brushing the golden tops of the grasses, leaving a yellow cloud in his wake.

"Reverend, we don't know anything about this planet," Nick said. "It would be better to stay close and not touch anything."

"God is great," Reverend said.

"Yes," Nick said. "And he'll still be great if you walk a little closer to me."

Reverend smiled, and drifted closer. "Dr. Paulson, you have opened my eyes. You are an instrument of God."

"How's that?" Nick asked.

"Without you, my people would have fought the Inhumans to the last man, woman, and child. I knew we could not win. Every time God's flock began to grow, the Inhumans culled the herd, and we were fewer. There were too many of them, and too few of us. That is why I thought God's fire in the sky—the asteroid—was our last hope. If God did not help us, we would be exterminated. But it made no sense to me. I kept asking myself, why would God bring us to this primitive land, only to let us be eaten by the beasts and murdered by Satan's two-legged demons? Thanks to you, I have an answer—this world. This virgin land is why we were brought back in time. This is where God meant us to go. I must bring my people here."

"Reverend, you're judging this ecosystem too quickly. Every plant here may be poisonous. What about bacteria and viruses? You could be wiped out by disease even quicker than starvation. What about water?"

"Trust God," Reverend said. "Why would God prepare a world for us that we could not survive in?"

Nick ignored the circular argument, knowing nothing he could say would cut through Reverend's self-assurance.

"Jeanette!" Carson yelled again, running toward the figures that had now spotted them and were waving their arms.

"Stop! Carson, stop!" Nick called.

Carson's keen sense of survival read the danger in Nick's tone.

"There's something coming through the grass," Nick said.

Reverend and Carson pulled their pistols simultaneously, Carson backing toward Nick and Reverend.

"I don't see anything," Carson said, still backing up.

"There!" Nick shouted.

Carson saw the movement in the grass, walking sideways now, pistol pointed. "What the hell?" Carson said, firing a shot into the grass.

At the sound, a dozen animals launched into the sky, flying away like giant bats, settling back into the grass a mile away. Carson tracked them with his pistol, making sure none flew toward him. Then he swept the grass again, aiming the pistol at every real and imagined movement.

"I saw something," Carson said.

"What?" Nick asked.

"Something that could eat us," Carson said.

Carson finished backing up, and then the three men stood back to back to back, forming a triangle, watching for movement in the grass.

"Here it comes," Reverend said.

A hidden creature was leaving a wake as it raced toward the group. Carson fired again, a few more flying animals taking to the skies. Whatever was coming deviated, circling—now spiraling in. Nick saw a head pop up over the grass, and then just as quickly drop back down. It looked feline, with huge square jaws.

"It's a lion," Reverend said calmly.

"Not a lion," Nick said, but had no idea what else to call it.

From the running women, Nick heard a musical call.

"Re, Me, Fa, So, La, Ti," one of the women sang out.

Watching for the approaching creature, Nick, Carson, and Reverend ignored the inexplicable singing.

"There!" Carson yelled.

Nick had already seen it. The lion creature appeared above the grass and then ducked back down again. Carson fired his pistol three times, then clicked on an empty cylinder.

"Reload," Reverend said.

Carson fumbled with his pistol, releasing the cylinder and trying to knock out the empty brass.

"Get ready," Nick said.

Reverend stood coolly in his black suit and sunglasses, arm extended, pistol steady in his hand. "Movement," Reverend said calmly.

Nick saw nothing until the lion leapt high, bounding toward them, clearing the grass, then disappearing in it, only to reappear again. Nick held his fire, the kangaroo attack made the animal impossible to hit. Reverend held his fire too. Given the animal's size, the pistols seemed pitifully inadequate. With seconds left, Nick aimed where he thought the lion thing would land just before it leapt on Nick, and gently squeezed the trigger. Before he could fire, velociraptors ran past, one passing between Nick and Reverend, brushing their legs.

"Raptors!" Carson yelled, dropping shells as he did, then snapping the cylinder back into place only half loaded, and then waving the gun back and forth, trying to pick out a target among the velociraptors as they disappeared into the grass.

The velociraptors tore into the lion, the hidden battle taking place in the tall grass. Snarling, snapping animals tangled, velociraptors bouncing above the grass tops seemingly randomly, but always coming down with legs extended, claws dripping pink fluid.

"Don't shoot!" the women yelled, coming fast with long leaps.

Recognizing one of the voices, Nick turned, shocked. Elizabeth was the woman with Jeanette. Arms wide, Nick caught her in a hungry embrace and then kissed her. Jeanette ran to Carson, Nick shocked to see she carried a velociraptor in a backpack like a mother would a baby. Gun still extended, Carson turned to her and then nearly jumped out of his skin when the velociraptor on her back leaned over her shoulder, sniffing at Carson.

Pointing his gun at the velociraptor, Carson said, "You've got a raptor on your back."

"They're our raptors," Jeanette said, breathless, pushing the gun away.

"Ours?" Carson asked, confused. "They're eggs."

"They were eggs. You've been gone for months."

"Months? What? They hatched?"

Now looking at Nick, Carson shut his mouth, turning back to the fight in the grass. Seconds later, the lion creature jumped high and then ran away with great leaps, pink blood dribbling down its sides.

"What are you doing here?" Nick asked, now angry with her.

"Looking for you, you liar," Elizabeth said, gasping for breath. "You said no more fieldwork."

"It was an accident," Nick explained.

"Later," Elizabeth said, turning Nick and pointing back at the hill. "We need to get out of here."

Silhouetted on the hill were four of the lion creatures.

"Let's get the ladies to safety," Reverend said, seeing the lions.

The velociraptors appeared one at a time, flopping down, licking wounds. The one in Jeanette's pack *awk*ed at the others, struggling to get free. Carson pointed his pistol at each arriving velociraptor, Jeanette having to reassure him over and over to keep Carson from shooting them. Elizabeth shrugged off her pack and pulled out a plastic bag of dog food, pouring a pile in front of each of the resting velociraptors. Then she took a cup, pouring water into it and offering it to each velociraptor.

"We don't want them to become hunters," Elizabeth explained.

"Elizabeth, what are you talking about?" Nick asked. "They are hunters!"

"These are pets," Elizabeth said, still wheezing.

Jeanette circulated, checking the condition of each velociraptor, the predators tolerating her attentions, some nuzzling her. Repressing a fountain of questions, Nick let the women work. While they tended to the velociraptors, Nick watched the creatures on the hill, the sun quite low, the lions now nothing more than black forms. They had not moved.

"They killed Sally," Jeanette said, turning to Carson, tears starting to fall.

"The raptors killed Sally?" Carson said, hand dropping to his pistol.

"No, the lions killed Sally," Jeanette said. "Up on the hill."

"What?" Carson said. "Why did you bring Sally?"

Bursting into tears, Jeanette wiped her eyes, turning away from Carson. The velociraptors stopped their eating, all eyes on Carson, who had upset Jeanette.

"Sorry, Jeanette, I didn't mean anything," Carson said, aware of all the predators watching him.

Finished with the raptors, Elizabeth put her pack back on, then comforted Jeanette. Wiping her eyes with bare hands, Jeanette composed herself.

"Re, Me, Fa, So, La, Ti," Jeanette sang, the velociraptors jumping to their feet.

"That's what she calls them," Elizabeth explained to Nick. "The one in the pack is Do."

"Music hath charms to soothe the savage breast," Reverend said.

"Who are you?" Elizabeth asked.

"I'm called Reverend," the man said, introducing himself. "I am pastor of a lost flock of sheep who are only now finding our way to the land God has prepared for us."

"Why are you wearing a suit?" Jeanette asked.

"As I said, I'm a pastor," Reverend said, as if that explained it.

"Let's go," Carson said, pulling Jeanette's arm.

With a lunge, the velociraptor named Do snapped at Carson, and then hissed.

"No, no," Jeanette said, scolding the velociraptor. "He's your daddy."

"Don't say that, Jeanette," Carson said, nodding toward Nick. "Dr. Paulson of the OSS might believe you."

"Oh," Jeanette said, now looking guilty.

Weapons ready, the group walked through the grass back toward the opening, Carson leading the way, setting a brisk pace.

"This is a good look for you," Nick said to Elizabeth.

Suddenly aware of her bare midriff and accentuated breasts, Elizabeth untied her blouse, letting it fall. "It was hot," she said, her breathing close to normal now. "And stop looking at Jeanette."

Nick did not bother to protest. He was guilty of checking Jeanette out. Even with dirt smudges on her face, her hair unkempt, Jeanette looked like a *Playboy* centerfold with a few more clothes.

"Oh no," Elizabeth said.

Nick turned to see what Elizabeth saw. The lions on the hill were coming, four shapes leaping through the grass.

"We gave you your kitten!" Jeanette shouted.

"Run!" Carson yelled, grabbing Jeanette's arm and yanking on it until Do snapped at him.

"Wait!" Nick called, stopping Carson. "We'd never make it."

"Re, Me, Fa, So, La, Ti," Jeanette sang.

Without more instruction, the velociraptors ran to the front, facing the onrushing lion creatures. Clearly exhausted, and injured, the velociraptors took positions between the humans and the attackers, ready to fight for the humans. Nick was stunned but grateful.

"There are too many," Jeanette said, rifle ready.

Jeanette and Elizabeth stood shoulder to shoulder, taking aim. Reverend and Nick stood on either side, pistols in hand. Behind them, Carson paced, unsure of whether to fight with the others or run. Then behind came a cacophony, like a symphony orchestra tuning up. The group turned to see Inhumans running through the grass, waving spears and fanning out. Fifty of them spread across the fields, continuing their earsplitting shouting. The lions stopped their charge, standing tall in the grass on bony legs, studying the mob. Then, one by one, retreating up and over the distant hill.

It was now getting dark, and the Inhumans formed two columns on either side of the humans, escorting them back to the dark shadow on a slope that was the passage back, and then letting the humans pass through first. On the other side, Nick discovered it was dawn. Passing through the hut, he led Elizabeth outside, and then looked at the sky.

"What are you looking for?" Elizabeth asked.

"The comet," Nick said. Taking Elizabeth's hand, Nick led Elizabeth through the village and up the hill to where the pyramid had erupted. That was the clearest view of the sky.

"What comet?" Elizabeth asked.

"That one," Nick said, shocked at how much closer it was.

The comet was the size of the moon.

"How long do we have?" Reverend asked, walking up behind them.

"Hours," Nick said. "A day at the most."

"Then we best prepare," Reverend said, falling to his knees and folding his hands.

Seeing the reverend on his knees, praying, Elizabeth said, "Oh, this is bad."

41

In Orbit

The three adventurous companions were surprised and stupefied, despite their scientific reasonings. They felt themselves being carried into the domain of wonders! . . . Their feet no longer clung to the floor of the projectile. . . . Fancy has depicted men without reflection, others without shadow. But here reality, by the neutralizations of attractive forces, produced men in whom nothing had any weight, and who weighed nothing themselves.

—Jules Verne, *From the Earth to the Moon*

Present Time
Earth Orbit

Locked in the cockpit, Commander Watson and Aurora pilot Rosa Perez-Roberts could do nothing but monitor the work of Mission Specialists Sarasa Chandra and Rick Maven. As promised, the Payload Assist Module was waiting for them, delivered on an Air Force bird out of Vandenberg. The PAM came equipped with a docking collar, so it was only a matter of attaching the twin cylinders to the collar and then lighting up the engines. The problem was working in zero gravity, where leverage did not come naturally. Any force exerted tended to put objects into a spin, since there was no friction or gravity to arrest motion.

Chandra and Maven worked with tethers at first, disconnecting cylinders to free them from the Aurora's cargo hold. Then they used a small hydraulic arm to lift them out. Now the two cylinders floated between the Aurora and the PAM, ready to be moved into place.

The astronauts pulled themselves into the hold, backing into the cradles for the MMUs (Manned Maneuvering Units). The units latched to the back of each astronaut's space suit. Powered by nitrogen gas, the MMUs would allow Maven and Chandra to maneuver the cylinders into position.

"We're set," Maven radioed.

The astronauts released the MMUs from their cradles and pushed off, floating out of the cargo bay.

"Let's give it a try," Maven said.

Everyone held their breath as Maven used the hand controls to release a jet of gas to propel him toward the near cylinder. Watching his monitor, Watson saw a small spray of nitrogen crystals from jets on the MMU, and then Maven shot across the gap, bouncing off the cylinder.

"Whoa!" Maven said, now floating back toward the Aurora. "It's not like the simulator."

"Arrest your rotation," Chandra said.

Maven touched his controls, and now he was rotating the opposite direction.

"Too much," Chandra said.

"Really?" Maven said, irritated. "The throttle isn't set up for the level of control that we need."

"Do we need to abort?" Watson asked.

"Have some faith," Maven said. "I'll get the hang of it, Commander."

It took Maven four more tries before he stopped his spin and then moved gently toward the cylinder. "Your turn, Sarasa," Maven said.

To Maven's embarrassment, Chandra managed to move away from the Aurora and toward the cylinder without running into it or putting herself into a spin.

"Nothing to it," Chandra said.

"Show-off," Maven said.

Using a fraction of the expected propellant, the astronauts positioned themselves at two points on the first cylinder, then moved it toward the PAM. The Payload Assist Module was simple in design, essentially a large cylinder with a rocket nozzle on one end and a docking collar on the other. Frustrated by being locked in the cockpit, Watson could only watch as Chandra and Maven maneuvered the cylinder into place. Normally careful, they were extra careful, since their MMUs were hypersensitive, the jets producing more thrust than they had trained for. Two hours later, they had both cylinders mated to the docking collar, the astronauts rechecking every connection and making sure all tools had been retrieved.

"Everything's nominal on this side," Chandra said.

"Everything's extra nominal on my side," Maven said.

"The PAM is responding," Perez-Roberts said. "All indicators are good to go."

"Houston, we are finished and retrieving our astronauts," Watson sent back to Earth.

"I'll let Dr. Puglisi know," West said. "As soon as you have retrieved your crew, move to a safe distance."

Watching Chandra and Maven return to the cargo hold using tiny bursts of gas, Watson questioned the decision to destroy the material they had gathered on the moon. The fact that Dr. Puglisi insisted on it made Watson wonder what else was going on. Given the recent history of the planet, it might be terrible indeed.

42

Column

The Indians surrounding the soldiers on Custer Hill were now joined by others from every section of the field, from downriver where they had been chasing horses, from along the ridge where they had stripped the dead of guns and ammunition, from upriver, where Reno's men could hear the beginning of the last heavy volley a few minutes past 5. "There were great numbers of us," said Eagle Bear, an Oglala, "some on horseback, others on foot. Back and forth in front of Custer we passed, firing all of the time."

—Thomas Powers

Sixty-five Million Years Ago
Unknown Place

If Leah was distressed over leaving Reverend's flock, she did not show it. After the first few miles, Leah drifted over, taking Jacob's hand and walking close, occasionally breaking into a smile. Bonnie had to be carried when she saw the Inhumans outside the compound, and Bea clung to her mother's hand. But after the Inhumans were out of sight, and no attack came, the girls relaxed, taking their cues from the adults. People whispered at first, as if afraid to be heard, and then chatted openly, speculating on what they would do back in the world. Children began to wander, farther and farther from the secure base of their parents, and soon the joy of anticipation infected the entire caravan.

"I barely remember the world," Leah said, squeezing Jacob's hand.

"It seems like a dream. Could it be as good as I remember it? I wonder if I can still drive a car? Do they have cars? We could go for a drive. No, let's go to a mall. Oh, I know, let's take the girls for ice cream. They've never had ice cream."

"Sure," Jacob said. "We'll need to get some money."

Leah pulled a thick wad of bills from her apron pocket.

"You still have money?" Jacob asked.

"I know we were supposed to turn all of our mammon in so the reverend could burn it," Leah said, "but I couldn't do it. I kept hoping we would get home someday, so I hid what I had and every time I found some, I added it to my stash."

"We can eat ice cream for a year with all of that," Jacob said.

"Dairy Queen," Leah said wistfully. "Would you mind if I put on a few pounds? I want to eat all the things I missed."

"On you, a few more pounds would look good," Jacob said. "On you, everything looks good."

Leah gave Jacob her full smile, and Jacob fell in love with Leah all over again. It wasn't just Jacob's love of Leah that made him happy; it was the sense of being useful again. He never had the skills to survive in the wilderness, but back in the world, he could make a living and provide for his family. Leah would not have to work herself into an early grave, and the girls could look forward to something better than a teenage marriage to a boy selected by Reverend.

"Can I walk by the horsie?" Bea asked, tugging on Leah's apron. "Sarah and Melanie are walking by the horsie."

Leah looked at Jacob, who nodded. "Careful with your dress," Leah said.

"I go," Bonnie said, wriggling out of Jacob's arms.

"Take your sister," Leah said.

Bea ran back, took Bonnie's hand, and the two ran alongside the column to the front, where Officer Conyers led her horse. Dr. Gah rode Torino, hanging on to the saddle horn for dear life. Children walked parallel to the horse, the officer answering questions, warning the children not to get too close. Ranger Wynooski and Crazy Kramer walked at the front with the officer, Wynooski's mouth running constantly. Wynooski was why the Lewinskis were deeper into the column. Jacob did not like the plump, know-it-all ranger.

"Do you think we could get a house? One just for our family?" Leah asked. "I love these people, but I want a place of our own. Is that selfish? I want a bathroom with a flush toilet and a shower. I want to sleep with you whenever we want and not have to wait our turn for some privacy."

"I was a Realtor," Jacob said. "I'll get us a house."

"Could you?"

"I won the Realtor of the Year Award, two years in a row," Jacob bragged.

"Even if you don't get us a house, I'll be happy. We could live in a tent or a trailer and it would be better than here. At least there won't be demons trying to kill us and dinosaurs trying to eat us."

"The only dinosaurs are in zoos, so I won't need this anymore," Jacob said, patting the rifle hanging over his shoulder.

"I wonder if my mother is still alive?" Leah said sadly, her mind wandering.

Years of hunting had sensitized Jacob, and now he felt movement in the trees. Instinctively, the rifle was off his shoulder before he realized it. Leah stiffened, seeing the look on his face.

"What is it? Dinosaur?"

"Maybe nothing," Jacob said, eyes on the trees.

The column was crossing a clearing and approaching another copse of trees.

"Maybe we should stop?" Leah suggested, looking ahead at the deep shadows of the trees.

"Yeah, maybe," Jacob said, eyes on the trees.

Jacob let go of Leah, separating from the column and walking a few yards into the clearing. Others noticed him, two other men with rifles splitting off, spacing themselves ten yards on either side of Jacob. Slowly, Jacob worked the bolt, loading a shell. Jacob's eyes fixed on the trees across the clearing, and darted from place to place at every little movement. He saw nothing, but the other riflemen were just as wary.

"Get the girls," Jacob said to Leah.

Without a word, Leah ran toward the front of the column. Person by person, word of what the riflemen were doing spread both directions in the column, reaching the front at the same time as Leah, who grabbed each girl by the hand, pulling them into the column, protecting her children with the bodies of other people. Conyers helped Dr. Gah off Torino, mounted, and rode back to where Jacob and the riflemen stood.

"What is it?" Conyers asked.

"Movement in the trees," Jacob said.

"Where?" Conyers asked.

"I don't see nothing," Ranger Wynooski said, marching up, then standing with her hands on her hips, staring at the tree line. "You've got everyone all riled up for nothing."

"See the gap between that clump on right and the rock with the tree behind it?" Jacob asked. "There's something in there."

Torino danced impatiently while Conyers studied the gap.

"Bring it on!" Kramer said, walking up behind Wynooski.

Gah hobbled over, and behind him, Willy and Mel Williams, with their bows and arrows. There were two more rifles in the column, three pistols, and very little ammunition, some of which was bad. Another fifteen men were armed with bows and arrows, but had few arrows left after the battle with the Inhumans who drove them out of their compound.

"There's nothing there," Wynooski said in a voice so certain that Jacob almost believed her.

"I saw something," Jacob insisted.

"I'll check it out," Conyers said, putting her white helmet on and snapping the chin strap.

With a light touch of the reins, Torino turned from the column and walked across the meadow toward the gap Jacob had pointed out.

Never a rider, Jacob nevertheless saw Torino as the beautiful animal he was. Unlike dinosaurs that specialized in ugly, mammals like the horse had symmetry, grace, and beauty.

With a hundred yards to go, Torino hesitated, dancing sideways. Nudged with the heels of Conyers's boots, Torino started forward, his neck bunched, his eyes wide and fixed on the gap. Jacob did not know horses, but he knew the horse did not want to keep moving forward.

"Come back!" Jacob yelled.

Conyers pulled up, turning Torino to look back at the column of refugees, waiting for word. "I'm almost there," Conyers said, then turned Torino, nudging him toward the gap.

Bucking gently, Torino refused to move. Just as Conyers started kicking Torino's haunches, an Inhuman burst from the shadows, spear in his hand. Taking her pistol, Conyers held her fire, pulling Torino around and trying to steady the horse to get a clear shot. The Inhuman launched the spear, putting all its strength into the throw, nearly falling as it did. Kicking Torino, Conyers yanked on the reins, the horse jumping forward and right, the spear flying past his haunches. Kicking Torino into a run, Conyers raced toward the column.

Dozens of Inhuman warriors burst from the gap, spreading out, charging across the meadow, yodeling their battle cry.

"Circle up!" Jacob ordered, others echoing the cry.

The refugees pulled closer together, women and children on the inside, men on the outside, those with weapons separating to join the riflemen. Conyers reached Jacob and the others now forming a battle line. Fifty men made up the line, most armed with clubs, axes, hammers, and knives. A few, like Crazy, had machetes. Those with bows or guns bunched in the middle, taking aim.

"Hold your fire!" Conyers yelled, taking Torino to one end of the line of armed men. "Hold. Hold."

Crazy Kramer stood next to Jacob, dancing on his toes, shaking his machete. "Come and get some!"

Dried blood from the last battle still caked his machete, clothes, face, and beard. Crazy looked like the insane maniac that he was in the midst of battle.

Jacob estimated the spear range of the Inhumans, realizing they were getting close now. Much past that point, and they could throw over the human battle line and into the huddled women and children. Jacob hoped Conyers understood the danger.

"Take aim!" Conyers shouted.

Bows tilted up while pistols and rifles aimed straight.

"Fire!" Conyers said.

Arrows flew and guns went off in a disorganized broadside. The center of the Inhuman mob collapsed, squeals of pain heard above the battle cry. Those in back tripped over those in front, and the charge faltered, Inhumans piling up, stumbling, falling.

"Reload!" Conyers called out unnecessarily.

Jacob knew the riflemen had no more than five rounds each, the men with pistols a little more. Bowmen might have more arrows. Helping injured Inhumans back toward the trees, the Inhumans reorganized, still passionate about killing the humans. With the wounded out of the way, one Inhuman began yodeling, a sound pleasant to human ears and eerie at the same time. Others picked up the musical call, and then the Inhumans began bouncing on their toes, jumping higher and higher, at the same time working themselves into a skirmish line.

"They're going to charge!" Jacob called to Conyers.

"Take aim!" Conyers said repeatedly, riding Torino the length of the line and then pulling up at the far end of the armed men.

"Come and get it!" Crazy screamed, shaking his machete.

As if they understood him, the Inhumans launched their spears and then charged.

"Fire!" Conyers commanded.

Busy dodging incoming spears, the humans fired only some of their weapons, the bows doing most of the damage, the guns suffering from a large number of misfires. The Inhumans took the losses, and still closed the gap. Pistols fired until they were empty, and then the Inhumans hit the line and the hand-to-hand combat began. Stepping out from the rest, Crazy split the skull of the first Inhuman, and then slashed left and right, gashing one Inhuman, severing the arm of another. Using his rifle as a club now, Jacob knocked an Inhuman senseless, and then parried the thrust of a knife. Next to him, Mel Williams took a spear in his thigh, his brother Willy knifing the Inhuman, then pulling the spear out and using it to jab left and right, driving Inhumans back, protecting his brother.

All along the line the battle raged, men falling, the injured crawling out of the fray, others filling the gap. Four men were down with serious wounds. Others retrieved spears, using them to jab at Inhumans. The ferocity of the attack caught the humans by surprise, and they fell back, dragging their injured with them.

"Hold the line!" Jacob commanded, knowing it was about to break. If the Inhumans reached the women and children, the slaughter would begin. "Hold the line!"

Then Conyers charged through the Inhumans, Torino knocking bodies left and right. Inhumans fell, tripped over one another, and jumped out of the way. Taking advantage of the disarray, the humans re-formed their line, women and old men running forward to drag the wounded away from the battle. Conyers continued her drive, disrupting the full length of the Inhuman ranks. At the end she turned, making another pass, shooting an Inhuman trying to spear Torino, and then another who lunged with a knife. When Conyers turned to make another pass, the Inhumans broke, fleeing toward their hiding place, carrying their wounded with them.

"What's the matter? You chicken or something?" Crazy hollered, fresh blood spattered on his face.

Three Inhuman bodies lay at Crazy's feet, and two other Inhumans crawled away from him, bleeding profusely from gashes.

"Yeah! Run, you chickens!" Crazy shouted.

Conyers rode over to Jacob. Up close, Jacob saw cuts in the horse's sides.

"We need a more defensible position," Conyers said.

The officer's leg bled from a six-inch cut in her trousers. Blood dribbled into her leather boot.

"The hill where we found you is through those trees," Jacob said.

He and Conyers looked at the sky and then at the many wounded.

"Let's get there and then see how we're doing," Conyers said.

"I'll hold the Inhumans here while you take them to the hill," Jacob said.

Taking charge, Jacob shouted orders, dividing the men with guns and bows, sending half to lead the column and half to stay behind with him as a rear guard.

Wynooski came up, helping Gah, who was having even more trouble walking.

"You should have formed a vee, not a straight line," Wynooski said. "That way you can split their forces. Divide and conquer is the name of the game in war. Ever heard of it? Should have. It's common sense."

"Ranger, I need you to help Officer Conyers herd everyone through the forest," Jacob said. "Can you do that for me?"

"Any fool could," Wynooski said. "I'll get them there."

With the ranger out of his hair, Jacob organized his half of the men, taking stock of the weapons, redistributing bullets and arrows. There were four arrows per bowman, but only three rounds per gun.

"Why you?" Leah complained when she learned Jacob was staying behind.

Bea and Bonnie were hanging on to Leah again, once more terrified. It broke Jacob's heart to see them cowering. He had seen it too often. That was the only life they had known—a prehistoric war zone where everything in the shadows wanted to kill them.

"Who else, Leah?" Jacob asked.

Both Williams brothers were injured now, the only other leaders left among the men. The natural leaders among the women had taken charge of the nursing, cleaning and bandaging wounds.

"But we were going to get ice cream," Leah said, crying.

"We will," Jacob said. "I promise."

"Come with us, Daddy," Bea said.

Bonnie cried like her mother, unsure of what was happening.

"You go with Mom, and I'll meet you there," Jacob said.

"Dairy Queen," Leah said.

"The others are leaving, Leah. Stay with them. It's safer."

"I'm not going unless you keep Crazy," Leah said.

"Okay, sure," Jacob said. "Crazy, you're with me!" Jacob shouted.

"Right!" Crazy said, coming to stand with Jacob.

"Crazy, you take care of him," Leah said.

Big, strong, and dumb, Crazy shook his head enthusiastically. "Sure, Leah," Crazy said. "Anything you say."

"You bring Jacob back to me, Crazy, and I'll make you a pie when we get where we're going."

"All right," Crazy said. "For a pie."

Leah kissed Jacob, and Jacob hugged and kissed his girls. Then, taking the girls in hand, Leah hurried after the others. Jacob formed the men across the meadow, blocking the trail the humans were retreating down. The Inhumans could filter through the trees, but Jacob could see them grouping inside the trees on the far side of the meadow. To be safe, he sent scouts into the trees.

"I can see some of them," Crazy said in a whisper.

"Keep your eye on them," Jacob said. "Let me know if they head this way."

"Right," Crazy whispered.

With the sun low, Jacob did not know what to expect. The Inhumans could see some of the humans escaping, but they stayed in the trees. There was still time before sunset for another attack, but they were not forming up, not chanting, not doing anything they typically did when getting ready for war. Inhumans would attack at night, they had proved that when they drove the Community out of their Home Depot compound. But night attacks were rare. The Inhumans were waiting for something, but what? Two hours later, the sun was nearing the horizon, and still no attack.

"Let's start after the others," Jacob said, circulating among the men, most of whom were resting, some even sleeping.

Sending them in groups of five, they began withdrawing from their positions. They weren't particularly stealthy, so the Inhumans had to see them leaving, but still they held their position. Crazy, true to his word, was next to Jacob when he stopped to take one last look at the distant Inhumans. They were up now, gathering, but facing the wrong way. Then they parted, and Jacob felt a familiar distant vibration. Out of the trees came an Inhuman mounted on a triceratops. The Inhumans had brought in their armor.

43

Distant Thunder

The tyrannosaur family includes more than a dozen members, varying in size from the one-ton Nanotyrannus *to the forty-ton* Tyrannosaurus rex. *It seems evolution just couldn't stop creating superpredators.*

—John Roberts, guest lecturer,
Dinosaur Ranger Academy

Sixty-five Million Years Ago
Unknown Place

Lieutenant Weller moved down the line, whispering to each man, making sure they were awake. John was the last in line.

"Sun's coming," Weller said. "Time to get moving again."

They were miles off course, driven off the trail by a group of predators from the tyrannosaur family that settled for the night on their route. Forced to backtrack, the marines gave the predators a wide berth. Difficult terrain drove them even farther off the trail, but no one wanted to tangle with a single *T. rex* cousin, let alone three. Nightfall forced them to establish a defensible position and wait for morning light.

"I didn't think *rex*es hunted in packs," Weller said as the men ate MREs for breakfast.

"I've seen *T. rex*es hunt together," John said. "One of them stampeded a herd of *Monoclonius* toward two other *rex*es who were hiding in wait. After the kills, there was enough to eat so there was no fighting. When game is scarce, or small, then it's every tyrannosaur for itself."

"Sounds like the way raptors hunt," Weller said.

"Raptors are even smarter," John said. "They'll not only ambush prey, but bait them, chase them down, feign injuries, tail them, and split their forces."

"At least they're smaller," Weller said.

"Size isn't everything," John said.

They finished eating and then cautiously worked their way through the forest, trying to pick up the trail they had been driven away from by the tyrannosaurs. The morning was cool but not cold, and John was a little chilled. The rising sun eventually drove away enough shadows to warm their bodies, evaporating the night dampness. Exercise did the rest, and John was soon warm and on his way to hot.

Terrain made keeping away from the tyrannosaurs difficult, and they meandered, carefully working around where they had last seen the pack. They were making good progress, John estimating they would cross Nick's trail in another half mile or so. Then he heard gunshots, followed by echoes bouncing off rocks and distant trees.

"Which way?" Weller demanded.

Kelton and Snead pointed in roughly the same direction.

"Get us there," Weller said, and Kelton and Snead led the way, setting a brisk pace.

44

Siege

Miserable men indeed were they! whose distress forced them to slay their own wives and children with their own hands. . . . So they being not able to bear the grief they were under for what they had done any longer . . . They then chose ten men by lot out of them, to slay all the rest; every one of whom laid himself down by his wife and children on the ground, and threw his arms about them, and they offered their necks to the stroke of those who by lot executed that melancholy office. . . .

—Flavius Josephus, on the siege of Masada, A.D. 72

Sixty-five Million Years Ago
Unknown Place

Torino snorted a protest as Officer Conyers climbed into the saddle for a better look. The refugees from Reverend's church were huddled together on the top of the hill where Conyers had met Nick Paulson and the others. The creatures the church members called Inhumans were arrayed around the hill, cutting off all escape routes. Fear was thick in the air, and Torino reacted to it, now restless, dancing off nervous energy.

Patting his neck affectionately, Conyers tried to calm the horse. "I know what you're thinking, because I'm thinking the same thing," Conyers whispered into Torino's ear. "What the hell are we doing here?"

Dawn was breaking, and in the morning light Conyers could see the forces deployed against them. Seeing the strange creatures, Conyers understood why Reverend's people called them Inhumans. Dressed in loincloths and little else, the warriors were more lizard-like than anthropoid. The hairless heads, large eyes, and snouts triggered an instinctive loathing. Killing one would be easy, Conyers thought, at the same time realizing the Inhumans must react the same way to humans. When they took the hill, Conyers circulated, checking weapons. Only a few men had rounds left for their rifles and pistols. Conyers distributed the spare ammunition for her pistol. Prepped for crowd control, Conyers had carried only one spare magazine and a canister of Mace. Thankfully, Conyers saw no bows and arrows, or spear throwers among the Inhumans. Given the human position on the hill, the spears would be a manageable threat. With bows and spear throwers, the humans would have been facing artillery.

The bigger problem was the triceratops positioned at the bottom of the hill. With three horns, a neck collar, and standing seven feet tall at the shoulders, the ten-ton animal was evolution's battle tank. Jacob warned Conyers that the triceratops was attack trained, ridden into battle by an Inhuman. Like Hannibal's war elephants, triceratopses were used to trample the humans, smash through their lines, and scatter them, breaking them into smaller groups and making them easier to pick off. Armed as the humans were, repelling an Inhuman attack without the triceratops would a miracle. With the triceratops, the Inhumans would follow it right through the human line, flanking in both directions.

"Our best chance is to concentrate our fire on the triceratops," Jacob said, standing next to Conyers. "Luckily, there's only one of them."

"They have more?" Conyers asked, straining to see in the dark.

"Several more. Some are trained for a harness. I saw three in a column once, pulling carts."

"Why bring only one, then?" Conyers wondered.

The human lines rippled with whispering and pointing. Over the trees beyond the triceratops rose the asteroid, and it was huge.

"This can't be a siege, or we're all dead," Conyers said.

"A charge would be suicide," Jacob said, looking at the asteroid and then back to where his wife comforted his hungry children. "They'd get to our families."

Conyers studied the triceratops and the Inhuman battle line. To circle the hill, the Inhumans had spread their forces thin. The humans could race down the hill opposite the triceratops and punch through the Inhuman line, but the time passage that Conyers rode through was the opposite direction. The triceratops and the Inhumans would run them down before they could get anywhere near the opening.

"How fast is that thing?" Conyers asked, pointing at the triceratops.

"Faster than a human when they sprint, but they can't run for long," Jacob said. "But even if it slowed to a trot, we couldn't stay ahead of it."

"Gather up the ammunition for my spare magazine," Conyers said. "And get me one of those spears that the Inhumans threw."

"What are you going to do?" Jacob asked.

"Take out their armor," Conyers said.

Jacob ran from man to man, collecting Conyers's ammunition back. Most were reluctant until Jacob told them what Conyers planned to do. While Jacob gathered ammunition, Conyers shortened her stirrups a few inches and tightened the cinch. Once the magazine was reloaded, Conyers put it in her belt, unsnapped the retainer on her holster, and remounted, accepting a spear from Crazy Kramer.

"Give it to them good," Crazy said.

"Taking on a triceratops by yourself is nuts," Jacob said.

"Not by myself," Conyers said, leaning forward and patting Torino on the neck.

"Bring it across our line and I'll take it down," Jacob said.

"Save your ammunition in case this doesn't work," Conyers said, then pointed at the asteroid. "It's getting bigger by the second. No matter what happens, take as many as you can through the trees there, and then bear west to the hillside. I came out of a cave or a depression in the hill."

"Good luck, Officer," Jacob said.

Tightening her helmet strap, Conyers nudged Torino forward and then kicked him over the hill, trotting toward the triceratops. Frozen in surprise, the Inhumans stood like statues. Then one broke, running to the triceratops, and was boosted onto a saddle behind its neck collar by another Inhuman. Using a spear as a prod, the Inhuman turned the triceratops uphill, other Inhumans frantically prodding the triceratops into motion. Now the Inhumans chanted musically, sending their war beast into battle.

The triceratops picked up speed, climbing toward the horse and rider. Torino wanted to veer away, Conyers fought to keep him on course. It was a collision course the horse could not possibly survive. Hidden behind the neck collar, the only glimpse of the rider Conyers got was an occasional peek over the top. The gap closed quickly, the Inhuman glancing more frequently now, sure it would win the collision but fearing it anyway.

Spear in her right hand, reins in her left, Conyers pulled Torino left at the last second. Quickly bringing Torino back right, Conyers was briefly parallel with the triceratops and its rider, and she jabbed with the spear. Instinctively, the Inhuman dodged the spear, the triceratops responding to the rider's weight shift by turning left.

Packed on top of the hill, the humans cheered, as if the duel between the horse and the triceratops were a sporting event. In response, a musical chanting came from the Inhumans.

The triceratops circled, the rider twisting to see where Conyers was. Torino could turn on a dime compared to the triceratops, and Conyers used that advantage. Bringing Torino around, Conyers cut across the arc of the triceratops's turn, coming up from behind, jabbing at the rider. Again, the rider turned the triceratops away, starting another wide turn. More cheering erupted from the top of the hill; the chanting at the bottom got louder.

Again Conyers set an intersecting course, coming up on the rider's left from behind. With some experience now, Conyers stood higher in the stirrups, leaning farther out, ready for a serious lunge at the rider. This time the rider turned the triceratops into Torino before Conyers could jab. Torino twisted to get out of the way, but a massive shoulder knocked the horse into a stumble. Torino went down, the triceratops continuing. Conyers tumbled from the saddle, rolling to keep from getting crushed by Torino.

The Inhuman chanting turned into a raucous high-pitched squealing. The top of the hill was silent. Conyers got up, knee twisted, hurting. Torino kicked wildly, rolling completely over, then getting his legs under him and standing. Head hanging, the horse shuddered but stood in place. Conyers limped over, taking the reins before Torino came to his senses and bolted. The ground rumbled as the triceratops made its slow turn and bore down on them.

"One more time," Conyers said to Torino and then climbed into the saddle. The humans cheered when she remounted.

Using her heels, Conyers kicked Torino into a trot, noticing the horse's gait was off rhythm. Conyers's own knee hurt, but nothing would matter if the triceratops ran them down. Having lost the spear, Conyers drew her pistol. Swinging Torino wide, Conyers circled, leading the triceratops into a slow turn. Making nearly a full circle, Conyers waited until the triceratops was angled in the right direction, and then she cut across the turn, coming up behind the triceratops as before. This time she hung back, Torino's head just parallel with the rump. Feeling a sharp kick from his rider, Torino lunged.

Coming up parallel, Conyers shot the rider in the side and then jerked the reins, pulling Torino clear. The rider disappeared over the far side of the triceratops, the animal continuing to run without a rider. Conyers had timed it well, and now the triceratops was headed toward the Inhuman line. Dropping back behind the triceratops, Conyers shot it twice in the rump, the beast grunting and picking up the pace.

Conyers pulled up, and then waved at Jacob, pointing toward the runaway triceratops. Jacob was ready, and the humans charged down the hill, following the track of the triceratops. Inhumans scattered, falling over one another to clear a path for the triceratops. A few Inhumans stood their ground, waving spears, trying to bring the triceratops under control. Kicking Torino into a gallop, Conyers caught the triceratops just as it reached the line. Conyers shot right and left, wounding two of the Inhumans trying to stop the triceratops. The third waited too long, and the triceratops ran him over as if he were not even there. Oblivious of the musical shouts on either side, the triceratops continued its unguided run, finished crossing the meadow, and disappeared into the trees.

The humans reached the line before the Inhumans could re-form. Coming in two columns, Jacob led one, Crazy Kramer the other. They drove the Inhumans back in both directions, creating a passage through the lines to the trees. With their forces circling the hill, the Inhumans were outnumbered and the humans wounded or killed many.

"Get them through!" Jacob yelled.

The families flowed down the hill toward the trees, through the passage secured by the men. Fighting was hand to hand, the ammunition now expended. Inhuman ranks swelled as those who had circled the hill came to join the battle. Conyers used Torino to herd the Inhumans into a tight mob, trying to keep them from flanking the humans. With two fronts in the battle, it was impossible.

Crazy fought like the madman he was, anchoring the center of one human line, Jacob the other. The first of the families was down the hill now, trying to squeeze through the passage held open for them, but the humans were being pushed back, the passage collapsing. With a final push, the Inhumans closed the exit, the human escape route gone. Turning back, the families in the lead pushed back into those still coming down the hill. Now the humans clumped together, surrounded.

The Inhumans cheered their pending victory, a weird high-pitched yodel. The fighting diminished briefly as the Inhumans filled in their ranks, making sure there was no gap in their line. Still mounted on Torino, a newly acquired Inhuman spear in her hand, Conyers knew their position was hopeless. On Torino, she could break through the lines and make a run for it, but looking around at all the terrified families, she knew she would never do it. She would fight with them to the end.

Men, women, and children knelt, praying, their voices beseeching the heavens' divine intervention. Conyers looked at the sky, seeing only the asteroid. Strangely, she wished it would hit. They could use the diversion. The Inhumans were chanting again, the chants slowly working into unison and getting louder.

"Come and get it, you choir boys!" Crazy shouted.

A woman began singing. *"Amazing Grace! How sweet the sound."* Others joined in, and soon the humans were all singing. The Inhumans stopped their chanting, listening. For a full minute there was nothing but the sound of the hymn, and then the Inhumans decided they had heard enough and resumed their chanting, building to an earsplitting level. Then they pressed the attack.

The fighting was furious now, Inhumans and humans taking knife wounds, broken bones, cracked skulls. Hacking right and left, Crazy severed limbs, took hands, split skulls. Three Inhumans attacked him at once, and Crazy wounded two before the third pierced Crazy's side. Killing the Inhuman that speared him, Crazy stumbled to where Jacob still fought, clinging to the promise he'd made to Leah.

"Bring it on," Crazy said, pressing a hand to his bleeding side.

"Hang in there," Jacob said, backing up to stand shoulder to shoulder with Crazy.

Conyers dismounted. The Inhumans might spare Torino if they did not have to kill the horse to get to her. Spear in hand, she stood with Jacob and Crazy, facing out. Tasting victory, the Inhumans chanted, jumped up and down, and then pressed in. One, two, three humans fell, the line crumbling. Then there was a new sound—the chatter of automatic weapons. Confused, the Inhumans stopped the attack. The rifle fire continued, brief spurts of three to five rounds. Inhumans fell, their ranks thinned. Confusion spread through the Inhuman ranks as they searched for the source of the gunfire.

Emerging from the trees was a squad of soldiers firing short bursts at the Inhumans. Careful not to hit the humans, the soldiers fired point-blank, wide, or even over the heads of the Inhumans. Working themselves into a frenzy, the Inhumans bunched, ready to charge. Familiar only with the semiautomatic weapons of the reverend's people, the Inhumans had never faced automatic weapons. They learned a horrible lesson.

The Inhumans charged, and the soldiers opened up with full auto fire, mowing the Inhumans down. Stumbling over those in front, the bodies piled up, those in back pushing those in front forward. In a minute, the soldiers killed more Inhumans than the humans had in two days of fighting. Dying valiantly but futilely, the Inhumans finally broke and ran. Letting them go, the soldiers spread out, making sure there were no lingerers. Finally, two of the soldiers approached Conyers, who led Torino. Jacob and Crazy Kramer stood next to her.

A marine officer and a civilian stepped forward, eyed Crazy Kramer and the bloody machete in his hand, and then addressed Conyers.

"Officer, my name is John Roberts. I'm with the OSS."

"Officer Kris Conyers," she said, wiping blood from her hand before shaking his. "We are really glad to see you."

"I'm Lieutenant Weller, that's Sergeant Kwan, Snead, Kelton, Washburne, and the big guy is Tafua."

"You came for us?" Jacob asked, trembling with relief.

"We'll get you home," John said, taking in the large number of people. "But to be honest, we were following someone else—Dr. Gah, Ranger Wynooski," John said, seeing them hobble from the crowd. "We had no idea the rest of you were here. Are Nick Paulson and Elizabeth Hawthorne here?"

"They've gone to the Inhuman village," Conyers said. "That's what they call them," she said, pointing at the bodies.

"They were trying to kill you," Weller said.

"Not at first," Jacob said. "They came to tell us something about the asteroid, and Dr. Paulson, Reverend, and a man named Carson went to see what they wanted."

"Asteroid?" John asked.

As one, they all pointed at the sky where the glowing dot that had hung over the trees had stopped rising and seemed to have sunk toward the horizon.

"How long do we have?" John asked, quickly realizing the time period they had dropped into.

"I think we're about out of time," Conyers said.

"Anybody can tell that just by how low the asteroid is," Wynooski said. "You can see it's coming in at a pretty low angle. A little lower, and it would just skip right off the atmosphere and go back into space."

"It won't," John said.

"I'm just saying it could," Wynooski said, hands on her hips, looking defiant.

"Where's this village Nick and the others went to?" John asked. "I need to find them."

"Follow him," John said, pointing at the triceratops, its harness still intact, coming out of the trees and angling across the meadow.

"Lieutenant Weller, get these people out," John said. "That asteroid will hit any time now, and when it does, everyone and everything will die. I'm going to get Dr. Paulson and the others."

"Kelton and Snead will go with you," Weller said looking at the asteroid, and then John. Without a question, Weller called the men over and gave orders. "We'll come back for you if there's time."

"There won't be," John said, then turned, double-timing it after the retreating triceratops.

"The closest way out is that way," Conyers said.

"That might be a problem," Weller said. "We had to deviate around a pod of tyrannosaurs back that way."

"What choice do we have?" Conyers asked.

"Are you sure you can find it?" Weller asked.

"Yes," Conyers said.

"Okay, let's get them up and moving," Weller said.

"We've got several dead, and we're still bandaging wounded," Jacob said.

"Get them buried, because we're moving as soon as we patch up your people," Weller said. "Ranger, do you know first aid?"

"Of course I know first aid," Wynooski said, moving indignantly toward the crowd. "Any moron can do first aid."

Conyers looked at the asteroid and realized she could see it creeping across the sky, moving like the minute hand of a clock. Estimating the distance between the asteroid and the horizon, she wondered if they even had enough time for first aid.

45

Monitoring

They launched one of their secret ships out of Area Fifty-one. We have witnesses that confirm it! They are up there in orbit right now, doing God-knows-what! Well, I know what, and I am here to tell you. That's why you listen. The government is in orbit to meet with alien emissaries about why our trigger-happy government blew up their base up on the moon. All you listening out there better hope that whoever they sent up there is one smooth talker, or else it will be interstellar war.

—Cat Bellow, host of *Radio Rebel*

Present Time
Lake County, Florida

Emmett Puglisi monitored the loading of the Aurora remotely through a secure Internet feed. From cameras mounted around Cape Canaveral, Puglisi saw the Aurora land, and then camouflaged by ground crews. Then the cargo was loaded on the Earth-to-orbit aircraft. At the same time, Emmett monitored the opening at the Mills Ranch. Fanny and Marty Mills were infinitely cooperative, opening their ranch to marines and technicians, who had installed even more monitoring equipment. From his lab, Emmett could remotely measure every conceivable kind of radiation emitted from the opening, as well as sample gases and detect thermal changes.

Emmett's primary concern was that moving the orgonic material from the isolation lab to Cape Canaveral would affect the nexus. His worst fear was that shifting the orgonic material would move the nexus or, worse, close it. Knowing that orgonic energy was affected by form gave Emmett some confidence the material could be moved. Emmett suspected that it was the geology or the topography of the locations where the nexuses were located that anchored the phenomena, but it was little more than a suspicion. When the truck left Emmett's lab for Cape Canaveral, Emmett studied his monitors, detecting only minute fluctuations. Most significant was a perceptible change in the shape of the opening at the Mills Ranch. Surprisingly, the opening seemed to get bigger. It might have moved only inches, but the darkness that marked the transition to the other time now was not so far under the collapsed wall.

Emmett had made it clear to Lieutenant Weller that he and his marines had only a short time to find Nick and Elizabeth and the others, and to get them home. Based on what had happened to the moon tyrannosaur, and Emmett's own modeling, the time differential was fast disappearing, the two time lines becoming synchronous. By moving and eventually destroying the orgonic material, Emmett hoped to seal the nexuses before the time synchronization, fearing what would happen at that event. If Nick and the others were not back before synchronization, they would never get back.

With surprising speed, the canisters were loaded and the Aurora prepped for takeoff. Towed into position, the Aurora spent no unnecessary time on the ground, where passing satellites or night owl employees, might snap a picture of it. Accelerating like a navy jet launched by a catapult, the Aurora flashed past three cameras and was gone.

Emmett studied his instruments as the Aurora shot into orbit. There was a clear warming of the Millses' barn, and a slight increase in oxygen content. The Cretaceous atmosphere was richer in oxygen than the modern air, with 30 percent oxygen, compared to the 20 percent in the modern era. The increasing oxygen suggested the passage had changed in some way, perhaps becoming more permeable. Emmett turned to the camera view and was shocked. The blackness that was deep under the collapsed wall was now closer to the interior of the barn. The blackness had also reshaped to fill the opening at this end. Emmett could only assume the same thing was happening on the other end of the passage.

"Come on, John, get them out of there," Emmett said.

Lost in thought, examining his instruments for even tiny changes in readings, Emmett was startled when an alert buzzer signaled a connection with flight control in Houston.

"Dr. Puglisi, we have a secure link for you from Commander Watson," Connie West said.

West was deputy flight director and liaison between Area 51 and Mission Control Center in Houston.

"What's happened?" Emmett asked.

"The Aurora has a fuel problem," West said cryptically. "Here is Commander Watson."

"Dr. Puglisi?" a voice said through a static mask.

"Yes, I'm here," Emmett said. "What's this about a fuel problem? Is it the Aurora or the booster?"

"Dr. Puglisi, the problem is that the Aurora reached orbit by using only eleven percent of its onboard fuel," Commander Watson said.

Surprised into silence, Emmett's mind raced with the implications.

"I repeat," Commander Watson said, "the Aurora reached orbit with only eleven percent fuel consumption. We are assuming that the cargo is responsible for this effect. Is that a reasonable assumption, or will there be residual effects on our return flight?"

"Sorry, Commander," Emmett said. "This is incredible. I would say impossible, but clearly it happened. It's not instrument error?"

"No, sir. Our tanks are nearly full."

"The effect should be limited to the immediate area around the canisters, so your return flight should not be affected," Emmett said, making it up on the spot.

"What about the PAM?" Watson asked. "Can we expect the same fuel consumption economy?"

"Yes," Emmett said, uncertain.

"Would the effect be specific to the type of fuel?" Watson asked. "The Payload Assist Module uses solid fuel and burns aluminum with ammonium perchlorate as the oxydizer."

"Solid or liquid should not matter," Emmett said, growing in confidence. "The material in the canisters is affecting the space–time continuum in the immediate area."

"So we can expect similar fuel consumption?" Commander Watson asked.

"Yes," Emmett said. "Is that a problem?"

"There is no throttle on this type of PAM," Commander Watson said. "Once we light it up, it's going to burn through all of its fuel. Given the performance of our engines on the flight up, the PAM will burn ten times longer than planned."

"Can you adjust the trajectory to compensate?" Emmett asked, worrying the mission was at risk.

"Houston is solving that problem," Commander Watson said. "You should know that the payload is going to get where it's going a hell of a lot faster than you thought."

"That's not a problem," Emmett said, doing his own calculations in his head.

"There is one more thing," Commander Watson said.

"Yes, Commander," Emmett said.

"Are you sure you want us to complete this mission?" Commander Watson asked.

Emmett hesitated, thinking it a bizarre question. Then he realized what Commander Watson was getting at. The orgonic material in those capsules was the solution to the biggest barrier to space exploration. The material Emmett was about to send on a journey to the sun made boosting mass into orbit cost effective. Emmett looked back at the camera trained on the Mills Ranch opening, seeing how much it had changed. Weeks had passed since John had gone after Nick, and still not returned. They might never return, and Emmett had given them all the time he dared. If these were links to the Cretaceous–

Tertiary extinction event, they had to be closed before the Chicxulub impactor struck.

"Send it," Emmett said, even knowing he was about to destroy a technological wonder.

46

Panic

Many studies have suggested that early Mars was covered by large oceans and blanketed by a thick atmosphere rich in carbon dioxide. . . . Mars today holds vast stores of frozen water, at its poles and even in the ground away from the polar regions. Scientists think there used to be more, in part because of pictures that show what appear to be shorelines, riverbeds, and tremendous gorges carved by flowing water.

—Robert Roy Britt

Sixty-five Million Years Ago
Inhuman Village

Nick found the village in an uproar. Inhumans hurried to and fro, gathering belongings, tying up bundles, hitching triceratopses to carts.

"They use the wheel," Nick said, still amazed at finding a sentient species in the human past.

"They learned about the wheel from us," Reverend said.

"But they adapted it," Nick said. "They would rule the planet if that asteroid hadn't wiped them out."

"It wasn't God's plan," Reverend said.

"We need to take them with us," Elizabeth said. "Back to the future."

"That's not God's plan," Reverend said in his preaching voice, his eyes wandering to the frantic preparations.

"What do you know of God's plan?" Elizabeth demanded.

"I know God's plan for these creatures because he has revealed it to me. They are to be killed by the cleansing fire of that asteroid."

"I've got a plan," Carson said. "It's get the hell out of here."

At the sound of falling timbers, Nick and the others turned, seeing the hut that sheltered the opening to Mars come crashing down, ropes cut, fronds removed, poles carried away and tossed unceremoniously aside.

"We're going," Carson said, grabbing Jeanette by the arm and dragging her along.

Velociraptors jumped to her defense, hissing and snapping at Carson. Even Do, still in Jeanette's pack, snapped at Carson.

"Jeez," Carson said. "Jeanette, call them off."

"Re, Me, Fa, So, La, Ti," Jeanette sang. "It's okay. He's not hurting me. Easy, Do. He's your daddy."

"Don't call me that," Carson said, stepping away from Jeanette and her velociraptors.

Inhumans hurried by, barely glancing at the humans, or even the velociraptors that they feared.

"I'm going, Jeanette," Carson said. "Are you coming?"

"Yes," Jeanette said. "Elizabeth, come with us."

"We're all going, right, Nick?" Elizabeth said, taking Nick by the hand.

"Yes," Nick said, glancing at the sky.

"I must get my people here," Reverend said, distracted by the activity of the Inhumans.

"You can see it for yourself," Nick said, pointing at the sky. "This age is coming to an end."

"And a new one is beginning," Reverend said. "I'm going to bring my people here and to the new land."

"There isn't time, Reverend," Nick said.

With the hut removed and the entrance revealed, Inhumans lined up, a large group of armed men at the head. Then, after an unseen signal, the warriors moved through the opening, to the world on the other side.

"We must stop them," Reverend said, realizing what the Inhumans were up to. "Mars isn't for them. It's for me and my people!"

"It's not for anyone," Nick said, indicating the stream of Inhumans going through the passage. "You know what Mars becomes. The same thing that is going to happen to Earth, happened to Mars but much worse. What strikes Mars is a planetoid the size of Pluto. The planet's surface is decimated, the atmosphere ripped away, the seas vaporized. Mars won't be able to support anything more complicated than bacteria."

"But when?" Reverend asked, pulling his attention away from the fleeing Inhumans. "You said that the Mars we visited is at least sixty-five million years in the past. When does the planetoid hit? In a year? A hundred years? A million years? Look what humanity accomplished in the few thousand years since their creation, and we did that outside the loving embrace of our Creator. What could we accomplish living in harmony with God? Over a million years? Why, in that much time, we could conquer the universe."

"Reverend, Mars is a dead end, for them, and for your people if you take them there."

"No, Mars is our future," Reverend said stubbornly.

"We're going!" Carson said emphatically, waving for Jeanette to follow him, but careful not to touch her.

Velociraptors eyed Carson suspiciously, keeping close to Jeanette.

"Yes, I must get my people," Reverend said.

Having served their purpose, the Inhumans ignored the small group of humans who pushed their way through the throng and past the giant spikes protecting the village. Hurrying down the trail, Reverend stayed with Nick and the others until he could split off toward his compound.

Moving at nearly a run, they fled down the well-worn trail, occasionally passing groups of Inhumans moving toward the village. Velociraptors orbiting Jeanette, the Inhumans gave the humans a wide berth, ceding their own trail. Carson suddenly pulled his gun, slowing, aiming at a small group of Inhumans coming toward them. Two Inhumans supported a third between them, the middle Inhuman bleeding from a wound in his side. Seeing the humans and their velociraptors, they stiffened, stepping off the trail, the two healthy Inhumans lifting spears with their free hands.

"Put your gun down," Nick said as they passed.

Carson ignored Nick, his gun pointed at the Inhumans until they were past. Shortly, they passed more straggler Inhumans, several injured, Carson as wary of them as they were of the humans.

"They look like they were in some kind of battle," Carson said. "And lost."

"Oh, I hope not," Nick said to Reverend. "You don't think they attacked your people, do you?"

"That's why they split the column," Carson said.

"What other people?" Elizabeth asked. "What's going on?"

"I'll explain as we go," Nick said, urging the others to hurry.

Moving as fast as they could, they raced down the trail, passing more Inhumans—many of them wounded, all of them wary. The trail narrowed, smaller branches splitting off. Nearing the point where Reverend would turn off for his father's church compound, they spotted a triceratops coming directly for them. Clearing the trail, they let it pass, the triceratops wary of the velociraptors but keeping to the trail.

"Nick Paulson, is that you?" Nick heard.

Behind the triceratops, Nick saw John Roberts and two marines. The marines spread out, slowing, guns on the velociraptors. John broke into a smile as he approached, coming straight toward Nick but wary of the velociraptors. John's eyes took in Elizabeth, Carson, and then lingered on Jeanette, as men's eyes always did. Then John saw Reverend. Suddenly, John diverted toward Reverend, his arms going wide.

"Cubby, is that you?" John asked.

"John?" Reverend replied, incredulous.

Then the two men embraced and slapped each other on the back.

"I thought you were dead," John said. "How'd you survive that nuclear blast?"

"What nuclear blast?" Cubby asked. "All I remember was trying to get into Portland but having no luck, and then suddenly I was inside and me and the whole city were here!"

"I can't believe you're alive," John said.

"What happened to Ripman?" Reverend asked. "Did he make it?"

"Yeah, he got me out of the Portland quilt in one piece. After that, he lived with me and my mom for a while, and then he became a hunter and guide," John said, ending the story of their mutual friend with him alive and well.

Nick knew John was leaving out part of the story. Ripman was part of the team that John led to the Yucatán to explore a newly discovered pyramid. Through that pyramid, they traveled back in time to the Mayan past. Ripman never returned and was trapped in the past, or some alternative time line, when the time passages were destroyed by a terrorist's nuclear device. Nick let the two men exchange stories, using the time to catch his breath. As the oldest of the group, Nick was having trouble keeping up with the others, even with an oxygen-rich environment. Elizabeth was hanging back with him out of pity, clearly not as tired as Nick.

"What's the deal with these raptors?" one of the marines asked, rifle pointed at the nearest. "Do we shoot them, or what?"

"Don't shoot!" Jeanette said, stepping between a marine and one of her chicks.

Reacting to Jeanette's emotion, the velociraptors all went into attack mode, heads down, tails straight. From the backpack, Do leaned over Jeanette, hissing at the marine.

"Don't move," Nick said.

With their rifles ready, fingers on their triggers, the marines were a second from starting a fight they could not win. With six velociraptors poised for attack, the marines might get two before they were torn to pieces.

"Enough of this," Carson said, careful not to touch Jeanette. "Remember the asteroid thing? Running for our lives?" Carson pointed at the sky where the asteroid had been— It wasn't there.

"There it is," Elizabeth said, pointing low in the sky.

"It's brighter," Reverend said. "Much brighter."

Nick saw it dropping, seemingly picking up speed.

"Is it my imagination, or is it going faster?" Carson asked out loud.

Before Nick could answer, the asteroid turned into a small sun that dropped out of sight.

"This is it!" Nick said.

Everyone held their breaths, even the velociraptors sensing danger. Seconds passed. Carson grew restless, then confident. Then the ground shook, enough to stagger everyone except the velociraptors, whose tails acted as balancing poles. Then the velociraptors started squealing, and then snapping at one another. Jeanette and Elizabeth clapped their hands to their ears and opened their mouths, their faces contorted in pain. The marines and Carson then did the same, with Reverend and John quickly following. Nick heard it last. A deafening high-pitched ringing that soon settled into a lower-frequency tone, as if a massive gong had been struck. Abruptly, the tremor ended, but the ringing continued, everyone pressing their hands to their ears. The pain ended, the tone dropping to low frequencies, and then was nothing more than a vibrating bass that faded away.

"What the hell was that?" one the skinnier marines asked in a near shout.

"The asteroid struck," Nick said. "It rang the planet like a bell."

"Planets do that?" the marine asked.

"That's it?" Carson said. "I thought all hell would break loose."

"There!" Reverend said, pointing across the meadow, above the trees where the asteroid had disappeared.

Bright streaks were shooting into the sky, spreading in all directions.

"That's not anywhere near here," Carson said. "Just what were you selling us?"

Everyone turned toward Nick.

"What you are seeing is the ejected matter being thrown up by the impact. Some of that will be orbited, but most is suborbital and will bombard the planet for thousands of miles in all directions. Forests and grasslands will ignite, burning out of control. The high atmospheric oxygen content will make it burn like no fire you've ever seen. But the worst is yet to come. There is a blast wave coming at us at five hundred miles an hour that will pulverize trees and rock. While we wait for that, ejecta will continue to bombard the planet, creating a massive firestorm that will suck the oxygen from the air."

"So we should run," Carson said, reaching for Jeanette but stopping short when Do leaned over her shoulder, the raptor's eyes on Carson's hand.

"How long do we have?" John asked.

Nick looked at the streaks fanning out in the sky like spokes of an umbrella. "Maybe two hours, maybe less," Nick said.

"We're double-timing it," John said to his marines. "Kelton, take point."

Two Inhumans came from the trees, one wounded, supported by the other. The marines covered them as the Inhumans hobbled past, nervously glancing at the raised weapons.

"God forgive me for my ignorance," Reverend said suddenly. "I'll never make it to my church and back, will I?"

"No," Nick said. "The rest of your Community can't be saved, but you can come with us. The ones who went with Officer Conyers might make it."

Reverend looked pained, and then a deep calm settled in. "Goodbye, Dr. Paulson," Reverend said. "Whether you meant it or not, you were an instrument of God's plan."

"What are you saying?" John said, putting his hand on Reverend's shoulder.

"It's clear to me now," Reverend said. "God did not call me to lead his people; he called me to be a missionary."

"Missionary?" John said, confused.

"To those who do not know God's love," Reverend said, indicating the Inhumans hobbling away.

"Come back with me," John said. "There are plenty of people who need saving there. You can keep the family business going."

"I go where God calls," Reverend said, shaking John's hand. "I'm glad you found your way, John. Be happy that I've found mine."

"They hate you," Nick said. "They'll kill you."

"My life is in God's hands," Reverend said, hurrying after the Inhumans.

As Reverend approached, the uninjured Inhuman pulled his black knife, jabbing it at Reverend to ward him off. Reverend opened his palms, spreading his arms wide. Walking slowly, he went to the injured Inhuman and lifted him in his arms, and then hurried down the trail toward the Inhuman village. Wary at first, the other Inhuman kept his knife out, following closely, and then put the knife away and trotted along behind Reverend.

"Can we go now?" Carson asked, inching down the path.

"Kelton, the point!" John shouted.

Then they were jogging, Kelton setting a brisk pace, but slow enough for the weakest member of the group to keep up—Nick. They ran, the velociraptors keeping close to Jeanette, Carson with Kelton in the lead, occasionally glancing back for Jeanette. Elizabeth came next, then Nick and Snead, the trailing marine. After a mile, Nick settled into a rhythm, jogging at his own pace, breathing deeply, but not out of breath. Keeping track of his troop, Kelton adjusted his pace so that Nick could keep up.

Running behind Elizabeth, Nick found himself thinking about his life, and how much of it he had spent alone. Elizabeth changed that. Even though they were both career focused, they found ways to spend time together, even if it was only for walks, trying new restaurants for lunch, or taking in shows. Once, they went to New York, seeing three musicals in two days. Nick remembered it as the best time of his life. There could have been more of those times, Nick thought, and there would be in the future if they made it home. The grade rose and became rocky, forcing Nick to focus on his footing. Soon Nick was puffing loudly. Eventually, the grade leveled out, Nick's respiration slowing, allowing him to talk.

"If we get out of here, I'm joining a gym," Nick gasped as they jogged, thankful for the oxygen-rich atmosphere.

"Save your breath," Elizabeth said. "You might join, but you'll never go. You're a workaholic."

"Look who's talking," Nick said. "We could go together. I'd like to spend more time with you."

"Very romantic, Doc," the marine taking up the rear cut in. "Folks, you better settle this soon 'cause we've got incoming."

Arcing overhead was a fireball trailing black smoke. It crossed their track at an angle, whistling to an impact far to their right. A sharp crack followed a loud thump, a fireball rising above the trees in the distance.

"Pick it up, Kelton," Snead called to the marine in front.

Taking a deep breath, Nick fought to keep up, the gap between him and Elizabeth slowly increasing.

"Incoming!" Snead shouted.

This fireball hung in the sky, not moving, just growing larger.

"Get down!" Snead shouted, tackling Nick and covering his body.

Nick felt the heat of the bolide as it whistled overhead, striking in the trees just ahead. The explosion was the loudest thing Nick had ever heard, the pressure wave rocking them as they lay on the ground. Shredded trees, earth, and burning debris rained down. Covered by Snead, Nick was protected from most of the fallout, but the others brushed burning material from one another and patted out flames.

Snead got off, letting Nick up. The path they had been following led into the trees ahead, which were now an inferno.

"Incoming!" Snead yelled, and tackled Nick again.

47

Obstacle

It is impossible for a man of average sensibility to observe closely and to note the painful expression and the intelligence of these creatures [horses] . . . to witness their sufferings [and] the brutal treatment which they too often meet from ignorant and cruel men; it is impossible for him to see these things without sorrow, without endeavouring to alleviate their agony. . . .

—Sir F. W. Fitzwygram

Sixty-five Million Years Ago
Unknown Place

On Torino, Conyers could have reached the passage home long ago, but would never leave the people in her charge. Walking as fast as they could were men, women, and children. Small children were carried, and older men and women were assisted. They had no wagons to carry the old and the injured, so the pace was slow. Dr. Gah was one of the injured, his ankle getting worse with each mile. Wynooski supported him with an arm around his shoulder, but the price was endless pontificating from the overconfident ranger. Many had wounds from the Inhuman attack, bandages seeping from the constant motion. Some might bleed to death before they reached the passage, but every time someone pleaded to stop, Dr. Gah would insist that they would all die if they did not get out of this land soon.

Conyers regularly rode ahead of the column, checking the route, scouting for danger, and then rode back to report to Lieutenant Weller, who kept the people moving. Marines were positioned around the slow-moving group, watchful for Inhuman activity. Now a half mile ahead of the column, Conyers reined Torino in as she came through a particularly dense stand of the peculiar palm trees. Torino gave a soft whinny and danced sideways, resisting moving forward. Stopping, Conyers peered through the deepening shadows. Late in the day now, there were only a couple of hours of sunlight left. While Conyers was sure she could find the exit in the daylight, she was equally confident she could not find it in the dark.

One of the shadows moved, and Torino bolted. Jerking the reins, Conyers turned Torino 180 degrees and kicked him into a gallop. At a piercing screech, Conyers looked over her shoulder to see a *T. rex* run from the forest, and it was moving fast. In open terrain, Torino could outrun it, but on an uneven surface, Torino had to pick his footing, jump logs, and sidestep boulders. The *T. rex* crushed or bulldozed everything in its path. The trees hampered the *T. rex,* so Conyers left what little trail there was to race through the trees. Angry at having its meal delayed, the *T. rex* roared its frustration, terrifying Torino.

Fighting to keep Torino's run under control, Conyers kept a tight rein, guiding the horse into a wide zigzag. At best, it kept the *T. rex* at bay, but the damn thing would not give up. Then the earth shook, and Torino stumbled, nearly fell, and then caught himself, stumbling sideways and grazing a tree, crushing Conyers's leg. With a wider stance and more mass, the *T. rex* seemed unaffected by the earthquake, closing the gap now. Struggling to stay on the back of the staggering horse, Conyers felt a shooting pain cut through her head, her ears ringing with the deafening bonging sound. Instinctively, Conyers clapped her hands to her ears, just as Torino bucked in reaction. Conyers fell, bounced off Torino's flank, and tumbled to the ground, thankful for her helmet.

As the ringing stopped and the ground settled down, Conyers poked her head above the patch of ferns where she lay. The *T. rex* was disoriented, walking in circles, shaking its head. Conyers touched the grip of her pistol, but then smiled at the silliness. It would be like shooting a whale with a BB gun. As if it had forgotten it was in the middle of pursuit, the *T. rex* stood stupidly, occasionally shaking its head. Carefully, Conyers looked for Torino, but he was gone. Keeping low, she studied the *T. rex,* which had its head high, sniffing, searching for a scent. Now the *T. rex* walked a few steps back the way they had come, repeating the sniffing routine.

Conyers inched away, her left knee hurting when bent. Biting her lip against the pain, she crawled through ferns and around the trunk of a tree, where she sat with her back against the trunk, letting herself breathe deeply. Her pants were torn, her knee exposed. There was no blood, but when she lifted her leg, sharp pain shot through her knee.

"Great," Conyers whispered. "Just when I might need to run."

Once she caught her breath, Conyers looked back around the tree, seeing the *T. rex* still sniffing. Now Conyers stood, keeping her weight on her right leg, and hopped away from the tree, keeping it between her and the *T. rex*. Reaching another tree, she inched around it and then repeated the routine. Angling away, Conyers put several trees between her and the *T. rex,* grimacing at every step with her left leg. Finally feeling safe, she turned and hobbled carefully and silently away, frequently checking over her shoulder.

She found Torino in a large clearing, grazing as if nothing had happened.

"I wish I had your memory," Conyers said.

Taking the reins, she hopped to Torino's side and then stopped. Her bad knee would not support her weight in the stirrup. Hanging on to the reins, Conyers limped to the other side and tried mounting from the right side, confusing Torino, who turned when she tried to mount. Falling from the stirrup, she landed on her rump, her left knee slapping the ground, and she gasped, stifling a scream. Letting the pain pass, she screwed up her courage, stood again, and talked to Torino as she tried mounting again.

"Easy boy," Conyers said. "Just let me get into the saddle from this side one time."

Confused, the horse began rotating again, looking to see what she was doing. Then she heard commotion in the trees. Fearing the *T. rex,* she held the saddle horn and leaned, looking under Torino's neck. Weller was there, leading the column of refugees. Waving her arms, Conyers hobbled across the clearing, making shushing sounds and leading Torino.

"There's that police girl!" Crazy shouted, waving his machete in greeting.

"Quiet!" Conyers replied as loudly as she dared.

"What?" Crazy hollered, Weller putting a hand on his shoulder and whispering something to him.

Then as one, the column froze, eyes wide. Conyers turned to see the head of the *T. rex* poking between two trees. Then it bellowed satisfaction. It had found its prey

48

Cousins

Imprinting *is a process where right after hatching, newborn animals attach to their mother—well, usually their mother. Actually, chicks will imprint on anything that moves or makes noise. I've see baby ducks swimming after a man they think is their father. Since birds descended from dinosaurs, we know that dinosaurs imprinted, just like birds do today.*

—Carmen Wynooski, Senior Dinosaur Ranger

Sixty-five Million Years Ago
Unknown Place

The fires flushed hidden creatures from the forest. Pterosaurs took to the air, disappearing into the murk. Small bipeds and quadrupeds ran past, oblivious of Nick and his group. Larger quadrupeds crashed through the forest. The earthquake, disorienting Earth-ring, and now fire put the herbivores in flight mode.

Ejecta continued to fall randomly, most of it nothing more than a distant boom. The size of the bolides reassured Nick, reasoning that the smallest mass would travel the farthest. Still, Nick stood by his guess of a couple of hours before the blast wave hit them. In the meantime, the spreading fires were the bigger danger.

Landmarks were disappearing, either burned or obscured by smoke. Fleeing dinosaurs crisscrossed trails, and the falling ash accumulated like snow. Snead, at the front, moved quickly, with a preternatural sense of direction, the others following blindly in faith. Jeanette's velociraptors were strangely vigilant, hissing and snapping at unseen dangers in the gloom. A sudden squeal in the distance, followed by snarling and a roar, told Nick at least one predator was in attack mode. The velociraptors ran a few feet off the trail, heads low, tails straight, oriented toward the distant fight.

Jeanette stopped for her velociraptors, Elizabeth, Nick, and Kelton, the marine taking up the rear, also stopping. Nick had his hands on his knees, breathing deeply. He felt like he was running a marathon he'd never trained for.

"Keep moving," Kelton said gently to Jeanette, careful not to touch her.

Do, riding in Jeanette's pack, eyed Kelton, jaws open slightly, showing razor-sharp teeth. Jeanette lifted the straps on her pack, relieving the weight on her shoulders. In addition to Do, Jeanette carried a rifle. Elizabeth had dropped her pack but kept her rifle. Nick realized he had been carrying nothing but a pistol, while Jeanette carried a rifle and a velociraptor on her back. Yet Nick was the most tired.

"I am joining a gym," Nick said, wiping sweat and ash from his face.

"We're joining a gym," Elizabeth said, smiling, helping Nick clean gray mush from his brow.

"Ma'am," Kelton said gently to Jeanette, "would your raptor let me carry him?"

Jeanette stood tall, arching her back, accentuating her voluptuous figure. She smiled at the kindness, revealing a small gap in her teeth. Covered in sweat and ash like everyone else, Jeanette somehow managed to make it look sexy.

"That's kind of you," Jeanette said. "But I don't think Do would like it."

"Yes, ma'am," Kelton said. "We need to keep moving."

A distant boom, and a bright flash startled everyone.

"That was a big one," Elizabeth said.

Nick realized Snead, John, and Carson had disappeared through the trees and gloom.

"Let me lead until we catch up," Kelton said, taking the point.

Then they were moving again, jogging, coughing, and wiping the mix of ash and sweat that dripped into their eyes. Like Snead, Kelton set a pace designed to keep the group together. After a few minutes, Nick began to wonder if they had taken a wrong turn, since they did not catch the group in front. Then they heard gunfire.

"Stay here!" Kelton shouted, and then took off at full speed.

Nick, Elizabeth, and Jeanette paused, breathing deeply and looking at one another, and then at the dark forest all around them.

"The hell with waiting," Elizabeth said.

Nick and Jeanette silently agreed, and they ran toward the gunfire. A few seconds later, the gunfire ended. Then they found the others, Snead on the ground, bleeding from a badly mauled leg, and John dumping the contents of a plastic first aid kit. Carson was holding the injured marine's rifle, jerking it around to point at Nick and the others when they came out of the gloom.

"Don't shoot!" Nick said.

Carson went back to pointing the rifle randomly at shadows. Lying nearby was the body of a velociraptor. Jeanette's flock trotted to the body, hissing and sniffing. Do struggled in his pack, trying to join his brothers and sister. Ignoring Do, Jeanette squatted, helping John bandage the young marine's leg. John ripped open two large gauze bandages pretreated with antibiotics and painkillers. Snead grimaced when John applied the first bandage, wrapping it tight with rolls of self-sealing gauze. By the time John applied the second bandage, Snead merely flinched, the painkiller from the first bandage already being absorbed.

"My leg's going numb," Snead said with relief.

Looking at the depth of the wounds, Nick wondered about what the bandages had been saturated with.

"Give him three of these," John said, handing Jeanette a small plastic bottle.

Jeanette scooted to Snead's head, lifting it and then resting it in her lap, leaning over his face to protect him from falling ash. Do looked over Jeanette's shoulder at the bloody leg, his tongue slithering in and out. Jeanette shook out three pills, gently pushed one in Snead's mouth, and then lifted his head to drink from her water bottle. The side of the marine's face pressed against Jeanette's bosom as she helped him. She repeated the process twice more.

"I feel better," Snead said when she finished.

"I bet you do," Nick said softly.

Elizabeth elbowed him in the side.

"It was a pack of their cousins," John explained, indicating Jeanette's velociraptors as he gathered up the remaining first aid supplies. "We crossed paths, and a fight started."

Nick inched closer to the velociraptor carcass, Jeanette's flock still surrounding it, sniffing and nudging it.

"Have they ever encountered another velociraptor?" Nick asked.

"No," Jeanette said, gently lifting Snead's head from her lap and then putting it down.

"Could I have another drink?" Snead asked.

Jeanette handed her water bottle to Snead, who was visibly disappointed.

"Maybe you better get them away from the carcass," Nick suggested.

"They're just curious," Jeanette said.

"He's afraid they may be choosing sides," Carson said. "Let's shoot them before they figure out they're not human."

Carson aimed at Jeanette's flock, which still surrounded the dead adult velociraptor.

"Carson!" Jeanette said, shocked. "They saved my life. No one is going to shoot them."

Jeanette's rifle slipped from her shoulder. Seeing the move, Carson swung his rifle away from the velociraptors and toward Jeanette.

"Easy, everyone," John said, stepping between the couple. "We're almost out of here. It can't be more than another half mile or so."

"Just a klick," Snead said, pulling at the bandages. "These are too tight."

"Leave them alone," John said.

"Look at the velociraptors," Carson said, his rifle now aimed back at the flock.

Heads down, tails straight, the velociraptors were focused on the shadows of the trees. Ash fell like snow, making it even more difficult to penetrate the forest. Slowly, everyone but Snead raised a rifle, pointing where the velociraptors were focused.

Four velociraptors appeared from the shadows, heads low, in attack mode. Spreading out, they came slowly, puzzled by the scene ahead. The lead velociraptor kept glancing at Jeanette's flock. Twice the size of Jeanette's velociraptors, these were experienced hunters, driven to the point of madness by the holocaust around them.

"Nick and Elizabeth, take the one on the left, Jeanette the next, I'll take the one in the lead, and Kelton and Carson, you take the one on the end. Nobody shoots until I do."

Nick aimed his pistol, knowing the velociraptor had little to fear from him. Elizabeth's rifle packed more punch, but Elizabeth was no marksman. Jeanette had trouble steadying her rifle, Do, struggling to get out of the pack, ruining her aim. John seemed confident of getting the lead velociraptor, and Kelton and Carson might get the raptor on the end.

"Re, Me, Fa, So, La, Ti," Jeanette sang. "Come," she said, singing their names again.

Jeanette's velociraptors stayed where they were, ignoring Jeanette's call.

"They ever do that before?" Nick asked Elizabeth softly.

"No," Elizabeth said, worried.

Holding their position, the pack of velociraptors studied the humans and the velociraptor chicks surrounding their dead mate.

"Re, Me, Fa, So, La, Ti," Jeanette sang again.

Jeanette's velociraptors ignored her call.

"We can't just stand here," Carson said, a distant boom serving as an exclamation point.

"Don't move," John repeated. "Kelton, Carson, you may have to cover the velociraptor chicks."

"They won't hurt you," Jeanette insisted. "Re, Me, Fa, So, La, Ti."

The stalemate continued until a small bolide struck somewhere behind the adult pack, and they jumped, triggering an attack. With no defined source for their fear, the velociraptors focused on the humans, as if killing them would end the horror their world had become.

The humans opened fire, but velociraptors leapt when attacking, and the humans fired wildly, trying to hit the moving targets. John wounded the lead raptor, but could not stop its momentum, and John stumbled back, firing his big bore rifle again. Holding his fire, Nick tried to track his raptor as it leapt once, and then twice. Then, midleap, a smaller velociraptor met it, claws extended, just missing the neck of the big raptor and raking its side. The impact from one of Jeanette's raptors knocked the big one off stride, saving Nick's life. Now there was a melee, with raptors fighting one another, clawing, leaping, jumping in and out of the fray. John's wounded velociraptor died first. Already bleeding from a chest wound, one of the raptor chicks managed to slash its throat, the big raptor bleeding out in seconds.

Carson fired indiscriminately, until Jeanette tackled him, his rifle flying from his hands.

"You shot Fa!" Jeanette screamed, pummeling his back.

Rolling over, Carson kicked Jeanette in the stomach and then the face, Jeanette curling into a ball. With a screech, Do wriggled violently, getting out of Jeanette's pack, crawled over Jeanette's shoulder, and then charged Carson. Grabbing the rifle, Carson brought it up just in time, shooting Do. The raptor's momentum carried it into Carson, but the little raptor was dead. Wiping blood from her nose, Jeanette crawled to Do, cradling the velociraptor, crying, even as the fight continued.

John and Kelton resorted to bursts of automatic fire over the heads of the tangle of velociraptors, the big ones finally turning tail and retreating, leaving another dead one behind. The skirmish was over. Three of Jeanette's velociraptors were dead. Carson had shot two, and little Ti was killed by one of the adult velociraptors. Another of Jeanette's flock lay badly injured, struggling to get up. The remaining three were on guard, eyes fixed on where the adult raptors had retreated. Like the velociraptors, John and Kelton stood guard, watching for another attack. Elizabeth moved to Jeanette, comforting her while Nick carefully approached the wounded velociraptor.

Nick did not know its name, but it hissed when he came near. Moving slowly, Nick knelt, seeing a gash that cut deep into a thigh.

"John, have you got another of those bandages?" Nick asked.

John took Snead's pack, dumped it, and came up with another bandage. Nick peeled off the protective coating, revealing the pretreated side of the bandage and the adhesive edges.

"Nick, are you crazy?" Elizabeth asked softly from where she held Jeanette.

Very slowly, Nick leaned over the velociraptor, placing the bandage over the gash and pressing down. The raptor snapped, Nick jerking back to save his fingers. Waiting a few seconds, the velociraptor seemed to settle down, and Nick reached in again, the raptor watching his every move. Gently, Nick pressed the adhesive edges to the raptor's skin. He finished with his fingers intact.

Jeanette was up, now mourning the loss of Ti, Fa, and Do, and then checking Nick's work on Me.

"Thank you for what you did for Me, Nick," Jeanette said, hugging him.

Nick accepted the hug, but broke it as quickly as politeness would allow, checking Elizabeth's expression to see how she took it—she took it well.

Jeanette then moved to La, Re, and So, who were all injured, but not badly. Elizabeth had dumped the dog food with her pack, so the velociraptors licked their wounds by the light of an approaching forest fire.

"I didn't mean to shoot your raptor," Carson explained, approaching Jeanette. "They were all mixed up."

"You shot Do too," Jeanette said, refusing to look at Carson.

"He tried to kill me," Carson whined.

"You kicked me in the face," Jeanette said.

"I'm sorry. You were all over me, and the raptors were attacking."

"Go to hell," Jeanette said.

"We don't have time for this," John said, interrupting the argument. "Nick, help me with Snead. Kelton, take the point. Elizabeth and Jeanette, I need you two to protect the rear. Carson, give me that rifle and you walk in the middle."

"I'm keeping the rifle," Carson said, hugging it to his chest.

"If you fire that weapon without my permission, I'll shoot you myself," John said.

"Wait," Jeanette said, taking off the pack that had carried Do. Elizabeth held it open while Jeanette gently lifted Me in. Then Nick helped Elizabeth lift the pack so that Jeanette could put it on. Me squawked annoyance, but did not seem to be in any pain.

"Let's move," John said.

With Nick under one of Snead's arms, and John under the other, they supported the marine, who was feeling no pain but whose leg could not carry any weight. Kelton led off, somehow picking his way through the forest, now lit by an approaching fire. At the back of the pack, Jeanette's three healthy velociraptors kept near Jeanette, one on either side, one trailing. Occasionally, one would stop, turn back, and freeze, then a few seconds later, trot to catch up. The velociraptors seemed to think that something was following the fleeing humans.

49

The Long Journey

On average, the distance between the Earth and the sun is 93 million miles, or 8.3 light-minutes. Unfortunately, a spacecraft sent to the sun could not travel in a straight line. Typically, space probes of this mass can be accelerated to 5.2 kilometers per second, which means it would take the better part of a year for transit.

—Emmett Puglisi, Special Consultant to the OSS

Present Time
Earth Orbit

Mission Pilot Rosa Perez-Roberts moved the Aurora away from the PAM to the recommended safe observation distance. With no ports, the observations were from external cameras, Perez-Roberts and Watson with their own monitors, Chandra and Maven sharing a screen in the cargo hold. Houston controlled the PAM, and now they saw puffs of gas from around the perimeter of the PAM, starting a rotation. The PAM used spin stabilization, the rocket and its payload now rotating rapidly. Rotation distributed and nullified any mass differences between the two cylinders, and compensated for potential uneven burn of the solid fuel, creating a clear center of gravity.

"Houston, she's stable," Commander Watson radioed.

"Roger that," West said.

Now the PAM engine ignited with a blinding flash, and then a steady burn, hot gases spewing from the nozzle. Quickly, the PAM sped away, the trajectory modified because of the newfound power of the booster. Previously, the plan was to accelerate the cylinders around the Earth, and then slingshot it toward the sun. With ten times the power, the trajectory was recalculated and the cylinders blasted out of orbit, not bothering with the slingshot effect.

"Houston, she's on her way," Watson said with a pang of regret.

"Houston, how's that software update for flight control coming?" Maven asked.

"We're sending it now," West said.

Watson watched the white dot of the PAM shrink to a pinpoint, and then lost it. Then Perez-Roberts turned the Aurora and executed a gentle burn, the spaceship dropping toward Earth on its way to being an airplane again.

50

Escape

As the middle of the proud ceremonial column leveled with the vehicle, the explosion was detonated. . . . Seven horses were killed. . . . Sefton suffered multiple deep wounds to his neck. . . . [One] 2 × 1 shred severed his jugular vein. Five four-inch nails were implanted . . . into his face, one spiked his back. His stifle and flanks were gored by searing shrapnel from the car. . . . [Eventually] Sefton returned to his duties. . . . The Household Cavalry recorded that he was a horse of great courage and character. Trooper Pederson reported that Sefton responded so bravely when the bomb exploded that there was no chance of being thrown from him.

—Cheryl R. Lutring

Sixty-five Million Years Ago
Unknown Place

With the column strung out over half a mile, only those in front saw the *T. rex*, but everyone heard it bellow. Turning to flee, they ran into and over those behind, hampering the marines from getting forward. With Sergeant Kwan, Washburne, and Tafua fighting their way upstream through the panic, Weller had the only weapon with ammunition between the *T. rex* and its prey. Crazy Kramer stood his ground, machete in hand, dried blood in his beard, wild look in his eyes.

Whether the *T. rex* saw the panicking crowd or not, it showed no interest. Instead, its eyes were fixed on Torino, who now danced around in a circle and reared, getting ready to run. Dragged by the reins, Conyers hung on for dear life and then lunged for the saddle horn, jammed her bad left leg into the stirrup, and threw herself into the saddle. Something in the knee tore, but fear helped control the pain, and she was in the saddle again. Bulldozing two trees, the *T. rex* broke into the clearing, coming straight toward Torino.

"Get out of the way!" Weller yelled, trying for a clear shot.

Given his head, Torino bolted, needing no kicks to get to a full gallop. The *T. rex* closed fast, sprinting across the open space, angling to cut Torino off. Weller opened up on full auto, the *T. rex* taking hits but ignoring them. Judging the speed and mass of the *T. rex*, Conyers cut inside his angle, forcing him to turn. For something that huge, it was nimble, but Torino was faster, the *T. rex* lunging when the horse made its near pass, the huge feet of the *T. rex* throwing mounds of turf into the air as it dug for traction. Its jaws snapped closed just over Conyers's left shoulder.

"Bring him around!" Weller shouted.

The other three marines had arrived, kneeling, taking aim. With the *T. rex* closing, Conyers rode parallel to the marines positioned in the trees. All four opened up on full auto, this time getting the *T. rex*'s attention. Veering, the *T. rex* charged the marines, running right into the weapons' fire. The marines broke, running left and right. The *T. rex* snapped up one, biting him nearly in half, his pelvis and legs dangling from huge jaws by sinew and a shredded uniform. With a jerk of his head, the *T. rex* swallowed the rest of the marine, and then looked for more. Gunfire gave away the position of another, and the *T. rex* attacked, the marine rolling away, crawling behind a tree. With a head butt, the *T. rex* knocked the tree askew, seeing the marine crawling away.

Kicking Torino furiously, Conyers drew her pistol, charging the *T. rex* from behind.

"Yah, yah, yah!" Conyers yelled, shooting at the *T. rex*'s spine.

Either the sting of the bullets or the bang of the pistol caught the attention of the *T. rex*. Seeing Torino, the *T. rex* went for the larger meal, burying the fleeing marine in dirt and turf as it dug in and turned. Conyers had a head start, racing across the open space, heading for the trees on the other side. As before, she planned to zigzag through the forest. Torino was tiring, partly from the exertion, but mostly from crippling fear. Conyers had to find some way to end this. If the marines could not kill the monster, then she had to lose it. Nearing the trees, she saw movement. Two more *T. rex*es came from the forest, attracted to the bellowing and shooting.

"Damn!" Conyers said, pulling hard right.

The trailing *T. rex* paused only long enough to bellow a warning at its brothers, which set off a squabble. The other predators came on, ignoring the warning, jostling for position in the chase. Out of ideas, Conyers decided to lead the *T. rex*es away from the others, giving them a chance to get away. Now chased by three of the monsters, she headed for the trees, Torino nearly exhausted, his terror keeping him running.

Then overhead Conyers saw a fireball coming straight for her. Kicking Torino furiously, Conyers eked out a bit more speed, and they reached the trees just as the fireball hit behind them. The explosion nearly knocked Conyers over Torino's head, but she landed on his neck, heat singeing the horse and rider, burning the hair from the back of Conyers's neck. Torino screamed with pain and fear, but kept running, dodging trees, letting them absorb as much debris, heat, and flame as they could. Then a new horror, as meat and scorched *T. rex* parts rained. Bits and pieces spattered horse and rider, bigger chunks landing right and left. To the right, a massive haunch hit and tumbled, creating a pinwheel of blood. To the left, a small *T. rex* arm spun down from the sky like a whirlybird. Then the head of a *T. rex* fell through the trees, knocking off limbs and burying itself in the soft ground, blocking their flight. Conyers pulled up, Torino rearing, whinnying, and staring wide-eyed at the gaping jaws and dead eyes.

Looking back, Conyers saw a fire in the meadow behind them and heard the screaming of an injured *T. rex*. Letting Torino walk off his exhaustion, Conyers circled wide, eventually finding the refugees crowded together, Weller and Jacob Lewinski trying to calm them and keep them from running back to the church compound.

"It's a sign from God!" someone shouted.

"He blocked our way!" another shouted.

"We should have listened to Reverend. We've got to go back."

"Don't be stupid," Wynooski could be heard saying. "There is no God. There are no signs."

"You need to get moving again!" Weller shouted. "We're almost there. We can get you home."

"This is our home," came a frightened voice.

"Quiet!" Conyers shouted, coming through the trees.

It had to be the horse that gave her authority, but the crowd settled down, listening to her when they would not listen to Lieutenant Weller and his men.

"God didn't block your way," Conyers argued. "God cleared the way. Who do you think sent that fireball?"

"She's right!" Jacob shouted. "God saved us from the beasts that plague this world."

Uncertainty spread through the crowd, some still arguing to go back, others listening.

"Look at the sky," Conyers said.

The people looked to see black streaks spreading from some distant point.

"This age is ending. God cleared the way for you to go home. Disobey God at your own peril."

Then Conyers pushed through the crowd, letting them fall in behind Torino, and angled through the trees to skirt the burning meadow. Behind, some followed immediately, while others hesitated, arguing and pleading with others to go back. Children cried in fear and uncertainty; husbands and wives bickered. Then all argument ended when another fireball fell from the sky, exploding a mile behind them. The forest between them and their church was now ablaze. Instantly, all the remaining people fell in line, now urging those in front of them to get out of the way, or to hurry.

Distant thumps announced more impacts, and soon smoke rose from a half dozen sites all around them. Soot fell thick as a blizzard, people coughing and complaining of the smoke. Taking her knife, Conyers pulled the tail of her shirt from her pants and cut it off. Soaking it in water, she made a bandanna, tying it over her mouth and nose. The spreading smoke hastened night, and soon they were hiking through a toxic gloom.

"Lieutenant Weller, I'm going to push ahead. I think we're close, but I need to find it before it's too dark to see."

Weller waved her on, and Conyers urged Torino into a trot, as fast as she dared go with limited visibility. Guided by her last visual reference, and her instinct, Conyers kept as straight a line as she could, passing through alternating meadows and small stands of trees. Finally, she came out of a stand of trees and rode for half a mile through ferns and palms the height of a fire hydrant. Then the slope changed, rising sharply. This had to be it, but was the valley she and the Stripys had come out of to the right or left? Conyers guessed right, riding partially along the hill, one eye on the distant tree line, fearful of what might be hiding in the trees. After half a mile, she found the cleft. Riding a few steps into the opening, she saw that the shadow was still there, an irregular blackness filling the small canyon from side to side. Afraid to dismount with her bad leg, Conyers tossed her handcuffs into the blackness. They disappeared.

"Let's hope that goes where I think it does," Conyers said, and then turned Torino and began retracing her steps.

Leaning out, Conyers kept her eyes on the ground, following her own trail. Torino huffed and coughed now, his lungs irritated by the thickening smoke.

"Hang in there, boy," Conyers said. "Just a little longer."

Following the trail through the meadow was relatively easy since a horse and rider chewed up soft turf. In the trees, the shadows made it even harder to see, and she rode slower. To the left, another fireball hit, turning a small fire into a forest fire. Wind direction was bringing it their way.

"We've got to move faster," Conyers said, nudging the exhausted horse.

Leaning out nearly to the point of falling off, Conyers watched the trail, awkwardly guiding Torino around trees and through small clearings. Once she lost the trail and circled, spiraling out, until she saw a clear hoofprint; then she was back on the trail, leaning low, trusting Torino to find good footing. Then ahead, she saw Weller coming through the trees, people trailing, holding hands, afraid of losing their way.

"This way, I found it!" Conyers called.

Weller smiled at seeing the officer, and passed the word behind him, voices spreading the news all the way to the end of the column to Sergeant Kwan.

"All right!" Crazy Kramer yelled, stepping out, covered from head to toe in soot but acting as if he were walking in the rain. "Bring it on!"

They hurried now, Conyers and Torino leading the way, the trail twice traveled by Torino now much easier to follow, even though it was near dark. Using her flashlight, Conyers lit the path, the light easy for the others to follow. The forest fire was burning its way toward the column, threatening to cut it off, more soot and flaming material raining, starting small fires. Finally, they emerged from the last of the trees, and Conyers left the trail, cutting diagonally toward where she knew the cleft would be. Looking back, Conyers could see how badly the group was strung out, with gaps between clumps of people. The stragglers would be lucky to get out of the forest before the fire reached them. Then the cleft appeared, Conyers's dead reckoning dead-on.

Conyers rode to the opening, positioning herself on the far side, waving the others forward.

"This it?" Weller asked, stopping next to Conyers, looking down the passage at the opening.

"Yeah, it's how I got here," Conyers said, realizing something had changed.

When she had first looked back after riding out of the opening with the Stripys, the blackness had filled the entire cleft near its widest point. Now the blackness had moved deeper in, where the passage was narrower.

"Crazy, you keep them coming," Weller ordered.

"All right!" Crazy said. "Keep them coming."

"You two, move on through," Weller said.

"We're the Browns, Betty and Lincoln," the old woman said. "Through that? But it's so black. Where does it go?"

"It's your ticket home, ma'am," Weller said, taking Betty's arm and walking her into the cleft, her husband following. "Now go. You back there, follow."

Cautious and slow, the Browns were the first through, a young couple with three school-aged children following. Then, as another clump of five men and women started in, the first group came rushing back out of the shadow, the Browns coming last, falling over the children who tripped as they were dragged out of the opening by their parents.

"It's hell!" Betty shouted. "The reverend was right. That passage leads to hell!"

"What are you talking about?" Jacob Lewinski demanded, pulling his wife and daughters to the front.

"It's awful," Betty said. "Better to die here than in that devil's playground."

"She's right," the mother of the children said. "It's not a fit world for raising children."

Seeing that the fire had finished consuming the forest and was now racing across the meadow after the stragglers, Jacob turned to Leah. "Wait for me," he said, and plunged into the blackness.

51

Closing Time

Until the time of Einstein, we thought that mass and energy were two separate things. Until we rediscovered the power of pyramids, we thought form and energy were two different things.

—Nick Paulson, Director of the OSS, testimony to the Senate Armed Services Committee

Present Time
Lake County, Florida

"Dr. Puglisi, we had a successful PAM burn, and your payload is on its way," West said over the secure link to Houston.

"Was the booster burn unusual?" Puglisi asked.

"Consistent with revised expectations," West said.

"Thank you," Emmett said, and disconnected.

Watching his monitors, Emmett saw readings from the Millses' barn changing rapidly. Atmospheric carbon dioxide was increasing, particulate matter flowing through the nexus into the Millses barn, and the temperature rising. That combination indicated fire. At the same time, the nexus had reconfigured again, creeping out nearly to the standing interior wall. The opening was not only moving, but also becoming larger. Theorizing in the dark, Emmett had no idea of the significance of the change, but he was sure of one thing: With the orgonic material leaving orbit, its influence would soon come to an end. Emmett called the marines standing guard around the Millses' barn and ordered them to move well back.

John, if you're going to get them out, do it now, Emmett thought.

52

Exit

Self-sacrifice is the real miracle out of which all the reported miracles grow.

—Ralph Waldo Emerson

Sixty-five Million Years Ago
Unknown Place

"I think we're being followed," Elizabeth said to Jeanette.

Carson overheard, looked back, and then slowed to get closer, testing Jeanette's mood with a smile. Me leaned over Jeanette's shoulder, snapping at Carson.

"Good Me," Jeanette said, and rubbed the little velociraptor's snout.

Carson jumped back and then jogged a couple of steps to catch up with the leaders, the murk so thick now, he nearly disappeared.

"Those raptors wouldn't follow us, would they?" Jeanette asked.

"I don't know," Elizabeth said. "Nick says velociraptors are very intelligent and more humanlike than any dinosaur. Maybe they want revenge. Maybe they think we caused all this. Maybe having the world fall apart around them is making them crazy."

Carson disappeared into the gloom, and they hurried to catch up. Jeanette's surviving velociraptors kept up their strange stop-and-watch behavior, unnerving Elizabeth. The climate was already tropically hot, and the heat of the approaching fire made it even worse. Dirty sweat ran in their eyes, and they wiped their faces over and over. Suddenly, something the size of a truck ran from the trees, crossing their path.

Elizabeth grabbed Jeanette's shoulder, pulling her back, and they went down, falling on their rumps. Without slowing, the huge quadruped stampeded across their track and into the trees on the other side, bulldozing a path as it ran. Behind it, three smaller animals followed single file, all with bony neck collars and one long horn.

"Thanks," Jeanette said, getting up.

Re hissed a warning. Based on the behavior of Jeanette's velociraptors, Elizabeth believed Re was the new top raptor. Re was certainly the largest.

The women turned, rifles ready, trying to see in the gloom.

"You see anything?" Elizabeth asked after a minute.

"No," Jeanette said. "But they do."

All three healthy raptors were frozen, pointed in the same direction.

"What should we do?" Jeanette asked.

"So, Re, and La will watch for us," Elizabeth said. "Let's find the others."

Elizabeth half turned, trying to find the path and keep a watch behind them at the same time. Jeanette did the same, the two women crossing the track of the quadrupeds, stumbling over deep hoofprints. They were out of sight of Jeanette's velociraptors after a few yards. The women moved slowly at first, and then picked up speed.

"Re, So, La," Jeanette sang.

Two of the velociraptors came through the smoke and soot—So and La.

"Re?" Jeanette sang, but the raptor did not come.

"We've got to go," Elizabeth said, pulling Jeanette. "Re will catch up."

They hurried as fast as they dared, trying to follow the general direction Kelton had been leading them. Elizabeth knew the risk, since it would be impossible to walk a straight line without distant landmarks. With a flash and then a boom, another fireball impacted to their left, bright light and heat radiating through the forest, feeling like the heat of an open oven. In the flash they saw Re, and behind him two large velociraptors. So and La turned, going into attack posture, Re trotting between them and then turning, taking a position behind.

"Weren't there three of them?" Elizabeth asked, checking on either side of the two visible velociraptors.

"Yeah!" Jeanette said.

Studying the posture of the adult raptors, Elizabeth realized their heads were high, their tails low. "I don't think they're going to attack," Elizabeth said.

"Maybe," Jeanette said, seeing their posture. "Let's go while we can."

They resumed trotting through the gloom, the velociraptors picking up their seesawing, protective routine. Just when Elizabeth thought they were lost, Kelton appeared in the forest, calling to them.

"This way!" he yelled.

The women followed him, running as best they could. A short distance later, they broke out of the forest, coming to a hill. Carson was at the top, supporting Snead, while John and Nick waited at the bottom. Nick hurried to Elizabeth, taking her in his arms.

"Nick, the raptors are back," Elizabeth said, pushing him away.

They all turned to see two adult raptors pacing back and forth in the flickering shadows of the fires.

"Get up the hill," Nick said.

"Not without Jeanette, and if she goes up, her velociraptors will too," Elizabeth said. "You go up with John, and we'll come last. You can cover us from the top."

"I'll stay with you," Nick said.

"I'll stay with Jeanette," John said.

"Go, I'll be okay," Jeanette said. "Re, So, and La will protect me."

Elizabeth relented, letting Nick help her up the steep hill, and then all of them except Snead aimed their rifles over John and Jeanette's heads. Jeanette and John climbed quickly, Jeanette's velociraptors climbing behind and next to her. The adult velociraptors advanced to the base of the hill, where they stopped, watching the humans. Coated in gray ash, the velociraptors were nearly invisible.

"Wasn't there one more?" Carson asked.

"Let's go," John said.

With John and Nick supporting Snead, they hurried along the top of the hill. The view from the hill showed a nightmare world. The forest below them was spotted with fires, some merging into larger fires. Distant fires were nothing but glowing spots. What was clear was that eventually they would all merge, turning into a super firestorm.

"It's spreading so fast," Elizabeth said.

"It's the high oxygen content," Nick said. "It's like lighting a fire in an oxygen tent."

"Carson, take Snead," John said.

"Why me?" Carson asked.

"Just do it."

Freed from helping support Snead, John led, stopping occasionally to look over the hill. Finally, he stopped, looking down.

"This is it," John said. "Straight down here and then through the cave. Carson and Nick, you help Snead down."

"I won't go without Elizabeth," Nick said.

Touched by his protectiveness, Elizabeth wiped grime from her face so Nick could see her smile. "I'll be okay," Elizabeth said.

"She'll come next, I swear," John said. "You can wait for her at the entrance while Carson pulls Snead through."

Nick relented, and Elizabeth watched him slip down the hill to the cave, careful not to slide by it. Below the hill the slope got steeper and was impossible to climb. Reaching the small ledge, Carson backed into the opening, dragging Snead behind him. Looking over the edge, Elizabeth saw Carson and Snead entering the opening, Carson bent over as he dragged Snead, but standing. Elizabeth did not remember the entrance being that spacious.

"Send Elizabeth!" Nick shouted.

"Elizabeth, you and Kelton next," John said.

They both put their rifles over their shoulders, and then carefully half-walking, half-sliding, worked down the hill, occasionally reaching out to steady each other. Nick hovered by the opening, looking like he might try to catch her if she fell. Just as they reached the ledge, there was shooting at the top, and the sound of velociraptors fighting.

Kelton unslung his rifle, looking uphill, and then turned to Elizabeth and Nick. "Get through the opening," the young marine said.

Then there was a commotion below, and Elizabeth turned in time to see the third velociraptor bounding up the hill, its clawed toes digging deep.

"Watch out," Elizabeth said, pushing Nick aside. The velociraptor had Kelton by an arm before he could move, pulling the marine off the ledge and tumbling down the hill with him. Elizabeth raised her rifle, but had nothing to shoot at, since Kelton and the velociraptor were tumbling together. At the bottom, the velociraptor came out on top, ripping Kelton's intestines from his body. Kelton gave one scream before the velociraptor clamped down on his neck, nearly severing his head.

"Get inside," Nick said, pushing Elizabeth toward the opening.

"We have to help him," Elizabeth said.

"He's dead," Nick said.

Automatic fire sounded above, and then everything was quiet, except for a distant roar, growing rapidly louder.

"We killed one, but the other ran off," John called from above.

"It was a trap!" Elizabeth shouted back up, barely heard above the roar. "There's one at the bottom too. It killed Kelton."

The roar was much louder now, Nick suddenly stiffened, looking into the distance. "What do you see?" Nick called up the hill.

"Something's coming," John said. "It's the blast wave."

"Get down here!" Nick shouted. "Hurry."

John and Jeanette came recklessly, Me still on Jeanette's back, but only one other velociraptor chick at her side. Elizabeth thought it was So. Elizabeth and Nick reached out, taking their hands, pulling them onto the small ledge.

"The opening's bigger," Elizabeth said, bending to enter.

"That may be bad," Nick said, barely heard above the growing din. "Go, go."

Then a velociraptor had Nick by the leg, clamping down so hard Elizabeth heard a bone break. Nick gasped as he was pulled over the edge. Elizabeth grabbed an arm as Nick fell, and she was dragged over the edge. John fell on her legs, wrapping his arms around them, arresting her fall. They lay there on the side of the hill, the velociraptor trying to tear Nick's leg off, Nick screaming from the pain. Elizabeth held his arm, and John her legs or she would go over the side. It was a stalemate, but Nick would lose his leg and his life if it went on much longer. Then So attacked, bounding down the hill, nearly out of control, leaping at the last second, clawed feetfirst. The adult velociraptor released John's leg, instantly sliding down the hill, snapping at So.

Jeanette and John pulled Elizabeth up, inch by inch, Elizabeth holding on to Nick for dear life—his life. Using his good leg, Nick pushed as well as he could. At the bottom of the hill, the raptors fought, a fight that little So would lose. Elizabeth made it over the ledge and then helped drag Nick up and over. He was bleeding profusely, a piece of bone poking through the skin of his leg.

"Leave me," Nick said, face contorted from pain. "It's coming."

The roaring was deafening now, and Elizabeth could see a boiling cloud towering a mile into the sky.

"Follow me," John said, taking Nick by the armpits and dragging Nick into the cave.

"So," Jeanette called down the hill, looking for her velociraptor.

In response, the adult velociraptor bounded up the slope. Jeanette raised her rifle, firing nearly point-blank as the velociraptor reached the top. The bullet hit midchest, the raptor dropping dead and tumbling back down the hill.

"That's for So," Jeanette said, sobbing.

"Come on," Elizabeth said, putting her arm around Jeanette, who was crying uncontrollably.

"They saved our lives," Jeanette said.

Me leaned out, rubbing his snout against Jeanette's cheek.

"You still have Me," Elizabeth said.

"Awk," they heard behind them over the approaching din.

The women turned to see an injured So struggling up the hill. Jeanette started down, but Elizabeth stopped her.

"You'll never get back up!" Elizabeth said, shouting to be heard.

The blast wave was towering above them now, approaching at the speed of a jet.

"Come on, So," Jeanette called. "You can make it."

The little raptor clawed its way up the hill, slipping back a foot for every three feet gained.

Elizabeth's eyes darted between the onrushing fury and the struggling velociraptor.

"Come on, So!" Elizabeth screamed, and then threw herself over the hill, landing flat, feet holding her on to the ledge.

Sensing its last chance, So lunged, Elizabeth grabbing it by the head with both hands, pulling its bloody snout toward her face. So scrambled up, stepped on Elizabeth's head, and then walked up her body to Jeanette. Elizabeth felt every claw cut into her back. Then Jeanette was pulling Elizabeth by the waist, helping her back to the ledge. The forest was exploding now, flaming trees thrown into the sky, the blast wave so high, Elizabeth could not see the top. They had only seconds.

"Hurry," Elizabeth said as Jeanette helped her to her feet.

Elizabeth turned to find the opening as big as a picture window. Behind them the last of the forest was pulverized, and as the women and velociraptors stepped toward the opening, the onrushing hell caught up with them.

53

Distortion

The Boonoke Fire in 1987 burnt out 120,000 hectares in the Riverina, New South Wales, and is one of the fastest recorded grassland fires. The midday temperature was 40.6°C, relative humidity of 7%, wind speed of 44.5 km/hr, and had a head fire rate of spread of 23 km/hr.

—Liam Fogarty

Orlando, Florida
Present Time

Jacob emerged in a room lit by light from high windows. It was thirty degrees cooler in the room, and relief from the heat made him pause.

I forgot how much I miss air-conditioning, Jacob thought.

The floor was concrete, with remnants of green paint. The Realtor in him estimated the room at twelve by fifteen. He saw nothing like the "hell" that Betty had described—until he looked straight ahead at a new door in a freshly painted wall. A poster next to the door showed male and female musicians dressed only in strategically placed strips of leather, and wrapped in chains, playing penis-shaped guitars. With heavy black makeup, obscene tattoos, and multiple piercings, the musicians looked demonic—at least to the Browns. Next to this was a poster for TWISTED GERBIL, showing the lead singer biting the head off a rodent—probably a gerbil. Turning, Jacob saw the rest of the walls were older, and layered in posters. More of the Poppa's Kum and Twisted Gerbil posters sprinkled the wall he had just passed through, as well as Bust-A-Cap, Devil's Mistress, and Wet Dreams posters.

"No wonder they went back," Jacob said, realizing rock music had devolved while he was gone.

Jacob ran to the door and tried it, but it was locked. Then he turned to the poster nearest the door to try to rip it down, but found it glued to the wall like wallpaper. Scratching at the edges, he peeled off strips of the offending poster. Finally obscuring enough of the offending instruments, he worked on the poster next to it, trying to create a safe zone for the Community. Then he realized the room was filling with smoke—could it pass through? If so, could the fire? Hurrying now, he ripped off a couple of more strips, realizing he could never scour the room of all the obscene images. Giving up, Jacob went back to the wall he had passed through, and stepped through it, emerging back in time. Hot air hit him like a slap in the face. Caught by surprise, he gasped, sucking in smoke and then coughing. His eyes watering, he rubbed them clear enough to see what had been a forest fire was now a prairie fire and closing in on his family.

"It's not hell," Jacob said. "They were just posters for some kind of music group."

"You saw them!" Betty wailed. "They were . . . male members."

"I tore them down," Jacob said. "Hurry now, we must go."

"I won't go to a world that gave itself to the Devil."

"What a lot of hooey," Wynooski said, pushing through the crowd. "You turn tail because of some sort of posters? With that kind of thinking, the world would be better off without you. Do me a favor, and stay here."

"You hear that?" Jacob shouted. "The fat ranger wants you to stay here."

"I'm not fat," Wynooski said, fists planted on her ample hips.

"Ranger Wynooski is trying to talk us out of going through this passage," Jacob shouted to all who could hear. "The ranger wants us to stay here. Look around you. Isn't this hell?"

Those that heard erupted into discussion. Those that could not hear got a secondhand account of Jacob's speech.

"I'm big boned," Wynooski said, still perturbed with Jacob.

"Crazy, I need you," Jacob said, and then turned to the crowd, shouting so that as many as possible could hear. "Choose who you will follow! The ranger wants you to stay here and not seek a new life. I believe God is waiting for us through this passage. I can't tell you what to do, but as for my family and me, we choose to follow the Lord. Those choosing the ranger's path, step aside. Those who believe that God loves us enough to rescue us from this hell, follow me."

"I didn't tell them to stay here," Wynooski said.

"Crazy, come on," Jacob said.

"Let's do it!" Crazy shouted, joining Jacob by the black opening.

Jacob picked up Bonnie and took Beatrice by the hand. With Leah right behind him, he walked into the opening and straight through to the door on the other side, Crazy following. Leah and the girls looked around, amazed.

"Whoa!" Crazy said, looking at the posters.

"Crazy, get that door open," Jacob said.

"All right," Crazy said, first trying the handle. "Stuck."

Taking his machete, Crazy hacked at the door with powerful blows. As he worked, more and more people flooded the room, bringing clouds of smoke. With Crazy wielding his machete wildly, everyone gave Crazy plenty of room to work, and the room quickly jammed with people, preventing others from coming through from the other side. With a clang, Crazy's machete split the wood clear to the handle. A dozen mighty hacks and he had several holes. Then he resorted to kicking out chunks of wood.

"What the hell's going on?" a woman said from the other side of the door.

"There's someone out there," Crazy said.

Before Jacob could stop him, Crazy put his machete arm and face through the opening he had created, blood-crusted beard and all, and shouted, "Bring it on!" shaking the machete at whoever it was.

The woman's scream and retreating footfalls were the last Jacob knew of her.

"Funny," Crazy said, pulling himself back in.

"Just get the door open," Jacob said.

Jacob helped now, grabbing the edges of the wood and breaking away pieces. It was a solid wood door, not like most interior hollow-core doors that Crazy could have crashed through easily. Alternating between hacking and prying, Jacob and Crazy tore the middle of the door away clear to the frame, finally breaking it in half, and creating an opening wide enough for a single person.

"Get on the other side," Jacob said to Crazy. "Help people through."

Crazy climbed through the opening. "Cool," Crazy said from the other side.

Jacob helped Leah through to Crazy, and then handed Bonnie and Bernice through to their mother.

"Come, Jacob," Leah said as she stepped through. "You promised us a house."

"I have to help the others," Jacob said, the next family already crowding forward and squeezing into the opening, cutting him off from his family.

With his family safe, Jacob felt overwhelming relief, and he stood for a second watching person after person squeeze through the broken door. Dr. Gah hobbled through, and out to safety. Other injured men and women came through, and a lot of women and children. By twos and threes, people were being saved, and Jacob wept with relief. Leaning against the wall, Jacob spotted a ceiling light, and then found the switch by the door, turning it on. Seeing the ceiling light fixture light up at the flick of a switch felt like a miracle. With the smoke getting thicker, the light helped illuminate the room. Now looking back at the opening in the poster-covered wall, Jacob realized it had changed. It was smaller and irregular, and fewer people were getting through.

"Hurry!" Jacob shouted, squeezing through the packed room to the back wall and pulling people through and then shoving them forward. Soon, there was nowhere for them to go. The bottleneck was the small hole in the door where people exited. Only one person at a time could get through, and the injured and old, many of whom were exhausted, had to be helped through the small opening. Given the size of the room, there were only so many people who could pack in to wait their turn. Helping another person through the passage in the back wall, Jacob realized the person's back was warm.

"Hurry it up, Crazy!" he shouted.

Whenever there was a free space, Jacob pulled another person through and shoved them forward. When he had to inch forward to reach the next person, he realized the opening was closing even faster. They weren't all going to make it. Pulling one of Mel Williams's little girls through, Jacob noticed her back was hot to the touch, and she winced when he pressed the back of her dress to her skin. Looking at the opening, Jacob could see it beginning to glow. Picking up the little Williams girl, he pushed through the crowd, yelling at the top of his lungs.

"Crazy, I need you!"

54

Bolide

The asteroid that killed the dinosaurs was . . . roughly 10 km in diameter and it hit with 100 million megatons of force. More than 50% of the world's different species were killed off because of the climate changes caused by the dust that was thrown into the air. . . . Acid rain and fires would have finished those that did not die from the initial impact.

—Jerry Coffey

Sixty-five Million Years Ago
Unknown Place

Conyers sat on Torino on one side of the opening, Weller standing on the other. Sergeant Kwan was in the meadow, and Washburne was with the tail end of the stragglers. Tafua had been killed by the *T. rex*, a loss that weighed heavily on the marines. "No man left behind," was an empty phrase when the lost marine had been eaten.

The marines shepherded the civilians across the meadow, ahead of the oncoming fire, and into the opening that led back to the present. An opening that continued to shrink back into the cleft of the hill. As the opening moved back, it continued to conform to the shape of the hillsides that it clung to. It was like a soap bubble stretched across an irregular wand. Conyers only hoped this bubble would not pop before they all could get through. Behind the fleeing refugees, part of the irregular edge of the forest fire reached the edge of the forest and now burned across the meadow, pressed by the wind. Smoke and ash obscured Conyers's view, but she estimated they would all make it.

What worried her was getting Torino through the constantly shrinking opening. She could not choose to save a horse over a person, but she was determined not to have to make that choice. There was time for both. She delayed sending him through, however, since without the horse, her leg made her another invalid, and she would not leave until all the civilians were clear. Instead, Conyers kept watch on the height of the opening, planning to send Torino through before the opening was too small for him, and that would be soon.

The last clump of refugees was nearly across the meadow. Two men walked with an exhausted pregnant woman, who must be near term. Conyers was amazed that she had managed their arduous journey without delivering. Now she could have her baby in a clean, modern facility. Judging the size of the opening, Conyers decided there was time to let the pregnant woman through, and then she could ride Torino into the opening, Wynooski and the marines going last. Conyers was about to interrupt the flow and send Torino through when she spotted animals stampeding across the meadow, coming straight toward the opening—they were Stripys, running for the valley they had used for escape before.

"Trouble!" Conyers yelled, pointing at the stampeding herd. "Give me your pistol," Conyers said. "Get as many out as you can."

Weller tossed her his weapon. It was a Beretta, and Conyers was familiar with it. Conyers kicked Torino into a run, heading straight toward the herd. The Stripys were twenty or thirty feet long, and three-ton animals, but herbivores. Like cattle, if Conyers could turn the leader, the rest would follow. Torino's trust in Conyers was tested again as they closed on the herd. Bred for racing, not cattle herding, the Thoroughbred nevertheless had the courage of a warhorse. As close as she dared now, Conyers swung left, shooting at the leader. Stung by a lucky hit, and surprised by the noise and the charging horse and rider, the lead Stripy deviated, now leading the herd parallel to the valley.

Conyers let the herd catch her, keeping between escaping humans and the fire burning ever closer. It was a narrow strip now, and

Conyers could see ahead that the fire was already up the hill. The leader would see it soon and turn again. Conyers drew up close to the leader, shooting it twice in the rump. The Stripy jumped, bucked, and then reflexively turned away from Conyers, toward the burning side of the meadow. Conyers turned away, pulling up, letting Torino rest, and the herd pass. When the leader realized his mistake, he tried to turn again, but the mass of confused animals pressed forward. The leader stumbled just short of the burning edge and was trampled, striped animals falling, squealing, and tumbling into the fire.

It was horrific sight, and Conyers turned away, looking to see how the evacuation was going. Just as she did, a fireball struck at the edge of the forest, the blast shredding trees and sending slivers of wood in all directions. The flash-bang startled Torino, and he reared. Conyers hung on, leaning into the horse, but then a wall of hot air struck. Torino stumbled and fell on his right side. Conyers yanked her right leg up and rolled off to keep it from getting crushed. Now flaming chunks of wood rained, and Conyers covered her face, brushing furiously at material. She heard Torino's pained squealing, then the horse struggling to get up. When she felt it was safe, Conyers uncovered her face and brushed matter from her filthy uniform. Torino had trotted a few yards away, and stood, head low, no energy or spirit left. Conyers's once beautiful mount was filthy, covered in ash, mud, and now blood that dribbled down his left shoulder.

Smoke obscured the gap in the hills that was their only way home, so there was no way to know if the passage was still there, or how big it was. Hurting from head to toe, Conyers tried to get to her feet, only to collapse. Her ruined knee could not support her. Shifting her weight, she got up on her good leg and then hopped toward Torino. Three hops and she tripped, dropping face-first into a patch of ferns and big white flowers. Waiting for the pain in her knee to subside, she spit out flower petals and rolled over, moving her left leg with both hands. Turning backwards, she used her arms to scoot up the hill toward Torino.

Torino stood, head down, breathing like an asthmatic. Conyers reached the exhausted horse, studying the gash in his shoulder. It was bad, but not fatal. Conyers could not mount Torino anyway, so there was no question of riding the injured animal. Using a stirrup, Conyers pulled herself up on her good leg, and then high enough to grab the saddle horn. Hanging on the side of her mount, Conyers said, "Time to go home, boy." Then clicked her tongue to get the horse moving. It took three tries, but finally Torino took a step. Managing a slow walk, the shell-shocked horse moved through a landscape of shattered trees and small fires, dragging Conyers along with him.

Remembering the shrinking exit, Conyers clucked her tongue again, encouraging Torino to move faster.

"Hurry, Torino," Conyers said. "Please hurry, like your life depends on it."

55

Demolition

Just as Jesus sacrificed Himself for us, I would sacrifice myself for any of you. And each of you should be prepared to sacrifice yourself for the good of the Community.

—Reverend

Present Time
Orlando, Florida

Tapping along the freshly painted wall, Jacob was a Realtor again—he knew about these things. The wall was sheetrock over wood studs set sixteen inches apart. Because it was an interior wall, there would be no insulation. There were two outlets along the wall, and no plumbing. Pushing through people to the opening in the door, he yelled out to Crazy.

"Break through the wall, Crazy. Walk over five paces, and break through the wall."

"Bust it down?" Crazy yelled over the din.

"Chop through it!" Jacob shouted back. "Make another hole."

"All right," Crazy said.

A few seconds later, Jacob heard furious hacking on the wall about where he intended—past the last electrical outlet, and far from the door. Smoke filled the room now, people choking, coughing, children crying, rubbing their eyes. Kicking at the wall opposite where Crazy worked, Jacob found the particleboard harder to break up than he expected. He cracked it on his first kick, but it took five hard kicks to make a hole. He was enlarging it when Crazy's machete broke through, nearly cutting into Jacob's shoulder. Jacob backed up as far as he could in the crowded room. Crazy was frenetic, if not systematic, and holes appeared here and there.

"Take a break, Crazy!" Jacob shouted.

The hacking stopped, and Jacob and other men kicked, punched, and ripped away particleboard. Crazy worked the other side like the maniac he was. Soon, there was enough wall removed to allow people to squeeze between studs. Jacob kept working, with Crazy on the other side, helping clear another opening between studs. Now people flowed steadily out of the room, the logjam broken. Grandma Reilly shuffled by, too exhausted to notice Jacob. Surprised at the toughness of the old woman, Jacob thought Leah would be glad that her sewing teacher had made it. Watching families move from the room, Jacob felt some relief. Then he realized the flow through the back wall had slowed, helping account for the clearing of the room. Pressing on the back wall, Jacob measured the opening, realizing it was half the size of what it had been. Estimating the size, and thinking of Torino, Jacob thought he might never see that horse again. Then Jacob realized the flow of people from the other side had stopped. In the confusion, Jacob had no idea of how many people had come through, or how many had been in their group. What he did know was that neither Ranger Wynooski nor Officer Conyers had escaped yet.

"Crazy?" Jacob called across the fast-emptying room. "I'm going to the other side."

Without waiting for an answer, Jacob passed back through the shrinking opening.

56

Inferno

About sacrifice and the offering of sacrifices, sacrificial animals think quite differently from those who look on: but they have never been allowed to have their say.

—Friedrich Nietzsche

Sixty-five Million Years Ago
Unknown Place

It was like stepping into an oven, Jacob throwing up his arms to deflect some of the heat. There was a crater from a bolide strike just inside the tree line. It had pulverized trees, sending flaming shrapnel in all directions. Two men and a pregnant woman were down—it was Nicole Schwimmer, her husband Mitch, and his younger brother Paul. Nicole wept as she pulled burning splinters from the backs of Mitch and Paul. Wynooski was flat on her back, unconscious, and Weller was sitting up, bleeding from a head wound, his clothing smoking. Washburne was unconscious, his legs on fire, while Sergeant Kwan beat at the flames with one hand, the other arm limp, pierced clear through by a narrow sliver. Torino and Conyers were nowhere to be seen.

Jacob hurried to Nicole's side, quickly pulling the rest of the big splinters from Mitch and Paul. Mitch came to as he did, but was groggy, mumbling something that made no sense.

"Can you walk, Nicole?" Jacob asked.

"Yes," she said sobbing. "Help Mitch."

Helping Nicole to her feet, Jacob then pulled Mitch up. With his pregnant wife guiding her husband, Jacob sent them through the passage, Mitch about as steady as a drunk. Next, he took Paul by the armpits and dragged him toward the opening. Even as emaciated as the rest of the Community, he was a heavy man, and Jacob struggled to move him.

"Let me do that," Crazy said, appearing from the passage and pushing Jacob aside.

Much stronger than Jacob, Crazy dragged the still-unconscious Paul through the opening. With the Schwimmers safe, Jacob went to Wynooksi, who was sitting up now, pressing her palm to a gash on her cheek. Blood soaked through her shirt over her left breast, slowly spreading. Jacob helped her up and toward the exit.

"I'm not fat," Wynooski said.

"No, just big boned," Jacob said.

Jacob handed her off to Crazy when he appeared, and then hurried to Sergeant Kwan, helping strip the smoldering trousers off Washburne's blistered legs. Then it was time to take him through.

"Can you help carry him?" Jacob asked, looking at the sergeant's pierced arm.

"This arm's still good," Kwan said.

Together they dragged Washburne to the exit, where Crazy took him, Sergeant Kwan following. That left Lieutenant Weller, who was up and walking. Taking him by the arm, Jacob got him to the exit.

"Where's Officer Conyers?" Jacob asked.

"She headed off a stampede," Weller said cryptically.

Jacob let Weller enter the passage on his own, realizing the opening was barely above his head and had shriveled deep into what was now nothing more than a crevice. Longing to be with his family, but concerned for the officer, Jacob lingered, walking to where the meadow began, searching through the smoke for the officer. Conyers's horse appeared a minute later, stumbling through the smoke, the officer hanging on to the saddle, being dragged along. Looking back at the opening, and then at Conyers and her horse, Jacob hesitated, calculating.

"Sorry, Leah," Jacob said, and ran for the officer, jumping small fires and chunks of logs.

Falling debris started scattered fires, so some of the fires served as backfires, leaving blackened ground. Jacob used these areas, winding around fires to reach the officer and her mount.

"Let go of the saddle," Jacob said. "I'll carry you."

"I won't go without Torino," Conyers said.

"It's too late," Jacob said. "The passage is too small."

"Not without Torino," Conyers repeated.

"Then go," Jacob said, lifting Conyers by the waist and letting her swing her leg over the saddle.

Conyers gasped when she hit the saddle, reaching for her left leg and squeezing it just above the knee. Examining the leg, Jacob found a dirty, tattered pant leg with small scratches, but no major blood loss.

"Go, go, go!" Jacob shouted, slapping Torino on the rump.

Torino jumped, and then managed a trot. Jacob ran too, the horse easily outdistancing him. Dodging fires, Jacob zigzagged through terrain resembling a battlefield. Torino and Conyers reached the opening, riding into the cleft. Jacob got to it a couple of minutes later to find Conyers sitting on Torino, staring at the opening.

"It's too late," Conyers said, looking at the opening.

The opening had shrunk to the dead end of the small ravine, now stretched between one wall and a pile of rocks that had fallen from the other wall.

"The opening's too small for Torino," Conyers said.

"But we can get through," Jacob said, reaching up and helping Conyers down, letting her lean on him.

Another bolide struck on the far side of the hill, the sky lit bright as day, and then fading to a dull orange, the thunder of the explosion rolling over the hill and echoing off distant features.

"You can't save him," Jacob said, putting an arm around Conyers's waist and lifting, carrying her to the opening.

"Stop it," Conyers said, wriggling loose and pushing away.

Jacob released her, and she collapsed, grabbing her bad knee.

"He saved our lives," Conyers said. "How can we leave him?"

"Because we'll die too, if we stay," Jacob said. "Look, that opening is about gone, and I've got a family on the other side. I promised them I would get them a house and take them to Dairy Queen. I'm going to keep that promise. Are you coming or not?"

Conyers looked at Torino, and then back to Jacob. "Help me get to him," Conyers said.

Jacob helped her up on her good leg, and then to the horse, where she hugged his neck, crying. Wheezing with each breath, his head hanging, Torino seemed not to notice the hug, but when Jacob started to help Conyers toward the opening, Torino nuzzled Conyers's side. Conyers turned, stroking Torino's muzzle, then let go reluctantly, letting Jacob help her walk away from the horse. She was crying hard when he started to help her get down to crawl through the opening. As they bent, Crazy came through, machete in hand.

"Who's next?" Crazy said.

"We're the last," Jacob said.

"Why is the police girl crying?" Crazy asked.

"She has to leave her horse," Jacob said. "Now, help me pull her through."

"Leave the horsie?" Crazy asked, frowning deeply.

"The opening's too small," Jacob said, frustrated with Crazy's interference.

"Make the opening bigger!" Crazy said.

Crazy was a man of few words, and this was one of the longest conversations Jacob had ever had with him.

"We don't know how," Jacob said.

"Do you know how to make it bigger?" Conyers asked, hopeful.

"Sure," Crazy said, turning to look at the opening. "See, it sticks to the wall here and the rocks here?"

Crazy traced the edges of the opening with his machete. On the left, the opening clung to a vertical rock face about three feet high and then recessed a few feet before becoming a vertical wall towering above them. On the right, the opening conformed to the irregular curves of a pile of rocks that had fallen from somewhere high above.

"Move the rocks," Crazy said.

Jacob understood. Without the pile of rocks, the opening might stretch to the vertical rock wall, which rose twenty feet before recessing somewhere out of sight.

"But it's shrinking fast," Jacob said.

"Please try," Conyers said.

"All right," Crazy said. "For the horsie."

Before Jacob could argue, Crazy was at the rock pile, using the machete to pry rocks loose, and then throwing them down the ravine. Parking Conyers and Torino on the far side, Jacob helped Crazy as best he could, staying clear of the manic machete work.

"Dig here," Jacob said, studying Crazy's random excavations.

Directing Crazy's digging, they undermined the top boulder, and then Jacob and Crazy climbed up and behind it, wedging themselves between another rock behind the boulder. Placing their feet side by side on the boulder, they pushed with all their might. The boulder slid, and then tumbled off the pile, rolling down the ravine a few yards. The passage instantly reshaped, now running over the top of the lower boulders, and then stretching up the rock wall to about six feet.

"That did it!" Conyers shouted, excited.

Jacob and Crazy had to climb up and over the ravine wall to the hill, then down and back in the passage to get to Conyers and Torino. The sky was a solid black cloud, the smoke thick. Fires lit their way, the ravine filled with flickering orange light.

"Crazy, take her through," Jacob said. "I'll bring Torino."

"Thank you, Crazy. Thank you both."

Sure Torino would follow, Conyers handed Jacob the reins, and then let Crazy put an arm around her waist, and then half-carry her into the passage. Looking at the oddly shaped opening, Jacob knew there was only a narrow passage high enough for the horse, and it was quickly shrinking. Just as he started forward, he heard a distant roaring. Looking down the ravine, Jacob saw the horizon rise up in a boiling black mass—this was new.

"Giddy up," Jacob said, pulling Torino by his bridle.

The horse let himself be led, but when they came to the passage, it was too narrow for them both to pass through. It was also barely high enough, even with Torino's drooping head. Releasing the bridle, Jacob left Torino facing the opening, and then walked to his rear, slapping him on the butt. The horse shuddered, but would not move into the opaque wall facing him. The roaring was getting louder, and Jacob did not have to look to know what was coming. Jacob walked back a few steps, picked up a fist-sized rock, assumed a pitching stance, and then reared back, and threw a fastball, striking Torino on the right haunch. The horse jumped forward, and was gone. Without looking back at what was coming, Jacob ran to the opening, bent low, and dived through.

Jacob landed at Torino's feet, Conyers's arms around the injured horse's neck. Weller and the marines were there, sitting against the wall Crazy had chopped a hole through. Crazy was looking down on Jacob, smiling.

"All right!" Crazy said.

"Yeah," Jacob agreed. "Everything is finally all right."

"Question?" Crazy said.

"What?"

"How do we get the horsie out?" Crazy asked.

Jacob rolled up onto his knees and looked at the people-sized opening hacked in the door, and those in the wall. Then he laughed long and hard.

57

Report to the President

SARA CONWELL: *Is it true that the ticker tape parade in New York made your horse sick?*

OFFICER KRIS CONYERS: *Torino is fine. He ate some of the shredded paper, and got a bit constipated, but we got him flushed out.*

—***Orlando Sentinel***

Present Time
Washington, D.C.

"There was no way to cover this up?" President Brown asked.

"No," Nick said. "Those returned from the past had to be reunited with their families. So, unless we intended to confine them indefinitely, it would be impossible to keep them from telling their stories."

"We also lost marines," John said. "They deserved to be recognized for their sacrifice."

John Roberts and Nick were in the Oval Office, President Brown sipping tea, Nick and John sitting on a leather couch, drinking coffee from cups with the presidential seal. With his lower right leg in a cast, Nick had it stretched out, his crutches leaning against the end of the couch. This was Nick's first in-person visit with the president since returning.

"Yes, of course," President Brown said, "but now there are consequences that are difficult to deal with. The return of survivors from the Portland quilt has raised the hopes of people all over the world who lost family and friends in the Time Quilt, and now they have unrealistic hopes of getting them back. The State Department has been inundated with calls from foreign ambassadors, demanding to know how to recover their own people. Our most faithful allies are accusing us of holding back technology."

"We've held nothing back," Nick said.

"Haven't we?" President Brown said.

"We knew almost nothing about the properties of the orgonic material that we recovered," Nick said. "At least not before this. Even now we know precious little. However, if you believe it is best, we could release what we have learned. The fact that exposure to this material was necessary to pass through nexuses should reassure the public. It's not as if someone could wander through accidentally."

"And we've disposed of this time-bending material?" President Brown asked.

"The biggest portion of it," Nick said. "The remaining material is dispersed for safekeeping."

President Brown frowned, pausing to sip her tea before continuing. "The other problem is that people have stopped trusting in their future—or, more accurately, they don't know what future and past mean anymore. Have you seen the polls? Only thirty-eight percent of Americans now believe that it is inevitable that they will move from the present to the future. Forty-two percent believe that they are just as likely to move from the present to the past as they are from the present to the future."

"That's just silly," Nick said.

"Is it?" President Brown asked. "The Lewinskis, and that cop and her horse, are the darlings of the talk show circuit. The more they tell their stories, the more people believe that time has been irreparably damaged. And if Americans aren't sure they are going to have a future, they don't plan for their future. There has been a ten percent drop in university applications and a seven percent drop in the amount Americans save each month. And you know what's happened to the stock market."

"It's temporary," Nick assured the president. "When nothing else happens, people will forget and move on with their lives."

"Can you assure me that nothing more will happen?" President Brown asked.

Nick squirmed, and then drank some coffee, taking several small sips as he composed his answer. "What I know is that time is a complex entity, with texture and strong and weak points, and that it interacts with both matter and form. Black holes distort time, transient dense matter creates time waves, and these waves travel forward and backwards in time. Holes can be punched in time, and the flow of time can be slowed, sped up, and even stopped. Knowing all this, we have taken every reasonable precaution to eliminate man-made time disruption, but as I said, time effects move both forward and back. The sins of the fathers may still be visited on the sons."

"And daughters," President Brown added.

"Yes, of course," Nick said.

"So what do I tell the people?" President Brown asked.

"You give them something else to focus on," Nick said. "Give them a new goal. Something that will distract them."

President Brown looked surprised. Like all presidents, she wore the stress of the job in the new wrinkles around her eyes, and on her forehead, and the gray in her hair. She wrinkled her forehead now, looking puzzled. "Where are you going with this?" President Brown asked.

"Do you remember the preacher that we met on the other side?" Nick had picked up the media habit of calling the piece of the Cretaceous past they had visited the "other side."

"The one they called Reverend? Yes."

Opening his briefcase, Nick took out two sheets and handed one to the president and one to John. Each sheet had two images of the same man. "We have no photos of Reverend, but using descriptions from the survivors of his congregation, we created a digital image of what he looked like the last time he was seen, and what he might look like twenty years later. Does that look like him, John?"

"Yes, that's him," John said. "I knew him in high school. Everyone called him Cubby back then."

"Why the interest in this man?" President Brown asked. "He never made it back, and neither did half his people."

"The last time we saw him, he was helping an injured Dinosauroid toward his village."

"What Reverend and his people called Inhumans," President Brown said.

"Yes, and that's actually accurate nomenclature, although meant to be derogatory," Nick said. "They certainly weren't human, but they weren't subhuman, either, as the name suggests to some. They were evolution's first attempt at a sentient species. I saw these people up close, and visited one of their villages. They were an intelligent, adaptable species that shared many human traits including speech, capacity for community, and the ability to domesticate animals. Like humans, the family unit was the basis for their social structure. Until a random cosmic event wiped them out, they were following an evolutionary path similar to humans."

"Speculation about that is all over the talk shows too," President Brown said. "It has stirred up a theological hornets' nest."

"Reverend would have been right in the middle of that debate, if he were here," Nick said. "He is the one who first called them Inhumans, and labeled them demons. He once believed it was his destiny to cleanse the Earth of the Dinosauroids. But like Saul of Tarsus, Reverend had his eyes opened. The last time we saw Reverend, he was heading to their village to preach the Word of God to a people he considered heathen. He became a missionary."

"Missionaries can do as much harm as good," President Brown said.

President Brown was a Christian, Nick knew, and regularly attended a predominantly African American Baptist church in Washington. While a believer, she was also familiar with the risks of sending missionaries to developing cultures.

"At first I did not think Reverend had a chance of getting to the village before the asteroid hit, and even if he did, I was sure that the Dinosauroids would kill him," Nick said. "Reverend had been their tormentor and nemesis for nearly twenty years. Now, however, I think he did make it to the village, and in fact went through the passage with the Dinosauroids to survive the Chicxulub impactor."

"How could you know this?" President Brown asked.

"There is evidence, of a sort," Nick said. He pulled two more photos from his briefcase, passing one each to President Brown and John. "You may recall that during the Viking One mission to Mars, the orbiter returned an image that included a human face," Nick said. "This is the so-called face on Mars."

President Brown and John looked at their photos of the Martian surface, showing a man's face, with deep-set eyes and a wide forehead.

"That was just an anomaly," President Brown said. "It's a trick of light and shadow produced by natural rock features."

"That's what I thought," Nick said. "Now, I'm not sure. Take a look at this photo." Nick handed out two more photos from his bag. "The face is nearly three kilometers long and either naturally, or artificially, carved out of rock. It has seriously eroded over thousands of years, but you can still see the major features, including eyes, nose, and mouth. I had a series of photos produced, showing what the face might have looked like with different levels of erosion. What do you think, John? Is that your friend Cubby?"

John stared long and hard, moving from face to face on the sheet, finally resting on the representation with the least erosion. "It could be," John said. "I think it might be."

"There's another reason to think that Reverend and the Dinosauroids made it to Mars. The face on Mars is located in a region called Cydonia. That face sits very near what used to be the shore of an ocean. It's the kind of location where primitive people would settle."

"Beachfront property," President Brown said.

"Exactly," Nick said. "You have the advantages of the abundance of the ocean, and also what the land can provide, all in one place. I expect there was a river near this location too."

"Very interesting," President Brown said, "but if they did make it to Mars, with or without the reverend, they are long gone. Mars is uninhabitable."

"Yes, Madam President," Nick said. "But I was thinking about something Reverend said before he left us. We don't know where in Mars's past they went. I have a dozen mathematicians trying to solve that problem, but we are eighty percent confident that it was at least sixty-five million years ago. If they did make it through to Mars, and had the time and resources to carve a monument to Reverend, then what else might they have accomplished? What archeological treasures are buried under the sands of Mars? And what about the biology of the Martian flora and fauna? Some of what we saw was unlike anything on Earth."

President Brown was watching Nick's face closely, but giving none of her thoughts away.

"And there is another remote possibility," Nick said. "With the knowledge of Mars's future that Reverend brought, and a clever industrious people like the Dinosauroids, and thousands of years to develop technology, it is possible that the Dinosauroids found a way to survive what happened to Mars."

"By going underground?" President Brown suggested.

"Possibly, but more likely by leaving Mars," Nick said.

"How? To go where?" President Brown asked.

"The only way to know is to go there and look around," Nick said. He dug into his bag again to pull out a thick bound document, and handed it to President Brown.

"You're proposing a mission to Mars?" President Brown said, looking at the cover. "A mission to Mars is proposed every few years, and presidents reach the same conclusion every time. Such a mission is technologically premature. Not to mention the cost of such a mission."

"The biggest hurdle has been the weight/fuel problem," Nick said. "Boosting ships into orbit is expensive, and a Mars mission means sending up the Mars Command Module, the lander, the Mars Habitat, and enough food and oxygen to keep a crew alive for the three years a mission would take. Then there's the fuel to send the ships to

Mars, the fuel for the descent and ascent phases, and enough fuel to get everyone home. Costs have been prohibitive, especially with the disaster relief needed because of the time quilting, so we've been waiting for advanced technologies to reduce the weight of the ships. If lifting mass were not a problem, we have the technology to go today. The good news is on page fifteen of my proposal. You can see that we may have solved the boost limitations. On page twenty, you can see that this solution drops the cost of the Mars mission by fifty percent."

President Brown scanned the pages, her face reshaping into deep concern, and then relaxing. "I'll consider it," President Brown said, her tone telling Nick the meeting was over.

"Thank you, Madam President," Nick said.

John stood to leave, helping Nick up and getting his crutches.

"I hear you are spending a lot of time in Florida," President Brown said.

"I'm going back for the weekend," Nick said.

"Has there been any change?" President Brown asked.

"Nothing perceptible," Nick said.

"I see," President Brown said, putting her hand on Nick's shoulder.

"There is one more thing," Nick said, leaning on John and taking one last paper from his briefcase. "If you would grant security clearance for another visitor, I would appreciate it."

President Brown read the cover letter and then gave a sad smile. "Does he understand the situation?" President Brown asked.

"Yes," Nick said. "As well as we could explain it to someone with his security clearance."

"Then, if he wants it," President Brown said, and signed the form.

58

Love Is Patient

> *Love is patient, love is kind. It does not envy, it does not boast, it is not proud. It is not rude, it is not self-seeking, it is not easily angered, it keeps no record of wrongs. Love does not delight in evil but rejoices with the truth. It always protects, always trusts, always hopes, always perseveres.*
>
> **—I Corinthians 13:4-7**

Present Time
Mills Ranch

Fannie and Marty Mills had the old barn torn down and replaced with a small guesthouse, with two bedrooms, two baths, kitchen, living room, and the room where Nick now sat. A wide paving-stone path now connected the guesthouse with the main house. Nick had dinner with the Millses, eating shrimp on the deck and enjoying the evening and their company. After dinner, Nick excused himself, taking the new path to the guesthouse, more confident now on his crutches. Nick would stay the weekend, and then fly back to Washington, D.C., for a few days, to do things in person he could not do digitally. He would fly back Wednesday night, to keep his vigil.

Nick had a stack of newspapers and, one by one, was reading them out loud. Elizabeth was a news junkie, and followed politics like men did football, so he read every editorial, which he seldom did for himself. Nick had finished with the *USA Today,* and had just picked up *The Washington Times,* when the doorbell rang. Nick was expecting the caller, and used his crutches to get to the door. Deputy Les Wilson was there, wearing shorts, sandals, and a University of Florida T-shirt. He was carrying two pieces of cheesecake on china plates with forks.

"The woman—Fanny—she made me bring these."

"Come on in," Nick said.

Nick and the deputy sat at the breakfast bar, eating the dessert, Nick explaining what the young man was about to see. Nick gave him details about how Elizabeth and Jeanette spent their last few hours, and how heroic they were, including saving Nick's life. Then, when Fanny's cheesecake was gone, Nick had the young man take two beers from the well-stocked refrigerator and led the way. Just as Nick had been, the young man was shocked by what he saw. There in the room were Elizabeth, Jeanette, and a velociraptor. Another velociraptor looked over Jeanette's shoulder.

"Are you sure they're alive?" Deputy Wilson asked.

"Watch them closely," Nick said.

"They're moving," Wilson said after a minute.

"Yes, and I think they might be aware that we're here," Nick said, "or at least they will be as their time and ours come closer together. That's why I spend as much time as I can with them."

Nick let Deputy Wilson study the women, who were dirty and trapped in a slow-motion run. Deputy Wilson walked close, trying to touch them, but finding he could get close, but not quite reach them.

"Sit down," Nick said.

There were two recliners in the room, a table between them, and a wicker lamp. Deputy Wilson sat, and handed Nick one of the bottles of beer.

"You didn't know Jeanette for very long," Nick said.

"Long enough to fall in love with her," Wilson said. "I met her when the department busted a meth lab on the farm next to hers. She was beautiful, and funny, and interesting, and I acted like a fool every time I was around her. We didn't spend a lot of time together, but I couldn't stop thinking about her, even on the job. I kept finding reasons to stop by and check on her. I wasn't fooling her. She knew why I was coming to see her, but she didn't tell me to stop, so I kept coming."

Nick smiled, sipping his beer. "Sounds like love," Nick said.

"What about you?"

"Elizabeth and I are past the falling-in-love stage," Nick said. "We are . . . comfortable together."

"That sounds good," Wilson said.

"It is, and it isn't. It wasn't until I lost her that I realized how much she meant to me. I was taking her for granted, when she deserved better. She was there when I needed her, but I'm not sure I was there when she needed me. Now that she's out of reach, I've had time to think about how I treated her, and honestly, I have no idea whether I was meeting her needs or not. She didn't complain, but what does that mean? Probably nothing. She wasn't the complaining type. She should have been the center of my life, not an appendage. Now, I can only hope I get a second chance. "

They were silent now, watching the women and the velociraptors in their endless slow-motion run.

"How long will they be like this?" Wilson asked.

"Maybe forever," Nick said, "but there is reason to believe they will get free someday."

Nick looked at Deputy Wilson, wondering if he had misjudged the young man. Wilson had learned of Jeanette's plight from Carson Wills, when the deputy persisted in looking for Jeanette. When Carson did not produce Jeanette, Deputy Wilson suspected Carson had killed her. Carson spilled the story just to get Wilson off his back. When Wilson showed up at the Mills Ranch, he had been turned away, and then referred to Nick, who discovered the deputy knew more than he should. Touched by the deputy's feelings for Jeanette, Nick eventually explained Jeanette's situation, then at Wilson's insistence, got him permission to visit. Now, the deputy seemed impatient, already asking about how long he might have to wait. It suggested he lacked the kind of commitment he had expressed to Nick.

"Someday?" Wilson asked. "Like days from now? Or are we talking weeks or years?"

"I have a friend who is studying this," Nick said. "He thinks it will be between one and three years. I can't give you details, but we sent something toward the sun. Sometime after it's destroyed, they could be free."

"Oh, thanks," Wilson said.

"You don't have to stay. I know you're disappointed."

"It's not that," Wilson said. "I was just thinking about how to arrange my vacation days so I can spend time here."

"There's no guarantee," Nick said. "It could be longer, or it could never happen. The only thing I know for sure is that it's going to be a long wait."

"Yeah," Deputy Wilson said, his eyes on Jeanette, "but some things are worth waiting for."

"Yes, they are," Nick said.